Twenty Grand
a love story

Twenty Grand
a love story

AUSTIN McLELLAN

Wild Caught Press

Twenty Grand, A Love Story
Copyright © 2015 by Austin McLellan

None of the material contained herein may be reproduced or stored without permission from the author under International and Pan-American Copyright Conventions.

Published in the United States by
Wild Caught Press
PO Box 17114
Memphis TN 38187-0114

ISBN-13: 978-1496119292
ISBN-10: 1496119290

This book is a work of fiction. References to real people, events, establishments, organizations, or locales are intended only to provide a sense of authenticity, and are used fictitiously. All other characters, and all incidents and dialogue, are drawn from the author's imagination and are not to be construed as real.

"Twenty grand. That's a lot of money in a place like Sloetown. 'No tellin' what folks might do for money like that."

—— spoken by a man on a street corner in
Memphis, Tennessee

TWENTY GRAND

ONE

Karl Orion reached for his fountain pen and checkbook. The pen was small and delicate in his strong, thick hands. He dated a check as the late afternoon sun forced its way past the dark curtains in his office. From his desk, he could see down a long hallway, where he noticed movement in a distant room. His wife Gloria was still working even though it was getting late. Gloria didn't have many responsibilities at the Orion Pallet Company, though Karl paid her well. It was an allowance mostly, but he was glad to do it. He loved his wife, and would have done anything for her . . . except tell her the truth.

On the check, Orion entered the name of the payee. He shifted uneasily in his leather chair that always felt too small, thinking *I really should get up from this desk more often, get back to the factory and check on the employees. Making pallets is hard work, and it never hurts to visit the warehouse and say Hello to the men. It's hot, dusty, and loud back there, and Lord knows they don't make much money.*

Karl Orion couldn't pay his employees much even if he wanted to. The wood pallet business earned little profit these days, though at one time Orion Pallet supplied customers in nine states. In recent years, sales had dwindled until now his company relied entirely on a handful of local accounts. Orion often considered selling the entire operation and retiring to Florida, especially since he turned seventy last winter. But nobody wanted to invest in an old, dirty industry with shrinking receivables, a decaying property in a tough neighborhood—Sloetown. Yes, he could hit the road, make a few calls, and drum up new business; but he had to admit, his old drive, the old desire, were gone. And he hadn't been feeling well lately. It felt like something else. Like pain.

Karl Orion entered the amount on the check: $20,000. Then he signed it, his hand tremulous and determined at once. In fact, the harder he gripped the pen, the shakier his grasp. Finally, he reached for an envelope and wrote the girl's name on it.

* * *

That same afternoon in another part of Sloetown, Lester Lewis sat on the hood of an old car in Jackson Park, thinking. It was summer, he had finished high school, and there wasn't much else to do on a hot day in July. The young man was thinking about money, how to get some, but nothing came to mind. A few guys he knew had joined the army, and one girl in his graduation class was going to college. Others had taken work over at the Orion Pallet factory, but he didn't want to work there. He'd heard bad things about that place.

So Lester sat on the old car with his thoughts. The car was a red Cadillac convertible, now spotted with rust, which belonged to his older brother Michael. Years ago, when Lester was a boy, Michael took him and his big sister Cheryl for rides through Sloetown on warm summer nights. The electric top never worked right, so to keep out the rain Michael always parked it under the big trees in Jackson Park. That was a long time ago. Now weeds grew through the floorboard, the windshield was shattered, and a door was gone.

Michael was gone too. He used to work at Orion Pallet but never came home one day. Lester heard stories: there was an accident, a big fire, but he wasn't sure. It was years ago. He was a child then. Now brush and small trees grew up around the car, children played on the swings nearby, and the older boys shot hoops on the court by the street. But the Cadillac remained hidden in a green corner of the park. Lester liked to hang out here. He wasn't sure why, but his head felt better when he visited Michael's old car, as if he was having a talk with his lost elder brother, getting some advice. And afternoons were always cooler in the deep shade of Jackson Park, a good place to escape the blistering sun of late summer. Sometimes Lester stretched out on the hood of the old convertible, closed his eyes, fell asleep, and dreamed.

TWENTY GRAND

* * *

Late that night, not far from Jackson Park, a young woman named Mira Ogilvy sat in her white BMW in the darkness. The street where she waited was deserted. It was almost midnight. She wasn't afraid, though it occurred to her that fear was entirely appropriate right then. After all, she was in a section of the city where bad news is no surprise, an old neighborhood of unpainted houses, vacant lots, liquor stores, one-room churches, and industrial ruins. The official name was Sloetown. That's how they spelled it: with an O and an E like the gin drink, sweet and fizzy with a kick at the end. No one could say for sure where Sloetown actually began, or ended, but you knew when you were there.

No, Mira Ogilvy wasn't afraid. She wanted to be there and knew Sloetown well enough. Everybody in town knew about the old neighborhood near the river, maybe even before they were born, as if their ancestors had passed the knowledge down to them. But it was no place for a solitary woman, and hardly a place for anyone so late at night.

She waited in her car before a neat, graying house. The woman inside would come soon. The clock in the dashboard read twelve now, later than before. As Mira squinted in the darkness toward the house, a light flickered in the window.

OK, she's home. Why doesn't she come? What is she doing?

Relax, the young woman told herself. She looked at her pretty face in the rear-view mirror and waited. Her fingers teased her dark hair, she checked her makeup. She had always taken pride in her appearance. In her youth, her father doted on her, remarking on her beauty every day, and she grew up believing it. Dating began at sixteen and Mira could hardly wait, back then, though it had brought her more trouble than happiness over the years. In an instant, a succession of men, boys really, flitted through her consciousness. At thirty-two, Mira Ogilvy was unmarried but didn't think about it much.

She looked in the mirror again, adjusting the pearls around her neck. Something was there. In the mirror . . . in the street. Movement outside the car. Her hands gripped the steering wheel and she peered into the darkness, down the block where broken streetlamps bathed everything in gloom. No, it was nothing. Only shadows. She checked her doors—locked. She glanced toward the

house and felt her pulse quicken.
Why doesn't she come?

* * *

Inside the house, Cheryl Lewis sang a lullaby to her restless baby girl. Maybe the child will sleep now, she thought, as a smile broke across the infant's chubby face. But when she moved away from the crib, the crying resumed. Cheryl looked at her watch—after midnight now. She sang again, knotting her hands and perspiring in the warm summer night. Then she walked quickly to the living room and parted the curtains. Out front, the white BMW waited near the sidewalk. She flicked on a lamp. Maybe the woman in the car would notice and be patient a minute longer till the baby stopped crying. It wasn't a good place for her to wait, at that hour.

Cheryl Lewis looked up and down the street. Everything appeared quiet, but she knew that silence could deceive in Sloetown.

* * *

Not far away in the humid darkness, four young men crouched low behind thick honeysuckle that covered an old chain link fence someone had pushed down years ago. They knew that lady would come here tonight in her fancy white car. That's what they heard. That's what people been saying up in Sloetown.

But it was late and the heat and mosquitoes had found them. They sweated and slapped at the bugs. Empty beer cans lay nearby. One man cursed while another told him to shut up. Another man stood up and walked into the shadows to pee. A fourth man felt the hardness of a pistol against his waist, pulled it from his trousers and laid it on the ground. He had never used a gun before, and he wasn't sure he could use it now. But he'd seen a boy get shot during a fight on the basketball court in Jackson Park, so he thought he knew how a gun worked. He'd even watched the man who sold it to him load the bullets. He looked at the black pistol lying on the ground, waiting for him. All the young men smelled the honeysuckle and breathed the thick night air.

"There she is," one of them whispered harshly. A white BMW had come to a stop before the Lewis house. The man who went to pee ran back to join the others. They jostled each other as they crouched together, as if they sought reassurance from the bodies next to them. The young men watched the car. The woman inside was doing something.

"Let's come up from behind," one said. "She won't see us then."

"Who cares if she see us?" the youth with the gun said. "I don't care 'bout nuthin but the money."

"What if she ain't got no money?"

"Shut up. Les go round back and come up quiet. Then she won't see us and drive off." It sounded like a good idea, but no one moved.

"What if her windows is roll' up?" So one man showed a chunk of brick in his hand. Then they saw the light flicker at the house.

"Look."

"Move!" someone grunted, and they rose from behind the fence and walked down the street, clinging to the dark spaces beneath the broken streetlamps. They approached the expensive car that looked out of place in Sloetown. One young man gripped the brick he carried, another fondled the gun. The woman inside the BMW examined herself in the mirror. She heard something. The pearls around her neck swung wildly as she turned to face them.

* * *

At the end of the block, a homeless man pushed a shopping cart along the sidewalk, eyeing the gutter for empty bottles, aluminum cans. He'd collected several already. They made a tinkling sound in his cart as it bumped across tree roots which had busted through the pavement. The bottles and cans would bring a few cents each. If he could find enough that night, he could redeem them at the junkyard in the morning and get enough money for a sandwich or a drink. But it was late now, he was tired, and needed a place to lie down. *Maybe back up in the bushes somewhere around here?*

Then he heard something. He looked up toward the sound. Something was happening at the far end of the street . . . men running, a white car, voices.

The homeless man rubbed his eyes. The beers he drank earlier made him dizzy. He looked again into the night—the men, the white car were gone now. He wiped his eyes again. No, they were still there! He squinted, staring into the darkness at the end of the block: more voices, louder, then a woman's voice. It didn't sound good.

"Trubble," he muttered, and spun the cart around. He disappeared into a vacant lot.

* * *

The baby cried again in the gray house. Cheryl Lewis went to her quickly as she glanced into her younger brother's bedroom. Past midnight and Lester wasn't home yet. Where the hell was he? She had to work early tomorrow, and he'd have to watch the baby in the morning. That was fine. Lester did have a nice way with the little girl, and knew how to calm her when no one else could. But it was late now. She'd have a talk with him when he came home.

Cheryl sang to the child, rearranged her little blanket, and leaned down for a kiss. Then she hurried to the front of the house thinking *Mira can't wait much longer, and dammit, it's not a good place to park anyway, not this time of night.* She unlocked the front door and stepped onto the porch, her breath pounding. Her eyes narrowed, searching for the white car in the night.

But all she saw was darkness under the broken streetlamp that fizzled and spat.

TWO

The next day at the Orion Pallet factory, Gloria Orion stared at a column of numbers in a ledger—and blinked her eyes. It had been a long time since she reviewed the accounts, but she had a good picture of the company finances. She thought.

She blinked again, then stood up and circled her office. When she came back to the numbers, they hadn't changed. Her breath raced as her fingers tapped the calculator. Everything looked accurate—it just didn't add up. The business was going downhill. What the hell was going on?

She noticed her husband Karl Orion in his office at the far end of the hall. Why hadn't he informed her? She trusted him, but knew the man kept things to himself. Well, he's got a lot on his mind, she concluded, and Karl was seventy now. People forget. Or maybe he didn't want to tell her.

But then, Gloria Orion didn't need anyone to tell her anything. She knew how things worked, knew since the day she married Karl years ago and he made her Vice-President of the Orion Pallet Company. It was a position with few responsibilities, but that was the point. Her husband was her senior by a couple of decades, and most of his hair had disappeared, but he was good company. He adored her, of course, and in their first year he showered her with expensive gifts, took her to Europe and the Caribbean. At forty-five, Gloria Orion had never been out of the

United States.

She examined the ledger again. Something was missing. Orion Pallet was almost broke, which meant she and Karl were also—no, she couldn't imagine it. Her head throbbed. She got up, left her office, and went outside in the sunshine.

It was a hot, sweltering afternoon. Gloria stood in the shade under a big metal awning that covered the loading dock. She lit a cigarette and brushed away a strand of the blonde hair she wore long because her husband liked it that way; though now in the summer heat she had gathered it up, leaving damp wisps along her brow and neck. The VP could've passed for a kindergarten teacher, a librarian, or a church secretary, except her green eyes were restless and intense, constantly in motion, appraising, evaluating. Her nose was strong and straight without any upturn whatsoever like she noticed, and disdained, in the pert noses of the tiny blonde nothings that passed for wives at the country club where Karl liked to dine on Friday nights. Those women had grown up here in the city, and rarely invited her to anything, but she didn't care. 'Just *girls*, she observed. They didn't work. They merely lunched, or planned parties all day long, which bored Gloria Orion to tears. She was not like that. She was a Vice-President at a big company . . . even if all she and Karl did out there in Sloetown was turn discarded wood into pallets, or paid other people to do it.

Now, as she took in the big parking lot and the warehouse beyond, something felt different. Orion Pallet was in trouble. She was in trouble. The finances weren't as they appeared. As she stood on the dock smoking, heat danced on the black pavement before her, like a mirage. A stench of creosote filled the air, made her slightly dizzy. She saw workers moving about in the warehouse—she had always felt like a big sister to them. They called her *Ma'am*, even though she wasn't old enough to be addressed that way. But now, with their dirty hands and sweaty clothes, the men looked ugly and stupid.

"I'll find out what's going on," she muttered. Then she finished her cigarette, threw it onto the pavement and ground it beneath her shoe, careful not to soil her glossy black pumps with ashes.

* * *

TWENTY GRAND

Cheryl Lewis spent most of that morning cleaning house and thinking about Mira in her white car. She must have got tired of waiting last night, and driven home. They had missed each other before, and the young woman had always called or returned later. But it felt different this time. As Cheryl vacuumed her living room, she stopped at the front window and stared outside. Another bright and sunny day. The street was empty.

Noon came, time to dress for work. She had traded the early shift at the restaurant for the afternoon slot, which gave her time to spend with her infant child, who had slept most of the morning. As she got into her white slacks, she heard her brother Lester snoring in the next room. The young man had been out late. She went to his room and stood in the doorway, eyeing him as he shifted under the blanket. Slowly, he became aware of her.

"Where you been?" Cheryl asked, as her brother rubbed his face. "It's about time you got up to watch the baby." Lester didn't answer, his hand over his eyes. "What were you doing last night?"

"Jus' hangin' out."

"Hangin' out where? With who?" It had been seven years since her older brother Michael had disappeared and she missed him at times like these. Michael had kept an eye on Lester, and it was her job now even though the young man was old enough that a big sister's words didn't carry much weight. But Lester was good with the baby, when he wanted to be.

"There's no reason to be out that late, not in Sloetown," she said, and flicked on the light in his room. The youth groaned. "You got your alarm set? The baby will be hungry when she wakes up. Or you want me to call you?"

"Ah get up," he said.

"I have to get going so don't go back to sleep."

The young man rolled over.

"Lester? You awake? The baby."

He mumbled something. He'd get up. She was okay with that, though she'd call him later to make sure. She went to the front porch to check the weather. Hot again. She looked out toward the street where Mira had waited the night before. Wrinkles appeared around her eyes.

Then Cheryl Lewis left home and drove into the city to work, thinking about the money she would earn that afternoon at the restaurant. It would be about the same as the day before, she reflected.

* * *

Later that day in a different part of town, Richard McDermott, Esq. stood before the big windows in his suite on the top floor of McDermott Center. An appropriate name, he thought, since he owned the building. He gazed out across the city, sighing at the lovely view before him. He hoped his clients liked the view also, though he really didn't care as long as they were suitably impressed. Good impressions count, his late father believed, and the son agreed. *Big man on top*, he remembered Father saying, with a laugh. It was important to look good, and the view from Twenty, the top floor, was excellent. Though at that moment, the landlord worried it might soon all disappear.

McDermott turned away from the window and faced the conference table in his office. A man and a woman, his bankers, sat there. He didn't know their names, nor did he care to. It was a hot afternoon and the man was fat. He had removed his jacket, and his arms swelled in the sleeves of his shirt. His stomach pressed against the table edge, cutting his tie in half. He said, "Well, Mr. McDermott . . . sir . . . maybe you can make some type of . . . uh . . . *arrangement*. On your mortgage."

The woman at the table spoke. "We can live with your principal in uh . . . abeyance. But we really need to get something done with the interest payments on the property." She wore a drab suit that looked as if it was manufactured in a poor Asian country. Her hair was cut into a rigid plainness and McDermott wondered if she was a lesbian; then he realized he'd never met a homosexual person. He paused, wondering if he'd seen enough of life. It was a great view from the twentieth floor, but maybe it was narrow, circumscribed, or even—he shuddered—obsolete.

McDermott had kept the slim profile of a younger man, his shoulders and face angular and sharp for a man approaching fifty. His black hair was thin, but enough body remained so that a good shock hung on his forehead like a fat comma; in fact he liked brushing it away when it fell forward, which it did when he was angry or upset. His eyebrows were dark, his skin light, pale almost, though it quickly reddened with feeling. His mouth was cut straight, but there was something fragile in it if one looked closely, like steel without any tempering, the mouth of a man used to having his own way. He stared at the bankers.

The fat man and the hard woman held their pens in mid-air, waiting for him to respond. Their bank occupied the first floor of McDermott Center . . . his building, he reflected. He had torn up their lease earlier that year, forgiving their rent to satisfy his mortgage, but it wasn't enough and now he was months behind.

McDermott turned back to the window and his panoramic view. Outside, tall buildings reached to the blue sky while the rooftops of new suburbs rolled to the west. Farther away stretched a carpet of green—the big trees of Sloetown. Beyond, the river glittered in slow motion under the bright sun of August. McDermott thought he heard birds outside but realized, on the twentieth floor, there were no song birds. He was dreaming.

"Sir?" the fat man said.

"Is Tommy Jameson still down there?" McDermott said brightly, referring to the man who owned the bank, its largest stockholder, who'd given his father the money to build McDermott Center years ago.

The bankers looked at each other. "Uh, yes, Mr. Jameson is still with us."

"Great guy, Mister Tommy. Super guy!" McDermott said breezily. "This city owes him a great deal, and he's a helluva golfer too. Just outstanding." Then he turned away to the lovely view at the window, the infinite sky. The bankers regarded his back. They were silent but they knew the truth: Thomas Jameson was eighty-seven years old. He only came to the office a few hours a week. The secretaries helped 'Mr. Tommy' with his mail and his coffee.

The fat man spoke: "I understand, Mr. McDermott, a few of your partners have moved on." He was nervous, as if something ugly wanted to burst from his tight, starched shirt, but he held it down under a veneer of solicitation. McDermott nodded. Yes, two partners and a paralegal had resigned from his law firm in the past month.

"We were thinking," the woman said, "that might free up some extra space here on Twenty. Usable space, leasable space." Her eyes were slits behind tiny wire-rimmed glasses that needed cleaning.

"Well, like a *sub-lease* actually," the fat man added.

The word pinched at McDermott. It wasn't a term he liked to hear. He could only imagine strangers occupying the suite. It wouldn't be comfortable. He'd have to make accommodations. He wanted the right sort of professional here, on the top floor, not just anyone. Impressions still counted.

"A way to generate revenue," the woman explained. McDermott showed a fake smile, thanking her for stating the obvious. She continued: "Or maybe you have other credit lines? I'm sure there is funding you could access."

"Well, let me see what I can do. I'm sure we can work something out."

"Well, Mr. McDermott, that's why—"

"—that's why we're here!" the woman interjected. "To work something out. Today." It felt to McDermott as if she had been waiting for this moment her entire life. He said,

"Well, it's going to take a while longer."

"We need to agree on *something*, sir," the fat man insisted. It was almost a whisper.

"'Agree on a date. Soon." the woman said.

"A week," he said. "Give me a week. I'll come up with something." The bankers looked at each other. They heard the air conditioner. It was blowing hard but the office was still warm.

"We need something now," the woman said. Her glasses bounced up and down on her nose. "We have obligations to our investors."

McDermott heard it. He caught it right then—the bank owed people too. They had to pay somebody. He remembered what his father told him years ago: at some point, the lender needs the borrower more than anything else. The bank needed him now; the woman had shown that card. The tiniest smile formed on the edge of his mouth. He said:

"You need something *today*? Oh, I really don't know." The bankers squirmed. McDermott felt it. "That's simply not going to be possible. Perhaps if you'd come sooner—"

"You're aware of the terms!" the woman exclaimed, but the fat man cut her off.

"A week or so will be fine, Mr. McDermott," he sighed.

"Okay. A week," McDermott said. The bankers scribbled on their legal pads.

"But we'll need the full amount then," the woman insisted.

TWENTY GRAND

The landlord didn't say anything. He strolled to the window, took a deep breath and said, "Such a beautiful view!"

The bankers looked at each other, then began collecting their papers. Soon they were gone. McDermott didn't see them out. They knew the way downstairs.

He crossed the room to a bookcase that displayed a set of law books in crimson and gold, and a crystal bar service. He poured a scotch from the decanter and wondered how he was going to find the money he promised these bankers, the little worms. One could always extract more rent from the tenants, but there were no leases to renew in McDermott Center. In fact, several floors of the building were empty. Any other assets he possessed were tied up with his wife. He had been married a long time, and separated a long time too, though he and Elizabeth were unable to effect a final divorce. It was all too complicated, and he disliked speaking with his wife. But he realized, as he sipped his drink, she felt the same way about him. His son and daughter were at college in New York and Boston but they rarely spoke either. He nurtured a hazy vision of his children's eventual marriage, family formation, and maybe a grandchild or two, but it gave him little hope and less comfort. Would they invite him to Christmas? Thanksgiving? Birthdays?

He didn't know. McDermott emptied his glass and poured another.

* * *

That afternoon in Sloetown, at the Orion Pallet Company, Gloria Orion left the shady loading dock and returned to her office. She stared at the ledger again. It stared back at her with numbers that screamed *bankruptcy*. Perhaps there was some error in the past? She reviewed the sales figures and expenses. She dug up older files, poring over each line in the reports, but everything seemed to be in order. Then it hit her. A name stood out, written in the jittery cursive of her husband's hand, *Mira Ogilvy*. It felt like a slap in the face. And beside the name . . . a debit, a payment . . . of twenty thousand dollars. Each and every month!

She got up, circled her desk, rubbed her eyes, sat down again. She peered at the name, the numbers. There was no reason, no explanation, no nothing . . . only *Mira Ogilvy*, the amount, and her address, 420 Lafayette Place. And the payments went back years, adding up to hundreds of thousands of dollars! It felt like electricity in her body.

She got up and marched down the hall, bearing down on her husband, taking long strides on the carpet, heat rising in her face. She would find out what this was all about. She would get to the bottom of it. Karl would tell her, by God.

Then she saw him. His eyes were big, watery, dim, and carved deeply into his face. His arms hovered over the desk as if they were robotic, controlled by an unseen power. His skin seemed to be made of white stone. When his wife appeared in the doorway, he didn't look up.

"What is it dear?" he murmured.

"Honey, I—"

"What?"

"The financials, Karl. Have you seen them lately?"

"Of course. What's the problem?"

"Problem? They don't add up. Orion Pallet is . . . not showing any profit, the revenue —"

"Don't worry about it."

"Karl, the numbers don't make sense."

"They make sense to me."

Her eyes were like hard glass. "I hope you know what you're doing."

He smiled. "Haven't I always?"

"Well then why are we showing a deficit for the year?"

"We've got money, Gloria."

"Karl, the books don't reflect ..." but he ignored her, shuffling some papers on his desk. "Karl?" She sank hard into a chair before his desk, searching the man's face. Her foot tapped the floor.

"Look baby, we're doing fine," he explained, refusing to look up. "Don't worry. Sometimes there are ups and downs. That's the pallet business. It'll all work out."

"Karl, who is Mira Ogilvy?"

He winced, looked up. "A consultant."

"A consul—?"

"That's right. She did some things. The company owed her."

"Did some *things*? Some *work*?"

Karl Orion stood from his desk and went to his wife. He

leaned and kissed the top of her head as a big hand patted her shoulder. "Honey it's not a big deal. 'Promise. Don't worry about it."

"Twenty grand is a big deal," she exclaimed. It stung him. He moved to the window and looked outside. She rose, pacing the floor of the office. They were like two boxers in a ring. She said, "All that money. Every month!?"

"The company owed her, Gloria. It's a payment."

"A payment? I don't care what it is. But the ledger is filled with red ink. We can't . . . the company can't keep going like this!"

Orion went to his desk and sat down heavily, as if he were getting into a bunker. He resumed his paperwork.

"Karl?"

"Dammit Gloria don't worry about the company."

Her eyes blazed. She came forward and leaned over his desk, trembling. "This company . . . this God-forsaken place . . . I work here, Karl . . . it's my money too . . . I'm your wife!"

"Well don't forget it!" He made a deep, vicious sound. She turned and walked out down the short hallway that suddenly felt a mile long.

Back in her office, Gloria Orion paced the floor, the name *Mira Ogilvy* burning in her mind. A consultant! And Karl wouldn't talk. He was shutting her out. She bit her lip until she tasted blood.

She heard the men at work out in the warehouse, their hammers banging against wood pallets, the whine of forklifts driving by. Orion Pallet was simple and coarse but it had been good to her. The big factory was a long way from where she grew up: a little town in eastern Kentucky where she said good-bye to her tearful mother a decade ago. She remembered the dying village with its single drugstore, lone gas station, and the McDonald's by the highway where the old men gathered in the mornings for coffee. She visited her mother once a year, maybe, in the country of dark hills and sullen forests. Her husband Karl had never been there.

Mira Ogilvy . . . the words screamed inside her head. She recognized the name, from somewhere. A party, maybe? A vague image of an attractive young woman came to mind, then faded. She grabbed the phone, called an operator and got her number—then her fingers hesitated. Karl is hiding something, she thought. Something is wrong, something he doesn't want me to know.

Maybe there's a good reason. She chewed a nail. But twenty thousand a month? That's my money!

She dialed Mira's number . . . no answer. She cursed, then noticed the ledger again and Mira Ogilvy's name, mocking her. Karl gave her the company's money. He spent Orion Pallet funds without permission! It must be fraudulent, illegal somehow. A lawyer, that's what she needed. She would go see her brother, Richard McDermott. His law firm had done a little tax work for Karl in the past. He'd know what to do. He'd get to the bottom of this.

The noise from the warehouse died as the hot day drew to a close at the Orion Pallet factory. Late afternoon would find Richard McDermott in his office downtown, on the top floor of McDermott Center. She would go there. If her husband wouldn't tell her about Mira Ogilvy, maybe her brother knew something.

And 420 Lafayette Place, Mira's home, is on the way. Maybe I'll just stop by there, and say Hello to that girl.

* * *

Downtown, on the second floor of McDermott Center, Baker Davis, PI, looked over his messy office as the day ended. It was late Friday afternoon, a good time to clean up for Monday. He had just returned from a long vacation, and his office looked that way—disorganized and dusty. But then, he remembered, he had no appointments scheduled for Monday, nor any day next week.

The investigator picked up his mail from the floor and stacked it on a desk. He wasn't ready to face it. Messages waited on his answering machine. No, not now. They were probably bill collectors anyway. A potted fern needed water. Maybe he could do that.

Then Davis noticed the pictures on his wall were crooked. He went to straighten them: the aging college diploma, testimonials from the police department, an 8x10 of his father shaking hands with Lyndon Johnson, a tableau of friends at a dinner party. His Private Investigator's license hung there also in a black frame. He took it down, noticing the safe hidden behind it where he stored valuables, except he had no valuables these days.

Davis examined the license. It was yellowing, and he wondered if he should take it down . . . now that the state had suspended it. Yes, he had helped the police put an end to the heroin trade up in Sloetown last year. He remembered that night in the old neighborhood when he faced down the big dope dealer, a thug who had shot one cop already and was reaching for his gun when Davis got the draw on him, putting his revolver right between the man's eyes, and keeping it there till the cops took over.

"That took guts, Mr. Davis," the police lieutenant, that Foster woman, remarked later.

His weapon wasn't loaded that night.

But then the cash they found on the dealer went missing. Yes, Davis had seen it, and everyone knew he'd seen it, even though he wasn't the only one to see it. But it didn't look good for the PI: the money was evidence, he had access to it, the money disappeared. Lieutenant Foster told him there would be no charges against him, but she didn't want him working. The police were content the heroin trade was finished, for now, in the old neighborhood. She added that if he was smart (and she *knew* he was smart), he'd lie low for a while, get out of town, take a long vacation. In the big picture, it was good advice. The months he spent out West visiting his brother were a nice break. Now, back in the city, Baker Davis planned to keep quiet, like the Lieutenant said.

He wiped dust from the framed license. *Suspended*, he whispered. He shouldn't display it, and held it over the garbage can. No, it was still his career, still who he was. The investigator had never known another line of work. He reached to hang the frame back on the wall—then noticed the safe there. He spun the dial. It opened smoothly.

Inside was his revolver. He withdrew it. The steel was cool and heavy, the grip solid. The last time Davis handled the gun was the night he drew on the heroin dealer in Sloetown. Maybe he would need it again sometime, or maybe he wouldn't. He couldn't see how a weapon would help much now, as he tried to earn a living without a license. He remembered that joke about how a man could steal more money with a briefcase and a lawsuit, than with a gun and a fast car, but it wasn't funny now. Davis put the revolver back in the safe, locked it up. Then he returned his license to the wall, straight this time, as he heard a voice from up front. His office partner Grayson Prince, was on the phone:

"If I said the money was going to be there, it's going to be there. Well, yeah, the check will be *dated* for next week, but you can go ahead and *access* it. Just don't *cash* it."

Prince occupied the front room of the suite. He was no detective, but ran his own operation, or *action* as he preferred to call it, dealing with people and companies in trouble. Auction houses, factoring agents, title loan shops, failing banks, and every creditor and debtor this side of the usury laws were his market, his *action*. Prince knew what was legal, and what could be evaded, in all fifty states. Illegality wasn't a fixed concept in his mind. The afternoon when Baker Davis showed up two years ago, he didn't rise from his desk, or offer a hand, but simply presented a card: *G. Prince, Investments.*

"Prince? Prince? I've heard that name before," Davis said then. "You been around here long? I mean, here in the city?"

Prince offered a smile that was sympathetic, almost condescending. "How many generations can you count back?" He sighed and leaned back in his chair, the springs creaking. The man was coming into middle age, softening now around the middle, but his easy manner looked more the result of rich food and good drink, than laziness. Yes, the family went back over a century, he said, and was once prominent and wealthy, but there was no money now. "Gone with the wind," he exclaimed with perfect serenity.

Baker Davis recognized the situation. Many of his father's clients fit the profile: an old family trust conservatively stocked with bonds, real estate, and other assets, but the annual income wasn't very much after they paid taxes and doled out the remainder to the siblings. In New York or Chicago, they'd be nobodies, but around here it was more than anyone else had. The money at least kept a man like Prince free and clear of normal employment; kept him invited to the better parties if that's what he wanted; and usually guaranteed he'd never do anything interesting in life let alone useful. It brought them heartache sometimes, but the money was there (they never lost *all* of it), so why fight it? Davis knew this. He also realized Grayson Prince knew it long before he did.

"My girlfriend teases me," Prince said that afternoon. "She says my work is bottom feeding, and maybe she's right, but mostly the distressed parties I deal with are big shots who overplayed their hands." Again he came with the knowing smile. "And me? I come in to help them out—or at least help them *get* out. With discretion of course. My lady friend calls me the Gray Prince since I operate in the gray areas. And your line of work?"

TWENTY GRAND

"Investigations. Private, you know," Davis replied.

"Private, huh? That might work out just fine."

That was two years ago Davis remembered as he watered the fern, though not everything had worked out fine. The PI had been successful in the past, investigating people and usually, their finances. That's what they said, *finances*, though it invariably became 'money' or 'cash' or 'dough' or something more vulgar yet. The work was honorable enough, but could turn gritty: following people, gathering hotel receipts, taking photographs. It almost made sense when they were guilty as hell—of adultery, larceny, fraud, etc. But sometimes Davis wanted to quit, and go sell used cars, peddle burial insurance, or deal cards at the casino. He'd read about some religious cats in a monastery down in Louisiana who rarely spoke, got up with the sun, worked in the fields all morning, made bread in the afternoon, and went to bed as the sun set. They didn't talk much either. One could do worse. He wondered if there was some kind of admission procedure, a test to pass. He could fake some prayers, he thought, at least until it felt right.

But detective work was all Baker Davis knew. His father had bequeathed him the agency and a list of clients. Most of them were dead now. And now he would have to manage without a license. That was okay. He could play it any way they wanted.

* * *

Upstairs at McDermott Center, on the twentieth floor, Richard McDermott heard the intercom buzz in his office. His secretary. He put down his drink and pressed the button.

"Yes Gail."

"Someone here to see you, Mr. McDermott."

"I don't want to see anyone."

"It's Gloria Orion, sir."

"Oh. All right. Show her in."

She entered on a wave of tension. McDermott could feel it, but he was relieved to see his sister. It had taken a long time, but he'd come to trust this stranger who appeared in the city years ago with no money and no plan, with nothing at all except she knew him. He remembered the afternoon long ago when an attractive woman came to see him. He received her and she started to talk, coloring in a rumor McDermott had heard all his life—that his father was unfaithful to his mother. She explained how her own mother Agnes Finch had been in the city decades ago, young and impressionable, seeking legal advice from McDermott, Sr. Soon they were involved, on some level, and Agnes was pregnant. The story became hazy then, but Agnes left the city, going back home to Kentucky an unwed mother, but not ashamed, not hiding it. She gave birth, raising her daughter as Gloria Finch, who didn't learn about a father in a faraway place until she was almost twenty-five, though by then he was dead.

But one day Gloria came to the city, and looked up her father's son. In McDermott's office that afternoon, she presented a hotel receipt, showing the guests as Richard and Agnes McDermott, Sr. The date fit perfectly with her story, and McDermott knew the hotel; still, his legal mind rebelled. The receipt could be a forgery, but he didn't object. He did pour himself a glass of scotch. Then the woman reached into her purse, withdrew a cufflink, and handed it to him. It felt like fire in his hand. His father had one just like it, a unique design of a silver golf club bearing a small emerald. But he only had one! McDermott never saw his father wearing the complete pair.

It was too much to believe, so McDermott kept silent, thinking it over, trying to get his mind around her story, trying to accept that a sister, or a half-sister at any rate, sat before him in his office. In truth, he didn't know what to say. Gloria Finch was silent too, staring at him calmly. Then she said,

"Does the phrase *Big man on top* mean anything to you?"

McDermott froze. No . . . no one else had ever heard his father say that. It was a little pet phrase, intimate, familial. It was the clincher. The lawyer finished his drink, poured another. All the evidence was in now. Gloria Finch was a McDermott too.

So he helped his sister out. He found her a job keeping the books at a hardware store. She settled into the city and McDermott didn't see her for months. And yet, over time and a few lunches, they grew closer, though she never crowded him, never asked for a thing. He showed her around town and found, to his surprise, that he could trust her. She became simply, his sister Gloria, family. Then, at a party, McDermott introduced her to his client Karl Orion, an older man with a factory out in Sloetown. Gloria Finch took it from there. The years passed by.

Today she entered his office and threw herself in the armchair as if she owned the place. It amused McDermott and he smiled. Most of his visitors were like those bankers—taut, officious, angry.

"Hey how are you?" he said, but she looked at the ceiling. "Gloria?"

She stood in a huff and marched toward the big windows that looked out over the city. The glass showed her reflection and she took advantage, smoothing her hair and correcting the collar on her blouse. She turned back to her brother.

"Richard, there's a problem down at the company."

He smirked. "Well, it's always something."

"Will you listen? There's a problem, at Orion Pallet, with the books."

McDermott went to his bookcase, reached for a glass there and raised an eyebrow at his sister. She nodded *sure*. He splashed scotch into the glass, added water, then brought her the drink where she stood at the window. He said,

"A problem, huh?"

"Yes. A big one." She sipped her drink. "Have you ever heard of Mira Ogilvy? She lives over on Lafayette Place."

"Mira Ogilvy? Ah yes, a minor heiress. Her father was a doctor here in town."

"An heiress. Really?"

"Well, her daddy had a large medical practice. He was quite successful, until he died that is. Mira came to that dinner party at my house last year. Don't you remember? I didn't invite her, somebody brought her. I can't recall who."

"A young woman? Pretty? In pearls?"

McDermott returned to his bookcase, withdrew a large album, and flipped through pages of photographs. "Here she is . . . Mira . . . at my house."

Gloria reached for the picture of the young woman. "Can I have this?"

"Sure," he said, removing the photo. "So what about her?"

She examined the image, then turned away to the window. "I don't know Richard, but Miss Ogilvy is mixed up with Karl somehow. The books at the company . . . show that woman has been getting a huge payment every month, twenty K, for the past several years. It must be hundreds of thousands of dollars by now. You've done tax work for Karl, right? Have you got any idea . . . ?"

"What are you talking about?" McDermott went to his desk

and found a cigarette.

"Richard listen. I was going over the financials this week. The rotten pallet company is broke. The numbers are in the red, and a big part of it started years ago, with huge payments to Mira Ogilvy every month. I don't know why I didn't catch it before. You've been doing the company's taxes, right?"

"Well, I've filed some documents for Karl . . . but the details, I'm not sure. How much did you say it was?"

"Twenty thousand a month, for years."

McDermott let out a low whistle. Gloria Orion came to the desk and took a cigarette from her brother's pack. She lit it and blew smoke across the room.

"All that money! What the hell for? What is that woman doing?"

"I hate to say it Glo', but maybe Karl has . . . you know . . . a girlfriend."

She evaluated the question like a business issue. "I doubt it. Mira's young, nice looking. I'm sure she gets plenty of attention. She wouldn't need that from Karl."

"But she might need money," McDermott said.

"True. But that much? What for? It can't be right. Something's wrong."

"Well, if Karl wants to give his money away, there's no reason why he—"

"It's my money too, Richard," she said bitterly. "It's the company paying her. It's my property too. He's my husband."

"Well then, Karl's hiding something."

"It's fraudulent, I tell you. It's got to be illegal. Karl can't give my money away. Isn't it common property or something?" She crossed the room to the window, smoking. Her brother's mind shifted gears when he heard the words *fraudulent* and *illegal* and *property*. There might be something here, the lawyer thought. Maybe this was something actionable. It *was* a lot of money, and his sister might well have a claim to it. Then he remembered his bankers. Their note, *his note*, was due in a matter of days.

"I don't know why Karl is paying her," Gloria exclaimed, "but Mira shouldn't have that money!" Her eyes were hot. "It must be a crime if she took it."

Again her brother's mind raced, fueled with booze and cigarettes: *Yes . . . if a gift was made under duress, or was deceptive in some way, or improper to the point of fraud . . . it could amount to extortion.*

"We've got to get that money back. If we can't, I don't know about the company or about me for that matter. Orion Pallet is circling the drain, and Karl won't tell me anything."

"Let me look into it," McDermott said, his face steady and dark. "But if we can get the money back, Gloria, I'm going to need help. I've got payments due on the building."

"Payments?"

"Yes, the mortgage on McDermott Center. The money is due in a week." He finished his scotch and ran his fingers through his hair. "I won't make it."

"You're kidding."

"No, dammit. The bank is going to foreclose."

In a corner of the room stood a faux fireplace, richly adorned with a mahogany mantle. Gloria Orion approached it thoughtfully, her arms folded, staring at the ceramic logs. Her brother's situation didn't surprise her. It felt like one more crisis to deal with. She had heard the gossip in town anyway: tenants were leaving McDermott Center and her brother was leveraged to the eyeballs.

"Don't worry about it," she said. "If we can get that money from Mira, somehow, it may be enough for both of us. 'For a while anyway."

"All right then. Let me see what I can do. I'll have a little talk with Ms. Ogilvy."

"I don't know, Richard. I don't know where you're going to find her."

"Mira? She's here in town."

"Maybe. I've been looking for her. I called her, or tried to, but no answer. I even drove by her house over on Lafayette, but it's dark there. No car, no lights, and several days' worth of newspapers lying on the porch."

"So she's missing?"

"I don't know, but something's wrong. Her house didn't look right. It didn't feel right." She stared into her drink.

"I'll look into it," he said.

"Maybe she took all that money . . . and left town. You can get pretty far with that kind of cash."

"I'll make a few calls."

"If Mira doesn't turn up soon, the police will be looking. We don't need them involved. Maybe we need some help, before that happens. Isn't there some kind of investigator downstairs here in your building? Don't those guys track down missing persons and all that?"

"I said I'll look into it."

"What the hell are you going to do?"

His face got hard. "A private detective, huh?"

"Yes, Richard, your tenant. I think he's on the second floor of your building, downstairs."

"That guy? On Two? I think he lost his license or something, and he's behind on the rent."

"No license, huh? So he's not legit? Interesting." Gloria Orion finished her drink and killed her cigarette in the ashtray. "What's his name?"

"Davis or something."

"You know his number?"

"Gail has it, but it's late you know." He reached for the intercom.

The tall blonde woman returned to the window and gazed out across the city at the dying sun that was turning the skyscrapers outside, the suburbs beyond, and even Sloetown in the far distance deep orange, violet and blue. Soon it would be night.

Gail's voice came through the intercom. "That line is busy, Mr. McDermott, so Mr. Davis might be there."

"Okay, thanks."

Gloria Orion noticed her reflection in the glass, touched at her hair, smoothed her hands across her hips, her skirt. "All right then. Let me pay that detective fellow a little visit."

* * *

Gloria Orion left her brother's office on Twenty, got into an elevator, and punched the button for Two. McDermott Center felt quiet, almost empty as she descended. It didn't take her long to find what she was looking for. It rarely did.

She saw a figure through the frosted glass of an office door. She tapped once, turned the handle, and went in. A man sat behind a clean desk, staring out the window. He wore a nice suit, but didn't seem to be doing anything purposeful. When she said *Hello*, he didn't even look at her. Gloria Orion was used to having men notice.

"A fine day," was all the man said. He seemed like a slightly annoyed concierge in a run-down hotel, a guy maybe used to better times who wanted you to know it.

"Well, it's a bit humid for my taste. I'm looking for a Mr. Davis."

"Lady here for you Baker!" Prince yelled.

"Hello," came a voice from the back. She heard steps; then he appeared, a man who didn't look like an investigator, to her. There was some experience about him, but it didn't seem related to crime. He was a decent six feet with hair that was once blonde, a good chin and firm eyes with a touch of melancholy. She expected something uglier, rougher. She also expected a warmer greeting, but it wasn't coming. The man stood there with his hands in his pockets.

"I'm Gloria Orion," she announced, extending a few fingers.

"Nice to meet you," he said, accepting the fingers, feeling her eyes sizing him up. "I'm Davis." She wore a dark skirt and a silk top full of curves, her blonde hair pulled back. She clutched a large purse that looked like a weapon. The woman wasn't young, but it was clear a second act remained even if the role she desired, her lines, were vague. She wanted something. The investigator saw this. He saw it all at once.

She presented a card. "My husband's a manufacturer here in town. The Orion Pallet Company. Do you know it?"

"Yes, I've heard of it," Davis replied. *Husband? Manufacturer?* It sounded presumptuous for a guy who made pallets in a big factory where no one likely earned a penny over minimum wage. He examined the card: *Gloria Orion, Vice-President, Orion Pallet*. And what did a *Vice-President* do there all day long? Well, he noticed, she is very attractive.

"I'm glad you're still here, Mr. Davis. I know it's late. I was hoping you might have a minute."

Davis glanced at his watch. He didn't want to see anyone, but a little work couldn't hurt. There could be a retainer here, a payday. And a client that looked like Gloria Orion had its advantages.

"I've got a minute. Come."

She followed him through a hallway to his office where a large desk stood before a mismatched credenza. Books, mail, and folders were piled on the desk with an air of neglect, the clutter reflecting no actual business activity. But nice bookshelves lined one wall while a row of windows in venetian blinds gave a view to the street. Davis motioned to one of the leather armchairs; in fact, he held it out for her. She noticed this too, and wondered if this was part of the man's experience, with women. It was something her husband had stopped doing long ago, and she missed it. The PI got into his chair and they regarded each other for a moment across the big desk. She spoke first.

"I don't know where to begin, Mr. Davis. I've been real anxious lately. My friend . . . an acquaintance really . . . I haven't seen her in several days."

"Sorry to hear that, Mrs. Orion."

"Gloria. Please."

"Gloria then."

"It's just that I can't reach her . . . can't find her. Mira that is. Mira Ogilvy."

"The name sounds familiar."

"Well, she lives here in the city. Her father was a Doctor Ogilvy. Maybe you've heard of him?"

Davis nodded, remembering the doctor. A local man, Winston Ogilvy had become a national authority on respiratory problems, established a successful clinic, and acquired a small fortune by the time he was fifty. Then, the story went, he took to drinking for some reason. His wife, Mira's mother, left him in a quiet divorce and resettled on the coast. Then the clinic deteriorated and so did the doctor. The man was dead in ten years. Mira was an only child, so the big question in town was the extent of her inheritance. The doctor's estate could have been significant, but with the messy decline of his final years, no one knew for sure.

Davis said, "How old is your friend, Mrs. Orion?"

"Mira's not much past thirty, I think."

He wrote something on a pad and said, "And when was the last time you saw her?"

"Oh, I haven't seen Mira at all, Mr. Davis, not lately. But I tried to call, and I drove by her house." Her posture grew rigid; her fingers squeezed the handle of her purse. "There was no one home. No car, no nothing, and the mailbox was overflowing. I'm anxious. Worried."

Baker Davis noticed her face. The investigator had seen fear before—and seen it faked too. And now this woman is concerned about someone she hasn't seen at all, hardly knows her age. All

right. Maybe. Davis stood and crossed the room to the windows, where he stared outside at the fading afternoon and said,
"Have you known Miss Ogilvy for a long time?"
"No, not really," she said. "We're not even that close. She was part of a group of people I know. We got together for an occasional dinner, drinks, that sort of thing."
"Was?"
"Was?"
"Yes, Mrs. Orion, you said Mira *was* part of . . ."
"*Is*. I meant Mira *is*. Sorry, I'm just worried, that's all."
"What are you worried about?"
"Oh I don't know!"
Davis studied her. "Well, you know . . . missing persons actually turn up okay most of the time."
"I hope so," she said. To Davis, this was a little too quick, simply a remark, a polite word. He looked into her face, trying to weigh the statement, get at her real meaning, but it wasn't easy. Her eyes were opaque.
"Do you think you can help, Mr. Davis? You know . . . find Mira?"
He returned to his chair. "Maybe. I can certainly look. Where does your friend live?"
"Out in the Palatine, 420 Lafayette Place."
He wrote it down.
She said, "You're familiar with this kind of thing? I mean, you're like . . . qualified, right?"
He stared at her. Clients normally didn't ask this. Qualified? Sure, but his license was no good now. He noticed the faded certificate on the wall and said, "Well, yes, I've been in the business for a long time. Sometimes it feels like forever." He gave an ironic smile.
"You think you can handle it?"
His smile became a frown. "What's to handle, Mrs. Orion?"
"I don't know. I'm just a little afraid. Is it dangerous, your line of work?"
"Not usually, but I've encountered it. Generally, it's not my style."
"Do you have a gun?"
"Do you think I need one?"
"But . . . well . . . you've handled—?"

"—the tough cases? Are you looking for a tough guy, Mrs. Orion? Is that what you want?"

"Oh all right," she said, annoyed. She wasn't used to being questioned. "What about the police, Mr. Davis? Should we contact them?"

Davis flinched, remembering Lt. Foster's advice to lie low, take a break. And then his license, suspended indefinitely. Still, it sounded like routine work . . . find a missing person . . . no criminal activity involved. It should be quiet, neat, unlikely to draw the cops' attention. And likely to bring in a little money.

"Let's leave the police out for now. We'll contact them later, if we need to."

Her green eyes shined. It didn't sound entirely right and she liked it that way. Her brother wasn't going to find Mira Ogilvy anytime soon. She brightened and said, "Well all right then. Great. I suppose you have a fee or something, Mr. Davis?"

"My normal retainer is a thousand dollars, but half that would be okay, for now."

She withdrew a check from her purse and filled it out, signing her name with a flick of the wrist. She handed it over, then reached again into the purse and produced a glossy photograph.

"Here, Mr. Davis. It's Mira."

Davis took the picture. The young woman's hair was as dark as the black dress she wore. There was a low neckline, the collar a delicate pattern of tiny scallops. There were pearls too. Her fine features suggested a world where there was little to worry about, perhaps even a world of leisure or wealth. It was a face of possibility, a face that received the hard edges of life gracefully, and didn't fight back too much. A face a man could marry, even love, but there was no sex in it, not in this picture. Davis guessed her age was about thirty.

"Very pretty," he observed.

"Yes she is."

"Well, all right Mrs. Orion. Let me see what I can do."

"Gloria. There's one more thing, Mr. Davis." She stared straight ahead, into nothing, her fingers gripping the purse as her voice fell. "We've got to hurry."

Something dark filled the warm room, as if a cloud passed by outside, obscuring the light from the window. It was uncertain, vague, but hung in the air like cheap perfume.

"*Hurry?* Any particular reason why?"
"Because there's not much time." She looked away.
Davis waited, but she said nothing. Then Gloria Orion stood up, smoothing her skirt as if she was trying to be rid of something. Davis came from behind the desk and received her hand, a smile. He followed her out, down the hallway to the front. She stopped at Prince's desk and said, "You can reach me with the numbers on my card. Call me if you learn anything, anything at all." She opened the front door. "And please, Mr. Davis. Hurry."
She left. They watched her go.
"Something's eating at her," Prince said.
"I know. That's all right. Whatever's going on, she won't be able to hold it in. They never can, in the end."
Prince's phone rang. He returned to his action: "You bet your ass it's good paper! Those guys in Kansas City 'been doing this for years, so there ain't no better rate." Then he waited. "Listen, if you don't want in, there's plenty other guys who want some."

* * *

That evening, Lester Lewis was glad when his sister Cheryl finally arrived home. He was tired of babysitting and couldn't wait to get out of the house. He was anxious to get to Jackson Park where his brother's Cadillac lay moldering in the brush. Earlier that week he had spotted weeds growing up through the floorboards, and finally guessed what they were—marijuana plants. He'd seen a TV show where the cops busted some hippies out in California, and the green plants they confiscated looked like the weeds growing in the old convertible. He got a book with pictures and double-checked. Yes, it was pot.
Lester ran from the house as his sister came in. She called to him, but he didn't answer. The young man walked quickly through Sloetown to the park. He guessed Michael had smoked the stuff, and he remembered the funny smell in the car when they went driving, the smile on his brother's face, and his bloodshot eyes. It was possible Michael stashed his weed or seeds in the car; then, maybe the pot somehow fell to the ground and took root after Michael disappeared and the vehicle was abandoned, left rotting in the park. Maybe. That was the only explanation Lester could see. In any case, marijuana was growing there. He didn't really want to

smoke any, but it could be worth money, he heard.

That Friday night in the park at the Cadillac, the young man clipped the leaves carefully, as the book said, and stuffed them in a backpack. When he got home, he stashed the backpack under his bed and thought about the money he would make.

THREE

On Sunday morning, Cheryl Lewis sat in her pew watching people enter the sanctuary. She knew most of them and nodded as they took their seats. It was peaceful and quiet now, a good time to rest until the Pastor came in and the preaching and singing commenced. She had always enjoyed coming to this little church, where she'd been attending services and Sunday school since she was a girl. A few years ago, the congregation purchased a larger, modern church in the city, and most of her neighbors went there now. She'd visited the new place a few times, and it was nice, but she preferred the smaller chapel in Sloetown.

Only a few dozen folks attended the morning service now. The wooden pews were smooth and worn, the hymnals and Bibles soft and frayed. It felt like home. Her mother and father were buried in the cemetery out back. She wondered sometimes if they should also place a marker there for her brother Michael. It was seven years now since anyone had seen him. But no, she wouldn't give up hoping. Maybe something happened. She knew about the fire at the factory, as much as anyone, but what difference did it make? Michael was gone, no one knew how exactly. Maybe there was trouble, and he had to get away from Sloetown. And maybe someday there would be a knock on the door or a phone call. So, no, it wouldn't be right to put a stone in the cemetery for Michael yet. But seven years was a long time. It would be nice to have a way to help remember him.

* * *

Later that morning, Lester Lewis rolled over in bed and rubbed his eyes. He'd been up twice already with the baby, feeding her, playing with her, but now the child was sleeping again. It was going to be a long Sunday hanging around the house, watching the child. His sister Cheryl wouldn't be home till afternoon. Those people can sit in church all day, he thought.

His arm fell over the edge of the mattress onto the floor where he could feel under the bed. He touched it—his backpack. He withdrew the bag and squeezed it to make sure the contents were intact. He opened it and inhaled the fragrant smell of the weed, then fell back onto the bed and stared at the ceiling. How was he going to turn it into money? If he sold it, what could he buy? Images filled his mind: a new TV, a stereo, clothes, maybe even a car. But who would buy the stuff? How could he get some more? And how dangerous was it? He thought of getting arrested, and jail. Maybe the dope would get stale and lose its power. How much time did he have? And then Cheryl might find it.

Sell it soon. He knew a few guys down at the basketball court who liked to smoke. He pushed the backpack under the bed again and went to check the baby.

* * *

Baker Davis liked driving around Sloetown on Sunday mornings because it was quiet then. It also felt cooler under the monstrous oaks that covered everything in green shade. The investigator had no particular destination, cruising along in his Buick that was new a decade ago, when times were flush; but now with the rust spots and a dent in the rear, the vehicle looked right at home on the worn streets. He took his foot off the gas and let the car roll forward. Some people thought Sloetown was a ghetto. Some called it a slum. But life was comfortable here, something one could trust. Davis wasn't sure why. Maybe because the old neighborhood had been there so long.

A sermon trickled from the car radio, broadcast from one of the black churches nearby, the rise and fall of the Pastor's voice the only sound in the Buick. The words weren't really important, just an earnest melody to keep a man company. The Pastor was calling the lost that Sunday morning, and Baker Davis may have looked that way. Maybe he *was* searching for something: drugs, money, or a woman. If so, he was in the right place. Or if a man needed a job done, some business too awful to handle alone, there were men in Sloetown ready to help. Eager to help. One could imagine any number of reasons why a middle-aged white man was driving around Sloetown, none of them good. But no, Davis wasn't lost, nor was he looking for anything. He liked the cool shade, the peace of Sunday morning, and the sermon wasn't bad. So when he passed the vacant, weed-choked lot on Vinson Street and saw something white and motionless in the grass beside the vacant diner there . . . he kept driving. But in the next block, he stopped.

What the hell was that? Davis wiped his eyes as sunlight danced on the hood of the car. The image simmered in his mind, something pale and still in the tall grass of the empty lot. Was it alive? Dead? No. 'Must have been a piece of litter, a board, a stick, an old t-shirt or something. That's all. But his thoughts raced. This was Sloetown. Last night was Saturday night and it was hot, the middle of summer. Things happened. He cut the radio and lit a cigarette, hoping to forget that image, whatever it was. It would dissolve and fade. But no.

Davis circled the block, easing through Sloetown like an old man walking in a dark house, expecting to bump into something that would hurt. Sweat dripped inside his shirt. A few gaunt figures prowled the sidewalks: a grizzled white man in a red ball cap and a black man in a plaid shirt hanging outside his trousers. Davis zeroed in quickly on their hands, checking for a weapon or a bottle they might throw, but it was okay. He turned a corner, Vinson Street again. He listened. The silence was thick, but he felt his blood pounding behind his eyes. He let the Buick roll ahead. He didn't want the car to go forward, but it did.

And there in the vacant lot, something without motion and without color in the weeds. Davis pulled to the curb as the humid air brought a hard odor, hitting him like a sonic boom. If that smell had a color it would've been brown-purple or bronze, attractive and unsettling at once. He looked up and down Vinson Street, then opened his car door and stepped out. There was no one around. Newspapers tumbled across the black asphalt in the hot wind. Foam cups spun in the gutter. It was enervating. He crossed the street as a scrawny dog trotted from behind the old diner, then disappeared. Overhead, the trees were so big and old they were almost dead.

He approached the tall weeds of the vacant lot. It wasn't a decision. It wasn't something he planned. Sweat ran down his face as he stepped over bottles and cans. Then he saw a pale form taking shape in the grass. Long and lean. He stopped. His breath stopped. He squinted. The still, pale thing became a hand, almost reaching toward him. He parted the tall grass. The hand became an arm. His sweat turned cold. The arm became a shoulder . . . and then . . . there it was . . . the body of a woman.

She lay there peaceful, as if she was carved from marble. Davis wanted the body to scream, cry out, say something, anything . . . but all was silent. She was young, her face unlined, her hair still dark. She'd been shot, her blood dried black on her pale arms and legs. He couldn't tell how long the body had been there, but the stench hit him again. He gagged, moving away to gulp fresh air. He stumbled over to the abandoned diner at the edge of the lot, sat down hard on a pile of white-washed bricks. He lit a cigarette to drive away the smell of death and remembered something, remembered an image, a face. It was the photograph that Gloria Orion had shown him, the picture of Mira Ogilvy.

He wiped his brow and tried to remember. The photograph lay on his desk in the office, and he tried to recall it, but it wouldn't focus. And yet this poor girl, her face, her dark hair . . . . Davis took a few drags on the cigarette, steeled himself, and returned to the body. On the ground beside her neck, he noticed several round pebbles glinting in the sun. He kneeled, reaching for them. They were pearls. He remembered the beautiful necklace on the woman in the photograph. Suddenly, in an instant, he turned cold. His body tensed. Maybe he wasn't alone. Someone killed this girl. Maybe someone nearby.

Davis stood and backed away, letting the pearls fall into the grass. He scanned the vacant lot and Vinson Street. Everything was quiet, but he noticed a few men loitering at the end of the block. Davis walked quickly back to his car and got it moving, pushing the Buick from ten to twenty to thirty in a hurry. He rumbled along the old streets that were rough yet smooth like a face scarred by acne years before. Finally the trees gave way and the shade lifted. He reached a broad avenue, then the highway. It felt good to be moving again as the car hit forty then fifty. He rolled up the windows and let the air conditioner blast away as he mopped his face and rubbed his eyes to clear the image of the dead girl from his mind.

* * *

Davis drove back along the highway toward the city. A coffee shop was at the next exit and he went there, parked and tried to forget. He turned the radio on, then turned it off. Decay lingered in his nostrils and he wiped his face with a handkerchief. He tried another cigarette. It didn't work. The image of the lifeless body in the weeds revolved in his head along with the photo of Mira Ogilvy on his desk. What did Gloria Orion say? The girl had been missing for days, no lights at her house, no car in the driveway, the mail piled up.

Davis went inside the coffee shop. The teenager at the counter wasn't chatty, and she only nodded when he ordered a Coke on ice. That was good. He didn't want to talk. He felt if he started talking, he wouldn't be able to stop. In truth, he wanted to grab the lapels of the first person he saw and scream out what he found on Vinson Street, get it out of his system, exhale.

The teenager put the drink before him. He said, "Say, you got a sandwich or something back there?"

"We've got a little chicken salad made up."

"Great. Bring me some of that, on toast if you can."

"Coming up."

He drank the icy Coke, then glanced in his wallet to make sure he could pay. There was enough, barely. It made him remember that he had no license, little money, and now the image of a dead girl rotting in a vacant lot gripped his mind. He wondered how he got into this mess, how he landed on this square in life. Maybe Lieutenant Foster was right; it was time for a new career. But the bottom line was, Baker Davis didn't know how to do much except the detective work his father left behind, an inheritance he was still trying to figure out. He knew his old man had operated in the classic style, secretive, probing, even violent, helping out rich businessmen, professional people and politicians, and of course, their wives. He remembered Dad's library, the works of Dashiell Hammett and Earle Stanley Gardner lining the bookcases. Ray Chandler and Ross McDonald were represented. Davis never read these books, but he knew what they meant. But in all, the work depended on Dad's personality; and when he died, his clients found other ways to handle their problems. In fact, that was the issue—they were *Dad's* clients.

Still, the old man had left him something. The work itself had declined, become less fashionable, but there would always be philandering spouses, secret incomes, business scams, ancestral jewelry gone missing, or adult children who'd run away but remained connected to their parents' bank account. Then, many people simply needed to talk and needed a place to do it, which Baker Davis understood perfectly, even though he couldn't remember Dad ever teaching him this lesson. That skill was in his bones, and was required everywhere in the city—uptown, downtown, even Sloetown. Rich, poor, middle class. One could add a few zeroes to the financial statements, make the cast better spoken or better educated, but the plots and the motivations remained the same. Davis knew all deception bore the same fragrance, if one looked deeply. In all, the work kept him close to a power he didn't understand clearly, something elemental, hot, and chaotic. He needed to touch it, even though he wasn't sure why and had given up trying to figure out why.

Davis got up and went down the rear hall, toward the restrooms, where he knew there was a phone. He found Gloria Orion's card in his wallet. She picked up on the second ring.

"Mrs. Orion, it's Baker Davis."

"Oh . . . you. How are you?"

"I'm fine. Say, are you busy right now, this afternoon? I know it's Sunday."

"Well, yes, it is Sunday. I'm with my husband. What is it?"

"Well, I don't know."

"You don't know?"

"Are you busy? Now? There's something I want you to see."

She thought about it. "I can meet you."

"Good."

"Where?"

"In Sloetown." There was silence. "That's right. I think you better come."

"All right. The pallet factory is nearby, on the east side of Sloetown. I'll meet you there."

"That's good. Come now."

"Okay. It will take me about an hour."

Davis returned to his seat. The teenager came, set his sandwich on the counter, took his drink and refreshed it. The food helped, got him thinking: a body, a vacant lot in Sloetown. It happened, as it happened in any blighted neighborhood of a major American city. He knew that much. But not like this, not like this young woman in her pearls. She wasn't homeless, nor a wayward soul who got lost trying to score a dime bag in the back streets of the old district. Things like that weren't unusual in Sloetown. Whoever she was, it was no accident. Somebody put that girl in the vacant lot, with malice. It was murder. So yes, the police, and soon. Then Lieutenant Foster came to mind again, telling him to take a break, get out of town, stay out of her business. The cops never did find that junk dealer's money, the evidence, but a lot of people thought Baker Davis knew where it was. Important people. People who could hurt him. Okay then, he'd stay clear.

He finished the sandwich. The waitress came by, her eyes asking if he was done, or needed anything else. He shook his head.

"Six bucks," she said, laying a bill before him. He threw a five and couple of ones on the counter and thanked her with a smile. As he exited the restaurant, he stopped again at the phone in the hall. He picked up the receiver and dialed a police tip line. He knew on Sunday it would be a recording, though someone was likely monitoring it.

"Four hundred block of Vinson, in Sloetown, behind the old diner," he told the machine when it answered. The words struggled to come, but he got them out. He wanted to say more, but this much would get the cops to send a car around. They didn't need him. They'd find that girl. It was enough for now. Let it go.

* * *

Late that afternoon, Detective Lieutenant Doreen Foster was cooking dinner at home. For years, she'd prepared the Sunday meal for her family mid-day, but now with her son working and her daughter away at college, they wouldn't arrive until evening. That was okay. She liked having dinner ready for them whenever they could make it.

Her younger sister Della lived nearby and often visited. They spent the day in the kitchen drinking pink lemonade and talking.

The Lieutenant found it very relaxing, and a respite from her work in the Homicide Division of the Police Department—so Della refrained from asking about it. Idle family gossip, the languid, slow cooking, and the lemonade were sufficient. The sisters were trying to determine the exact amount of pepper required in the fried chicken batter when the phone rang. They looked at each other. They knew, and everyone who knew the Fosters understood, that Sunday afternoon was their time, their ritual, and there was no point in disturbing them. Doreen Foster sighed, but reached for the phone.

"Hello."

"Lieutenant?" Della heard the voice come through the receiver, a man's voice.

"Sorry to bother you at home, but we got a tip. And now . . . a situation."

"A situation, huh? Can't it wait till Monday?" She had been in homicide for three years. The tragic murders that occurred in the city over the weekend were by now little surprise to her. They were routine. She could deal with it later.

"Yes, I guess it could wait ma'am, but I wanted to let you know that . . . this one is different." Della watched the lines in her sister's face grow deeper as the man explained.

"In Sloetown?" the Lieutenant asked. "All right, I'll come on over. Are the forensics people there?"

"Yes," the caller said. "And the coroner is on the way." She put the phone down slowly.

"I'll finish getting this chicken ready," Della said.

Doreen Foster knew that Sloetown was no stranger to murder. She understood. She'd grown up there.

* * *

Baker Davis left the restaurant and drove back toward Sloetown and Gloria Orion. He took Kenner Boulevard, a broad, divided road which years ago had been County Road 18, then became state highway 74, then U.S. highway 33, and finally took the name of a Senator Kenner who went to Washington in the 1950's. Road signs for all these incarnations still dotted the shoulders, confusing visitors beyond hope. These markers bore shades of rust like an archaeological record, their true meaning a

TWENTY GRAND

mystery, but Davis knew them, knew them better than he wanted to.

He passed a long stretch of stores selling liquor, furniture, haircuts, pagers, payday loans, and hot wings; then he turned onto a street guarded by a faded taco joint and a used car lot. He was in Sloetown, and felt the heat of late afternoon giving way to the cool shade of the trees overhead. Most of the inhabitants had retreated to broad porches. If a man had a swing there, and rocked it some, he could stir up a little breeze. Some front yards boasted little plastic swimming pools filled with water from the garden hose. Children splashed in the water that always looked blue. Davis wondered how a corpse could lay decomposing a few blocks away.

In a few minutes the streets ended. He'd reached the east side and before him stood a brown brick building as long as a city block—the Orion Pallet Company. The old factory was immense, monumental, permanent, like something out of Egypt, and surrounded by a vast parking lot. Birds circled overhead, landed, then flew away. In the distance, at the end of the lot, a man pushed a shopping cart beside a chain link fence. It looked right. Also near the fence a late model SUV was parked. It didn't look right. Davis drove toward it. The window came down as he stopped beside the vehicle.

"You made it," he said.

"I came as soon as I could."

"I know it's Sunday, but I've—"

"No, no. If you've got something, Mr. Davis. I want to know about it."

"I do too."

She looked at him, puzzled.

"We better take my car," he said. "But lock yours up."

"All right." She gathered her purse, her sunglasses, and in a moment she was in the Buick. The summer humidity outside had loosened her hair so it curled on her cheek and clung to her neck.

"We shouldn't be long," Davis said.

"Oh, I don't mind." A faint smile appeared at the corner of her mouth. They left the parking lot, the huge factory receding behind them. Soon they were back among the old streets.

"I guess you know the neighborhood," Davis said blankly.

"No, not really. Karl and I . . . we come to the office, then we go home. But most of the guys who work in the factory, they live around here."

"I guess pallet work doesn't pay that much."

"It pays enough," she said, not defensively. "But those guys . . . they don't stay for long. They come and they go. They get sick, start drinking, gamble their paychecks away, fight, steal stuff. It never ends."

The shadows grew longer as the afternoon dwindled and the car rumbled across patches of brick in the street where the blacktop had worn away. Sloetown was very old. No one could remember a time when it wasn't there, when it wasn't like it always was, or any different. In a few minutes, they reached Vinson Street. Davis tightened, preparing himself. Then he slammed the brake.

"What in the …?"

Three police cars and a fire department vehicle blocked the street. The tip he called in had worked, better than he thought it would. The cops came in a hurry. He pulled his car over and stopped. Uniformed men stood in the vacant lot, searching in the tall grass.

"What's going on?" Gloria Orion asked.

"Come on," he said, exiting the car. "Say, do you have a Kleenex or something? Any perfume?" Her brows came together, her eyes narrow. Then she reached for her purse, withdrawing a tissue and a small bottle. He took the tissue and sprinkled perfume into it, holding it to his face. "Like this. You might need it."

* * *

In the vacant lot, Lt. Doreen Foster bent over a stiff body in the tall weeds with Officer Jeremy Wilson, who said,

"Gunshot. Looks like twice, in the neck and back, exit wound from the chest." Another cop, Angela Grimes, kneeled in the grass beside the dead girl in the black dress. Then the smell, rotten and curdled, almost waxy, opaque, like burnt wood, sour milk, wet dogs. Officer Wilson turned away, his hand over his mouth.

"Anything else?" the Lieutenant asked. She and Grimes had worked domestic violence in the past, and many rape cases. Grimes understood the question.

"Nothing I can tell right now, Lieutenant, nothing obvious. No struggle, no fighting I can see. Her clothing is kinda undisturbed, considering. Just the two gunshot wounds. She was

TWENTY GRAND

likely gone before she knew what hit her."

Wilson came back, paler but breathing easier.

"We did find these, Lieutenant." He held up a little plastic bag containing small glassy spheres. The Lieutenant took them gently, watching them flash in the sun.

"Pearls?"

"I think so, ma'am."

She withdrew one and rolled it between her fingers. A few of the pearls were soiled. "Only these?"

"That's all we found in the weeds."

"No string or a necklace anywhere?"

"Nope."

"Robbery then, maybe."

"I don't know, Lieutenant."

"If there's a few lying around, maybe they weren't snatched until the girl got here, in this lot." They were all quiet for a moment. "So they shot her first, maybe, and grabbed the necklace when they dumped her here, dropping some in the grass."

"Huh," Wilson said. "Like the pearls were an afterthought, maybe. Like robbery wasn't the main thing."

"Maybe not."

"Maybe they just wanted her dead."

The silence returned as they huddled over the dead woman. Again the smell of death began to overwhelm them.

"We'll figure it out. Let's get her in," the Lieutenant ordered. Two men came forward with a stretcher as the police withdrew. Lt. Foster stood and looked out over the vacant lot, at the empty, boarded-up diner before them, its whitewashed bricks turning gray. She surveyed the neighborhood, taking it all in, trying to understand how a young woman in a good dress and nice jewelry might end up in this part of town. She walked back to her car, thinking *No, the victim's final moments weren't here in this weed-choked lot. She didn't come to Vinson Street on her own. She was killed somewhere else.* But the Lieutenant felt . . . and it was only a feeling . . . that somewhere else wasn't far away.

Then she noticed a man crossing the street, approaching the scene, a man she knew. A tall, blonde woman accompanied him.

"Mr. Davis," she said as the PI came forward. "Not expecting to see you here in Sloetown."

"Just out for a Sunday drive, Lieutenant," he answered.

"Guess I wasn't expecting to see you either." The blonde woman shifted uneasily. Lieutenant Foster regarded them both.

"Sunday drive huh?"

"Sure Lieutenant. You know it's always cool and shady up here in Sloetown."

"I know all about it Mr. Davis. So you're not working today?" Davis knew what she meant. She told him a year ago he was due for a vacation, a long one.

"No, not me. I'm kinda retired these days, you might say. But we were driving around, turned the corner, and here you are. So what's going on?" They saw the coroner's men in black trousers and black t-shirts carrying a stretcher away from the weedy lot.

"I'm Gloria Orion," the blonde woman interrupted. The Lieutenant took the hand she extended.

"I'm Doreen Foster, homicide."

Davis felt his companion start. She asked "Is someone . . . was someone in that vacant lot?"

The Lieutenant frowned. She looked at Davis and the woman. "I wouldn't be out here on Sunday otherwise. 'Plenty of things I'd rather be doing this afternoon than finding a body in Sloetown." She remembered her sister Della making dinner and the cold lemonade she left behind.

Gloria Orion gasped. "Oh!"

"Any ID, Lieutenant?" Davis asked. The men with the stretcher opened the doors of the ambulance.

"Not yet, but we will."

"You mind if I take a look?"

The Lieutenant thought about it for a moment. "So you're not working, right?" Davis shook his head *No*. Again she considered it, squinting her eyes. "And I can count on you to keep quiet?"

"Absolutely, Lieutenant."

"All right, Davis. It'll be in the papers in couple days anyway." She yelled at the men with the stretcher. "Just a moment guys!"

The Lieutenant moved toward them. Davis led Gloria Orion forward, taking her arm. It was warm, trembling. He whispered to her, "I need you to see something."

The coroner's men paused, ready to push the stretcher into their vehicle. A skinny, red-haired cop stood nearby.

"It's not pretty," one of them said. "You sure?"

Davis nodded as Gloria's fingers tightened on his arm. The

man in the black shirt yanked the blue tarp which covered the body. The blood-smeared face of the young woman appeared. Gloria Orion shuddered.

"Mira!"

"What?!" the red-haired cop exclaimed.

"You know her?" the Lieutenant said.

Gloria Orion shook her head, covering her mouth. "No! Yes. I do, but not well." She took the perfumed tissue from her purse and brought it to her nose. She breathed deeply.

"You said *Mira*," the red-haired cop said.

"It looks like her."

The Lieutenant said "Mira—?"

"Yes. Mira. Mira Ogilvy."

"Ogilvy, huh? You're sure Mrs. Orion?"

"I believe so. She lives over on Lafayette, I think."

The red-haired cop perked up. "Well then, we're gonna need to ask you some questions ma'am." Davis glared at him.

"Oh, sure. Anything," Gloria Orion said, "but maybe tomorrow, if that's okay. Here." She withdrew a card from her purse, handing it to him. "Call me. I'll do anything I can to help." He took the card, then handed it to Lt. Foster. She thought about it for a moment, then nodded and said,

"All right, Mrs. Orion. We'll be in touch soon." She turned to the men: "Let's get this place cleaned up guys!" They drew the blue tarp back over the body and lifted the stretcher into the ambulance.

The Lieutenant watched Gloria Orion gather herself. Her reaction, her shock, appeared normal, but it was likely this well-dressed woman had more to tell. If she did, it would come out in time. She had learned not to suspect much until the evidence, the facts, were on the table.

"Ever seen anything like that, Mrs. Orion?" the Lieutenant asked.

"I'm afraid I haven't."

"And Mr. Davis. Did you find what you were looking for?"

"Yes. I mean no. I wasn't looking for anything, Lieutenant. Just curious, you know. It's in my blood, I guess. But I appreciate it."

She watched Davis and the blonde return to their car. The doors of the ambulance slammed shut and Doreen Foster knew that something was starting now, not ending, and she wasn't particularly looking forward to it. Baker Davis and this Orion woman turning up in Sloetown today didn't feel right, though it might be harmless. She didn't trust the PI. He didn't have a license anymore and shouldn't be working and maybe he wasn't. It didn't make much difference as long as he stayed out of the way. Private investigators—a necessary evil she thought, like defense attorneys, though she was never too clear about the necessary part. They were tolerable if they kept to the civil side, handling divorces, money problems and such; but she also knew them to hang around the periphery of criminal investigations, trying to *help*, trying to drum up a little business. Most of the time they were simply in the way.

But murder? No. That was her territory. And this one wasn't going to be easy. She got into her car, glad to be driving away from Vinson Street as day ended in Sloetown. She hoped Della got that seasoning right in the fried chicken.

* * *

Davis led his client away, his hand on her shoulder. She leaned into him, accepting the gesture but not relaxing. In the car they rested and smoked, watching darkness fall among the trees as the cops finished their work in the vacant lot.

"You've got to help me, Baker," she said softly. A dry sob came up, her voice fragile. She removed her sunglasses.

"What do you know about this?"

"I knew her, that's all. 'Merely an acquaintance. A sweet girl, a little messed up." Then she looked at him, her eyes saying *But who isn't?* The eyes were beautiful, vulnerable even for a brief second.

"No one deserves that," she continued. "Out there in a vacant lot, in this neighborhood. It's terrible. Awful!"

"Yeah it is."

"Do you think the police will find out who did it? I mean, it looks like a murder, right?"

Davis shrugged. "I don't know. But a girl like that . . . it will get their attention. And since you ID'd her, they've got to talk with you, too."

"I know. It's okay." She tossed her cigarette out the window, then collected herself, smoothing her hair back, patting at her blouse. She withdrew another tissue from her purse and daubed her moist eyes, then her lips.

"So we must hurry." Her face was blank.
"You wanted me to find her. That was Mira Ogilvy, right?"
"Yes. That was Mira, I'm sure of it. A terrible thing."
"Well, the cops will take care of the rest."
"I wanted to talk with her, Baker."

Davis eyed her. She looked away, asked for another cigarette, and said, "You see, there's a problem. Mira had money, but it wasn't hers. And no one can account for it." She lit the cigarette and blew smoke out the window up into the trees. "Certainly not now."

"So that's what you're looking for? Money?"

She shot him a sharp glance. "I said it wasn't hers."

"Then how did she get—?"

"Look, Baker, there's important people involved. They have a rightful claim to these . . . assets."

"Assets, huh? Nice term. So it was a lot of money."

"Yes."

"Do you have any idea . . . ?"

"A lot, hundreds of thousands."

"So you don't know exactly?"

"I said it wasn't hers!"

Davis let it go, but he wasn't surprised. When he learned the missing girl was Winston Ogilvy's daughter, he knew other issues would surface. He was used to working with people like the Ogilvys. He knew how they operated, their motivations, their sins of omission and commission; where they were hard and ruthless, where soft and sentimental. That was his experience. But then again, maybe Mira simply took a wrong turn in a bad neighborhood. That was Sloetown. He knew that too.

"All that money—" Gloria Orion said, staring out the window at the vacant lot.

The police were finishing up. One last car remained as the streetlights began to flicker in the gray twilight. Davis started the Buick and left Vinson Street as warm, tired air blew in through the windows.

"Maybe the police will find out," he said.

"The police. They can handle the murder. I don't care about that." The intensity of her words grabbed Davis, but he kept his eyes straight ahead. "No," she added. "I didn't mean it that way. I can't bring Mira back, not now. No one can. It's terrible about that poor girl."

"Somebody killer her, Gloria. Those were gunshots."

"But that money. It wasn't hers. And now I need your help to find . . . " She didn't finish.

Davis made his way through Sloetown, back to the pallet factory, thinking about Lt. Foster. She had seen him, knew he was back in town. Searching for a client's missing friend was one thing; he could do that under the radar. But now the missing friend was a homicide and the police were involved. If he got close, the Lieutenant would notice.

He glanced at Gloria Orion as they arrived back at the pallet factory. She was smiling, but her eyes were hard. She reached into her purse and grabbed her wallet.

"Here," she said, writing a check. "It's another five hundred."

"No."

"Baker you've got to help me. I can't help that Mira's gone, but that money wasn't hers. We've got to find it."

Davis stopped the Buick beside her SUV as he thought of Lt. Foster. She'd warned him, again, but maybe he could pull it off. It would be hard, but he knew he could play it, knew he could turn up something about this dead girl's money before they got wise. And the pay was coming easy, for now. Gloria Orion laid the fresh check on the console and said,

"Are you busy now? A lot of clients these days? You've got time, right?"

"Yeah, I've got time," he muttered.

She reached across the car and touched his shoulder. "I need someone. I can't do it by myself." Her hand lingered there as he parked next to her SUV.

"What did you say Mira's address was? Where she lived?"

"420 Lafayette, in the Palatine. I went there Friday, but it was all dark."

She opened her door, looking him full in the eyes. "I hope you can do something soon, Baker. If you need more money—"

"I'll let you know."

Gloria Orion stepped from the car, slammed the door and got into her SUV. Davis watched her drive away and suddenly it felt late. He felt worn out as he left the big parking lot of Orion Pallet. He couldn't remember doing much work that day, but the dead woman in the tall weeds was enough. It was good to be leaving

Sloetown.

When he arrived home, he picked up the Sunday paper on the sidewalk. Inside, the cat and dog greeted him, dancing around in circles with excitement. He'd been gone all day. He petted the cat and wrestled with the dog, letting them both out the back door as he fell into a chair with the newspaper. He skimmed the big stories on the front page, moving quickly to the sports. The AAA baseball team had left the city last year, and in August there was little news.

Drowsiness took over. The dead girl in the vacant lot swam heavily into his thoughts, like something washed up on the shore of a vast and melancholy ocean. Words careened through his mind: *body corpse cadaver remains stiff the deceased the departed* . . . but nothing seemed right. Then more words, *ashes dust earth dead.* And finally *money*.

Baker Davis fell asleep in his chair.

* * *

Gloria Orion left Sloetown that evening with a sick feeling about the young woman in the vacant lot. But she felt worse that Mira Ogilvy was not only dead but gone, and maybe her money was lost forever. It would be much harder now. Maybe this Davis character could help. He seemed to be comfortable working in the shadows, behind the scenes. Maybe he'd turn up something. If the man had no license, even better; then he would stay clear of the police. That was fine. It was messy enough without the cops. They could look for Mira's killer, and Davis could find her money. Neat.

It was getting late, but Gloria Orion didn't go home. She drove through the city to visit her brother. Time didn't matter. When she reached his house, there was a light in the living room.

Richard McDermott hadn't dressed that day. He spent the weekend thinking about his bankers, trying to think of a way out. He imagined his last day at work after they foreclosed on McDermott Center. He saw brown boxes strewn around his office suite, filled with his possessions, and beefy men in uniforms coming to roll them away to . . . he didn't know where. Nor did he know where he would go then.

McDermott sat in his house, smoking and drinking, one lamp on. When he heard knocking at the front door, it came as a relief. He looked out the window, saw his sister's car in the drive and let her in. She entered without a word, her face drawn up and narrow. She fell on the couch and kicked off her shoes. The Sunday paper covered the floor. The room smelled of alcohol.

"Keeping the Sabbath?" she asked, nodding at the scotch and cigarettes on the table.

"Of course. Join me?"

She got up and poured a drink. "Why don't you turn some lights on?" she asked, flicking on another lamp.

"It won't do any good." He ran his fingers through his black hair.

She returned to the sofa, sank into the cushions, and stared at the ceiling. "You're not going to find Mira."

"I told you, I'll make some calls."

"No, Richard. She's gone."

"It's only been a few days. Relax." He went to the table, lit a cigarette.

"No." She sipped at her drink again. "Mira's dead."

His mouth opened and his eyebrows came together.

"They found her, Richard. Up in Sloetown. Somebody killed her."

"Killed? What the hell? What happened?" There was urgency in his voice, but no feeling.

"Somebody murdered the woman. That's all I know, all anyone knows right now. The police found her on Vinson Street, in Sloetown." She drank the scotch, feeling it warm her empty stomach, settle her nerves. Her feet and legs felt heavy, tired. It wasn't unwelcome.

McDermott drew hard on the cigarette. He splashed more scotch into his glass, tossed it back. Then he stood at the fireplace, drumming his fingers on the mantle. "Damnation. You sure it was Mira?"

"Uh-huh." She closed her eyes and whispered "All that money . . ."

"Damn. It won't be easy now. What about that detective? Davis?"

"I don't know."

"He's not entirely legit, you know. I checked. He's got no license, not right now. Is he going to be of any use?"

"Maybe. *I* don't know where to look for the money, so I paid him to help. A grand so far."

"Is that enough?"

"How should I know?" Then Gloria Orion sighed, rose from the couch and crossed the room to a window. She peered out into the dark, empty street. "I do know, however, that some men need a different kind of incentive."

AUSTIN McLELLAN

FOUR

The pain started in his arms and legs a year ago, but months passed before Karl Orion could bring himself to mention it—that he was hurting. He went to the doctor. He went to the specialist. He told Gloria there were tests, but that's all he could say. He didn't want her involved, almost pushed her away. But finally the oncologist called and since then he'd been living with the bad news alone. It was cancer. And it was very dangerous. Still, there was reason to hope. He would fight it.

That's how Karl Orion operated. It was his problem and he would deal with it. When he needed to put something out of his mind, he could build a wall around it. Solid. But the pills they gave him were tough. He vomited at the office, and last night he felt weak and went to bed early. It wasn't the right time to tell Gloria. He needed to sleep on it, and hoped he might wake up and discover it was all a dream.

Now it was morning, the sun bright already. When he awakened, Gloria was already out of bed and moving around. On Mondays, they took their time going to the office. As Orion got up and found his robe, pains shot through his legs and he sat on the bed for a minute. It was no dream. His wife was busy at the stove, making breakfast, and the smell of coffee helped. He gathered himself and went to the kitchen.

"Come here honey," he said. And as soon as he spoke, Gloria Orion knew something was wrong. She sat at the table with him. "I'm not going to the office today. You go ahead. I'm not feeling well."

"All right. Maybe if you eat—"

"No. The doctor called. The tests were . . . " he sighed heavily. "It looks like cancer, Gloria."

She opened her mouth. No sound came forth.

"That's right, baby. Cancer."

"Oh no! Oh, Karl," she said, reaching to hold him. She cradled his head in her arms and stroked his face. The man sighed deeply, but there was something in him that couldn't quite let go, couldn't let tears come and overwhelm them. It was a freedom he didn't really understand, but he held her tightly, his face buried against her shoulder. They embraced as the morning sun streamed in upon them.

Gloria Orion knew she would be with him, until the end, if that's what it took. It wouldn't be her first time, caring for the sick. She'd been down that road with an uncle years ago, and her grandmother before that.

"I'm sure it will be all right," she said. "I'm sure it'll be fine."

"Well, the doc said there's reason to hope, with this type of cancer. We can fight it." His voice was shaky but she knew her husband was a strong man, stronger than she was in many ways. And she knew that if fighting was required to beat this, Karl Orion was the right man for the job.

"Sure there's hope! Don't worry. It's going to be okay." She held him tighter, as the sum of what he meant for her life washed over her like ocean waves: her escape from Kentucky, the time they met, the years together at Orion Pallet, their beautiful home. There was so much life in her husband. He was so much more than sickness or disease. Still, as she sat with him at the kitchen table that morning, Gloria Orion couldn't help but wonder if she held a dead man in her arms.

"I'm going to Mercy Hospital next week, for chemotherapy," he said.

"Oh, they're the best. We'll get the best help we can."

"I don't know, Gloria."

"Oh yes, don't worry. It's going to be all right. I know it."

"It's going to be rough, this treatment. I'm going to be sick for a long time."

"Shhh," she whispered in his ear. "Don't worry. We'll do everything we can. Everything."

"I don't know."

"Stop it, honey. It's going to be fine."

"No, not the treatment. I can deal with that. The doctor said it's promising. It's just that, well, I'm not sure we can—"

"Can't what? Look, I'll be there with you. Stop worrying. It doesn't help anything." She kissed him on the temple.

"I know I know. But I'm not sure we can do everything, you know, with the treatment."

"Sure, we'll do everything possible, Karl. It's going to be all right."

"No, Gloria. Maybe we can't." She withdrew and looked into his eyes. They were empty. "These treatments are very costly. Thousands and thousands . . ."

"I know, I know. But they can deal with it. The insurance will take care of it."

"No, honey. They won't."

"Sure they will. That's what insurance is for, for this kind of thing."

"Gloria," he said, as he tried to stand, but his breath fell short and he sank more deeply into his chair, as if he couldn't get up. "Glo—"

"Karl?"

But he couldn't speak. He looked out the window at the morning sun and said,

"There isn't any."

"Don't be silly."

Again he tried to get up. This time he made it, and stood over her at the table. He surveyed the kitchen, the den, and looked out the window to their beautiful garden, and thought how within days he must trade it all in for a hospital room, a room where he would be sick, and maybe die.

"There is no insurance."

"No ins—?" Her lips parted.

Karl Orion shook his head. "I couldn't pay them Gloria, the premiums. There's no money. The policy was cancelled last month."

* * *

At police headquarters that day, Lt. Doreen Foster frowned at the homicide reports piled on her desk. They seemed to be waiting for her. There could be one or two, or she'd seen as many as four reports come in after a long, hot weekend in the summer. She always tried to guess how many deaths had occurred by the size of the pile, but she never got it right because sometimes the write-ups were lengthy and detailed, other times brief and to the point. Occasionally nobody knew anything. There was nothing to say.

But the Lieutenant supervised the Homicide Division, and it was her job on Mondays to get formal investigations started. It was a strange business, but she accepted it now. At first, three years ago when she took the position, it didn't make sense that anyone except God Almighty would make decisions about such matters. Yes, eventually her men followed up on every incident, but there were priorities to be set, resources to be allocated. So when a report involved a homeless man found stabbed under a bridge, it got pushed down the list. Chances of solving a crime like that were remote, she knew. Then there was always a shooting over a dice game in an alley. That got pushed down the list too because, frankly, nobody cared. And there was little need to move quickly on domestic violence, men and women killing each other, because the guilty party always thought they were justified anyway, so they rarely fled. She simply dispatched a patrol car to pick them up.

But this weekend a young woman turned up dead in a vacant lot up in Sloetown. Homicide gave every crime its due, and she was proud of that, but this one was different. It wasn't routine. It bothered her.

She reached for her coffee and the reports when Officer Jeremy Wilson appeared in the doorway. He was one of her new detectives. She liked him, but he had a lot to learn, she thought. And he ought to hit the gym, or the buffet table at least. He was too skinny for a cop.

"I've got a little bit on that woman we found in Sloetown, Lieutenant, if you're ready."

"Sure."

Wilson came in and took a seat in her bare office. "The medical exam was inconclusive," he explained. "But it doesn't look like a sex thing, no evidence of an assault, anything like that. Just a couple of gunshots so far. And no slugs turned up, but the wounds were consistent with something common like a .38 or a 9mm."

"Belonging to whom, Detective?"

Wilson sighed.

"Any drugs or alcohol?"

"Not yet, Lieutenant. Right now, we're looking at why she was there, in Sloetown."

"You think she had a reason, Mr. Wilson?"

"I don't know. But you know Sloetown is a dangerous place. Not the best neighborhood."

The Lieutenant was tempted to roll her eyes, but she held back.

"I'm familiar with the neighborhood, Wilson. My point is that a woman like that . . . you're saying she had a *reason* to be there? That she died right there, in that vacant lot? That's where somebody shot her? Is that what you're saying, Detective?"

He didn't answer.

"How do you know they didn't kill the poor woman somewhere else, then dumped her out there in the weeds?"

He couldn't answer.

"Wilson?"

"I'll look into it Ma'am." He scribbled something on a pad. "If the woman didn't have a reason, maybe she took a wrong turn, got lost or something."

"Maybe. Was she driving? Is there a car?"

"We did a look-up at Motor Vehicles. Miss Ogilvy owned a white BMW."

"Well, where is it?"

Again Wilson had no answer.

"Another angle to work then," she said, drumming her fingers softly on the desk. "Look, Detective, all I'm saying is . . . a woman like that, a white woman, a pretty young girl in a nice dress, wearing pearls . . . women like that have no reason to visit Sloetown. At all. Ever."

"Right." Wilson replied. He wrote on his pad.

"And what about those pearls we found?"

"Yes, it was the victim's blood on them."

"That's not surprising." The Lieutenant glanced at the report on Mira Ogilvy, then at Wilson. "Well, anyway, you'll have to go up to Sloetown and take a look around. Let's find her car. The girl *did* end up in that lot. Maybe she did have a reason for being in Sloetown, I don't know. And have you been out to her house yet?"

"I'm going there today."

"All right. And what about that Orion woman? The blonde

who ID'd the body for us yesterday?"

"She's on my list too, Lieutenant. I'll be talking with her. Soon."

"Keep your eyes open, Detective."

"Always, Ma'am." He rose to leave.

"And let me know if you see that PI snooping around. That Davis guy."

* * *

Best Diner was home style, serving food which didn't have a name other than what it was: roast beef, chicken, fried fish, pork chops, vegetables, spaghetti (on the side), and 24-hour breakfast. The restaurant was quiet that morning and Cheryl Lewis liked it that way. It meant fewer tips, but the slow pace gave her time to read her assignment. She was enrolled at the evening college downtown, working on her teaching certificate. Alone in the waitress station that morning, she hid a textbook under the menus and read between customers. Only an elderly couple occupied her section of the big dining room. She read a few more pages in her book, then noticed a solitary man in a distant booth—he was simply there all of a sudden. She grabbed the coffee pot and a water.

Richard McDermott hadn't slept well. It was Monday and he didn't want to go to the office; in fact, he didn't want to do anything except relax in a booth at the Best Diner. He had cleaned up that morning but feared the scotch he drank the night before lingered in his skin. He hoped it would dissipate by the time he reached McDermott Center. But at the same time, he didn't care.

With a shaky hand, he scribbled numbers on a napkin. These were his finances. But no matter how he added the figures, the result was the same: there wasn't enough money for the mortgage payment, not by the end of the week, nor the week after that. Key tenants in McDermott Center had left the past few years and he'd been unable to replace them. Entire floors in the twenty-story building were dark and empty. During the holidays, the tenants normally decorated their offices with red and green lights. Parents brought their kids to see it. But last Christmas, the dark, empty floors made the whole building look sad, and no children came.

McDermott looked up and saw the waitress notice him from

across the room. He returned to his numbers, worrying about his reputation. He imagined voices at the cocktail parties, in the better restaurants, and in the pews of the Episcopal church; the voices that wondered, that speculated . . . *How is Richard doing? He's really taking a hit these days. 'Such a nice man. I wonder how much longer he can hold out. It's a pity. He was a smart guy—once.*

But McDermott knew they hated him, knew they celebrated his bad luck. He knew the secret joy which lay behind the long faces of pity and commiseration. He wasn't sure why, except that he'd been their landlord for so long, *the big man on top*. Then he remembered the bankers who came to see him yesterday. Years ago, it would have been okay to go see Tommy Jameson, the antiquated owner of the bank, and plead his case to the old guy. They could drink a beer, reminisce about McDermott's father, play a few holes of golf, then cut a deal. But negotiating with the fat man and his bitchy sidekick—McDermott couldn't accept that. A bitter taste rose in his throat. He glanced once more at the numbers on the napkin. They were unchanged.

Then the waitress approached his booth, disrupting his attention. McDermott hadn't seen anything quite like her in a long time. No one teaches women how to walk anymore, not formally he reflected, and maybe that was a good thing, but this one didn't need any lessons. She came toward him, quiet, smooth, and composed, with a coffee and water glass balanced perfectly in her hands. She was confident, but not athletic like a man. *Graceful* was the word that came to him. It was not a quality the lawyer normally associated with a black woman. He knew it. He wasn't proud of it, but there it was. Then he realized he enjoyed watching her. He forgot about the numbers on his napkin.

Cheryl Lewis noticed this customer's nice suit jacket as she placed the water on the table before him, but his face was drawn and worried, as if he'd had a rough night. Though it was warm in the dining room, the man remained in his coat. He should relax, she thought. His hair was dark and slicked back like a TV anchorman's. She wondered about white people's hair sometimes. It would take her all afternoon to get hers to do like that. This customer didn't look up, but merely nudged his cup forward as if that was all he could manage.

"Thanks," the man whispered hoarsely as she poured the coffee. "Have you got an egg maybe? A piece of toast?"

Her eyelids fell forward. She looked him over. "Yes. Sure you don't want anything else?" He shook his head. "We've got blueberry pancakes on Monday." Again he shook his head, closing his eyes. He rubbed his face and reached for the coffee. His hands were white and fine as ivory. And they appeared strong, but not muscular.

McDermott wanted to say something to her, but his lips were dry, his mouth tight. Then she left to place the order. He watched her walk away as he sipped at the coffee and returned to his numbers. 'Still the same. How to get money, he wondered. Maybe a mortgage on the house? No, no one would lend to him now. They knew he was in trouble, and even then, it would only raise a little cash. Then he remembered . . . Mira Ogilvy has money, or did, and maybe Gloria has a right to it, especially if her husband was skimming it from Orion Pallet, their company. That's it: Karl has been stealing from common property! It's a fraudulent conveyance, a misappropriation of funds, invalid.

But what the hell had Mira done with the money? It might add up to hundreds of thousands of dollars. If he and Gloria could find it, and get it, he could write a fat check to that fat banker and throw it in his face. But the girl was dead. Gone. She wasn't coming back and the prospect of finding that money felt remote, but maybe . . . .

Then he wondered if this is what delusion felt like.

McDermott looked out across the big dining room at the few customers who lingered there and wondered how it all happened, how it came to be that he sat there, alone, waiting on a stranger to bring him something to eat. Best Diner was a decent place, but it felt like a hospital. He heard soft music trickling from old speakers in the ceiling. It was an ancient jazz tune, a cloying sound that reminded him of better days when he was . . . yes, he had to admit it, when he was young.

The waitress returned. Jesus, she looked good. She said, "Here's your toast. And I brought you some pancakes, just in case you want to try 'em."

McDermott noticed the woman's smooth neck as she leaned over the table and placed the food before him. Her blouse was tight and he heard it move against her skin.

"I'll get you some more coffee," she said.

"Thanks," he croaked. She left again. Slowly he nibbled at the egg and toast. It went down easy. Then he looked at the pancakes. He couldn't remember when anyone had made anything like that for him. The blueberries smelled great.

The waitress was back. "Sure you don't want to try those pancakes?" she asked, pouring him more coffee.

"I don't like to talk much in the morning."

"Oh all right. I won't bother you."

"No, I didn't mean it like that." He looked up from his coffee, his eyes almost crawling up her figure. She was young but not a girl any more. Not by a long shot. "I guess talking with customers—it's part of the job, huh?"

"Yeah, it is," Cheryl Lewis said, smiling. "Monday mornings are slow." She noticed the man held his fork in a proper way, with his fingers, not with his fist like most men who came into the restaurant. She saw the numbers he'd written on the napkin. No one ever did that in Best Diner. She lingered.

McDermott looked down at his coffee again, slowly letting his eyes wander over the shape of the woman. "You work every day?"

"Mostly, but at night I'm in school, at the college downtown."

"Downtown? I work there too."

"Oh yeah? Whereabouts?"

"My office is there."

Cheryl Lewis didn't know what to say next, but something held her at the table with this man. The people she normally waited on had nothing they would call *my office*. They ate fast and reported to jobs somewhere. But this customer . . . it seemed as if he could sit here all morning. She put her hands on her hips, as if she was frustrated, couldn't figure this one out.

McDermott noticed her again. He caught her nametag—Cheryl. "College, huh? What are you studying?"

"Education. I'm working on my teaching certificate."

"That's great. You'll be good at that." He meant it. The woman smiled. It was a beautiful smile. Her teeth were brilliant. "I bet you're good at a lot of things." He didn't know why he said that; it simply broke free of him. The words touched her. She shifted uneasily, but she liked hearing it from this man. She believed him. Then she remembered the other customers.

"You better try some of those pancakes," she said lightly.

"Yes, miss teacher," he said, and Cheryl Lewis laughed softly, moving away to the other tables. McDermott was glad when she left so he could watch her, the way she walked, her legs moving against the polyester of the uniform that clung to her like sticky tape. The woman was really good looking. His suit jacket suddenly felt warm and he removed it. He took a bite of the pancakes, then another. Then he tried to recall the name of that fat banker but now it escaped him.

When the waitress came back across the dining room with the coffee, McDermott tried not to notice her. Slowly, she refilled his cup. Then she looked at him and his eyes were on her. She smiled nervously, her lips parted. The eggs and toast and pancakes were gone. He'd eaten everything.

"Your 'cakes were great," he said. She saw his white shirt now. Without the jacket, his shoulders looked straight and strong. His eyes were lively and dark.

"Glad you liked them." Cheryl Lewis didn't know what to say next. He sipped at the coffee, and again lifted his eyes to her.

"Did you make them?" he asked, getting another smile from her.

"No, 'course not."

"You work all day?" She thought it was a silly question.

"Just through lunchtime, but then I have to study and get ready for class tonight."

"So you're busy all day then, huh?"

"I guess so. Except tonight's class is statistics. I'm not very good at math. We have a test."

McDermott rifled through his brain for some memory of that subject from his undergraduate days. There was something there, but it wouldn't come into focus. Still, it was enough.

"Math was my favorite subject in college," he said, and he held up the napkin where he'd scribbled his depressing finances. Her eyes opened wider—and prettier, he thought.

"So you're good with numbers. Are you smart?"

It was McDermott's turn to smile. He looked good that way. He said, "Mostly *smart aleck*, my mother used to say." Other customers had come into the big dining room, but the waitress didn't move. "And you've got a test tonight? Downtown, right?"

Cheryl Lewis sensed the man was trying to say something. "Yes, at six."

"Well, you know, I work downtown, right near the college, and I'll be finishing up about five. If you want some help studying—you know, for your math test—maybe I can give you a hand?"

It felt too nice. She didn't know what to say, and asked, "Don't you go home after work?" She'd already noticed he wore no wedding ring. In fact, there was little sense of a woman, or any female presence, in the life of this man. He *felt* single, to Cheryl Lewis. In fact, the man *felt* alone.

He said, "We could get a little bite to eat or a drink before class, if you want." She knew what the man was asking now. "And study," he quickly added.

"So you're good at math, huh?" She tried hard not to smile.

"Oh yeah. Your test is on *statistics*, right?" He made the subject sound awful, and it was true—she dreaded it.

She brushed a strand of hair from her face; her eyes were light, playful. She agreed to meet him at a café downtown before class and review for the test. McDermott watched her leave the table, gazing at her figure in the tight slacks as she moved away, wondering what he had done. He didn't know where it would lead. He certainly didn't know anything about statistics. But he was sure of one thing: this woman made him forget for a while.

* * *

Baker Davis didn't want to go to work that day. It was too hot and, except for Gloria Orion, he had no business. Nobody wanted to pay for his services. The investigator sat at home, sipping coffee, wondering why more people didn't try counterfeiting. Jail, he concluded, was the reason. But still, if one could print enough cash to get through the day, only a little, just fives and tens, escaping the notice of the police and the banks, using the false bills only in smaller shops to acquire the most inconsequential things . . . then maybe, for a while anyway. Then stop doing it. That would be key: to stop doing it, stop while you were ahead, let it be a masterpiece of self-restraint. It could be thrilling.

At least Gloria Orion had money. Davis had cashed the checks she wrote and there might be more. Finding Mira's money wouldn't be easy, but it was a safe gig if he could avoid Lt. Foster. Then he realized her detectives would be checking out the dead girl's house soon. He finished the coffee, got dressed, and left the house. Baker Davis wasn't sure what he was looking for, but the victim's address wasn't hard to remember, 420 Lafayette Place.

* * *

Lester Lewis spent most of the day looking after his sister's baby. Monday was Cheryl's busy day, with work in the morning and school at night. Normally, he didn't mind. He enjoyed playing with the little one and spent most of the day watching TV anyway.

But today Lester Lewis couldn't sit still. He had talked to a few guys about the weed. Wesley wanted some, but he didn't have any money and asked if Lester could 'loan' him a little. Omar said he'd trade a bicycle for a bag full, but Lester didn't need a bike and suspected Omar had likely stolen the bike anyway. Finally Antonio said he'd give him fifty bucks for it, which sounded about right. They were going to meet last night in the park, but Antonio never showed up.

Lester looked again under the bed. The backpack was safe, for now, but he couldn't leave it there. Cheryl would find it eventually, or the baby would pull it out when she was crawling around. He tried to think of a place to hide it, but his sister knew the house like the back of her hand, knew every inch, every nook and cranny. He went to a spot in his room where the floorboards were loose, and he pried one up, but there was no room beneath it. He examined the TV and other appliances. Maybe he could stuff the bag inside something like that? But no, it might burn up in there. Maybe he could bury it in the yard? It would be safe there, but it would be hard to get at later, and he didn't feel like digging a hole. Someone might see him.

It all made him jumpy and nervous. He could hardly watch TV that day, and when the baby started crying, he wished the child would shut up. Maybe he could hide the dope somewhere in Sloetown.

* * *

Baker Davis reached Mira Ogilvy's house about noon. Her residence was in the best or at least the better part of town, in Palatine Hill, which wasn't a hill at all but simply a few square blocks behind the large estates and great lawns of the prominent families. The Hill (cynics called it the Lesser Palatine), was a collection of smaller dwellings where generations of the more fragile or impecunious members of these families lived out their lives. Here they lingered, generally without mortgages, twigs on the family tree, outside the gates, but within reach. A demimonde almost, but sporting distinguished lineage. Davis knew they weren't employed; they were largely unemployable. And they rarely advanced. Often they were merely colorful. But they didn't need to *do*, or *be*, anything else since they already presided in the fine old neighborhood. They clung to the past, which Davis knew *was* a kind of strength in its own way, and worthy of respect, but not envy. It was an independence fraught with hoary attachments and iron obligations, bitter grudges and implacable frustrations, and finally . . . shriveled horizons. Davis wondered if Mira Ogilvy was like that, if something here in the Lesser Palatine led her or pushed toward that vacant lot in Sloetown. Maybe she was trying to escape.

Her home on Lafayette was a small, fashionable house of red brick and white trim, Neo-Classical in style. A long porch graced the front, supported by white columns, Ionic order. It wore an eerie silence, like a memorial, as if it understood its mistress was gone. As he approached, Davis noticed a silver four-door parked in the street before the house. It didn't look right. Cars in the Palatine stayed in garages. Maybe the driver was visiting elsewhere. He drove past, left his Buick down the block and walked back, noting the tag number on the sedan.

He stood before the house, then scanned the neighborhood. Yard men clipped hedges that were already neat, raked lawns already perfect. The sunny afternoon was quiet, but Davis knew it was the kind of place where old ladies peered out from narrow slits in lace curtains, watching every move. Still, he had little choice, little time. Mira was dead, and if there was anything to be discovered about her money, it would start here. And soon, the cops would come.

Davis walked up the gravel driveway but the stones crunched beneath his feet so he crossed to the lawn for silence. He noticed the mailbox stuffed with letters that Gloria Orion had mentioned. The wide porch formed an elegant arcade beneath white columns. He imagined Mira Ogilvy there in the afternoon with a drink, laughing with friends; or alone watching dusk come, ice tinkling in her glass amid the scent of flowers. Now a layer of fine dust or pollen covered the porch, to be expected if she'd been gone a while. But then he noticed something else . . . prints in the dust. Footprints. One could see big shoes made them, a man's shoes, and they led right to the front door. Davis looked back at the silver sedan in the street.

He jumped off the porch into a side yard, passing through an iron gate that hung open. He was in the backyard, under a small grove of pines. Nearby, a stone bird bath covered in green moss stood amidst a disorderly bed of roses. A few dogs barked far away. He was alone. A row of dirty windows ran along the back of the house. The curtains were parted, so he approached. He moved closer . . . then stopped. Movement inside.

Davis pulled back, crouching behind the roses. Then, the memory of the dead girl in the vacant lot flooded over him. Maybe it was the fragrant roses, he thought, different but strong and powerful.

He watched the movement in the house. It was slow and heavy, like a man, even a sick man. He moved forward, easing up to the edge of a window, peering in. Yes, a man, a big man who seemed agitated stood over a desk, rifling through a stack of papers. Some fell to the floor. He ignored them. He jerked open a drawer and dug through it impatiently. He stood back, his face red and gleaming with sweat. He yanked another drawer, slammed it shut. With desperation in his eyes, the man searched the room, searched his own mind. Then he snatched up a pile of folders from the desk, looked anxiously around the room once more, then quickly moved toward the front of the house, as if he couldn't stand being there any longer.

Davis ran around the side yard, watching as the man came out the front door. He was an older man and lurched across the yard, his arms full. A manila folder tumbled from his grasp onto the lawn but he was moving too fast to notice. He reached the sedan and shoved everything he had taken from Mira's house into the back seat. Then he jumped in and sped away.

Davis wondered where the man was going, where he was taking the feeling, the anxiety, which gnawed at him. Something told the investigator it was something all his own, that only he knew and only he could exorcise. Or maybe he couldn't.

The neighborhood was still again. In the grass lay the manila folder the big man dropped. Davis looked around, then emerged from the side of the house and retrieved it. Inside were personal papers, Mira Ogilvy's papers. I'll look them over later, he thought, as he felt eyes watching from somewhere. Maybe it was a good time to leave, call it a day. But he'd come there for a reason: Gloria Orion hired him to find the money, her money. He had an invitation.

He noticed the homes across the street, the drawn curtains, and remembered his faded PI license, yellowing in the black frame on the wall of his office. If he went inside the house, it was burglary, breaking and entering at least. If he got caught, he could forget about getting his license back. What the hell, the damn thing was suspended anyway. And it was hot standing outside.

Davis tucked the folder under his arm, went to the front porch and tried the door, knowing it might lead to a place he didn't want to go or maybe even regret some day. The handle turned. The big man had left it open. Maybe it was unlocked when he arrived, but it seemed unlikely, even in a good neighborhood. Did the man know Mira? Have a key? He was certainly in a hurry. *In a hurry* . . . like Gloria Orion, Davis reflected.

The investigator took a deep breath, eased into the house and closed the door softly. He stood in a narrow foyer, paved with chipped marble that led down two steps into a den that was large, formal, feminine. He paused, feeling the silence. Two chintz sofas were arranged around a low, polished table that held a collection of art books and a vase of silk flowers. Rose petals, probably from the backyard, lined the bottom of a crystal bowl. It appeared to hold water, once, but was dry now, the petals faded.

He switched on a lamp, crossed the den, then walked through a pair of French doors into a library. Here stood the desk the strange visitor had torn apart. Davis examined a few papers scattered there: an invoice showing four pairs of shoes, delivered, almost $500; a page of minutes from a local symphony board meeting; an alumni newsletter from a college in the East he'd never heard of, its crest prominent on the letterhead; then a birthday card, unsigned. 'No telling what the stranger had sought, and Davis wasn't quite sure what he was looking for either.

He left the library and went to the rear of the house, the bedrooms. It was dim. He turned on all the lights. Everything was in order, untouched, a posed silence, though Davis knew most of the Palatine was like that. He breathed in the non-smell of rooms which had been empty for a while. No trace of the big man here.

He entered the master bedroom, Mira's room, where a suitcase lay in the middle of the bed while a hairbrush, shampoo, and make-up sat on the pillow. Mira was going somewhere, but didn't finish packing. Murder has a way of interrupting things like that, Davis reflected. Carefully, he nudged her bag. It wasn't locked. Inside, a few blouses and a pair of slacks lay neatly folded. He picked up the clothing—an envelope appeared in the bottom of the suitcase. He reached for it and felt a current jolt his arm when he saw his name. It was for Baker Davis, addressed to his office.

The improbability of it all hit him hard, the chances this letter, for him, turning up here, now. But he dealt with people in trouble, people trying to leave town. That was his job. A private detective was about the last guy to reach out to this side of the law, and he was one the few investigators working in the city these days, albeit without a license. The other guys had retired, grown sick of it, or settled into corporate security gigs, leaving Baker Davis as the only PI left standing in the market, so yes, it began to make a little sense. If Mira Ogilvy wanted help, where else could she turn?

The envelope was stamped but not postmarked. It never got sent. There was no return address. Davis opened it and withdrew a letter:

Mr. Davis, allow me to introduce myself. My name is Mira Ogilvy and I am a resident of this city. I am writing because I may need your help in the near future.

Over the past few years, I have been part of a project here in town that involves a large amount of money. Now the project is ending, and I hope to bring everything to a peaceful, orderly conclusion. While my work has helped some, I suspect that others may wish to disrupt it, or even undo the results. They could go to any lengths. Even violence.

I may need your help to achieve a good ending for all this, and I wanted to alert you in case anything unfortunate occurs. I've considered going to the police, but I prefer they not be involved. I'm sure their efforts would be heavy-handed and insensitive. I want to avoid that.

And though I seek a happy conclusion, it's not how something ends, but how it starts that guides our way. Trees, fruit, flowers . . . all begin as seeds, right? I have heard that you are the man to understand this, though I'm not sure why. I have done my research and, frankly, your reputation is hard to determine. But I'm not sure who else to ask.

I know this is vague, but I hesitate to add more in writing right now. I

will contact you soon, by phone, to discuss. (I have set aside money for compensation, of course.)
    Thank you in advance for your attention.
    Mira Ogilvy

    So there it was, he mused, *a large amount of money*, the money Gloria Orion sought, the money she claimed was hers. But for Mira, it was part of her *project*, some *work* she was doing, work she feared was dangerous. Maybe she was protecting someone, something? Then the police involvement: *heavy-handed and insensitive*. 'Strange, Davis reflected, that's what the cops do, how they operate, their job. Finally, Mira had set aside compensation for him, though he'd never see it now, but it didn't suggest a girl careless with money. In all, it looked as if the young woman knew what she was doing, and planned to keep doing it, even if it was dangerous. There was no date on the letter. 'Likely one of the last things she ever wrote, he thought.
    Davis placed the letter in the manila folder. The letter was his, addressed to him; the police could have it later. He imagined her friends sadly packing away the dead girl's clothing, emptying the closets, closing down the house; a few items set aside to be kept forever, the rest coldly organized for an estate sale. Then Baker Davis felt very alone. It wasn't his house. He shouldn't be there. The cops might arrive anytime.
    But in that moment, an overstuffed chair presented itself near the window and he took it. Something drew him. He rested in the frumpy piece of furniture, propped his feet on the ottoman, and felt the mid-day sun warming him through the curtains. He was alone in the room, knowing it was her room as he imagined soft voices, then breathed the fragrance of a woman's perfume. But no . . . Mira was gone and he didn't believe in ghosts. That was her body in Sloetown. He found it. He saw it. Gloria Orion identified it.
    The quiet washed over him. Again he felt Mira's absence, realizing he was one of the last people she spoke to, or reached out to with a letter, trying to connect. Now she was like a client retaining him from the grave. It felt like a heavy hand on his shoulders, and he wanted it to throw it off, push it away. He withdrew the letter from the folder and read it again. The *seeds* she mentioned—what were they? Beginnings, not endings, and she

thought Baker Davis might understand that. He didn't.

He rested in the chair. It only grew quieter. Mira wasn't coming back; her suitcase would be half-packed forever. More silence. Finally, Davis stood, left the bedroom, switched off the lights in the den, and exited the house. On the front porch, the air was warm and sticky but it felt good, felt like life. He crossed the yard again where the big man dropped the manila folder. A small indentation remained in the grass. As he reached the sidewalk, he turned back, pausing, scanning the neighborhood. Still quiet, still hot.

At the end of the block, he saw movement—two vehicles turning into Lafayette Place. They moved slowly, as if they were in no hurry. They came closer. He rolled the folder tight and stuffed it in his trousers. The first car was black and white, the police. The second car was white, unmarked, a government car. Davis wanted to move, to run, walk away quickly, but there was nowhere to go. The vehicles stopped at the sidewalk before him, and the skinny, red-haired cop bounced from the patrol car. Davis remembered him from Vinson Street. He said,

"Well, well, the private investigator."

"Afternoon," Davis mumbled.

"Here you are, once again," he sneered. "You got a pretty good nose for turning up in the wrong place." Another cop emerged from the driver's side. He was shorter, but thick, strong, brown, as if carved from oak. The white government car eased into Mira's driveway. Davis said,

"What's wrong with this place?"

"Shut up, smart ass." The red-haired cop faced him, one hand on his weapon. Davis saw his badge—Wilson. He stared hard at Davis in the hot sun and said, "What the hell are you doing here?"

"I thought you wanted me to shut up, Officer."

"I do. Just answer, dick."

Davis felt the other cop circling behind him. "All right. I'm standing on a public sidewalk. 'Minding my own business—"

The cop in back grabbed his wrist, thrust his arm up behind his shoulder blade. His other hand grabbed the back of his neck, pushed him forward. Davis's chest slammed against the squad car.

"*Your* business?" Wilson snarled. "This is *my* business, asshole. Police business."

"Good for you," Davis groaned. The short, thick cop pressed

him against the hot car.

"I said what are you doing here? You been in the house?"

"What house?" The cop twisted his arm. "Ahaaggh." Spit flew from Davis's mouth.

"Mira's house. You ain't lost asshole. What the hell are you doing here?"

"Payin' last respects," Davis grunted.

Wilson glanced at the other cop. He loosened his grip on the investigator. Davis fell back from the car.

"Well go pay 'em somewhere else."

Davis rubbed his shoulder. "Maybe I will." The cops glared at him, then turned their attention to Mira's house. He added, "But if you boys need any help figuring this one out, just tell your Lieutenant to call me."

The two cops looked at each other. Wilson feared Lieutenant Foster, and in Sloetown, he'd seen her talking with Davis. They knew other; there was history between them, somehow.

"Beat it, dick," he said.

Davis let them go. He walked down the street to where he left his car, got in and rested with the air conditioning blowing hard. He rubbed his shoulder and withdrew the manila folder from his trousers, unrolled it and laid it on the seat. After a few minutes, he started up and got moving, driving past Mira's house. The two cops stood at her front door. A fat man exited the white government car, hitching up his pants as he crossed the green lawn to the porch.

They should have brought a woman for this job, Davis thought. Tomorrow the newspapers would tell the world that Mira was gone.

* * *

Later that afternoon, Officer Jeremy Wilson felt better as he drove out to the Orion Pallet Company. Inspecting the dead girl's house earlier gave him the creeps. He was glad it was over. And that Davis fellow was annoying. He knows Lt. Foster somehow, the policeman remembered, but I'll fix him. He gripped the steering wheel tighter and drove toward Sloetown.

Wilson knew he wasn't the toughest man on the police force, or even in the Homicide Division, but there was little he truly feared. He was sure of it. He'd arrested some hard cases—gang bangers, wife beaters, thieves, even a few killers. He'd wrestled and cuffed men bigger and stronger than himself; though, he had to admit, other cops helped. Once he took a knife away from a guy, but the man was drunk, half-conscious. Then, another time, a towering biker dude took a swing at him, but Jeremy Wilson was quick; he simply ducked and the man slugged a concrete light pole and that was the end of that. Yes, he could handle most anything this city could throw at him, the policeman concluded, though he realized he'd only been on the job for three years. Then he spotted the Orion Pallet Company in the distance. Maybe he hadn't seen everything.

Wilson pulled into the lot of the big factory, coming to a stop before a row of windows that suggested the main offices. He went inside where an older woman greeted him from behind a counter. As he was introducing himself he heard his name spoken.

"Officer Wilson." He turned to see a tall, striking woman, and he felt something move inside his stomach that he didn't understand. She said, "I'm Gloria Orion. Thank you for coming by." She stood there in a silk blouse and a black skirt that looked expensive, as if she was going out for the evening even though it was only late afternoon. There were no women like that in the police department, Wilson thought.

"Sure," he mumbled.

"Won't you come back to my office?" she said, and disappeared into a hallway. Wilson followed her. He tried to remember why he had come to see her, the purpose of his visit, but he felt distracted.

"Please have a seat," she said, as he came into her office. It wasn't grand or elegant, but simple and business-like. She was the main thing in the room. "Can I get you anything Mr. Wilson?"

"Nope," he replied. "I came here to talk, Mrs. Orion. To talk about—"

"—about Mira Ogilvy. Yes. It's so terrible, what happened to her."

"*What did happen* to her?"

Gloria Orion looked him over. She had hoped the man wouldn't be like this, wouldn't be small and petty, but maybe he couldn't help it. Maybe he wanted to prove something. She'd seen the type. She put on a smile.

"Well, *you* know what happened, don't you Officer? You were there. In Sloetown, that's where you found the poor girl."

"Well, we are conducting an investigation Mrs. Orion."

"Gloria, please."

Wilson wanted to call her that, but told himself not to. "You ID'd her for us that afternoon. We appreciate that. I need to follow up. Can you tell me anything about Miss Ogilvy?"

"What would you like to know Officer?"

"Who put those bullets in her, for example."

Gloria Orion wondered if this was his idea of being strong, forceful. "I can't help you with that."

"But you were friends with Miss Ogilvy, right?"

"*Acquainted* would be more accurate, Officer. But yes, I knew her. I met her at a dinner party once. A lot of people knew Mira. She was popular, I think." She wished she hadn't mentioned the dinner party.

"May I ask where, Mrs. Orion?"

"Where?"

"Yes. The dinner party. Was it your party?"

"Heavens no!" she laughed, thinking of hosting a dinner party with Karl. She didn't know anything about food anyway. Wilson noticed her sparkling teeth against red lipstick.

"Well—?"

"It was a few years ago, at my brother's house, I think." She didn't want this to get out, but it came.

"You *think*?" He scratched a few notes on a pad.

"Yes, I think," she said, a little color rising in her face. "There were several people there. I can't remember every—"

"At your brother's, huh?"

"Yes."

Wilson kept writing. "Understood. His name, ma'am."

"Richard McDermott," she said quickly, to suggest there was nothing to hide. "He's an attorney. Will you be speaking with him?"

"Probably. We're talking to a lot of people."

"I don't think my brother, uh Mr. McDermott, invited Mira that night. Someone brought her."

Wilson wrote again on his pad. "You know, we were unable to discover anything about the victim's employment. Do you have any idea where she worked?"

"Worked? I don't think Mira had a job, come to think of it."

"Or what she did for money?"

Gloria Orion remembered the $20,000 her husband had been giving Mira Ogilvy every month over the years and felt sick. Her face twitched, and Wilson thought he saw it, but he wasn't sure. She was too good looking. He couldn't tell.

"Money? I don't know," she said dully. "Mira's father was Dr. Winston Ogilvy. I think people assumed she inherited something when he died."

"Is that what you assume, Mrs. Orion?"

"I never assume anything, Officer." Her eyes narrowed and her mouth tightened, and she wasn't pretty now, Wilson thought. He wrote again on the pad.

"Miss Ogilvy's last few days . . . any idea where she might have been late last week? What she did?"

"No, sorry. Like I said, Mira was only an acquaintance. I didn't really know her routine. She was single. I'm not sure if she had any family around here."

"Any idea why she might have been up in Sloetown?"

"I said I hadn't seen her. She wasn't my friend."

Wilson sensed that his interview had reached an end. Gloria Orion wasn't going to talk much anymore—something had changed. Something he said had touched her. He wasn't sure what it was.

"Well, I guess that's about it for now Mrs. Orion, but one last thing . . ."

"Sure."

"Sunday, in Sloetown, you came with Baker Davis.

"Yes."

"Can he add anything to the story?"

"What story? I don't know. Mr. Davis is simply—" she smiled again, "another acquaintance."

"All right." Wilson folded his pad and stood to go. "Please remember this is a criminal investigation, Mrs. Orion. Let us handle it. There's nothing here for a private detective."

"Is Mr. Davis a problem, Officer?"

"No, no problem. But we've had dealings with him before, in the Department. We don't need any help now, no interference."

"I see. I'm sure he understands. I thank you for coming by. I hope you can find out something about Mira. Poor girl."

"Oh we will, Mrs. Orion."

She escorted him back to the front office and said good-bye. She was polite, but stiff and formal now. Wilson concluded the woman was glad to be rid of him. Her manner was different. Maybe she was hiding something. Maybe he got on her nerves. That's all right, he thought, because like Lt. Foster always told him: *You're not there to make friends, Wilson.*

* * *

Downtown in a café that evening, Cheryl Lewis asked the boy who came to her table for a Coke. Then she opened her textbook. She examined the card the man gave her that morning at breakfast: Richard McDermott, Attorney at Law. What kind of lawyer was he? She thought about the men in courtroom dramas on TV. They were always smart, handsome, dashing. They wore beautiful suits and probably made a lot of money.

She stared at her book. He said this café would be quiet, a good spot to prepare for her math test. It wasn't a fancy place, but it wasn't right for a waitress's uniform either, and she was glad she had a nice outfit in her locker at Best Diner. The boy returned with her Coke as her eyes watched the front door of the café, waiting.

* * *

In McDermott's office on Twenty, the answering machine held nine messages. He watched the tiny light blink. Then he stood from his desk, crossed the room to the tall windows, and drank in the splendid view of the city. In the distance lay a horizon of green, the ancient oaks of Sloetown. That's where the cops found Mira Ogilvy. Appropriate, he thought. If one must die, let it be under the old trees, not in the city, certainly not a hospital.

Then McDermott's gaze wandered to the street far below, and the café at the end of the block where the attractive waitress he met at Best Diner would meet him soon. A good enough place, not too public, not too private. People would see him there, with a lovely black woman, but it would be okay. It wouldn't be okay everywhere in the city, he considered, and probably not okay in Sloetown either for that matter. The women he'd known, his wife, his girlfriends, even Gloria, wouldn't approve, wouldn't understand. She wouldn't fit into their view of things: the girl was black, worked in a diner. But so what? At least she wasn't one of those wretched bankers trying to suck his blood. Besides, that woman looked good. Really good. The lawyer said aloud *To hell with it all.*

McDermott left his suite, boarded an elevator, and descended to the first floor. In the lobby people greeted him and the security guard nodded. He raised the corner of his mouth at everyone, but it wasn't a smile. It was more like a smirk. All the landlord wanted them to see in his face was a hard question—Where's the rent? Richard McDermott didn't care about anything else, and he didn't want to be friends. Then he noticed the bank offices, and he considered that's all they cared about too, the money he owed them. He paused before the glass door of the bank lobby. Inside, the lights were dim and the tellers were locking up. His reflection stared back at him in the glass, so he smoothed his hair and thought about the woman at the café.

He got outside where pedestrians crowded the sidewalk, going home. He crossed the street and looked up at McDermott Center. It wasn't the nicest building in town, but far from the worst, and he remembered all the money he'd spent over the years keeping it up, the Italian marble which graced the lobby, the modern art he purchased for the hallways. Now the property was saddled with debt and obligations. If one added up the numbers, McDermott Center didn't really even belong to him.

He gazed up at the top floors and saw more lights flick off as people left for the day. The tower grew dark, and he recalled a story from English class in college long ago. Or was it high school? Something from Poe maybe? A tale about some nervous, sad guy in a big house or a castle? Or was Usher the author? In the end the entire place implodes and crashes into the Earth, taking the sad man with it. McDermott imagined a similar fate for himself and his office building; but so long as those bankers perished too, it would be okay with him. The ground could open up and the entire joint plummet to hell. He shrugged. Then he remembered the café.

* * *

The man looked better than he did that morning, Cheryl Lewis thought as McDermott walked into the café. She watched him approach the table. His step was lively and active, and she wondered if he had played sports as a younger man. 'Not football or basketball, but maybe a game like tennis or golf.

"Hey Cheryl, how're you doing?" he said warmly.

"You remembered my name," she said.

"Of course." They were at a four-top. She didn't know where he would sit, but she had been thinking about it. He took the chair next to her, his knee grazing her thigh. She pulled away instantly, but couldn't hide a smile. McDermott thought it was about the finest thing he'd experienced that day, or in months . . . years even.

"How'd everything go at the diner today?" he asked. "Were you busy?"

"It wasn't bad. Monday's are slow, but it gives me a little time to study." She glanced at her text book sitting on the table. They ignored it.

"You like working there?" And she told him how she felt, but he didn't hear what she said because he watched the young woman and she was too good looking. Dammit, he thought, they were different, black people. Their hair, their skin—they were so different. And sleeping with someone like that, waking up in the morning, bathing, dressing, everything all mixed together. Jesus Christ. He grew anxious and excited at once. As she talked, she moved her delicate, slender hands that weren't all of an even tone, like a white girl's. But holding those hands—now that would be sweet. Then it hit him: that's why he wanted her, the core of his desire. She was different.

"*Your* day, Richard. I asked how *your* day went."

"Uh—" he replied. "It went fine. I shuffled some papers, went to some meetings, talked on the phone. Routine legal work."

"Oh, I thought you were one of those fancy lawyers like on TV." She couldn't remember when she began to enjoy teasing him. As he told her about his work, Cheryl noticed the neat, straight line along his jaw where his dark beard met his white skin. It didn't grow like that on a black guy's face, not too often. White folks . . . so different, she thought, and remembered those pictures of Jesus that always hung on the wall in her Sunday school class. Back then, Jesus was always white; and she wondered why, if they were all God's children like the Sunday school teacher said, why the Lord wasn't black too. Then one day someone found a picture of a black Jesus and hung it up on the wall, but He never looked right up there. No one knew why. After a few weeks they took Him down and put the other Jesus back up. But He was tanned and dark for a white Jesus, even then.

McDermott went on about his work, his brown, liquid eyes darting back and forth as if they were trying to explain something complicated. They were quick and intelligent and Cheryl Lewis wished those eyes would slow down.

It flashed in her mind she knew how to make them slow down.

FIVE

When Baker Davis woke up the next morning, the shoulder where the cop had twisted his arm still ached, but felt better as he got up, got moving. After a second cup of coffee, the investigator's brain started to wake up with the rest of him. He opened the door for the cat and the dog and followed them outside to get the morning paper, hoping it contained no word of Mira Ogilvy yet. He wasn't ready to see her like that, not in the newspaper, but there it was at the bottom of p. 2, with a photo:

WOMAN IDENTIFIED—The police have identified the remains of Mira Ogilvy. She was the daughter of the late Dr. Winston Ogilvy. Ms. Ogilvy was active in society for many years, and served as a hostess of the annual Champagne Breakfast which supported the Symphony. She was also a painter, and had exhibited her watercolors in the lobby of Mercy Hospital, which the Ogilvy family had long supported. Funeral services are under arrangement.

The police are conducting an investigation. Persons with information about Mira Ogilvy should contact Lieutenant Doreen Foster at Police Headquarters.

Her photograph appeared contemporary, and Davis searched it for any clues about the victim's last week on Earth—the party that went too far, the boyfriend angry with love, the drinking or drugs, money problems—searching for any reason why a girl like Mira Ogilvy might end up in a bad neighborhood. But there was none, only a hopeful smile and her eyes bright with life for the camera. Then the image changed before him . . . there she was again . . . lying in the tall weeds in Sloetown.

The picture made him feel heavy and tired. He refilled his coffee and let the animals back in. Then, on the kitchen table, he noticed the folder the strange visitor dropped at Mira's house. Davis picked it up, examined it, sipped his coffee, then slowly opened it. Inside were tattered receipts, scribbled lists, a few business cards, a wrinkled dollar bill. Then a photograph caught his eye. It was a glossy halftone, clipped from a society magazine, showing a woman and two gentlemen in formal dress, arm in arm, cocktails in hands, smiling in a crowded ballroom where elegant dancers seemed to float in the background. The woman was Mira Ogilvy, and one of the men was a big man—the man he'd seen yesterday in her house! The caption below told the story: it was Karl Orion. Gloria Orion's husband.

Davis's eyes locked on the picture. The other man was Dr. Winston Ogilvy. So they all knew each other: the dead girl, her father, and Karl Orion. They looked very happy together then. Now only Karl Orion remained, and he'd been in the girl's house, looking for something even before the police arrived. The rest of the caption indicated that the ballroom scene was a party to raise funds for new construction at Mercy Hospital.

Davis shuffled through other papers in Mira's folder. In the back, several bank statements turned up. He skimmed the debits and credits when a pattern grabbed him: a $20,000 deposit appeared each month, followed by a regular $20,000 debit. The transactions occurred in pairs, twenty grand in, twenty grand out, month after month, but no check or payee was recorded for the twenty thousand. Apparently the big debits were cash withdrawals. Davis tried to imagine Mira Ogilvy needing that much money every month. Who could spend it all around this city, he wondered . . . let alone Sloetown.

And where did it all come from? Mira Ogilvy didn't work. The deposits might have been an inheritance, but the rumor in town was that her father the Doctor was almost broke at the end of his life. Nonetheless, there it stood in black and white: twenty K a month deposited, and twenty K withdrawn, like clockwork, year after year. So here was money, Davis realized, a lot of money, enough to bring people to desperate acts, even violence. Sums like this are bound to have strings attached, either coming or going. He remembered what his father used to preach: ultimately, there's no such thing as perfectly clean money, not when human hands touch it. Then the words from Mira's letter seized him: *it's not how something ends, but how it starts.*

Baker Davis gathered up all the statements and clipped the sad news article from the newspaper. He put everything into the manila folder. Then he finished his coffee, got dressed, took the folder and drove downtown.

* * *

At Orion Pallet that day, Gloria Orion spent the morning in her office thinking, and remembering the policeman who came to visit the day before. Wilson, the little jerk. She wondered how much money he made and concluded it wasn't much, a trifle more than the guys in the warehouse earned making pallets. But his questions were annoying, and she'd let it slip out about Mira visiting her brother's party. She'd have to call Richard.

Then she thought about Karl. The news he gave her was like a clenched fist deep in the stomach. She didn't want her husband to get sick. She didn't want him to die. She remembered caring for an uncle and her grandmother in their last days. She'd care for Karl, too, if that's what it came to, even if he didn't want that. She knew her husband was tough, but couldn't say where it came from. Karl wasn't patient, nor religious; maybe because he kept things to himself, kept it all bottled up. People said a man like that was ripe for an explosion, but she knew better. She knew men sometimes kept things to themselves until the end, the very end. And even beyond that.

Already Karl's medication was making him ill. He was consulting another specialist this week, and maybe they could find a cure. No, *remission* was the word they used, a vague twilight of anguish and hope. But she also worried about the care he might receive, or be denied, without any insurance. He hadn't paid the premiums! What the hell was the man thinking? Maybe he forgot. Maybe he really didn't have the money. Maybe he knew something she didn't—that his case was hopeless. It wouldn't be the first time he kept her in the dark.

At the end of the hall she heard Karl moving around in his

office. Her husband had never denied her anything, when she asked for it, but he never discussed their finances either. It was like a wall between them that she never questioned over the years. But there was little need to. They shared a beautiful home with more rooms than she could decorate. The house included three closets overflowing with clothes, and her safe deposit box at the bank overflowed with fine jewelry. Karl gave her five hundred dollars every week to shop.

But recently he said they wouldn't be making their Alaskan cruise this year, mumbling something about liquidity at the company. She was disappointed. It was their traditional summer vacation, their escape from the sweltering heat in the city. She had always looked forward to spending afternoons wrapped in a blanket on the deck of the ship, caressed by the cool breezes of the north Pacific. Evidently the figures she'd discovered in the ledger were accurate. Orion Pallet was in trouble, and Gloria Orion began to wonder if her entire lifestyle wasn't some house of cards Karl had fabricated—a house built from old, dirty, creaky pallets, ready to burst into splinters. She wanted to bring it up, to discuss it, but company operations had always been Karl's domain. Last Friday, he came to her with the shopping money, and his usual wink and smile.

"'Love you baby," he said, bending to kiss her uplifted cheek.

"'Love you too." She always said it, and meant it, even if she didn't feel it. But when Karl left and she counted the money, it wasn't the same. Only two bills this time. It made for a long weekend.

Finally Gloria Orion thought about Mira Ogilvy. Twenty thousand a month, year after year. What could the girl do with it all? And why the hell did Karl pay her? If she knew why, it might shed light on the situation. But after a while, reasons weren't important. She only wanted to know what Mira had done with the money. Where was it?

She phoned a friend who worked in a bank. The friend made more calls, but could find no mortgage recorded on Mira's house in the Palatine. She remembered the girl drove a white BMW, a nice car but not brand new. She didn't live extravagantly. Mira couldn't have spent all that money. It didn't belong to her anyway. It belonged to Orion Pallet—and to Gloria Orion. It couldn't just disappear!

She heard the men in the warehouse hammering and drilling, and forklifts rumbling by. She remembered the sounds she heard as a child at her uncle's sawmill in Kentucky. They all felt like sandpaper on her heart. Now everything seemed to be working against her. That little cop was annoying and she wasn't going on the Alaska cruise. Her husband had cancer and no insurance. The Orion Pallet Company was in the red, and Karl only gave her $200 that week. Sure, there's money all right, she thought, except Mira Ogilvy has it—or had it—somewhere. Karl gave it to her. And it's not hers. It's mine.

Now her head hurt. She reached into her desk for an aspirin but couldn't find any. She picked up the phone and called her brother.

* * *

Cheryl Lewis was due home early that afternoon, after she finished with the lunch crowd at Best Diner, and Lester was glad. He had looked after the baby all morning and itched to get out of the house. When his sister arrived, he barely said *Hello* as he ran out the door.

He had stuffed the brown sack of weed in his pants. He walked quickly down the street, passing houses where he knew most of the occupants. They had lived there for years; they had known Lester since he was a child. He eyed the windows and screen doors, thinking someone inside must be watching. His feet moved quickly down the sidewalk, almost running.

Finally he reached several acres of green at the end of Sloetown, Jackson Park, where the big trees created an oasis of shade. The rusty swing set here lay still, except when it creaked in the humid breezes coming up from the river nearby. The young man stood at the edge of the park and looked around. The old basketball court was quiet. There would be a game later that afternoon; he might come back for that. In places, crews from the city had cut the grass low, but big stands of honeysuckle, wild rose, and privet hedge six feet high covered the grounds. It was easy to get lost in Jackson Park, and Lester Lewis felt glad it wasn't dark yet. Still, the shade and dense growth all around created a gloomy scene. He reached for the paper bag in his pants. 'Still there.'

The young man walked to the end of the park where the trees

grew thickest. Beyond, the land sloped away to the river. No one ever visited this area. He parted the branches in a wall of brush, and there it was, Michael's Cadillac. His mind drifted back to his childhood days, when he was nine or ten or so, and Michael would take him cruising in the car with the top down. Cheryl would go too. They waited together on the porch of the house for Michael to come home from work so they could go driving through Sloetown in the hot afternoon with the wind in their faces, cooling their sweaty t-shirts. Lester could almost feel that breeze even now as he stood there before the old wreck. Then one day, Michael didn't come home . . . nor the next day or the day after that. There were no more rides in the convertible. In fact his brother never did come home from work, ever again. No one had explained it to him. He was a child then, but the older folks kept talking about Orion Pallet. That's where Michael worked.

Lester Lewis reached for the paper sack under his belt. Rust covered the old car, but the trunk still worked, and he popped it open and hid the bag inside. It will be safe here, he thought, like a memory.

* * *

When Davis arrived at his office downtown in McDermott Center, he saw three men swaying beside the dumpster near the back fence of the parking lot, Rico and his comrades. 'Not homeless men exactly, since they crashed in a rooming house nearby for five dollars a night, money they scraped together doing odd jobs, or by begging and hassling people on the street. Davis gave them a little work if they were sober, and sometimes when they weren't: sweeping the office, taking out the trash, picking up the parking lot. In fact, if Rico and his cronies saw anyone else working around the building, they'd get mad. That was money out of their pocket, as they saw it, and Davis couldn't miss the connection they had to the property, the neighborhood, this corner of the city. They had been here a long time, longer than he had, longer than McDermott Center even, and they would still be here when he was gone. So he paid them a couple of bucks for chores or gave them old clothes. One day, he noticed four of them hanging around, each man tricked out with discards from his wardrobe. They looked like Baker Davis's own private army. He wanted them all to beat it, but wondered . . . *Where would they go? And how? This was already their world.* In the long run, paying them was likely a good investment. After all, they kept an eye on the place when he wasn't around, watching out for him, somehow caring for the man in the office, or at least the place itself. So Davis gave them a few bucks, and they called him *Bawssman.* They were waiting on him as he rolled into the parking lot of McDermott Center. He wanted to avoid them today; he wasn't in the mood. He looked away as he stopped the car and got out. One came forward. The smell of beer came with him.

"Hey Hey Hey!" It was Rico. "Bawssman!" he cried, as if he recognized an old friend.

"Hey man," Davis muttered, putting on a hard face. Rico was short and wiry. Word on the street was that he'd played semi-pro ball once, was once a top shortstop in the league. But that was decades ago. Now he stood there in a tattered oxford cloth dress shirt Davis had left in the dumpster. A glittering necklace of cheap Mardi Gras beads hung from his neck. He was dirty and happy and a little drunk.

"Hey Bawss. Hey, I need a little help Bawss. Jus' a little—" He held out his hand.

"I ain't got nothing," Davis replied, reaching into his pockets as if searching in vain for money. Rico's rheumy eyes glistened in sun. A big wad of gum or tobacco or God knows what rolled around in his cheek, going up and down along his black, whiskered face. He smelled.

"Lemme pick up Bawss. Lemma clean up a little bit, come on now." Davis looked around and saw cups and beer cans and newspapers littering the lot. He squinted at Rico. The two men near the dumpster drank deeply from brown paper bags and smiled.

"All right. Here." Davis reached into his car and grabbed a fistful of change from the cup holder and gave it to Rico. "Get this litter picked up and throw it in the dumpster."

"Yeah Bawss, doan you worry none. I get it all up."

"How'd you let things get so messed up around here, Rico?" Davis asked, eyeing the debris in the parking lot. He knew Rico and his friends were likely responsible for it.

"I ain't been around here, Bawss." He pocketed the change and picked up an empty beer can at his feet. "Ah been gone."

"Gone? You on vacation or something?"

"I been gone Bawss. 'Ah been up in Sloetown."

"Uh-huh," Davis said. "Sloetown, huh?"

"Yeah Bawss. Up in Sloetown, dat's where I stay." He picked up a paper cup.

"You supposed to be looking after this parking lot, Rico."

"Doan worry none Bawss. I jus' been gone. I get it all clean'd up now."

"What you doin' up there in Sloetown Rico? You drinking?"

"Naw Bawss! Naw. I stay up there wit my cousin. I do me a little woik up there too." He bobbed around the lot, picking up litter, his colorful beads glittering in the sun.

"Work!?" Davis laughed. "What kinda work you do man?"

"Yay Bawss. I wurk in Sloetown, pickin' up cans, doin yard wurk, anything."

"Uh-huh."

"Looky heah Bawss" He dug around in his pocket. He pulled out a fist and slowly unfurled his thick fingers. In his palm rested two pearls.

Davis looked at his eyes. The eyes didn't look back at him, but remained fixed on the pearls in his hand.

"What you think dey wurth, Bawss?"

"Where'd you get those?"

"Dey wurff some money, ain't dey Bawss?"

"Where'd you get them Rico?"

He looked up at Davis. He chewed on his lip. "Up in Sloetown Bawss."

"Where, man?"

"I found em Bawss. While I was pickin up bottles on de street in Sloetown."

"What street, dammit?"

"Ah jus found em!" he snarled, and crammed the pearls back in his pocket.

"All right Rico. What the hell." Davis looked him over. "Just get all this cleaned up."

Rico returned to his chores, mumbling curses. Davis went to his office in McDermott Center. Inside, Prince was at his desk. He looked as if he'd been there all night.

"You all right?" Davis asked him.

"Never better," Prince assured him. "How about you?" Davis

answered with a shrug. He made his way to the back office. He found a space on his messy desk and laid the manila folder there, adding to the general state of confusion. Prince appeared in the doorway and said,
"There's coffee you know."
"Yeah, sure. Say, Prince, you ever hear of the Orions?"
A sad, knowing smile appeared on the man's face, as if he knew the entire story already and pitied Davis for not knowing it. "I've heard of them. They've got that old factory in Sloetown. They make something there—?"
"Pallets."
"Oh yes. Karl Orion, the pallet man." The corners of his mouth turned up again, without mirth. "Yes, I know him, or at least about him. My Dad knew him better, years ago. In fact, the land where his factory now stands used to belong to my grandfather, but Orion bought it long ago." Davis knew men who owned real estate, but Prince was the only man he knew whose family *once* owned property. The Gray Prince knew the story behind every parcel, development, or building in town, knew it in his bones. He continued, with a sigh.

"I guess it's a big operation now, but it wasn't always that way." He took a seat in the armchair in Davis's office. "Orion's father T.H. started the whole thing from the back of his pickup truck. He drove around collecting scrap wood from the lumber mills in the countryside, then nailed everything together to make pallets for the merchandise wholesalers in town, tradesmen who were a little higher in the economic order. That would have been in the late Forties. Then he bought my grandfather's land out near Sloetown for his factory. Over the years, Orion became the only game in town, for pallets that is, except most people still looked down on it." Prince smiled again. Davis realized it was Prince's own family that looked down on it.

"Pallets—it wasn't respectable," he added. "It was dirty, and white folks wouldn't work there. It was a low margin game, the wood on the bottom, so to speak, simply a place to stack the more valuable goods that people really wanted. I guess it's still that way."

"I get it," Davis said. They were quiet for a minute.

"Then old T.H. died and his son Karl started running the place. And to my knowledge, everything was fine until the big fire."

"Fire?"

"Yeah, about ten years ago, I think. The factory went up in flames, or most of it anyway. It was a huge mess. A lot people got hurt and Orion lost most everything, but somehow, he rebuilt. He was back in business within a year."

"That didn't take long."

"No, I guess it didn't." Prince stopped, a kind of melancholy in his voice, as if he wished he didn't know this story. There was more to tell, but his eyes were on a faraway place. He rose from his chair and left, walking back to his desk up front as Davis wondered *maybe that's why his name fit—the Gray Prince.*

Davis went to the little kitchen, poured a coffee and returned to his office, thinking about Karl Orion and his pallet factory. He opened the manila folder on his desk and withdrew the picture of the man at the charity event. There he stood, smiling in a tuxedo, with Mira Ogilvy on his arm and her father nearby. So Karl Orion knew the dead girl, was in her house searching yesterday. And his wife Gloria was a client. The old guy seemed to be in the middle of everything. Maybe it would pay to have a little talk with him. He'd dropped that folder in Mira's yard—maybe he'd like to have it back. Davis found the card Gloria Orion had given him and called Orion Pallet. A woman answered. He said,

"I'd like to speak with Mr. Orion."

"He's busy," she replied tartly.

"Relax. I only need a minute. I'm not a salesman."

"He's busy."

"Well, how long will he be there, at the office?"

"Until he gets finished."

"Finished with what?" That stopped her for a second, long enough for Davis to add, "I just need a minute. He's expecting me."

The woman paused. Davis heard her chew her lip. "Mr. Orion *always* works late. If he really knows you, then you would know that."

Now it was Davis's turn to stop. The woman chewed again, then sighed. "But if you come by later—"

"Okay. Thanks." He hung up, and for the first time in a long time Baker Davis tasted fear. Right there in his quiet office where bright sunshine crept through the drawn blinds, the investigator knew something was wrong. He wasn't sure why, couldn't name it, but something dark and strong pulled at him.

TWENTY GRAND

He grabbed his car keys and the manila folder.

* * *

Richard McDermott sat in his office on Twenty and stared at a letter from his bankers. It came as Certified Mail, even though the bank was right downstairs. Gail signed for it. The bankers wanted him to submit a written plan for making the mortgage payment. Their Committee needed details, the letter said. Could he please forward documentation? Documentation of what, McDermott wondered.

Then, earlier that day, he received word that a key tenant, Adams Financial, wouldn't be renewing their lease. They were moving, leaving behind ten thousand square feet on the sixth floor. It was another blow, making his chances of paying the bank even more remote. In fact McDermott had already borrowed against the Adams lease.

He knew the president of Adams Financial, Theodore Adams. They were in college together. McDermott called him that afternoon, talked about old times, then wondered aloud if there was any way to sit on the announcement, keep it quiet for a while. Maybe the bank won't find out. Sorry, Ted Adams explained, they must notify their customers about the move. Everyone in town would know.

McDermott thanked him and hung up.

He cast about, trying to think of a plan, a way out, a solution. Then he remembered Mira Ogilvy. She had plenty of money, even if she was dead. Karl Orion gave it to her. It was Orion Pallet money and it was Gloria's too. If he could find out what happened to it, and maybe get some of it back, it would sure help. It would get him through the end of the year with the bank.

Gail came through on the intercom. Gloria Orion was on the phone.

"Sure," he said, picking up the receiver.
"Richard?"
"Hey."
"Richard, the cops came to see me."
"What?"
"The police came to the office late yesterday, asking about Mira."

"Well, what did you expect? You ID'd the woman, right?"

"I . . ."

"Don't worry. You hardly knew her."

"Yes."

"What did you tell them?"

"Him. It was just one cop."

"What did—?"

"I didn't tell him anything, Richard."

"Nothing?" His sister fell silent. "Gloria?"

"Well, I had to tell the little jerk something. I said I'd met the girl before."

"So?"

"I met her at your house, Richard. Remember?"

"Uh—"

"But that's all I said. 'That Mira was there, that someone brought her to a party at your house."

"Well, hell."

"I'm sorry, but I had to say something."

"Don't worry. Listen. Did they ask anything about the money? Mira's money?"

"No."

"All right then. If they want to talk to me about Mira, and who killed her, I don't care. I don't know anything that, and I don't mind telling them."

"All right, but I'm still worried. We've *got* to get that money. Karl's—"

"Have you heard anything from that Davis fellow? He's supposed to be looking."

"No, I haven't," she said, as they paused for a moment. "All right, I'll take care of it."

"Good. Call me later." He hung up.

The lawyer rose and approached the windows that formed the west wall in his office. McDermott Center soared over most of the buildings downtown. Below, he saw people lounging on rooftop decks, sipping drinks, talking. They looked like tiny figurines in a toy village one could arrange and rearrange. Then suddenly, as he looked down, one of the figurines stood up and walked away, disappearing into a doorway. It didn't seem right, that they could do that in Richard McDermott's world; and he wondered if it was all slipping away from him, if this commanding view he enjoyed that moment would soon disappear. What could he do then? Where would he go? The word *failure* came to his mind, and it occurred to him that some people in trouble jumped out of skyscrapers. He'd read stories in the newspapers. But these big windows weren't the kind that opened.

He returned to his desk, opened a drawer, and withdrew a pint of vodka. He took a deep sip, grimaced, then put it away. What the hell, he thought. It would take them months to get him out of McDermott Center if he played his cards right. But those damn bankers—they were experienced foreclosure operatives. They knew how to do it quick, efficient, brutal. Maybe if he went somewhere, some place they couldn't reach him. He could leave town, maybe even go abroad. He thought of South America. Maybe Cheryl could go with him, and slowly a smile came to his face as he remembered her. How much fun she was to sit and chat with! 'Even if she didn't say much and when she did, she teased him. He noticed the letter from the bank open on his desk. He had no idea how to answer it. It made his mind reel, and he looked forward to seeing Cheryl again. She made him forget, if only for a moment. He was meeting her tonight in Jackson Park.

McDermott reached into the drawer again for the vodka, hearing her voice, light and smooth.

* * *

It was late afternoon when Baker Davis reached Sloetown. He turned his Buick onto a shady, unkempt street that had no name, no outlet. Orion Pallet Company sat at the end of it, a brown brick factory building a city block long—immense, monumental, and permanent, like an Egyptian ruin.

The investigator drove into the parking lot and stopped. He grabbed the manila folder, got out of the car and looked around. A hot breeze struggled across the pavement where he stood, bringing an odor of sawn wood, fuel, and creosote that he could taste. At one end of the lot, behind a chain link fence ten feet high, stood giant heaps of wood pallets as far as he could see, a gritty scene. Sounds rolled from the warehouse building: the voices of men, the whirr of equipment, but it felt as if the day was ending. It felt like exhaustion.

Davis ascended a few concrete steps onto a vast loading dock, then noticed a metal door flanked by windows—the offices. He pounded on the door. No answer, but the handle turned and he entered a large reception area. It was empty and quiet. He remembered the tart woman on the phone, but it was late afternoon. Maybe she had gone home. He looked around. A window in the back wall gave a view into the factory. To his left, a big door loomed, a rich door of paneled oak, slightly ajar. He approached and gave it a nudge.

The big man in the easy chair didn't look up. His shoulders filled the room, his cinder-black eyes fixed on the man who stood before him.

Davis's breath stopped. "Uh, Mr. Orion?" But the man's eyes didn't change. They stayed empty. "I didn't see anyone out front."

"Good," he said. His face was long and gray. A newspaper lay open in his lap.

"I hope it's not too late. I only need a minute."

"I've got time," he replied absently.

The big man didn't move as the investigator eased into the office. The room was dim, with the late afternoon sun streaming in around the parted curtains.

"I'm Baker Davis."

Orion didn't say anything but motioned to a chair across from his desk. He looked his visitor over and said:

"That's a nice jacket, Mr. Davis. I take it you're not looking for work. We make pallets here. You know . . . carpenters, painters, forklift drivers, guys that unload boxcars."

"No, sir, I'm not looking for employment. I wouldn't be very good at that. But I have something here, maybe something you're missing." He showed the manila folder.

"What? Where did you get—?"

"You dropped it last night, sir." He tossed the folder on Orion's desk. "At Miss Ogilvy's."

The big man grunted, reached for the folder and leafed through the papers inside. The emptiness came back to his eyes again; then he turned to a small table behind him. A bottle of amber liquid stood there. He said, "Drink, Mr. Davis?" He poured something that looked liked good scotch into a glass and handed it over, smiling.

Davis tasted it. Yes, good scotch. He said, "I guess you know then, about the young lady."

"I've heard," Orion said. He poured a drink for himself and reached into his desk for a medicine bottle. He shook a few pills out and tossed them back, washing them down with the scotch.

"Looks like strong stuff Mr. Orion."

"I like it that way." Then he shoved his newspaper across the desk, toward Davis. It landed open to the story about Mira, and her picture. "So you know anything about it?"

"Her death? I'm afraid not, Sir."

"Right. But you knew enough to be at the girl's house on Sunday, before it was reported."

Davis raised his drink. "Well, you were there too."

Orion sighed, looked into his glass, and said, "I have friends downtown, at the newspaper. They told me about it." He appeared older then, darker. "And you?"

"I have friends too, Mr. Orion. In Sloetown."

He smiled. "Well, then, we're both ahead of the cops, eh?"

"Sometimes that's not too hard. But the police are investigating a murder. They're looking for Mira's killer. And—"

"—and me? What am I looking for?" Orion put his glass down, added more scotch. "I might ask you the same thing, Mr. Davis."

The investigator considered his options. The room felt very still then, the muffled sounds of the factory in the background. "Mira had a lot of money, Sir."

Again the years seemed heavy in Orion's face. He stared across the room at nothing, and said, "Is that what you want Mr. Davis? Money? Are you some kind of . . . creditor?"

"No. I have clients. They're interested. I'm an investigator."

"Ah, a private dick?"

"That's a common term, not one I especially enjoy."

"Don't take it personally."

"I don't. But my clients, they have a claim on Miss Ogilvy's assets. That's why I'm interested."

Orion rose and crossed the room with his drink. He stood at the window, parting the blinds to look out at the waning afternoon, the coming twilight. He eyed Davis over his shoulder: "Mira didn't have any money. Not her own, anyway."

"Not her own?"

"No, not hers. Not really."

Davis eyed the folder on the desk. "But those bank

statements. The deposits—?"

"I know about them."

"You—?"

Orion's mouth became a hard line. "Yes, I know. I made them." He went back to his desk and sat down.

Davis took a moment, kept his eyes on Orion. "You gave her twenty grand?" he said, but the big man gave no answer. "All those years, every month?" Again, no answer. The office, the factory, the big man were silent. There would be no explanation. Orion sipped his drink. Davis tried a different tack. "I didn't realize there was that much money in selling pallets."

"I'm a successful businessman, Mr. Davis."

"Uh-huh. All the way back to eighty-four?"

Orion winced. His black eyes flashed. "Eighty-four?"

"Yes. Wasn't there a big fire about then? Or maybe in eighty-three? Here at Orion Pallet?"

"A temporary setback."

"I heard it was a minor disaster. A lot of guys hurt, your company almost destroyed."

"We rebuilt the factory."

"Got back to business as usual, eh?"

"All right. Yes, there were injuries. We compensated people. Is that why you came to see me? About that old news?"

"No sir. I just wanted to return your folder. Orion Pallet is your business."

"You're damn right."

Davis stood. "Well, sir . . . I appreciate your time." He turned to go. At the door, he paused: "But just one thing, if you will: That money you gave Miss Ogilvy, those deposits. What did the girl do with it all? What could she have possibly done—?"

"That . . . Mr. Davis . . . is something I'd very much like to know." The old man drained his glass and stared at nothing.

Davis left Orion's door open and walked back through the reception area. Afternoon was gone as he exited the building, with darkness gripping the parking lot as he found his car. The warm night settled in over the giant oak trees which surrounded Karl Orion's property.

* * *

Cheryl Lewis asked McDermott to come to Jackson Park—to

a bench on the corner near the playground. She thought it would be a good place to sit and talk that evening. The children had vacated the park, leaving their toys behind as they ran home to dinner. Balls and bikes and a jump rope lay in the grass. They were often stolen, but always re-appeared in a few days because that's where everyone in the neighborhood met to play. The streetlights flickered to life now, but it wasn't late.

She couldn't stay long tonight. She had work tomorrow and Lester was watching the baby, but the lawyer said he wanted to see her. She wondered what he did all day in that building downtown which had his name on it. Just then, a car appeared beneath the streetlight. She didn't see it coming down the street and her heart skipped a beat. It was a black Lincoln.

He parked along the curb, got out and came to her. He wore no jacket and removed his tie as he exited the car, tossing it on the seat. Cheryl Lewis had wanted to wear something nice, but decided jeans would be okay for a weeknight in the park. She ran her hands along her thighs to make sure the jeans weren't wrinkled. She'd selected a blouse of red silk. It was tight and she tried to decide how many buttons to leave undone at the top. She wondered if white guys cared about that kind of thing. They must, she concluded. They're men, aren't they?

"Hi there," McDermott said softly.

"How you doing?"

The lawyer stood there before her, looking around Jackson Park, noticing the toys nearby on the ground, the idle swing set, and the dark trees beyond. They were all alone. He sat beside her on the bench, near her. She didn't move.

"Say, you look nice," he said. She smiled at him, fingering the top of her blouse where she'd left a button undone. "Good to have a night off, huh?"

"Hmm, sure is. But I have to work tomorrow." She noticed him sitting forward on the bench, almost clenched, holding something inside. His eyes met hers, then looked away. She asked, "So how was everything downtown today?"

"All right. The usual." He sounded tired and worried, she thought. He knotted his hands then looked at her. "Well, there's a lot going on, to tell you the truth. There are some problems with the building, McDermott Center."

"Problems?"

"Yeah. 'With the banks and everything." McDermott leaned back against the park bench and sighed. He felt better telling her this, but wondered how much more to say, how much she would understand.

"Those banks!" she said, smiling. "I don't trust them. I never use them." She waved a hand in the air, dismissing the whole lot of them. Then it dawned on McDermott that some people operated with cash and money orders and things like that, especially in Sloetown. They had no checking accounts, no credit cards. She added, "They don't care about nobody but themselves."

"That's right!" he agreed. "They just don't care! I don't trust them either." Then laughter bubbled up from a place inside him, a place he didn't know existed. He heard the sound go out into the darkness of Jackson Park. Cheryl Lewis laughed too as she touched his arm. McDermott felt his breath moving easier through his body as he leaned back, extending his arms out along the top of the park bench, near her shoulder. She wore a nice fragrance. He didn't recognize it.

"So what are you gonna do with those bankers?" she asked.

"Something bad," he said cryptically, but the corner of his mouth formed a grin. "Maybe I'll take all my money out of their safe!" Cheryl Lewis didn't believe him, nor was she impressed, but she liked to hear him talk, so her eyes grew big, encouraging him. He said, "Maybe I'll kick them out of the building."

"Yes," she cried. "Kick 'em to the curb!"

"Kick 'em where?"

"To the curb!" And she poked out a foot as if kicking something. McDermott laughed again, imagining her shoes against the backsides of his creditors—and noticing her long legs. He liked women with long legs.

"Like this?" he asked, putting his foot out.

"Kick 'em," she said, kicking again. McDermott tried it again.

"That's right. You got it!" And they laughed together.

Then, his face turned gray and he stared into the darkness of the old neighborhood and said,

"Or maybe I'll go away."

"Away? Like leave town?"

"Yeah, some place where they don't know me, can't find me."

"Where?"

"I don't know, but far away."

Cheryl Lewis found it hard to imagine living any place else, but she tried. She visualized herself boarding a sleek jetliner, then enjoying sunny afternoons in foreign cafés, or strolling along a coastal promenade in a city by the sea, with this man at her side. She enjoyed the novel sights and sounds. But people there stared at them with cold eyes that didn't understand. And behind it all lurked something bitter and wrong, something she and McDermott couldn't escape, couldn't leave behind. Maybe they couldn't escape who they were. Or was it something about Sloetown? She couldn't tell exactly, but it would follow them everywhere, and they would never rest.

"Will that work, Richard? Going away?"

"Maybe."

"So those bankers . . . what do they want?"

"I don't think you'd understand, honey."

"Oh boo."

He looked at her, her brilliant smile, her red silk top, lovely neck. "You're beautiful. You know that?"

"You crazy," she said softly.

"No, I mean it."

"Hah. I'm not beautiful."

"Of course you are."

"No, I can't be. I don't have any money."

The lawyer paused. He had never heard it stated quite so plainly before. "Really?"

She smiled at him again, as if he were a child. "Don't you know that?"

"I guess I never thought—"

"Beautiful? With no money?" She laughed. "I'm a poor girl, Richard. I work in a restaurant. I have a little house Mamma left me when she died. I have a baby, and a little brother just out of high school. That's all I have. Beautiful? In Sloetown?" She laughed again.

McDermott recalled the women he'd known over the years, the fine women, the women with breeding and money. They weren't from Sloetown. Then he thought about his office on Twenty, the splendid view there at the window, a view that required no money to enjoy.

"I don't care. You're still lovely."

"Well, thanks, but you still crazy."

He sighed and looked away. "I know a place, Cheryl, where it's beautiful. You'll have to come and see it."

"Oh?"

"Yes, my office in McDermott Center. There's big windows. You can look out and see the city."

"The whole city?"

"Everything, baby."

"Even Sloetown?"

"Yes, and beyond, all the way to the river."

"Wow. I'd love to see that."

"We will sometime. Together."

The man and woman sat contentedly in the park. They were mostly silent, but sometimes they glanced at each other. He thought her eyes warm; she enjoyed his company. His hand touched her shoulder along the top edge of the bench. She didn't move.

At that moment, a sharp cry pierced the gloom in the park. McDermott shuddered. He knew somebody killed Mira Ogilvy, maybe not too far away from the bench where they sat. And this cry in Sloetown: it *must* be murder, robbery, rape, or worse. He sweated. His heart pounded. Cheryl Lewis stifled a yawn as she glanced at her watch. "'Guess it's getting kinda late. I've got to work early tomorrow."

McDermott exhaled. "Sure. Me too." They rose from the park bench. "Say, let me give you a lift home."

"That's all right," she said, looking at the toys on the sidewalk and the empty swing set under the trees. "I only live a few blocks away. I walk here all the time. I used to come to this park when I was little. My big brother played basketball here, and I'd come and watch." She slid her hands into her pockets and moved away, staring at the ground. McDermott noticed, and said:

"Your brother?"

But she wouldn't look at him, her eyes wandering out into the darkness. "Yeah. Michael. He used to play ball here. And in the summer, on warm nights like tonight, he'd take us riding around in a convertible he had back then." Again she looked at the ground.

"It's getting late Cheryl. Let me give you a ride home."

"Okay."

They went to his car across the street. As McDermott got behind the wheel, he said, "A convertible is nice in the summer.

Does he still have it?"

"Have what?"

"The convertible. Your brother."

"No. Michael's gone now."

"Gone? Where'd he go?"

She didn't speak, her eyes vacant as the Lincoln rumbled across the pavement under the ancient oaks and the breeze coming in through the windows. Then she said, "Michael's been gone a while now, since about nineteen eighty-four. He just never came back from work that day," she paused, "after the big fire at the pallet factory." The streetlights threw a lurid glare into the car.

"Pallet factory? *Orion* Pallet?"

But she wouldn't answer. Her eyes were moist. Better shut up, McDermott thought. He knew sadness when he heard it. He knew it because life wasn't easy for him either, not now. The bankers were scheming to take McDermott Center away from him. He owed everybody in town, and soon the cops would come to ask about the dead girl who attended his dinner party. Further back, he remembered his wife and kids. He knew where they were, but in a sense he didn't know what happened to them either. They were lost. He was lost. How did his life get so far off track? The world he knew was dissolving before his eyes, and now Cheryl's brother was gone and suddenly the lawyer didn't want the world to be this way. He wanted Michael to come back, and the bankers to go away, and this girl to come to his office and enjoy the view from Twenty, beside him, with him.

"To hell with everything!" he exclaimed.

"Whaaat?"

"Nothing, baby."

She wondered what was wrong with the man, what bothered him. He must have big conflicts at work, enemies even. It made her mad that anyone could trouble him so, or hurt him. If she could do anything for him, she would. But she wasn't sure what that could be.

They reached her house. McDermott stopped the car in silence. He was ready to get out and walk her to the door, but she didn't move. She reached for the purse that sat between them, and as she did McDermott put his hand on hers, covering it, holding it warm and steady. She smiled. They remained still, afraid to look at each other, his white hand on her dark hand, conscious of how it looked. It looked fine. Then she turned her hand over, and their fingers wrapped together. She felt his smooth palm and the pulse of the man, felt him move. Her lips parted and her eyelids closed as he drew near, slowly, as if he wasn't sure. She didn't know what to do and even tried to speak, but only felt her warm breath in her mouth.

His lips touched her neck.

Cheryl Lewis felt a tear rise in the corner of her eye, as if something hot and moist had been squeezed from her. She expected him to withdraw and lean back and say goodnight, but he remained at her neck, breathing. She thought he couldn't move, then he did. He kissed her cheek slowly. Her thighs felt heavy against the seat of the car. She turned to him and McDermott felt the woman's hands on his shoulders and then her mouth, parted, on his. He kissed her deeply.

They stopped. They withdrew from each other as if they had been shocked. They exhaled, filling the car with hot breath, steaming the windshield. The man coughed. She reached for the door handle.

"I've really got to go."

McDermott couldn't speak as he watched her exiting the car. He reached for his door.

"No, no need," she said, getting out of the car and smiling at him from the sidewalk. "Bye."

"Bye then."

Then she closed the door gently and in a moment she stood on the front porch of her house. She turned and waved.

McDermott nodded to her, then eased his Lincoln away into the darkness, tasting the woman in his mouth. He passed along the empty streets with his window down, letting the night air rush in and cool his damp shirt and face. Yes, it would be nice to have a convertible in the summer, like Cheryl's brother . . . that brother who never came back from his job at the pallet factory.

He drove on, then realized he was lost. Everything looked the same as he wandered through the old neighborhood. He drove past the Park again. Was he going in circles? His jaw tightened. Somewhere around here the cops found Mira Ogilvy. That's what Gloria said.

* * *

Officer Jeremy Wilson thought it would be stupid to wait much longer there on Vinson Street. It was dark and late, but Lt. Foster was anxious about the case. People were bugging her and she wanted results. "Find *something*, Wilson," she yelled at him as he left the office earlier that day.

So the policeman waited in his car that night near the vacant lot where they found the girl. Maybe it was true: criminals do revisit the scene of their crimes. He wasn't sure why, but he had his theories. Plus, a man did phone this one in on the tip line last Sunday. Some one knew Mira Ogilvy was dead that day.

Wilson sipped a Coke and smoked a cigarette, thinking Sloetown was not a good place to be at that hour. Someone could put a bullet in him as easily as they did that young woman, and they'd find his body slumped over the steering wheel sitting in a pool of blood. Why the hell did that girl want to come here anyway?

But Vinson Street remained quiet and deserted and soon Wilson considered it was time to go. He had to be in early tomorrow and report to Lt. Foster. He reached for the ignition when lights flashed into his rear view mirror. He paused, slid low in the seat. A car came up behind him, moving slowly, as if it wasn't going anywhere definite. It was a black Lincoln. Wilson could see a man inside, a white man, and he looked like an executive or businessman or something, not a rough character, not a killer, but who the hell knew? One thing was for certain, he didn't belong there in Sloetown at that hour. Not a guy like that. It was wrong, different, out of place, didn't make sense. The Lincoln rolled past, giving a good view of the man. There was little color in his sweaty face. His eyes were dark and restless. At the end of Vinson, the Lincoln paused. Jeremy Wilson scribbled down the license plate number. Then the strange car disappeared.

* * *

Baker Davis found himself in Sloetown that night after he left Karl Orion's office. He could have avoided it, taken a different way, but the old neighborhood lay spread out before him as if there was no other way. Along the streets, faded apartment buildings rose two stories high, a riot of electrical wires crossing overhead. The night air was humid, and curtains hung limp in the windows, while other windows held groaning air conditioners that appeared ready to fall into the street. From these rooms, voices trickled into the evening, the words a soft chatter. Most of the employees of the Orion Pallet Company lived here.

Davis stopped at a corner sundry, one of those joints announcing *Beer Cigs Cold Cuts Milk Ice* in big red letters above the door, as if here were the fundamentals of human existence, the eternal verities, all a man could ever need. Inside the little store, he bought cigarettes and a six of beer as the man behind the counter languidly dropped change into his hand and said *You ain't lost are you?* Except it wasn't a question. Davis said he didn't think so, but when he returned to his car, he realized the man was right. He didn't know a soul around here, couldn't find a landmark. No one knew him either, but the anonymity felt good.

Davis relaxed in his car, smoking, drinking a beer, thinking about Karl Orion. He gave Mira Ogilvy that money. Where did it come from? Did making pallets bring in that kind of dough? Of course, the old guy was a *manufacturer*, as his wife said. Davis finished one beer and opened another, watching men enter and leave the little store. The night was warm, the beer cold. Finally he started the Buick, easing away, unsure of his destination but feeling good about it, letting the old streets take the wheel. Where would they lead? It didn't matter. He rolled down the window for a breeze, hoping it was cooler. But in its place sadness flooded in, from where he couldn't tell, but he remembered the young woman lying in the empty lot on Sunday and maybe nobody missing her, no one to offer a few last words, a few tears. When was the funeral? Who would attend? And the man who shot her? Who knew? Maybe Sloetown knew. That was likely.

His car moved through the old neighborhood, going—well, it doesn't matter, he thought. I'll find my way eventually. He finished a beer, tossed the empty into the back seat, then started another, noticing his head go fuzzy though it felt appropriate that night. He turned down one street, then another. Each deserted block felt more lost, more remote from the city. He was getting farther away. No, closer to something, deeper—until he came to a dark street and three men under a streetlight. They stood in the middle of the road and weren't moving. There was no way to turn around.

Davis stopped the car, killed his lights. It didn't look good, but they were only teenagers, one tall, one short, one fat. Their bodies were taut, tense. They saw him too. And when he climbed from the Buick, they moved forward.

"You make a wrong turn somewhere?" the tall one demanded.

"Maybe," Davis answered. The youth shifted uneasily. Davis knew if it came down to it, he'd start with this one. Always take out the biggest one first, he knew, if you can. It sends a message to the others.

The chubby one jumped in. "Man, you lost?"

"I know where I am," Davis said. They stared hard at him with narrow-eyed toughness. It wasn't hatred, nor was it experienced, but the PI knew there was more danger in a youngster who was unsure, who wanted to prove something, than in a cold-blooded adult.

"You looking for somethin'?" the short one said, moving closer. His eyes were eager, cunning, hoping maybe this stranger wanted something he could provide—drugs, a woman, or worse. There could be money in it.

"I don't know," Davis answered. "What you got?"

"Anyting you want mister." Their eyes shifted quickly to one another as Davis recognized it was all new to them. More experienced eyes would've never left his face. This was only a game they'd seen their big brothers play—making a deal with a white dude in Sloetown. These kids likely didn't have a damn thing to offer, or sell, though maybe they could go and find something if they tried hard enough; but, pathetically, it would take them all night.

"What the hell you want?" the tall one demanded.

Davis made no reply. He sipped at his beer, then strolled across the street, ignoring them, looking around. He lit a cigarette and blew the smoke up into the branches of the trees.

"Y'all live around here?"

"'Course we live here," the short one sneered. He was wiry, angry. His head was shaved except for two streaks of hair along the side.

"In Sloetown, huh?" Davis said, with a few grains of contempt to let them know he didn't need to be friendly. He guessed this was an attitude, a rank appraisal, these young men had never heard about their neighborhood. "Some kinda place ..." he drawled. "And ya'll growed up around here?"

"Yeah."

"So you know about the neighborhood, huh?"

"Yeah, we know all about it."

Davis drew on the cigarette, looking out into the darkness. "Then ya'll know about that big factory over on the west side. Where they make the pallets."

"Hell yeah we know," the chubby kid blurted. "That factory ain't nothin' without Sloetown."

"I bet."

"What you wanna know?" the short, intense youth said.

"I heard it was a tough place to work."

"How come you wanna know?"

"Cause I'm interested."

The young men stared at Davis. No one spoke. No one moved. He said,

"All right. Maybe you don't know nothing."

"Oh we know plenty," the chubby kid exclaimed.

"Shut up," one said.

They stood there in the empty street. A cloud of insects buzzed in the warm glow of the street lamp above them. A minute went by like an hour. Davis felt sweat trickle down the side of his face. He said,

"Y'all thirsty?" He sipped his beer.

The teenagers looked to one another.

"Y'all want something to drink?"

One tried to speak. Another moved his feet. One scratched himself.

Davis went to his car, reached in and grabbed the rest of the six-pack. Sure, they're under age, he thought, but one beer isn't going to hurt them. And it sure as hell won't be the first alcohol they ever tasted. He returned to the boys.

"Here."

They didn't move.

"Here. They're cold."

The tall one came forward. His pulled a can from the plastic rings. The others crept up behind him.

"Here," Davis said.

Then they each had one. They popped the tops, the compressed air spewing into the night. They tasted the beer. Davis said,

TWENTY GRAND

"I hear that pallet factory is a tough job."

"It ain't tough," the chubby kid said, the can at his mouth.

"Huh. So you know folks who work there?"

Again there was silence. Davis watched them try the beer. The wiry youth with the shaved head spoke:

"My uncle used to work there, but he got hurt a while back. There was a big fire—a whole lotta folks got hurt. They don't work no mo'. They can't."

"No work? So what they do for money? For the rent and the groceries—all that?"

"They got some money from the factory when dey got hurt."

"Yeah," the chubby teen intruded. "That's why some of these houses 'round here look fixed up. Some of them had new cars too. But they ain't new no mo'!" The boys all laughed.

"Hell naw!" the tall one commanded, silencing them. "Ain't everyone got money from that. A couple of dudes didn't make it outta that big fire."

"Aw shut up," someone said.

"You shut up," he said back. He drained his beer, crumpled the can, and flung it into the gutter. "Those men got burnt up. Dead. They didn't get nothin." Then his voice settled into an unfamiliar depth. "I know. One of 'um was my brother."

Davis didn't say anything. He waited, sipping the beer. "So your brother's passed?"

The tall youth shrugged his shoulders. "'Don't know. But Michael never came back from the factory that day, after the fire. I was little then, but it was the last we ever saw of him."

Davis eyed the young men. There was no emotion in them. He said,

"And no money came from Orion Pallet?"

The chubby kid laughed: "Wass a dead man gonna do wit money?" The other boy laughed too, but the tall one stared them down and said,

"No. Michael was just gone."

"Sorry to hear it."

"He never came back."

Davis finished his beer and the cigarette, flicking it away, watching the orange ember arc in the night. He turned back to his car. The young men followed.

"Is this all you got to drive?" one said, noticing the old Buick.

They all laughed.

"It runs good," Davis replied, climbing into the car as they approached his window.

"Hey man, you got any more beer?"

"No. It's not good for you."

"Aww!"

"Hey what's your name?" Davis asked the tall youth.

"Lester."

"You got a last name?"

"Lewis."

"Y'all take it easy," Davis said, as he pulled away from the curb into the night. The boys stood there under the streetlamp watching him disappear into Sloetown as if he had never been there at all. The investigator left his window down, feeling the warm breeze pour into the car and onto his face. He drove through the quiet neighborhood, past frayed churches, weedy lots, and gloomy little houses. A few liquor stores and a solitary gas station were open but that was about it. Sloetown Elementary occupied an entire block, the schoolyard worn bare by the tread of countless feet avoiding the broken sidewalks. The school was an immense, stone ghost from the Nineteenth century, and resembled the Orion Pallet factory, which is where many of its students ended up: the school, then the factory, and finally they came back home. For generations it was like that. Then they died and got buried in Sloetown except for a few souls who never even made it out of the factory. Like that kid's brother.

* * *

Karl Orion was the last one to leave Orion Pallet that night. The men in the factory went home at four and it was almost ten when he left the building. It was dark and his sedan was the only vehicle left in the big parking lot. And he felt tired. The medicine he was taking made him nauseous and dizzy, and that PI fellow who came to visit earlier was annoying. But tonight he knew the homeless man with the shopping cart would be out picking up bottles and cans. He'd overheard guys in the warehouse talking about him—Rico. They said he could get anything you wanted.

So Orion sat in his car, waiting in the big parking lot. He smoked a cigarette, listened to the radio, and finally saw a dim figure moving along the chain link fence at the far end of the old brick warehouse. He started up and drove slowly in that direction.

The man turned violently when Orion pulled up beside him. He cried,

"Naw man! I ain't doin' nuthin'!"

"You Rico?"

"Hell naw. I ain't nobody." His eyes burned like red coals in his black, sweaty face.

Orion looked him over. He didn't know what to say. The man's legs trembled. He looked drunk.

"I heard you could help me out."

"Naw, man. Not me. I can't hep nobody. I'm just pickin up these cans."

"All right, I don't care. Take all the cans you want."

"Hhmm." The man's face began to change, thinking.

"But I need something to smoke. Maybe you know somebody."

"Know somebody? Who you lookin fo'?"

"I don't know. I don't care. I just need something good to smoke. I'm sick. I got money, good money."

"Smoke, huh?"

"That's right."

The man's eyes began to smolder again in his dark face. He chewed something, his jaw working up and down. He said "All right bawss. You come around here tomorrow."

"Tomorrow?"

"Yeah, 'bout midnight."

"All right then, midnight. You gonna be here?"

Rico turned back to his shopping cart and pushed it slowly along the chain link fence in the darkness. Orion heard the cans tinkling in the cart until the man disappeared behind the warehouse.

* * *

Baker Davis noticed the street lights burning brightly as he approached home late that night. Here the streets looked cleaner, the property fresher. He took a deep breath, savoring the prosperity around him, yet tasting the beer in his mouth and remembering the kids in Sloetown. Money dwelled in this part of the city, even if the PI didn't have any. Here people made it, spent it, fought over it, and threw it away. Modest, broad wealth suffused this neighborhood like an atmosphere. If a man sat very still here, he'd have some too—if he didn't say too much. It would come. There was no escape.

Davis turned onto his street, and saw a white SUV parked before his house. He slowed, noticing a woman inside the vehicle, blonde; then her window came down. Gloria Orion. He pulled into his driveway and got out. She smiled nervously as he approached.

"I'm sorry Baker. It's so late," she said, shaking her head. He glanced at his watch. It was almost midnight, but she looked good.

"It's all right. This is early for me," he lied. After Sloetown, it *was* nice to see her. She was like something shiny and fresh.

"Well, I needed to talk with someone."

"So I'm the lucky guy?"

"It's the police, Baker. They came to see me. I don't know who else to—"

"It's late. Why don't you come in for a minute?" Davis said, almost regretting it as soon as he said it. He helped her from the SUV, then heard the click of her shoes loud on the porch, realizing it was a long time since anyone had visited at that hour, especially a woman.

"Nice in here," Gloria Orion commented as they came into the house. She walked around the living room taking it all in, evaluating, appraising, and Baker Davis felt right then that this woman's engagement with the world was perfectly commensurate with the size of her bank account. She was no more or less than she could afford. It was a value system that made her instantly aware of where she stood in any situation, but was neither conscious nor premeditated nor malicious. That's how her money worked. She didn't judge, she measured. She rarely met an equal. She didn't believe in equals. So when she entered the investigator's home, she instantly knew his status, where he fit, the role he could play.

She perched herself on the edge of the sofa, crossing bare, tanned legs. Davis never knew how much to make of a move like that, but he assumed the worst. He unscrewed the cap from a bottle of wine and poured a few glasses. The woman's hair was pinned up, but a few strands had come undone in the humidity and clung to her neck, making big *S* shapes on her skin. Davis wanted

to brush them aside. He gave her the wine. She looked at him smoothly over the edge of her glass and said,
"Sure you don't mind me coming over? At this hour?"
"It's okay."
"You're alone, aren't you Baker? I mean, you're not married are you?"
"I don't think so."
"Do you have a cigarette?" He gave her one, and lighted it for her as her eyes sparkled. "So being alone here, with me, now, doesn't make you nervous?"
"It's late. I'm too tired to be nervous."
She uncrossed her legs and approached. She stood before him. "Past . . . your bedtime?"
He regarded her squarely. "Is it bedtime?"
She smiled, then backed off. She returned to the sofa, sank into the cushions, and sighed: "The cops. Jesus."
"Ah, the city's finest. They came for a little visit?"
She rolled her eyes, drank the wine. "I can't help them. I don't know anything about Mira."
"Well, don't worry. If they don't smell anything interesting, they'll wander off. Like dogs."
Her eyes slanted toward him. "It's funny, Baker. They do find *you* interesting."
"That so?"
"They seem to know you rather well. This red-haired cop—"
"We go back a ways," Davis said, remembering Wilson. Then he recalled the grim look Lt. Foster gave him Sunday afternoon in Sloetown, and further back, last year, when she advised him to take a long vacation or find another line of work. It might be the smart thing to do.
Gloria Orion got up from the sofa and came to him. "They said to stay away from you." Her hand reached up slowly, touching his arm. "Now why on earth would that be?"
"They don't like private detectives."
"You're not in trouble with the cops, are you Baker?" Her fingertips ran across his shoulder, then touched his neck. Her nails were blood red.
"No."
"No trouble with your license or anything?"
He tightened. "What about it?"

Her lips were at his ear. "Oh, nothing. I just don't want the cops to keep you from doing all you can . . . for me."

"I appreciate that."

Her fingertips caressed his skin. "And how much am I paying you Baker?"

"A thousand."

"Is that all?" she purred. "You know if you find that money, Baker, there's a lot more in it for you than a measly grand."

"I'm doing okay."

Her hand reached out to his chest, touching his heart. "And if you do find it, maybe you and I can—"

Davis stood up. "Is that the best you can do?"

She returned to the sofa and her drink, aiming a smile at him. "When are you going to start having a little fun?"

"I'm having fun Gloria." He looked at her legs and sipped his wine. It was bad wine, but they were good legs. "But I'd be having a lot more fun if you'd tell me about your husband."

"Karl? Can't we think of another subject?"

"I thought you wanted to find the money."

"I do. I've got to!"

"Then why didn't you tell me about Karl? He's the one who gave Mira that dough."

"What? How did you know about—?"

"You asked me to find Mira. I did. Then you wanted to find her money, your money. Okay, I'm on it. But I'm not going to get very far if you don't play nice."

"I've told you what I know."

Davis looked at his watch. "You know baby, it's getting late, past my bedtime, and I—"

"Okay all right. Yes, Karl gave Mira that money. I don't know why."

"So Karl knew her."

"Yes, I don't know why or how he knew Mira, but it all goes back a long time."

"Girlfriend maybe?"

"Maybe. I doubt it. Karl isn't like that. But to tell you the truth, I don't care." Her voice had the edge of a knife, sharp and clean. She sipped her wine. "But yes, he gave the girl that money. And it wasn't hers. The money belonged to Orion Pallet, so it's mine. I've got to find it."

"Look, if we know how Mira got the money, we might learn what she did with it, what happened."

"Karl—" she whispered, falling back into the cushions and gazing up at the ceiling as if it were the Milky Way. She closed her eyes. She was beautiful, Davis thought, in her unhappiness, or maybe even because of it. "I told you, Baker, I don't know why my husband gave Mira that dough. My attorney used to do some tax work for Karl, but he doesn't know either."

"You've hired a lawyer?"

"Well, no. My lawyer is Richard McDermott. He's my brother."

"McDermott? At McDermott Center?"

"Yes. He's your landlord, Baker." She said it with a twist, like she was sticking something in.

"Well, thanks for the information." Davis finished his drink, started a cigarette and looked her over. "But I don't think I see the family resemblance."

Gloria Orion looked away, her eyes distant. "Richard is only my half brother, different mothers. You know Baker, I haven't been here forever, in this city. I grew up in Kentucky, with my mother. She and McDermott's father were involved many years ago, but never married. I never knew the man. When I grew older, I heard that he lived in this city, but he died before I ever left Kentucky. Richard is his son, who I never met until I came here, as an adult, almost fifteen years ago."

Davis saw in her face that her past had been difficult, but she'd reached some acceptance. It hadn't been easy. He said, "So you and your brother . . . you both want the money?"

"Don't make it sound like that." She removed a wisp of hair that had fallen onto her cheek. "But yes, it's true. We've got to find the money. Richard's in trouble. His law practice is a wreck and he may lose that building. His family is estranged. He drinks a lot now. He's alienated a lot of people. He has no future."

"That's tough."

"And I have no past; except my late father lived here, and he's been gone a long time now." She drew on the cigarette and exhaled slowly. "Have you ever been to Kentucky, Baker? No, not the horse races and all that, but over in the east, in the hills near West Virginia, coal mines—Lewis, Macon, Greenup county?"

"Can't say that I have."

"And do you know what it's like to come here, unknown, without a thing, from a place like that? You don't, do you? No background, no past, nothing really to look back on, to draw on, to even help you remember who the hell you are. It's like waking up to life after a long sleep, maybe after many years, and forgetting what happened. And then nothing familiar here. No one to recognize you, no faces that I knew. Disconnected. It's like an emptiness you want to fill with something, almost anything. The only thing I was sure about—I couldn't go back home. I wouldn't!" Her eyes rested on a place far away, a time long ago.

"So when you got here, your brother like . . . took you in?"

"Something like that. And here . . . here I could be anyone, or anything. Anything I could dream. So, yes, my brother helped me out. He was all I had." Then she stood from the sofa, crossing the room to examine a painting that hung above the fireplace. "And Richard worked for this guy Orion. He knew the man was lonely so he introduced me." She paused, her face suddenly drawn and gray. "And Richard knew Karl had money."

"And that's why you married him? Money?"

She laughed. "You make it sound so simple. Karl's not a bad fellow. He was older, sure, but no one had ever been so nice to me before. He bought us a nice house; there were trips to Europe, all that. He gave me anything I wanted. I was somebody. And back in Kentucky, I didn't have much of . . . you know . . . anything. I know it's a trite story, but Mother wasn't educated and there was no money. I'd die there, with her. So maybe Karl *was* more a like a father than anything else, to replace the one I lost, or never had."

"Not unusual."

"I had a home, a place to go now." Davis saw pain in her face again. "Did I love Karl? Of course not, but I managed. Or I thought I did."

She returned to the couch, crossing her legs again as she sat. She picked up the glass of wine and finished the last drops. "Until I discovered what my husband was doing with our money. I keep the books at Orion Pallet you know, or most of them, and I finally discovered those checks he wrote to Miss Ogilvy. The size of those payments—my God! He's bleeding the company white. If Karl dies . . . when he goes . . . he's not a young man after all . . . there won't be anything left. No money for me, after all those years of marriage. Just that rotten pallet factory. And now Mira's gone and the whole business is in the red."

She stood and shouldered her purse, suddenly hard, her mouth a firm, bitter line. "Karl had no right to give that money away. Richard says it was illegal. You've got to find it, Baker, whatever Mira did with it. It's mine."

"You hired me. I'm on it." Then Gloria Orion approached again, her eyes on him. She clasped her arms around his shoulders in a warm embrace, facing him, her fingers entwined behind his neck.

"I know you are, Baker. Find the money—and part of it will be yours." She raised her lips to his cheek. Her legs brushed into him. Then her lips were on his face, whispering, "We could do so much." Davis wanted his arms to hold her, but they wouldn't. There was nothing soft about this woman anymore, not even her sweet perfume. He said,

"Knock it off."

"You really should lighten up," she said, pulling away.

"I'm working, Gloria, like you asked."

"Well, good." She turned to go. Davis went to open the door for her, but in an instant she was outside. He watched her cross the yard, get into her SUV and drive away in the darkness past the manicured lawns. He stood there on the porch, remembering Mira Ogilvy lying out in the tall weeds of Sloetown, and thinking about another young woman arriving in the city alone from the black, coal-veined hills of Kentucky. In the sky overhead, the investigator watched the stars struggle to shine through the haze that lay over the city.

AUSTIN McLELLAN

SIX

At Police Headquarters that morning Lt. Doreen Foster was in a bad mood. Her superiors in the Department were getting phone calls about Mira Ogilvy. Now they were calling her. They wanted to know about the dead girl. What was the Department doing about it? What happened? Were there any suspects? How long had she been missing? What about the evidence? Why was it taking so long?

From her office, the Lieutenant stared out across the big room filled with low cubicles, searching for Jeremy Wilson. She couldn't see him. It was a quarter past eight. She paced through the office, noticing who was there, who wasn't. She stopped at Angela Grimes's desk that was next to Wilson's.

"Where is he?" the Lieutenant growled.

"I haven't seen—"

"I want him when he gets in."

Officer Grimes blinked, thinking it better not to say anything right then. Lt. Foster returned to her office, noticing the lights flashing on her answering machine. She didn't want to hear the messages, and placed a folder on top of the phone. Maybe Wilson could use a little help with this case, she considered. He was still new and the whole thing was attracting too much attention. In a way, it made her mad. The city had plenty of homicides to worry about, including a random drive-by last night that left a teenage boy dead. He was somebody's son, somebody's brother, but the kid was in a gang and nobody cared. This girl found dead in Sloetown was another story—a physician's daughter, with social connections. People, important people, wanted results. Now. She sipped at her coffee.

Wilson stood in her doorway.

"Where've you been?"

"Down the hall at Motor Vehicles. I had to look something up. You need—?"

"Sit down and tell me what you got on this Ogilvy thing." Wilson sat quickly, fumbling with his pad and pencil. "Just tell me, detective."

"Uh . . . I talked with Gloria Orion. She's the woman who ID'd the victim the other day."

"That lady from Orion Pallet?"

"That's her, the one with the private investigator Sunday afternoon." The Lieutenant frowned, thinking about Baker Davis. Wilson continued: "It seems Mrs. Orion *did* know the victim, but not by much. They were acquainted, met at a party, ran in the same circles, that kind of thing."

"Uh-huh," the Lieutenant muttered. She heard Wilson say *Mrs.* and wondered if he was being too respectful, too easy on these people. This was a murder investigation. "Are you sure that's all?"

"Well, the Orion lady did mention one other person, her brother. It seems he knew Mira Ogilvy too. In fact, that's where Mrs. Orion met the victim, at her brother's house, at a party there. He's a lawyer. And there's something—"

"Good. So you've got another person to talk to."

"I mean . . . there's something else Lieutenant."

Her eyes narrowed on him. She wasn't much interested in theories these days.

"Well?"

"The brother, ma'am. I saw him last night."

"So?"

"At the crime scene, Lieutenant. Last night, about ten-thirty, in Sloetown."

Doreen Foster put her coffee down slowly. "In Sloetown? At the crime scene?"

"Yes ma'am. On Vinson Street, right near that vacant lot with the tall weeds. I saw his car, a black Lincoln. I got the plate number. It was Mrs. Orion's brother, Richard McDermott."

The Lieutenant stiffened. Wilson felt her eyes. "McDermott? McDermott?" she said. "Why does that sound familiar?"

"You know that building downtown, McDermott Center? He's involved with that somehow. His company or law firm owns it, I think."

"McDermott Center? What's a guy like that doing in Sloetown?"

"I don't know ma'am, but the word on the street is that he's in financial trouble."

She laughed. "Well, he's not going to find any money in Sloetown."

"I know ma'am. I was only saying—"

"I got it Wilson. Money troubles lead to motive, sometimes." She stood and stretched as if a burden was lifted. At least this might be an angle.

"I'll go see Mr. McDermott today," the policeman said.

"You do that. Now go."

* * *

Real detectives take care of business, Baker Davis thought as he showered that morning. They get the bad guy, save the girl, save the day. They have sharp clothes and fast cars, carry guns and kick ass. They inspire confidence in the weak, fear in the malevolent, envy in all the rest. They uncover all the clues. They master every situation. That what real PI's do. It sounded nice for a TV show.

Then Davis remembered that he was a real detective. His card said so, even though right now he had no license to operate legally. The cops were getting wise and he was broke. The money Gloria Orion gave him covered a few bills, but it was gone. Now she was promising more, considerably more, if he could find the money she claimed was hers. It wasn't going to be easy. Not even Karl Orion knew what Mira Ogilvy had done with all those deposits. And when Davis asked him about it, the old man locked up. It didn't make sense. Mira's letter said *it's not how something ends, but how it starts*. She'd heard that Baker Davis *was the man to understand this*. That too, remained a mystery to the investigator.

He exited the shower, dressed, and left the house, not ready for the bright, damp day yet, but resistance made it worse. He eased into it carefully, as if relaxing into a bed of clean, fresh sheets. He didn't want to mess it up and the only way to do that was slow. He drove downtown.

The Gray Prince was firing away when Davis came into the suite, chattering into one phone, listening on another. Prince claimed that if he kept at it long enough, made enough connections and got the right people on the line, a million dollars waited there for him like a pot of gold at the end of a rainbow. It was crazy but Davis believed it because he wanted to. He nodded as he walked by, took the final coffee from the pot, and got behind his desk. He moved a few papers around to get a little traction on the day but it didn't work. He felt like a man running in place, going nowhere. He sipped the coffee. It was hot but tasted bad. Then he became aware that Prince had grown silent. He went back up front.

"Say, Prince, you were telling me about the Orions the other day."

"Yep."

"—and their pallet factory, and the big fire."

"That again? You on to something?"

"I don't know. Maybe. I don't remember any fire in Sloetown."

"Well, it was simply another horror on the evening news back then. But yes, that factory burned. Afterwards, Orion tried to keep everything quiet. And you know what? I think he succeeded."

"Ah. Quiet. Why?"

"I don't know, but a lot of men got hurt in the fire, workers mostly. There were lawsuits." Prince leaned back in his chair, lacing his fingers behind his head. "Those guys all lived out in Sloetown, black folks I'm sure. That's who worked there back then. It's still that way, I think."

"Yes it is." Davis shook his head. "Burned. Damn. That's tough."

"Yeah. And the smoke too. You know those pallets they make out there? They contain arsenic, as a preservative."

"Like treated wood."

"Right. And when they burn, the fumes . . . well, they're toxic. The injured men filed lawsuits against Orion and his Company, but I think it all got settled early, long before it ever came to trial."

"I see. No judgment. No disposition."

"And no publicity. They just settled. You never know why. Well, money, of course. I bet Orion had good insurance. In any case, the men got paid and kept quiet."

"Nice and neat."

"Maybe, but the word back then was a few workers were missing. They never turned up that day."

"You mean were lost in the fire?"

Prince gave that look which was knowing and condescending at once. "That factory is a big place, my friend. I don't think Karl Orion, or anyone, knew every soul in the warehouse any given day. So you're right, *lost* might be the right word. Factory jobs like that—men come and go. They couldn't account for everyone. 'Still can't."

"Or don't want to. That *would* be a smart thing to keep quiet. Maybe that's how Orion played it: he simply didn't know every man on the job that day, nor who was missing."

"That's right. After all, they were only Sloetown guys, the sooner forgotten, the better. It's hard, but true, or so I hear."

"I don't believe everyone has forgotten," Davis said. He returned to his office and the coffee that was cold now.

* * *

It was late that morning when Richard McDermott arrived downtown. *But what difference does it make what time I arrive*, he muttered as he approached McDermott Center. In the parking lot, he saw a few idle men standing near the dumpster and he cursed to himself. Street people. He'd told Security to get rid of them more than once. He'd even yelled at them a few times himself, but screaming at winos made him feel guilty and vulgar. If he could avoid them, he would, and notify Security again.

He parked his car and reached for his briefcase in the backseat. As he climbed from the Lincoln, the odor of stale sweat hit him. Rico stood there under the hot morning sun.

"Hey bawssman!"

McDermott flinched. Stupid security guards, he thought. *Why can't they get rid of these people?*

"Hey sir. Suh!"

"Beat it," the lawyer muttered, smelling beer on the man's breath. A string of cheap plastic beads hung from his neck.

"Naw suh. I jus' need a little help."

"I said beat it. I'm busy."

"Awright bawss. Awright. I don't mean nuthin'." McDermott walked away, toward the entrance to the building. Rico followed his prey across the parking lot. "I jus need a few dollahs, suh. Get me sumthin' to eat. I ain't had nuthin to eat in two days bawss." A few people emerged from McDermott Center dressed in suits. They looked at the landlord and the tattered man together.

"Will you get outta here?!" McDermott shouted.

"C'mon bawss. Let me do a little woik. Make a few dollahs. I just need a couple dollahs fo a sandwich." The man smelled bad.

"I don't need any work done. Now get the hell away from me." McDermott lowered his eyes and plowed forward across the parking lot, thinking *if I can get inside the glass doors.*

"No woik bawss? Aw mane. Well looky hear then." Rico reached into his pocket. "Ah got sumthin fo ya." He withdrew two dirty pearls and showed them to McDermott. "These 'r real pearls, suh. How much you gimme for 'em?"

"I don't need anything, dammit."

"A couple dollahs suh. Gimme two dollahs for dese bawss. Dey real!" He shoved the pearls toward McDermott. The landlord looked at them sitting there in Rico's dirty hand. He felt a trickle of sweat roll down his temple.

"If I buy them, will you get the hell outta here?"

"Sure bawss. Yeah. Ah'll go and get me a samwich." McDermott reached for his wallet, found a couple of ones and handed them over. Rico offered the pearls.

"I don't need them. I've gotta go."

"Naw bawss! They yo's. You bought 'em. They real."

McDermott extended a hand and Rico dropped two dirty pearls into his palm. "All right. Now beat it."

"Sure bawss. Ah doan want no trouble. I'm gonna get me sumthin to eat now." He turned and shuffled away.

Thank God he's leaving, the lawyer sighed as he examined the dirty pearls. He stuffed them in his pocket. *I must get Security to keep the damn homeless away from here,* he said to himself as he entered the revolving glass doors of McDermott Center. He strode across the lobby and reached the elevator. When he got to his office on Twenty, he set his briefcase down next to his chair and removed his jacket. He felt the pearls again in his pocket and laid them on the desk. *Plastic,* he thought.

* * *

Officer Jeremy Wilson had never been in McDermott Center before, and he wondered if anyone from Homicide had ever been in there. The shiny tower wasn't the kind of place that harbored killers; maybe some bogus accountants, he guessed, or a few embezzlers. He knew the address, however. Most everyone did. The building was a landmark that was new in the 1960's, but still looked nice. As he entered the lobby that afternoon, he noticed the creamy marble floors and brushed aluminum trim. Rare plants, perfectly tended, grew from huge, glossy pots. The elevator whisked him upstairs.

Wilson exited the car into a short hallway where the lights were dim and the carpet worn. The top floor should be in better shape, he thought. A vague odor of cigarettes lingered. Then he noticed gold lettering on a big door at the end of the hall. As he approached, the sign read: 'Richard McDermott, Attorney At Law.' He raised a hand to knock, but stopped and reached for the handle instead. He managed to walk in steadily. Inside, a woman of indeterminate age sat stiffly behind an antique desk. She looked over her glasses and croaked,

"Yes?"

"Hi. Is Mr. McDermott available?" Wilson asked. She was thin, her blond hair silvery but attractive and curled up in a bob. Her gold earrings gave a soft glow. And like many women in these positions it wasn't so much what smarts they had inside their remarkable heads that mattered, that kept them ensconced behind those rich, mahogany desks, but who they were, how they presented, what they understood about the people who came through the door—even before they walked in. Wilson guessed that was smart enough.

"Do you have an appointment?" she asked.

"No. I'm with the Police Department. I only need a few minutes." She didn't flinch, made no motion at all, but lowered her eyes to an appointment book. Wilson could see it. The book had no entries.

"And your name, sir?"

"Wilson, ma'am." He presented his badge. She picked up the phone.

"Yes, with the police," she explained to her listener. "He only needs a minute." There was a pause, then she nodded toward another door to the right. "He's in there. Go ahead."

The office Wilson entered was appointed with oxblood leather armchairs that stood before a desk that would have looked about right in the White House. Heavy drapes the color of saffron hung in the windows, rich bookcases lined the walls, an exotic rug from the Orient lay beneath his feet. Everything was respectable, but it didn't feel like a place of business, where actual work was accomplished. McDermott was standing.

"How are you today?" the lawyer said. He came from behind the desk and extended a hand.

"Fine, sir. I'm Wilson, from the Police Department. I'd like to talk for a minute."

"I'm all yours," McDermott said, smiling. "Have a seat. Please."

"I'm conducting an investigation, Mr. McDermott," Wilson said, getting into the chair. "It's about Mira Ogilvy."

"Yes. Terrible news. I read about it in the newspapers."

"I understand that you knew the girl."

The lawyer paused, but didn't flinch, didn't move. "Yes. I met her once."

"So you knew her?"

"She attended a party at my house, Officer. Last year."

"That's all?"

McDermott stared. "Yes."

"So you don't know the people well at your . . . parties?"

"What did you say your name was?"

"Wilson."

"Oh yeah. Someone brought her to my house, Mr. Wilson. That's about it. I remember the girl, though. Very pretty."

"Right." The policeman wrote something on a pad. "You know, Mr. McDermott, Miss Ogilvy's remains were discovered in Sloetown."

"Sloetown?"

"Any idea why she might have been up there? It's not a good place for a young woman like that."

"Not a great place for anyone."

"Not even you, sir?"

"Me?"

"Do you know the area, the old neighborhood?"

"I beg your par—"

"Sloetown. You got any reason to be there?"

"Do you have a question, Officer, about Miss Ogilvy?"

"Just asking, sir. You were there however, in Sloetown, last night." Wilson saw McDermott tighten. The man didn't move, but it seemed as if he was trying hard to be still.

"Is that against the law?"

Wilson smiled. "No, not at all. But you were there, Sir, on Vinson Street, where that girl's body turned up. Any particular reason why?"

"I don't know anything about that."

"But you were there."

McDermott scratched at something along the side of his face then folded his hands on the desk, making a steeple with his fingers. "I was in the neighborhood, visiting a friend. I got lost for a minute. All those streets look alike, you know."

"No I wouldn't know. So you have friends in Sloetown?"

"Yes."

"That's a little surprising—a man in your position, with friends in the ghetto." Wilson looked around the nice office. "Anyone I might know?"

"I doubt it," McDermott said, glancing at his watch. Wilson waited. He crossed his legs as if he was content to sit for a while. The lawyer spoke: "You know, Officer, I've got an appointment in a few minutes. If there's anything else I can help you with—"

Wilson sighed and folded his notebook. "All right." Both men stood. The policeman noticed the pearls lying on McDermott's desk.

"Are you a collector?" Wilson said, nodding at the dirty gems.

"What?"

"Those pearls? Are you a collector?"

"No."

"Do you mind?" Wilson asked, reaching for one. "Where did you get them?"

"I . . . I . . . they were found in the lobby. I'm sure they're plastic."

Wilson rolled a tiny sphere between his fingers. "You know, Mira Ogilvy was wearing pearls when somebody shot her."

McDermott frowned. "How interesting. A lot of women wear pearls."

"You know, my daughter collects beads. She makes bracelets and stuff. These are unique."

"Take 'em."

"No."

"Take 'em."

"Well, okay," Wilson replied. "Just a couple. Thanks." He pocketed the pearls, leaving one on the attorney's desk. "Appreciate your time, Mr. McDermott," he added, turning to go. He paused at the door. "And I'd be careful visiting Sloetown after dark. It's not the safest place in the city, even if you do have friends there." The lawyer's eyes were black and hard.

Wilson smiled at the woman behind the antique desk as he exited the suite. She didn't smile back.

* * *

Baker Davis contemplated the quiet afternoon in his office. The setting sun crept through the venetian blinds, its light deepening into orange and red as he considered the story Prince told about Orion Pallet. A big fire. Many men injured. An insurance settlement. Others missing. And everything kept real quiet. The manila folder lay on his desk, containing the Ogilvy bank statements. Those deposits began about the time Orion Pallet burned, or not long thereafter. Maybe that's where Karl Orion got the cash, insurance. According to Gloria Orion, selling pallets never earned much. But that Lewis kid in Sloetown with the brother who never came home—he never got a cent. Mira Ogilvy ended up with all the money. And now she was dead.

It made Davis's head ache. He wanted to see it all clearly, to make sense of the world around him even if it was going to hell; or maybe, he reflected, the world had gone to hell years ago and he was the last to notice. Still, the investigator wanted everything to fit, to make sense, to be rational, orderly, even fair. But it wasn't that way—no, not even close. A dead woman, young and beautiful, killed up in Sloetown. Sad enough, but in the end a police problem. In the world Baker Davis occupied at the moment, people wanted money, not justice.

The phone on his desk rang. It was Karl Orion, his voice heavy and labored. He wanted to meet. Come to Roxanne's, the man said, anytime after six, and dinner's on me. Then he hung up.

Roxanne's, a strip joint out near the Army base. Davis didn't want to go there. It was another thing he didn't understand. But it was getting late and he was hungry, though he wondered about eating a plate of food with a naked woman nearby, or dining while seated next to a guy with an erection in his pants. Then, maybe the old man had something for him: a tip, a lead, some news about Mira Ogilvy. Maybe Prince would go along. Roxanne's wasn't a good place to visit alone. Davis went up front.

"Say, what are you up to?" he asked Prince.

"Thinking about going home."

"Let's get something to eat. Out toward the Army base."

"Why out there?"

"Why does anyone want to go there?" Davis asked, smirking.

"Kinda early for that."

"I've got to meet a man down there. He's buying. There's a buffet too, and of course there's—"

"I know I know. A floor show. All right. Let's go. I know a girl there."

* * *

Lester Lewis reclined on the hood of the red Cadillac, enjoying the late-afternoon shade from the big trees overhead. It was peaceful in Jackson Park. The humidity made everything still. Even the flies moved as if they didn't care to. Then Lester heard the tinkling of aluminum cans. He sat up, eyeing the man pushing a shopping cart filled with cans toward him. He said,

"I thought I told you to beat it."

"Aw man, I doan want no trouble," Rico said.

"Go on, get out."

"Naw man, c'mon. I got something fo—"

Lester made a hard face at him. "I don't want nothin."

"Looky here, man, looky here." He came forward, pulling his cart up to the red convertible. He hitched up his loose trousers. "I got a man, a friend. He want something."

The young man threw his legs over the side of the car. "I ain't got nothing."

"Aw c'mon. All he want is somethin' to smoke."

Lester stood, regarding the homeless man and his cart and cans.

"De man is sick. He needs a little something to smoke fo' his head. I saw him las' night."

He squinted. "Smoke huh? And he's got some money?"

"Aw yeah, he got money. That's for sho'."

Lester thought about the weed hidden in the trunk of the car. He wiped a trickle of sweat from his face. "Your friend, huh?"

"Yeah."

"What's his name?"

"Hhmm."

"What's his damn name?"

"Man, I doan know! He work over at the pallet factory, an old man, a big man. White dude."

"He a cop?"

"Aw man gotdamn!" Rico threw his hands up, his face twisting in anger. "He ain't no fuggin cop!"

"All right. Shut up."

Rico grabbed his shopping cart, turning away. He cursed.

Lester said, "Where is he?"

Rico stopped. "He's over at the pallet factory. He got a silver car."

"When—?"

"Tonight man."

"To*night*?"

"Yeah, around midnight. He's gonna be at the factory, in dat silver car." Rico stared, his eyes swimming in his sweaty face, saying "And you gonna help me, right?"

"Huh?"

"You gonna help me boss. You make a deal with dat white man, you got to help me out too." He showed a dirty palm. "I need a few dollahs."

"Maybe."

"I came here lookin for you. If you get a little smoke fo' that old man, you gotta help me!" He stood there, his hand out.

"All right, all right, I'll go see the man. But I ain't got no money right now."

"Boolshit."

"Now go on, get outta here."

Rico moved away slowly with his cart, mumbling curses.

* * *

TWENTY GRAND

Davis and Prince drove out across the city toward Roxanne's in the old Buick, watching the world pass by: buildings, parks, houses, the river. Prince knew a story behind each place. There stood a hulking old hotel, once owned by his great uncle. It was now a black church with a plywood sign out front: Mt. Zion C.M.E. Temple. But high above, on the roof, another sign read Hotel Frisco in faded, ghostly lettering. In 1968, the great uncle sold the hotel to the church for a dollar. The man owned several hotels and decided he didn't need this one as much as he needed comity among the races in the city during those tough times, so he sold or gave the church a hotel where once black folks hadn't been allowed to stay. Nowadays white people never went there even though they could attend service on Sunday morning if they wanted to but they never did. Prince still called it *Uncle's hotel*.

Then they passed a new glass office building that a local plumber had developed after he won twenty million dollars in the state lottery. Though planned as an impressive twelve story tower, it only rose four stories now because the plumber lost his money gambling and divorcing his wife. The mirrored walls of the lower floors reflected the sun beautifully, but the top floors were only steel girders, rising to the sky like an unfinished dream. And the place was empty because everyone knew the owner was a plumber and nobody who could afford a lease there wanted to rent from a guy like that. It would be low class.

Next they drove by a tidy park where a large smooth rock stood behind an ornamental iron fence. On this stone the city fathers had auctioned slaves before the Civil War. Prince's great grandmother had donated it to the city. Davis wasn't prepared to learn how she came to own that rock. A melancholy historical maker stood nearby. Tour buses never stopped here.

It was growing dark. The sun fell, lights began to glow, and the city cooled. Davis let down a window for some air as they drove toward Roxanne's. The topless joints were nestled close by the Army base like suckling pigs at their mother—a dark row of run-down properties made of brick or stucco painted in black and white, or pink and purple, and illuminated under neon signs which splashed a fantastic rainbow of primary colors across the big gravel parking lot which they all shared. It was a matriarchy: *Roxanne's, Tammy's Playpen, Justine's Happy Club* and *The Kitty Box*. One place was *Janes*. There was no apostrophe in the name and not because of a bad light bulb in the sign; they didn't know they needed one. Or maybe it wasn't possessive, but simply a plural that identified the ladies working inside . . . *janes*. As Davis pulled the Buick into the gravel lot where several dozen cars were parked haphazardly, he imagined the sweat on the dancers, the lurid faces of their customers, the smoke in the club—and his stomach moved.

"'Busy for a Wednesday night,'" Prince observed. They stopped, got out and approached Roxanne's under the hazy blue and pink and yellow light from the neon signs. Massive air conditioning units jutted from the sides of the buildings, droning a soft mechanical roar, mixing with the music that pulsed through the walls. Each AC unit dripped an oily puddle of condensation onto the sidewalk, reflecting prisms of light. Davis stepped into a pool of shiny water that splashed onto Prince's leg.

"Watch it," he said.

"Why? You meeting someone in here?" Davis asked.

"Yes, your mother," he replied. Davis was glad he brought Prince. He had the right attitude for Roxanne's.

At the door, a man with no neck wearing a leather vest squatted behind a plywood counter. *Eight bucks* he grunted, not even looking up. A girl in a brown bikini stood nearby. It looked like underwear.

"'Comes with a free drink,'" she announced. Davis wondered how the drink was *free* as he handed over his money. She asked, "What can I get you?"

"'How 'bout a beer?'" he replied, brightly, trying to drum up enthusiasm.

"Rum and coke," Prince said.

"Come on," the girl said, entering a hallway that was painted black. The floor was black too. A bare bulb dangled from the ceiling. The men followed her.

The hall emptied into the big main room of the club which, in the darkness, seemed to go on forever. One couldn't see into the corners, nor up to the ceiling that was clouded by cigarette smoke. A raised platform dominated the center, reminding Davis of an altar in a Protestant church. But there was no dancing right now and the music was low. He looked around, searching for Karl Orion, but could only make out groups of young men huddled at tables attended by girls moving in and out of the shadows. One couldn't see where they came from, where they were going.

"Sit wherever you like," the waitress said. "I'll get your drinks."

Prince walked to the back, Davis following. They got a table and, in a moment, the girl reappeared in her brown bikini.

"Here you go," she said, placing drinks on the table. Her top sagged as she leaned forward, displaying a good deal of her small breasts. Davis looked her up and down. She was long and rangy, not really shapely. She wore black, high-top tennis shoes and pink socks.

"Hey, I thought this was a topless joint," Prince said as she leaned over the table. He smiled, sipping the rum.

"The shows starts in a minute," she said, glancing at the stage, "Unless, of course, you can't wait that long." She bent over and placed her hands on Prince's knees, gyrating her butt in the air while she looked Prince deeply in the face, up close. He didn't flinch. He let it happen. But he didn't bite either. He knew that kind of show would cost.

"I came to see Kendra," Prince said, after milking the attention for all he could. "She working tonight?"

The girl stood up, all business now but not pissed. "She's in the back. You want me to get her?"

"I'd like to get you both," he replied, grinning foolishly, and Davis remembered Prince's *action* back at the office. He wondered if that's what it took for the man—the talk, the words themselves as intoxicating as any dream or even the real thing. That must be what felt best, or made him feel anything at all, to send a message and see what happened. The woman flicked her head and disappeared into the darkness in her pink socks.

"Hey, the buffet," Davis said. Next to the dance stage, a few men were lining up at a steam table. Prince and Davis got up, passing a few soldiers from the Army base who sat together, talking over their drinks. They weren't in uniform; their haircuts gave them away. One man perched a woman on his lap as she ran her fingers over his buzz cut and laughed. His arm was around her waist, holding her, with a lit cigarette between his fingers. At the steam table, heat lamps illuminated eager faces leaning in from the darkness toward fried chicken, cheese sticks, slices of pizza, a pyramid of tuna sandwiches. Then an older face moved into the light, a face Baker Davis knew. "Greetings," he said.

Karl Orion looked up, recognizing the investigator with his

eyes and making a vague noise. "Ah Davis. So you came," he said. "You alone?"

"I brought a buddy along," Davis said, nodding at Prince who was leaving the buffet with a heaping plate.

"Come and sit with me for a minute," Orion said. It didn't feel like a request.

"All right." Davis dragged a few slices of pizza onto his plate and followed the big man. The music came up louder and a young woman climbed onto the stage as if she was getting into the bed of a truck. She was short and pale and voluptuous.

"I'm sure your friend will be okay," Orion said, sitting down heavily at a small table.

"Prince? Sure. He has a girlfriend here."

"That's a good girlfriend to have," Orion said.

"Is that what you're looking for here, a girlfriend?"

His eyes narrowed. "I'm not really looking for anything Mr. Davis, but I like it here. Believe it or not, I think better in this place. Distractions help me focus sometimes." Up on the stage, the dancer wobbled on spiky heels but kicked them off after a few uncertain steps. Orion leaned forward. "To tell you the truth, I have as much fun watching the men, and all their weird little games, as watching that girl up there." He picked up a sandwich, pointing it for emphasis. "But you have to know how to play it, Mr. Davis, how to see things, to get any enjoyment from it all. Take that guy over there," he continued, jerking his eyes at a young man seated before the stage, his face lifted to the dancer. "He can't see anything, nothing at all." Orion yelled across the room at the man: "Hey. Hey!" There was no response. "See? That guy's blind. Love itself could walk right by and he'd never know it. He doesn't know how to look, how to play it."

"But you know how to play it, right?"

"Sometimes I do. Sometimes I miss it, miss things." Orion drank from a glass of wine. He was the only customer in Roxanne's with wine.

Davis tried the pizza. "But still, you *are looking* for something."

"Yes, Mr. Davis, I'm looking." The dancer began to spin and lunge about the stage, smoothing her hands across her stomach and thighs, screwing her face into a parody of lust and desire. "You came to my office yesterday with that folder, those bank records. I went through them. But no: I didn't find what I was looking for."

TWENTY GRAND

"You knew about the girl and the money. You made the deposits—"

Orion's face turned dark. "But not the withdrawals. Look, I knew Mira. I knew her lifestyle. Twenty thousand a month? For what? She didn't travel. That house in the Palatine? It has no mortgage, never did. All that money . . . the girl did something with it, and I need to find it. You seem to be good at finding things. That's your line of work, right?"

Davis finished his beer. "I'm already employed on that, sir. I have clients."

"Clients, huh?" he smirked. "So helping me would be . . .what? A conflict?"

"More or less."

"I see. The private dicks' code of ethics." he remarked, sarcastically. Then Orion put down his glass as the pounding music seemed to fade in the smoky room. His eyes were heavy and blank. He spoke clearly: "That's all rather scrupulous for a man without a license."

Davis glared at him, kept a straight face. "I do what I have to."

"And do these *clients* of yours know that Baker Davis doesn't have . . . let's say... the documentation required for operating as a PI in this state?"

"They might know. What about it?"

"Well, I'm sure they wouldn't mind if you did a little work for me."

"I said I'm busy," Davis said, his hand tightening on his glass.

"How about that Lieutenant Foster, down at Police Headquarters? She's investigating the murder. Maybe she'd like to know how *busy* you've been, how scrupulous, how delicate!"

Davis flinched. "How did you—?"

The old man laughed out loud in the dark club. His eyes danced, his belly shook. "I know everything in this city, Mr. Davis: downtown, Sloetown. Don't you understand that by now?"

"Well good for you." The investigator took a minute, lit a cigarette. "But you don't know about that money."

"You're right, I don't. But you're going to help me find it Mr. Davis, or else the Lieutenant and I are going to have a little chat."

"Go to hell."

"Hell?" Orion laughed again above the music. "What do you

know about hell? What could you possibly know about that?" A big smile rolled across his face. "Look, Davis, don't be stupid. You can be tough, or you can be smart. Like I said, it's how you play it. Mira did something with that money. She stashed it somewhere, a secret account maybe, or she gave it to somebody. You find it—I'll cut you in." Orion leaned back in his chair and finished his wine, a look of satisfaction on his face. "With money like that, my friend, you won't need a license again. Ever."

The woman on the stage had removed her top. She thrust herself out over the edge of the platform as if she was fornicating in mid-air. Davis stood up and said,

"You make quite a case for a man in a strip club."

"Like I said, I think better in a place like this. Everything's clearer."

"Enjoy the show, Mr. Orion." He turned away.

"Find that money, Mr. Davis, and call me. Don't forget. And don't forget Lieutenant Foster either." The old man laughed out loud. A few patrons turned around to look at him. The naked dancer completed her act in a fake orgasm. The younger men cheered.

Davis returned to Prince, half expecting to find him with his face buried in the cleavage of a waitress, or adjourned to a back room for natural sex. But Prince was sitting, relaxing and munching pizza, talking with a woman as if they were old friends.

"Baker, this is Kendra," Prince said, almost shouting over the loud music. The woman stood up quickly in her bikini and offered a hand as if she'd gone to finishing school, not shaking it, simply putting it out there gently. Davis couldn't help wondering where that hand had been.

"You havin' fun tonight?" she asked, drawling, betraying whatever refinement was suggested earlier.

"Great time," Davis said. "Good food," he lied.

"Kendra knows all the dancers here," Prince said. Their eyes went to the stage where a big, good-looking blond now commanded the attention of the room. She pulsed naked to the music, oblivious to everything but aware of her power. She knew exactly what each move of her body meant. Her eyes focused on nothing in particular. Davis wondered if that was how she endured it. Or captured it.

"That's Irene," Kendra said to Davis. "She's one of the best girls here, makes a lot of money. Maybe you'd like to meet her?" Part of Baker Davis certainly did. Yes, I *could* do that, he thought. But no. He didn't want to go there alone. And with Irene, a man would go there alone and be alone and stay that way. He knew that's what she offered: loneliness, solitude, isolation even, turning customers into subjects, counter-parties to transactions they didn't even know they were in. That was Irene's trade, her craft; and she was an expert, light years ahead of the investigator. But maybe, if he played it right, like Karl Orion said. If he could see it all clearly enough, maybe he could find something of value there, an acceptable residue. Davis stared at Irene moving on the stage amid the smoke and light. Her eyes were half-closed, simmering, but almost asleep too, and suddenly he thought about Gloria Orion. She was blonde too, and beautiful. Maybe. If he played it right. Davis looked at Kendra.

"Maybe another time," he said.

"You look like you're ready to go," Prince said.

"I'm getting that way."

Prince smiled at Kendra. "I'm gonna stick around awhile. I'll find a way home."

"Y'all have fun then. See you later." Davis got up and walked into the darkness of the club, making his way past the tables and the men captivated by the dancer. Near the buffet, Orion sat watching the show from his table. He looked entirely at peace. The music continued. The smoke had grown thicker. Davis inhaled deeply, wanting to feel all of it, remember all of it. On the stage, Irene was bent over, almost touching the floor with her face. He exited into the black hallway, moving toward the front door where the big man stood guard.

"You leavin man? Things are just gettin' warmed up."

"That's right," Davis replied.

"You coming back?"

He didn't answer. It felt good to be outside, even with the heat of the night and the sickly glow from the neon signs and the drone of the air conditioners. Davis crossed the parking lot in the humid darkness, then got into his car. The throbbing music faded. He drove away. He lit a cigarette and reached for the radio.

No, no music now.

* * *

It was almost midnight when Karl Orion left the club. The show never really ended at Roxanne's, not so long as customers, and their money, remained. But Orion had to meet someone. He said good-bye to the girls, tipping them generously. Outside, he felt better, but as he crossed the parking lot, pain surged in his arms and legs. The wine he drank earlier didn't mix well with his cancer drugs. He grew faint and looked up at the stars. Blurry. Finally, he reached his car, waited a minute for the pain to pass, then drove out toward Sloetown in the darkness.

The night became cooler and quieter among the trees in the old neighborhood. He rolled down his window to get some fresh air, and as he did, he heard sounds he couldn't recognize—a man shouting, a woman screaming, the sound of a car? Something. He thought about turning around, forgetting about the whole thing. It was a crazy idea. He was okay, and Sloetown was dangerous at this hour. At an intersection, he stopped and reached down to make sure his revolver was still beneath the seat. As he bent over, the pain stabbed at him again and he winced. But he felt the steel of the gun too.

Soon he came to Orion Pallet, driving across the empty parking lot before the big factory. He stopped and looked around. The moon and stars were bright, but the place was deserted. *Damn, Rico was lying, and surely drunk. He doesn't know a man. Nobody's coming. This isn't going to work. It's crazy.*

Then Orion noticed movement at the far edge of the building, a dim figure moving along the fence in the distance. His breath stopped. Maybe this is how it happened to Mira, he thought. Maybe this is how she died. Again he reached under the seat for the gun, again felt the pain. He sat back and sighed. Just breathe, the doctors told him, just relax and breathe when you feel the pain.

The movement along the fence grew clearer. A man. Then he stopped, and a face looked up, noticing Orion. Both men waited. Neither moved. They were motionless at either end of the parking lot.

What the hell, Orion thought, Rico said the man would come tonight, a little after midnight. Who else would be here at this hour? Orion stared at the man in the distance. What the hell? He needed help. He eased his car forward, but the man didn't move. He came closer. The man shifted a little as he approached, but held his ground. Orion saw the man was young, tall and slim, a teenager maybe. He cut the headlights. The man didn't move. Orion pulled up beside him.

"Hey," he said.

The man didn't answer. Orion didn't know what to say. "Hey," he repeated.

"What's up?" the man said. He was young, barely out of high school maybe.

"You know Rico?" Orion asked.

"I don't know no Rico."

Orion realized it was a dumb question. He wasn't here to make conversation.

"Well, I heard you could help me out."

The youth nodded and looked Orion in the eye. Orion regarded him: the kid wasn't afraid, and he didn't seem dangerous. The young man reached into his pocket and withdrew a small, clear, plastic bag. Inside were two fat cigarettes. Orion reached out of the window of his car and took them. He held the little bag up to see it.

"These are gonna work, huh?"

The young man smiled. "Yeah, they work."

Orion examined the cigarettes. They were hand rolled. He didn't know what he was looking for, exactly.

"And they're okay, right? They won't hurt none?"

"Hurt? Naw. They fix you right up, Pop."

"Huh. All right. How much?"

"There's two in there. Ten bucks."

"What the hell." Orion reached for his wallet, feeling pain again in his arm. He gave the young man a ten. The youth stuffed the bill in his pocket and backed off.

Orion eyed him. "Smoke 'em like a cigarette, huh?"

The young man smiled again. "Yeah. That's right. Just hold it a little longer."

"And what's your name?"

"It ain't important, Pop."

He turned away. Orion watched him go. The youth walked back into the shadows under the trees. Then he was gone. Orion sat in his car and looked at the cigarettes. Weed. What the hell? The damn cancer drugs had vicious side effects and made him feel like crap; then the docs gave him more drugs to counteract the first ones and he felt sicker than ever. Ten bucks. Not bad, especially compared to the hospital dope that cost a fortune, cost him whatever money he had left in life. He looked out the window at the dark brick factory. He couldn't remember the last time he'd been here at his company, this late.

Orion withdrew one of cigarettes from the little bag and smelled it, a strange, sweet fragrance. He reached into his glove box for a lighter. Then he stopped, and looked around. The parking lot was deserted. No cops. No one at all. He lit the cigarette. It was poorly rolled and ash dribbled onto his pants and he brushed it off. He took a few puffs. It didn't taste bad. He drew deeply and held the smoke before exhaling, like the kid said. Then he rolled all his windows down. He didn't want to stink up the car. Gloria might recognize the smell, and he didn't want her worrying. He took another deep drag and held it. Then another. He started coughing. The smoke was hot and harsh, and he stubbed the cigarette out. He wondered if he should smoke the whole thing. Maybe, if this didn't work, he'd smoke the rest of it. And there was another in the bag.

Orion rested for a minute. He wondered when the dope would start working, and what it would feel like when it did. He waited another minute. He looked at his watch; it was very late. He sighed. *What the hell? I'll go home and see what happens.*

He put the car in drive and crossed the parking lot. He looked up at the bright stars and the silvery moon and it occurred to Karl Orion they had never looked quite so beautiful before.

SEVEN

Morning came again and Baker Davis didn't like it. He wanted to quit, sell his agency to whoever would take it and call it a day. It was too bad about that young woman, dead in a vacant lot in Sloetown, but that was police business, or God's business, or whoever loved her. Maybe Karl Orion loved her and gave her $20,000 every month. That's a lot of love, Davis reflected.

Now the old man wanted the money back, and so did Gloria Orion. They claimed it was theirs, and promised him a big cut if he found it. That would be nice. He could sure use it. He wasn't quite ready to sell his car, pawn his furniture and take a rented room somewhere, but maybe that was his future. Now this week the rent was due on his office at McDermott Center and he couldn't pay. He examined the contents of his thin wallet, a couple of tens and a five. He sighed. There wasn't much demand for his services these days. Nobody trusted a detective without a license.

He prepared for work: made coffee, ironed a shirt. At least he could show up. It was his only chance.

Then he remembered the other angle. If he *didn't* find the dead girl's money—Karl Orion would go to the cops. Gloria Orion might play that card too. The Lieutenant had told him to take a vacation, stay out of her business. If she thought he was meddling again, she'd be pissed and he'd never get that license back. It was a tight spot, Davis considered, a bitter mix. But then, he'd helped the police before. Without Baker Davis, that heroin trade in Sloetown would still be going strong. Maybe he could help the cops again.

Maybe it was time for an encore. Yes, he would find the man who killed the girl! Then Lt. Foster would be happy. And surely then, the money would turn up. If everything worked out, he would be tight with the Department and get a fat check from the Orions. He imagined a cabin in the mountains where he could spend endless sunny days wandering through alpine valleys under deep blue skies with clear upcountry air filling his lungs with the scent of pine and sage and juniper. And then afternoons soaking in a hot tub, writing haiku, going to bed early and listening to rain fall in the night. Every day would be like the one before and he could live forever.

If he could find the killer.

The police were doing their part, pushing hard, interrogating his client Gloria Orion, maybe her brother. They might get to Karl Orion if they discovered those fat deposits he'd been making to the victim's account all those years. And the state had resumed executions recently, so a needle might be waiting for the killer. Eventually, somebody would start to sweat. Whoever pulled the trigger would begin to hide, cover his tracks, create a diversion, run, get nervous, drink, drug, prevaricate, or maybe even strike again. It always worked like that. Davis knew murder was never an act which ended when the victim fell but was only a beginning. Killing was the simple part. Only afterwards do fear and desperation and hatred and cunning begin to manifest. Only then does sickness take up residence in the soul of the man who watched the young woman die, a sickness curled up and lying there reptilian and observant, almost inert, but over time craving attention, wanting a cure, a palliative, an excuse, a pardon, or even a prison sentence to lance the memory—anything to end it, even another murder to replace it. Baker Davis wanted it to go away too, the memory of that young woman's corpse in the tall grass in the vacant lot with no one to hear her final words, a scream without a sound.

He finished his coffee, dressed, and drove downtown in the bright, warm morning. When he arrived at the office, the temperature had climbed to ninety-two. A stiff breeze hit him when he stepped from the car, like exhaust from a blast furnace, a tough wind blowing from the West, rushing across the plains from far away, bringing something with it he didn't understand. It felt like dread. He leaned into it, trying to reach his office but something, someone blocked his way. It was Rico, wearing a white

T-shirt of an unmentionable color, his skin glowing like waxed mahogany, a string of Mardi Gras beads around his neck. He was chewing something, so that his gray whiskers rolled across his cheek like a fist moving beneath a blanket.

"Hmm . . . Bawssman," he mumbled loudly. "Hmm—" His jaw went up and down.

"'Ain't got no money today," Davis said, trying to get inside the office.

"Oh Bawssman. Ken I get a little?" He held out his hand. He was upbeat, happy.

"'Ain't got no money, Rico. I'm broke."

"Jus' a little. A dollah!"

"No money, man."

"Ken I getta little wurk then, Bawss? Jus' a little wurk." His voice modulated smoothly between insistent and pitiful. In the past, Davis had given him odd chores in the office for a few bucks; but it was often more trouble than it was worth, since Rico was frequently intoxicated and one had to stand over him explaining how to do the least little thing. "Lemme pick up 'round heah," he clamored, gesturing at the litter the wind had blown into the parking lot.

"You drunk Rico?"

"Naw, Bawss. No beeahr. No likker! Lemme pick up jus' a little bit."

"All right, come on in the office and get up all the trash."

He followed Davis into McDermott Center, mumbling *Hhmm hhmm* his jaw working up and down with the gray whiskers. Inside the suite, Davis pointed at the wastebaskets and said "Get all these, and take 'em on out to the dumpster."

"Ah get 'em up ah get 'em," Rico said, bustling around. Davis left him and went into the kitchen to make coffee. Prince hadn't arrived yet and it was quiet. In his office, he noticed the light on the answering machine, indicating messages. They'd have to wait for the coffee.

Rico came in. "Where's dat trash, bawss?"

Davis nodded at the wastebasket beside his desk. Rico shuffled forward. He reached for the basket, then stopped, his arm frozen.

"Hhmm."

"Just take 'em on outside Rico."

"Hhmm."

"Rico."

"That girl, bawss—" His eyes were vacant and still, seized by the photograph on the desk. He reached for it.

"Don't throw that out. I want to keep it."

The homeless man stared at the image of the young woman in her black dress and pearls. "She ain't coming back."

"No, she's not."

"She gone. Hhmm."

Davis looked at him. "Gone? How you know?"

"I jus knows. I seen her befoh, up in Sloetown."

"Sloetown? Man, what you doin' up there?"

"I tol' you . . . I go up there and do me a little woik sometimes, pickin up cans and bottles and stuff. I got me a shoppin cart. Hmm. An' de woman here in dis picture, she been up dere too. In the night. But she gone now. Hmm."

"You're drunk, Rico. What's a woman like that doing in Sloetown?"

"Naw, Bawss. I ain't drunk, naw. No beeahr!"

"All right. Settle down." Davis knew he was lying. He smelled like alcohol.

"I doan know why she come up dere Bawss, but I saw dat white lady, plenty of times. She had a white car 'n she came 'round 'bout every month or so, regular. She know'd somebody in Sloetown."

"Who?"

"Doan know, Bawss. 'Ain't nuthin' but niggas up in de Sloetown, but she come plenty of times. I know dat." He hung his head and stopped chewing. He stared into an empty place. "She gone now. Hmm."

"What happened to her?"

"Hmm." he mumbled, and reached for the wastebasket, chewing again, making the gray whiskers roll around on his face.

"Rico."

He turned away. "Ah take everything out to de dumpster, Bawss." He shuffled from the office as he had entered, though he seemed slower now, heavier.

Davis went to the kitchen and poured a coffee. *Plenty of times*, he thought. A young woman like Mira Ogilvy, with background, education, the daughter of a prominent physician . . . up in

Sloetown. Repeated visits? It didn't fit, didn't make sense. Everyone knew Sloetown to be the place where one could find a little weed, a little coke, or *a little sumthin'*, as Rico might say. Most of the young and privileged from the respectable side of the city had visited Sloetown at least once, but these were teenage escapades, college pranks, bored kids seeing how far they could go. After one visit, they never returned. They were done. But not Mira Ogilvy. She had been there *plenty o' times*.

Davis returned to his office and clicked the answering machine. The first message was from a credit card company, the voice filled with urgent concern, inquiring about that month's payment, which they had not received. He deleted it. The next message was from Gloria Orion. Halting and unsure, she thanked him for listening last night, and for "putting up with her" at so late an hour. It quavered at the end with a coy vulnerability that pulled at him hard. He wanted to call her right that moment. Then he remembered the beautiful woman reclining on his sofa, her bare legs crossed, and the game she was playing. He wanted to play the game too, but couldn't imagine how it might end, or if he could extricate himself from it if he wanted to. He didn't blame Gloria Orion, didn't judge her. He knew desperate straits led to desperate acts. He deleted her message.

The final recording scratched to life: "Mister Davis? This is Lieutenant Doreen Foster with the Police Department. I'd like to meet and talk with you as soon as possible. 'Just a few questions. Please call me at four five eight six thousand."

Davis winced. She didn't sound happy. Wilson probably told her he'd been at Mira's house. Or maybe Karl Orion got impatient, called the police. Maybe Gloria reported something about his *activities*, just to show she cared. The Lieutenant wasn't a good woman to cross. She had a homicide case to crack, a job to do. Davis knew if he got in the way, the Lieutenant would make a phone call and it would be a cold day in hell before he ever got his license reinstated. He picked up the phone to call her—then thought it best to go in person.

Davis saved her message then went back to the front. Rico was finishing up. Davis handed him two dollars. "Here. Now get this trash outside. I gotta go."

"Two?!" Rico cried.

"Yeah, two."

"Three."
"Two."
"Three, Bawss. Three."
"That's all I got. Two."
"Three Bawss. I need to get me a little sumthin'." His cheeks rolled around. "C'mon now." It was a little game Davis knew all too well, so he always held a little something back. Then he considered the man *had* worked hard that day, so he handed over another dollar.

"And don't forget that garbage in the kitchen."

"Ah get it Bawss. Ah get it. Doan worry none." He left, carrying the trash away.

Davis went back for his keys. He didn't want to go and see the Lieutenant, but he remembered Karl Orion sitting in Roxanne's and saying *it's all in how you play it*. He hoped he could play it right now. He grabbed the keys, locked the office and left.

Outside, Rico rested in the shade beside the dumpster where he'd thrown the trash. A brown paper bag was beside him on the ground. He drank from it and glared at Davis.

"Hey Bawssman!" he hollered across the parking lot. "Dat girl ain't comin back. She gone!" he yelled with a note of mockery, as if he were laughing at all the efforts of the police and Gloria Orion and Karl Orion and Baker Davis too. But the voice also held a note of despair, something vague and lost, even fearful. "She ain't comin' back Bawss. Never!" Rico cried, reaching for the brown bag. He knew something, but Lt. Foster waited.

Davis jumped into his Buick and left.

* * *

Cheryl Lewis sat at her breakfast table late that morning. She picked at the eggs on her plate and knew it was over. Her tea was cold and Mira was dead. She'd heard the rumors, then seen the girl's picture in the newspaper. She wouldn't come again like she had every month for the past seven years.

Now Cheryl would have to tell the others. It wasn't going to be easy even though Mira said it was ending someday. They'd have to make do. That part was okay. They could make do in Sloetown. They always had. The money helped but it always felt like a gift, something extra. They never relied on it because they didn't trust it even while they accepted it and appreciated it. But money was good to have, helped to soothe the memories and the pain.

She rose from the table, her food unfinished, and prepared to go to work. She was taking the afternoon shift. As she dressed, she remembered Mira waiting in the white BMW in front of her house that night when the baby was crying. That wasn't a good place, a good time to wait—in Sloetown on a Saturday night. Someone killed the young woman. It felt hard, as if such an act was inevitable there in the old neighborhood, and she and her neighbors couldn't get away from it no matter how hard they tried.

Mira's death troubled her but she wouldn't tell Richard McDermott. He wasn't part of that, wouldn't understand it. She was sure he had never experienced anything like that from the twentieth floor of that building he owned downtown. Richard was different, far away, almost like a dream she didn't want to wake from. And he kissed her. She remembered his strong hands, the taste of his lips.

But she had to tell the neighbors. On Sunday she would see them in church.

* * *

Baker Davis drove out toward Police Headquarters. The city had been warming all day, the buildings and the land absorbing heat like a sponge that could never be saturated. And he wondered if the people here in these parts were the same: absorbing and soaking up life and death like a sponge that could never get enough, filled to overflowing, as they waited for something or somebody to release the heat, the life, the suffering, even the joy. Maybe there was no release, only renunciation, or forgetting. Maybe some didn't care, or couldn't. But no one escaped. Not Karl Orion nor his wife nor Richard McDermott. They all dwelled here. Their lives were all mortgaged. Even the Ogilvys, except they were dead.

The mercury climbed to about ninety-five under the pitiless sun. Today would be like other days, Davis thought, the heat conjuring up a storm in the afternoon, filling the sky with dark clouds, electricity, and wind . . . but no rain. His gut rumbled as he approached downtown and the marble and granite edifices of government. The courthouse and the county archives loomed ahead, strong, imposing structures, evoking awe and expressing authority. The investigator felt small near to them, especially the jail, a brown brick tower the size of a stadium with slits for windows and tiny doors where an unending stream of people in various states of guilt poured forth as if from a giant hive. They were mostly men, who were mostly black, entering grimly in a measured pace with sullen faces, their heads low. And then a crowd of similar men, even the same men, walking lightly almost running as they left the building, free. As they got away from the enormous jail, they ran out into the street like wild cats, ignoring the crosswalks, and traffic be damned. A few women milled about, busy and filled with worry, and then the occasional lawyer, usually a man, usually white, whose chalky face and hard suit stood out among the teeming mass as if he were a piece of Styrofoam bobbing along on the dark river of people flowing by.

Nearby, Police HQ occupied a building clad in smoky glass that worked hard to look modern, efficient. Davis parked on the street and made his way through the sweaty afternoon mob and got inside, passing through a set of revolving doors and a metal detector before reaching the elevators that carried him swiftly to the third floor where Lt. Foster and her crew managed homicide investigations. A few perfunctory *Hellos* greeted Davis as he came off the elevator. Several officers knew him, but no one smiled. 'Not going to be my day, he thought.

"Lieutenant Foster around?" he asked a cop at a gray metal desk. The man looked up, refused to answer. "I'm Davis. She's expecting me." The officer got up and disappeared into a hallway. Davis looked around—everything was hard, built to last, easy to clean, and cheap. He wondered if the people here were like that too. One officer questioned a dirty man who slumped in a chair. A woman cop sorted through a file cabinet. Another man held a phone to his ear, taking notes. One read the sports section of the daily paper. There was no visible process to discern, nothing which pointed toward a concrete goal. Davis imagined that if there were no crime, no felonies to investigate, they would have nothing to do. They would sit here and wait, forever. But people kept killing each other, and business was usually good in the summer.

The Lieutenant appeared.

"Mr. Davis," she said flatly. "Back here." She led him down the hall to her office. "Let me put this away," she said, gathering papers and shoving them into a file cabinet. Davis took the chair opposite her desk. He guessed the Lieutenant wasn't quite fifty, but she was close. She was big around the waist, maybe from having a few children, and was likely a wife, a mother, a person around whom other worlds revolved. It was a curious role, investigating homicides, for a woman like that; but then he thought, *how suitable*. A mother is a natural judge and jury, a legislature, a court, and executive all rolled into one and maybe better set up than any man could ever be to know what's right and fitting and just.

"How have things been going, Mr. Davis?" she asked, settling behind her desk.

"Nice and quiet, just how I like it."

She narrowed her eyes. "Quiet, huh?"

"Yes, I had a nice vacation, but it's good to be home."

"And you're taking it easy these days?"

"Yep. The rat race—who needs it? I'm thinking of going into business with my brother. He has a ranch out West. Do you know anything about investing in farmland?"

"A ranch, huh? Farming? That's nice." She folded her hands before her, looking at Davis with large, sad eyes. "So we don't need to discuss your work here in town, do we?"

"Like I said, I'm taking it easy."

"Good. Then we don't need to talk about Mira Ogilvy, right?"

"I don't think so. But we can talk about anything you like, Lieutenant."

She frowned. "Good. I suppose you had a good reason for being up in Sloetown on Sunday."

"I enjoy a quiet drive in the old neighborhood," Davis replied truthfully. "It's restful up there, at least on Sundays."

"Or in the Palatine, on Lafayette Place?"

Davis gripped the arms of his chair. He had no explanation for his visit to Mira's house, none that he wanted to share. He kept silent, hoping the Lieutenant wouldn't see his jaw getting tight.

"Mr. Davis look, I don't really care what you were doing in Sloetown, nor at the dead girl's home, unless you're a burglar. Believe me, we've got better things to do than check up on you. You're no killer. But we are interested in some of . . . your friends."

"I don't have many friends, Lieutenant."

"Gloria Orion?"

"I know Mrs. Orion. She's not a friend."

The Lieutenant smiled without mirth. "Mr. Davis, please let me remind you of what I'm sure you already know: this is a serious investigation. Someone's been killed. We are going to arrest someone for it. The closer you are to all this—"

"I'm trying to stay out of the way, Lieutenant."

"Well try hard. This case is difficult enough as it is. We don't need any complications." The Lieutenant stood and came to Davis's chair, looking down, lowering her eyes. She folded her arms. "It's a murder, Mr. Davis. You know what that means. We suspect everyone. Anyone. I've got my hands full, so I don't need any *help*."

"Gotcha."

She returned to her chair, her big eyes on him. She drew something on a pad aimlessly and said, "But can you tell me anything about Richard McDermott?"

"I thought you didn't need any help."

"I don't. I'm asking a question and I'd appreciate a straight answer. He's been up in Sloetown. A strange place to be, for a guy like that."

"McDermott's my landlord. That's all. Is he a suspect?"

"Like I said, we look at everyone."

"You think a guy like McDermott, a man in his position, could do something like that? Kill a girl in Sloetown?"

"What do you think, Mr. Davis? You've been in this business a while." Then she leaned forward, her voice dropping, almost to a whisper. "Look, I know you're taking it easy these days, and that's exactly what you should be doing. But we don't have much on this Ogilvy situation right now. If you know anything—"

"Sorry. McDermott's my landlord. That's all."

She rose and came from behind the desk again, approaching him. "Farming, huh? Out West? You know, Baker, you don't look like much of a cowboy. I'm thinking one of these days you'd rather get back to your detective work, get your PI license reinstated."

"I've considered it."

"Well consider that I might be able to help you with that, when the time comes."

"I will."

"So. Mira Ogilvy. Anything else?"

Davis considered it. The Lieutenant had been okay with him over the years. She had a job to do, and she was good at it. He remembered the pale, thick, bloody corpse in the vacant lot on Vinson Street and the smell. Whoever shot Mira and left her in the weeds ought to be hanged. If McDermott had any connection to it, so what? The man could rot in jail. He didn't care. But Davis also knew he was tied up with Karl Orion and Gloria more than he wanted to explain to the police right now. He rubbed his forehead. No, he wasn't going to be a farmer or a rancher anytime soon. He wasn't a cowboy. He squirmed in his chair. There was a question before him. Answer it, he thought, and move on.

"Mira Ogilvy had money."

"I guessed that."

"No Lieutenant. She had a lot of money. Cash probably. It may have something to do with her death."

She scribbled on the pad. "Go on."

"That's about all I know."

"Where did she get it?"

"I don't know. But she didn't work."

"All right. And what was Miss Ogilvy doing with all this money?"

"Don't know that either, but there might be a motive there for you."

"Frankly, it doesn't look like a robbery so far. What else?"

He hesitated. "Well, Sloetown."

"Yep. That's where we found her. You were there Sunday."

"No, not only then Lieutenant. Mira Ogilvy had been there before, in the old neighborhood."

"In Sloetown?"

"That's what I hear. The girl had been up there before, more than once."

The Lieutenant jotted a note. "Doing what, I wonder."

"It's just what I hear, a little noise from the street, all second hand."

"Well, that's something. We'll check it out. Thanks. How about Richard McDermott? You hear any *noise* on him?"

"No, nothing. Are you looking at him?"

"We've questioned him. That's all I can say. You know the rules, Mr. Davis, but there could be an arrest. Soon."

"Yes. I hear you." Davis rose to leave. "If there's anything else I can do—"

"No, don't do anything, Mr. Davis. Stay out of it. Let me

handle this. Just keep your ears open."

"I always do, Lieutenant." He stood to go.

"Like I said, the fewer complications—"

"—the better." he said, finishing her sentence. Davis exited Lt. Foster's stark office, walking out into the main room where the activity had picked up. He recalled the words from Mira Ogilvy's last letter: the police, *heavy-handed and inconsiderate*. He turned it over in his head. But that's what the police do, that's who they are. He nodded to a few of the uniformed cops behind the steel desks; then he was on the elevator, feeling the descent and glad to be out of there even if part of him wanted to stay with the Lieutenant. She was solid and real, at the center of things, not out on the periphery, the outside, like he was. Maybe it was the imprimatur of sovereign government, but she made sense. Baker Davis admired her for it, and part of him also wanted to be earnest and busy and important, but he knew he could never do it, not like the Lieutenant. He was free to roam about town, lighting where he would, moving along the edges, searching and usually, looking in. It suited him, though he was afraid to think about where it would lead, where he'd end up. Maybe in Sloetown, maybe with Gloria Orion, maybe back in the office watching the days unfold and slip away as he talked it all over with Prince. Or perhaps he'd simply keep moving forever to the end . . . like maybe everyone does, he guessed.

* * *

Day was ending when Davis left Police HQ. The minor chord hues of evening—deep reds, violets and grays—colored the city as he skipped down the steps to the sidewalk and crossed the street. People walking by looked tired. They'd been tangled up all day in the jail or the courthouse or the archives and now they were going home. He'd been there too, an oppressive, serious world of sharp but hollow edges where blunt force reigned.

A block away a man came into view, approaching the Headquarters building, going against the tide of weary pedestrians. He walked with purpose, as if he was moving toward something. He came closer. Then Davis recognized him.

"Mr. McDermott," he said.

"What? Davis. What are you doing here?"

"A little business. Over there." He nodded at the police

building.

McDermott frowned. "Shouldn't you be out looking for something?"

"I'm okay. I'm taking a break."

"A break? That's not going to turn up anything about Mira Ogilvy's money."

"Ah, I see. So you and Gloria . . . Mrs. Orion . . . you're both in this."

"Don't worry about that."

Davis kept quiet, lit a cigarette. McDermott's face got hard. He said, "Mrs. Orion paid you, right? That money isn't for standing around."

"I know what it's for. Look, Miss Ogilvy's death is a murder investigation. The cops are all over it. A man has to be careful."

"A man without a license should be careful."

"Don't crowd me, sir. I'm not in the mood."

"So how about some progress?"

"Look. Somebody killed that girl, in case you forgot."

"Yes, tragic," McDermott said acidly.

"And whoever killed her might have something to do with that money your sister, Mrs. Orion, is looking for."

"I could've figured that out myself."

"Then why didn't you?" Davis paused, letting it sink in as he drew on his cigarette. The men eyed each other. "You know any reason why Mira Ogilvy might've been visiting Sloetown?"

"Sloetown? Why the hell would anyone want to go there?" And as he said it, the lawyer remembered Cheryl, and meeting her there, and her warm lips. And he remembered the annoying red-haired cop in his office, asking about his car on Vinson Street.

"I don't know why," Davis said, "but the girl went there sometimes, before she got killed."

"Where'd you hear that?"

"I know people. I find things out. That's what your sister is paying me to do."

The lawyer smirked. "I almost forgot."

"Mira Ogilvy may have simply got lost one night and made a wrong turn in a bad neighborhood, but if she was visiting Sloetown for some reason—maybe it's connected to her death. And that reason might involve money. Money and murder . . . they're old friends you know."

McDermott's eyes turned bitter and black. "That's nice, Davis. Look, just find out what Mira did with that money, what happened to it. I really don't care *why*, and I don't care how you do it. Just get it done." Then he turned away, resuming his march down the sidewalk. Davis watched him leave as he finished the cigarette. It was good to be rid of him. But as McDermott came to the end of the block, he stopped at the intersection and looked around, searching. He plunged his hands in his pockets, withdrew them. He wiped his face, looking around again. What was he doing, Davis wondered. Suddenly, McDermott crossed the street—then bounded up the steps of the County Archives, almost as if he were running away. He disappeared into the building through the big glass doors.

The man is up to something, Davis thought, and it might pay to find out. The investigator took a walk around the block as night fell. He stopped and bought a newspaper from a machine, then paused to chat with an elderly cop reading meters. Soon he was back at the Archives, but McDermott was nowhere in sight. He circled the block again, strolling past the big Courthouse, enjoying its huge Ionic columns in the twilight, taking in the obligatory statue of Justice, her eyes covered with a limestone blindfold. 'Might be better that way, he thought—she didn't have to see what was happening.

As Davis came around the corner, he saw the Archives in the distance. He stayed back. Soon McDermott emerged from the building, walking down the long steps. He paused on the sidewalk, looked up and down the street, then left with the same purposeful movement as before, as if he had accomplished something. Davis waited a minute for him to disappear. Then he moved toward the Archives.

Inside the glass doors, the smell hit him first, the fragrance of time and decay emanating from papers and documents and books and maps and photographs going back two hundred years. Davis liked it and inhaled deeply. An older woman staffed the desk. She wore a lot of hairspray.

"Hi, how are you?" he said warmly.

She peered at him over her glasses. "We're about to close, sir."

"Uh, right, sure. But I'm looking for someone. I'm supposed to meet him here." Davis looked around the big room, the rows of shelves and tables.

The woman frowned. "This is an archives, sir. For research. All we have is books."

"Of course. But have you seen a man in a suit jacket, no tie, dark hair?"

She rose from her desk with grudging efficiency. Her hair didn't move. "A nervous-looking fellow? He went to look for something. He may still be here." She led Davis into a hallway lined with books that reached to the ceiling. They came to a little alcove that hosted a table where one of the chairs had been pulled away. A large book sat in the middle of the table.

"Well, he was here a minute ago," the woman said. "I don't know where he went. Maybe he left. I didn't see him."

"That's fine. Thank you very much," Davis replied. "Maybe I'll look around a little bit." The woman frowned again. "I'll only be a minute."

She left. Davis approached the book on the table, noticing the title, a bound volume of the local newspaper from 1984. He picked it up and set it gently on its spine, removing his hands and letting the book fall open slowly as the yellowed pages fanned apart. It didn't work, revealing only a sports section, baseball scores, ads. He tried again, more gently. This time the book fell open to a news article and a photograph of a building in flames. It was the Orion Pallet factory.

Davis looked around. He was alone. The archives were quiet as death; only the smell of the aging books was alive. He looked at the picture again. Flames leaping from the old building illuminated the scene, throwing light on the fire trucks and emergency vehicles in the parking lot. Smoke framed the entire image. The news story indicated several employees and firefighters were injured, but the building was saved. Then the final sentence: *a few men remained missing.*

Davis looked around again, anxiously, as if somebody was watching. No one. He examined the photograph again, a terrifying picture of people running amok in horror and pain. But in the smoky chaos, he discerned an ambulance, its doors flung open to receive the injured. On the side of the ambulance it read *Mercy Hospital.*

Davis whetted his index finger and drew a line of saliva along the inside edge of the open book. Then he gently tore the page away and tucked it in his pocket. He returned the volume to the shelf where McDermott had found it and went back up front through the musty stacks.

"I guess my friend isn't going to show," he said to the woman at the front desk.

"I hope you found what you're looking for," she said, tightly.

"Yes ma'am. Well, I'm not sure exactly." He exited the glass doors and found himself outside in the darkness. He gazed out across the big civic center plaza before him; the Police HQ and the courthouse stood in the distance. No, Baker Davis wasn't sure. He didn't know what he was looking for any more, but a week ago he found a corpse in Sloetown. Then he took a call from a pretty woman, from Gloria Orion, and accepted her money. Now her brother, his landlord, was piling on and Davis owed him rent for that month. Finally, an old man in a strip club wanted to nail him to the wall with the police.

It was getting hard. He was comfortable in his office downtown. He could sit right there with the Gray Prince and watch the world go by. But this terrible fire in eighty-four. The ambulance took the injured men, Karl Orion's men, to Mercy Hospital. Some of them got well, some got paid, some went missing. Davis remembered that Lewis kid in Sloetown, and his brother who never came home. He remembered the dead girl in the weed-choked lot. The world felt disrupted, uncertain, even broken, and it was hard to deal with, hard to watch. He didn't want to look, didn't want to know—like the blindfolded Justice. He wondered about a way out.

The sun was gone. The streets were empty. He descended the steps of the Archives building and walked past the spot where he met McDermott earlier. The night felt darker here. Then he found his car and drove away.

* * *

Richard McDermott considered the newspaper image he'd discovered in the Archives as he drove through town that evening: the big fire, the burning factory. It looked like a total loss, but he remembered Karl Orion got back in business again quickly, making pallets. Maybe the old guy had good insurance. Maybe that's where the money trail started, for soon thereafter he started giving Mira Ogilvy twenty grand a month. And Davis said the girl had been visiting Sloetown. Well, what the hell, McDermott thought. I go there too.

The lawyer stared ahead as his headlights pierced the night on the highway. He thought about Cheryl. He would go see her. When she was with him, all his troubles faded. What if he did lose McDermott Center? It was his father's building, truth be known, not his. The law practice might go, even his home. The police had seen him up in Sloetown, but so what? What the hell was a cop doing there anyway, in the middle of the night?

But Mira Ogilvy was still dead. Finding the money seemed remote as ever. Paying his bankers felt delusional. Maybe there was a way out, a place he could go where the cops and the bankers couldn't find him: South America, Europe, or a quiet spot in the Caribbean—a place where no one knew Richard McDermott. Could he make a life in a foreign land, a strange, sun-washed place? Perhaps he'd take a new name. Could he ever return to the United States? Maybe Cheryl could go with him. Yes, Cheryl would have to go.

It was late when he reached Sloetown. The lights along Kenner Boulevard subsided as he approached the big trees of the old neighborhood; and as he turned, he plunged into darkness. But he wasn't afraid. In fact, he felt better suddenly, and wondered why when there was a good chance Richard McDermott was the only white man around. Well great, he thought. He'd been among white people his entire life, and it hadn't done him any good. The lawyer loosened his tie, threw it in the backseat and rolled the windows down. The air was cooler here. The fragrance of magnolia and honeysuckle, old and tired but still rich, came in with the breeze. He inhaled deeply and relaxed. For a while, he would forget.

Cheryl Lewis was glad to be at home Thursday night. The restaurant had been busy that day and she was tired, but there was a movie on TV. Her cousin Sheila the next block over had taken the baby for the evening. Cousin was sixteen and liked kids and was glad to have a few dollars for babysitting. Now Cheryl could relax on the sofa and watch a good show, but she kept looking outside for her brother Lester. The boy raced out the door when she got home that afternoon and she hadn't seen him since. She had made a pot of spaghetti. The leftovers waited on the stove for him. She began to wonder if she ought to put the food in the refrigerator.

The movie was boring. She got up to look outside. Lester would come home late again. Maybe I should impose a curfew on him or something, she considered, but knew that Lester was getting a little too big for that. Still, there was nothing good for young men late at night in Sloetown. She peered out the window through the trees in her yard to the street in the distance. A lone streetlamp illuminated the sidewalk there. That's where Mira Ogilvy had waited. That's where her white BMW was parked the last time Cheryl saw her. It may have been the girl's last night alive, she reckoned, and she hoped, wherever Mira was now, God was with her.

A long black car appeared under the streetlamp. Her heart jumped and she felt something in her knees. It was him. The car stopped and sat there, as if the driver didn't know what to do, whether to stop and get out, blow the horn, or drive away. But he was here. Now.

She walked quickly into the bathroom and looked at herself in the mirror, took a pinch of toothpaste and cleaned her mouth. Her spaghetti had a lot of garlic. She went back to the front door, almost running. He was still there! She opened the door, her breath pounding. The heat remained from the day, and as she got outside on the porch, Cheryl Lewis felt as if she was jumping into a warm bath, like swimming. She approached the Lincoln. The electric window came down.

"Hey," she said softly, leaning in at the door.

"How you doin?" McDermott asked, almost laughing, but nervous and relieved too.

"What are you doing out here, driving around?"

"Oh, I don't know. I left work. I didn't want to go home. I came here."

"You know it's late Richard."

He didn't remember her saying his name like that, but hearing it now, in the humid August night on the empty street in Sloetown felt like someone pouring warm syrup.

He shrugged and drew on a cigarette. "Late. Yes. You tired?"

She shook her head as light from the streetlamp danced in her eyes.

"Well, don't just stand there. Get in."

Cheryl looked back toward the house. Lester would come home sometime. The boy was beyond her control now, and food was on the stove. She opened the car door and got in. McDermott drove away, the breeze coming in again.

"Just thought I'd come by," he said after a while.

"Uh-huh," she said, as if he didn't need to explain. McDermott let the car wander along the old, worn streets, past the school, past Vinson Street, past the old junkyard by the river. Finally they came to Orion Pallet at the end of the Sloetown. From her window, Cheryl saw the old factory, now dark and silent. McDermott eased the Lincoln into the vast, empty parking lot and stopped. They got out and came to each other, leaning against the hood of the car, side by side, gazing at the giant brick warehouse in the distance under bright stars.

"That's where the fire was, huh?" McDermott said.

"You remember."

"I was just thinking. That's what you told me."

"Yeah, that's right. Mike worked there."

"And he just never came back?"

"No." She looked at him with pain in her face, and longing too, as if she wanted someone, maybe a man like Richard McDermott, to know about Michael Lewis, to know what happened to her brother in Sloetown a long time ago.

"And no one ever told you about it? What happened to him."

"No."

"Nothing?"

"Well, some of the men who were hurt in the fire got help. They got money." She looked away, staring across the parking lot at the dark factory building as long as a city block. "But the ones who didn't come home—we never heard about those guys, or what happened to them."

"There was more than one?"

"Seven men were missing that day, Michael and six others. They all lived in Sloetown. Their families still do."

McDermott stood and walked away from the car, away from her. "And no one ever did anything? Never told the police?"

"I was barely a teenager then, so I don't remember. I do know the police came around about that time, and some guys from the fire department—asking questions. But after a while, it was like they gave up. We all guessed those men died in the fire, but no one ever told us anything about it. They weren't like *employees*; they just showed up to work some days. In the end, there was nobody to talk to, so we never knew, for sure."

McDermott approached the woman, her eyes feeling warm to him in the darkness. He stood facing her, then caressed her bare arms. She felt her own hands reach for his shoulders, as if she couldn't make them stop and then they were around his neck and she felt him against her thighs and her breasts, kissing her. They remained there in the night, falling against each other. He kissed her neck and Cheryl felt her knees relax as McDermott held her tighter, his hands caressing the small of her back. She looked out over his shoulder at the old brick factory vivid under the summer moon.

Then she eased away from his embrace. "And not long after that, that's when the girl started coming around to see us. In Sloetown."

"What?"

"After the fire, a year or so later, Mira started coming to visit." Cheryl Lewis walked away, looking down at the pavement. "But she's gone now."

McDermott froze. "What did you say? Who—?"

"I ought to go home now."

He grabbed her arm. "Cheryl."

She looked at him. He let go. She reached for the car door. "It's late. I have to work tomorrow at the restaurant."

McDermott drove her back home. When they reached the house, a thin, solitary figure waited on the sidewalk, a young man. He didn't move as the black Lincoln stopped at the curb. McDermott's hands gripped the steering wheel, but Cheryl knew the boy. Her window was down and she said, "Lester."

The youth didn't say anything. He walked forward slowly, approaching the car. His eyes were big, curious.

"Who dat?" he said, leaning in at the window. He stared at McDermott.

"My friend Richard," Cheryl said. She nodded at McDermott. "And this is my brother Lester. He forgets his manners sometimes."

Lester didn't say anything, but his eyes got bigger. McDermott managed a grim smile.

"What you doing out here? So late?" Cheryl said, addressing the youth.

"It ain't late."

She looked over at McDermott, then reached over and touched his hand and said, "I've got to go."
"All right."
Cheryl Lewis exited the car. "It's almost midnight," she said to Lester. She took him by the arm and they went into the house as McDermott watched.
Yes, the woman said *Mira*. He was sure of it.

AUSTIN McLELLAN

EIGHT

Lester Lewis didn't sleep well that night. He was agitated. He didn't like that man who brought Cheryl home yesterday. And dreams filled his sleep. He wanted a car, but all he had was ten dollars from the marijuana. He also wanted a new television. Cheryl would like that, and the baby too. He had a little more weed, and maybe he could sell it, but he didn't know anyone with any money except that old man. His sister was moving about in the kitchen preparing breakfast. He smelled bacon. He stretched and groaned.

"Is that you Lester?" Cheryl called out. "Are you getting up? I've got to go to work, you know."

The young man mumbled something.

"Come on and get something to eat. You want some toast?"

He shuffled into the kitchen, half asleep, and sat down heavily at the table.

"You look like an old man," she said lightly. "What time did you go to bed?"

"I dunno," he replied. "I didn't sleep good." She placed a glass of orange juice before him. He drank while his sister moved the bacon around in the frying pan.

"You're too young to be tossing at night. You worried about something?"

"Naw." His eyes opened a bit. He drank the juice. "Who was that last night?"

She didn't look up. "Who?"

"That man in the car."

She eyed him over her shoulder. "Is that what you're worried about?"

"You was in the car with him."

She lifted the bacon dripping from the skillet onto a paper towel. "He's just a friend."

"He was white."

"So?"

Lester didn't say anything, but rose from the table and went to the refrigerator and got more juice. "White dude," he grumbled.

Cheryl set the plate of bacon on the table. "Don't worry about it. Just eat. You want some toast?"

"I ain't worried about it," he said, sitting and reaching for the bacon. He ate quietly for a moment. "What's he want?"

"Nothing."

"Yeah, white dude."

"Don't talk like that. He's a friend. His name is Richard."

"He wants something. I can tell. 'Ain't no reason for him to be up in Sloetown. He don't belong here. This ain't no place for him. He's lookin' for something."

Cheryl Lewis fell quiet and stared out the kitchen window into the backyard. An old swing set stood there, its paint chipped away. She hoped to fix it up in a few years so the baby could play on it.

Lester said, "Either that or he runnin' away from something."

"Eat your breakfast, boy. Your cousin Sheila's bringin' the baby back this morning and you've got to look after her. I'm working today."

* * *

Lieutenant Doreen Foster was at her desk late Friday morning thinking about lunch when Officer Jeremy Wilson came into her office. He held up a little plastic bag for her to see. She looked at him like *So?*

"Pearls, ma'am," he said. She stood and examined them. "Like the ones we found in Sloetown, in that vacant lot."

"With the late Miss Ogilvy?"

"Yes ma'am. Like that."

"Where did you get——?"

"Not in Sloetown. These are different."

"They look the same."

"No . . . I mean yes, they're the same, but I got them here, downtown." She looked at him gravely. "I got them from Richard McDermott."

"McDermott?"

"Yes ma'am. When I went to question him, he had these." The Lieutenant fondled the pearls in the little plastic bag, thinking it over. Suddenly she didn't feel like lunch anymore.

"And they're the same? The same as the ones we found in Sloetown with the dead girl?"

"Maybe. I'm taking them to the lab now. They might match the others we found there, and the soil on them—"

She held the tiny spheres up to the light. "It's not soil, Wilson." They were silent, their attention on the pearls. "It's blood." The policeman looked at her, color rising in his face. "And Mr. McDermott . . . you say these were in his possession?"

"Sitting right on the desk in his office." Wilson took the pearls back from her, noticing her face alert and sad at once. "I'll have the lab check it out," he added, turning to go.

"You do that." She sat and looked at the Ogilvy file on her desk. Well now, maybe this was something, these pearls in the lawyer's office. They could place him at the crime scene. And Wilson had seen him there too, on Vinson Street, a man who had no reason to be in Sloetown late on a Tuesday night, no good reason. Then his sister, Gloria Orion, knew Mira Ogilvy; and the victim had even been in McDermott's house at a party or something, so he knew her first hand. But why? Mira was young and attractive —maybe the love angle? The Lieutenant knew love made people crazy, especially in Sloetown, if *love* was the right word for it. Then Baker Davis mentioned the girl had money, a considerable amount. And if McDermott needed money, like Wilson said, then maybe . . . .

* * *

When Baker Davis woke that morning, he knew the day was hot already. Even from his bedroom, the sun felt like a brass band clamoring to get inside his house, inside his head. He longed for a cool, dark, quiet place where he could hear his own thoughts, apart from clients trying to sell him a story, or creditors trying to work an angle, or the cops trying to push him against a wall. It would be nice to get everyone off his back.

Maybe food would help and he went to the icebox. It was

empty. He reflected that some people went to the store with lists and coupons and purchased groceries which they brought home to prepare and consume. It all seemed remote and strange but Davis knew some people lived like that. He just knew it.

He phoned the Gray Prince. It was early but Davis remembered his office partner operated better with less planning. He talked him into breakfast. Then he showered and gathered up the images he'd collected: the Ogilvys with Karl Orion at the fine party years ago, and the lurid scene of the burning pallet factory he'd taken from the Archives. He left the house.

When he reached the Trade Winds apartment building, he honked the horn. After awhile, a door opened and Prince emerged, unsteady. As he got into the car, Davis said, "So you finally got out of Roxanne's, huh?"

"That was two days ago."

"Well, you looked real comfortable there when I left."

"No. It was bad. Bad!" But Davis knew that. He knew when he left Roxanne's it would be bad. "It took me forever to get home," Prince said, shaking his head. They drove with the air-conditioner blowing hard, keeping the heat of the day out. It was almost noon.

Davis asked "Whatcha hungry for?"

"Coffee. Eggs. Toast. Coffee."

"Well, there's only one place. The Best."

The city passed by as Prince narrated the tale of his time at Roxanne's. When they came to Best Diner, they saw a crowd seated in the big dining room through the front windows. Everyone was eating. They all looked fat. "A good sign," Prince commented. They entered and found a quieter table in the back. A young black girl appeared from nowhere. She was tall, with her hair pulled back to reveal large, shining eyes. She set two glasses of water before them in an elegant manner that was completely untaught.

"You doin' all right today?" Prince drawled.

"I'm okay," she said. "An you?"

"Can you bring us a little coffee maybe?" Davis asked.

"Sure." She placed a few menus on the table.

"What's your name?" Prince asked.

"I'm Cheryl." She glided away. They sipped at the water, condensation trickling down the side of the glasses.

"This isn't Roxanne's," Davis said.

"I was being friendly."

They studied the menus. Prince continued his tale about the club, "And then she asked me for a hundred to help her make the rent next week. I didn't know what was gonna run out first—her love or my money." As he talked, Davis withdrew the pictures from his pocket, smoothing them on the table. Prince stopped. "What's this? You been stalking people again?" He ran his hand over the wrinkled images. "Ahh, Orion again, but with the Ogilvys this time, at some nice party, black tie. And what's this? The pallet factory, on fire. Where did you find these?"

"They found *me*," Davis replied. "You know how I like to get to the bottom of things."

"Yeah, that's your problem. You need a night at Roxanne's. Why can't you let things alone?"

"I don't know."

"It doesn't pay, you know," Prince said, examining the images.

"I know it doesn't, but it might. This time." Davis nodded at the photo. "You see the big fire?"

"Yeah. At Orion Pallet." Prince mumbled, without looking up.

"Read the caption."

"... *many workers injured and a few men reported missing*. Looks like everyone didn't get out."

"Some made it, some didn't."

The waitress returned, sliding two coffees onto the table. "Here you are."

"I'm gonna need a little cream," Davis said, but the young woman didn't hear. She'd become still, unmoving, noticing the photographs. "And maybe a little sweetener," he added. But she was lost.

"What's up baby?" Prince asked softly.

"You know this?" she asked weakly, her eyes on the images on the table. Her voice trembled. The men exchanged glances.

"It's just some old pictures," Davis said. "From years ago." The young woman twisted her hands in knots, her face hard with anxiety as Davis asked, "Do you know—?" But she couldn't answer, couldn't move, as if the images held her in place, nailed to the floor.

"Maybe we could get some eggs?" Prince interjected. It broke the spell. She pulled a little pad from her pocket, scribbled an order and retreated to the kitchen.

"Something here got her attention," Prince said, picking up the image of the burning factory. "What a mess."

"The ambulance. Check it out."

"So what?"

"The name on the ambulance—Mercy Hospital. That's where they took the injured."

Prince looked up. "Well, all right. So you call 9-1-1, and somebody shows up. Could've been the Baptist hospital or that hospital out in the suburbs. 'Coulda been anybody back then."

"Yeah, okay, maybe it's nothing."

"What are you thinking?"

"Not sure." Davis picked up the other image, of Karl Orion in formal wear, one arm around the shoulder of Dr. Winston Ogilvy, his other arm around Mira with a glass of champagne in his hand. He handed it to Prince, who said,

"Karl Orion and the Ogilvys. A big party. Okay."

"Look what the party is for."

Prince read the headline: *Charity Event for Mercy Hospital.* "It looks like a swell time. Orion and the Doc must have been pretty good friends—" His voice trailed off into thought and the men found themselves on an island of silence in the middle of the busy restaurant. The waitress came with their breakfasts.

"Y'all want ketchup with that?" the young woman asked, setting plates before them. Again the photographs on the table seized her attention. She coughed nervously as a line creased her brow. She swallowed hard and spoke. "Where did . . . you . . . get that?"

Davis nudged the pictures to the edge of the table where she could see them clearly. Her eyes flashed. "From an old newspaper," he said. "Maybe ten years ago. You know about—?"

She picked up the image of Orion Pallet in flames. "This one. Yes, I think so." Her voice was deep and steady. "I remember."

Prince and Davis looked at each other. The woman stood before them and suddenly Cheryl Lewis wasn't young anymore. She spoke in a tone ancient and timeless, as if revealing a truth ten thousand years old:

"I remember. I live in Sloetown and that's the pallet factory. We saw smoke from miles around, rising over the neighborhood.

We always played outside and the smoke came over the trees. The smell—"

"Lotta people got hurt," Davis said.

She stared at the photograph, knotting her hands. "Yes. I was about fourteen, and I had an older brother Michael. He used to give me and my little brother Lester rides in his old Cadillac. It was a convertible, a beat up old thing, and the electric top wouldn't go up, so he parked it under the trees in Jackson Park when it rained. But when the sun came out and the seats dried off, he'd take us riding around Sloetown." A weak smile appeared on her face, but her voice sounded far away. Her hands became still. "Michael saved up all summer to buy that car. He worked at that factory." Then she dropped the picture onto the table. "Ah'll get you some ketchup."

"That's all right. Forget it," Prince said.

She didn't move. Davis picked up the photograph. "Your brother Michael," he said. "Does *he* know about this? What *happened* at the factory that day? This big fire?"

The young woman knotted her hands again, taking the picture gently from the investigator. She looked at it again deeply.

"That day—" she said, her voice dry as wood, "that day was the last day we ever saw him." She dropped the image.

"Ah."

"His convertible is still there under the old trees in the park, right where he left it about ten years ago."

Then Cheryl Lewis picked up the other picture, the scene of Karl Orion and the Ogilvys in glossy black formal wear, the sparkling drinks in their hands. She stared at the image.

"Who are these?" she asked, her head tilting to one side as if she was trying to recognize an unfamiliar sound.

"Just some folks," Davis answered.

"That girl," she whispered, eyeing Mira Ogilvy between the men in the picture. "That girl!"

"What about her?" Davis asked.

"Ah'll get more coffee." She walked quickly away.

"Hey!" But the young woman disappeared into the kitchen.

Prince said, "That picture of Miss Ogilvy got to her. She's the one they found in Sloetown last week, right?" Davis nodded as they finished their meals. The waitress never returned. Finally, an older man wearing a stained tie came from the kitchen, looking like a manager.

"You guys all right?" he asked. "Need anything else? More coffee?"

"I think we're about done here," Davis said.

"Our waitress—hey is she all right?" Prince asked.

"Uh . . . she's on break right now," the manager said. "I'll get your check."

"Nice girl. She did a good job," Prince said, flipping a ten onto the table. Davis gathered up the photographs.

"Thanks. I'll tell her."

The manager left and returned in a moment with a check. They paid at the counter, and were soon outside the Best Diner. They found the Buick.

"It felt like that waitress had never told anyone about that before, about her brother and the fire," Prince observed as they got back in the car. "Just *missing*, huh?"

"Yeah, that's what the newspapers said, *missing*. You know that company has over a hundred guys making pallets in that warehouse any given day, most all of them from Sloetown. They don't know who's working, who's not. They're day laborers, paid in cash."

"That waitress knows," Prince said. "What was her name? Lewis?"

"That's right, *Lewis*. She said she lived in Sloetown, and mentioned a younger brother too, right?"

"That's what she said, a little brother. Lester, I think it was."

Lester. Davis remembered the kid he met in the park a few nights back, the one whose brother turned up missing.

They drove out onto the highway. Afternoon had arrived and a milky haze filled the sky.

"I guess after a while they stop looking for them, the missing." Prince said.

"Yeah, that's how it usually happens. Those men are nobodies. Untouchables. After a while it's like they never existed. Nobody cares. And finding out what really happened turns up more problems, for someone, than anyone wants to deal with. So the cops or the fire department or the pallet company or the insurance people . . . they stop looking. Too much trouble, grief, fear, whatever. They give up, and hope it will all go away."

"Maybe that waitress, Cheryl Lewis, gave up too," Prince said.

"Finally gave up waiting for her brother to come home."

"Maybe. Maybe not. She remembers his Cadillac parked under the trees in Sloetown. She remembers waiting for him to come back and start it up and give everyone a ride on a warm summer night."

"How do you ever stop waiting? Or forget that? Maybe the waiting gets to be like scar tissue, smoother and smoother and fainter over time, until you can hardly see it."

"But it's still there."

"Still there."

Davis wondered how long Cheryl Lewis would wait. Maybe forever, he thought. They grew silent, enjoying the ride. Davis reached for the radio but Prince said he liked it quiet. They drove on. The investigator remarked,

"That waitress, Cheryl Lewis. She knew the girl in the picture too, the dead girl. She knew Mira Ogilvy."

"Let the police handle it," Prince said.

Davis turned it over in his mind. Prince was right, let the police find the killer. It's their problem. But when that waitress saw Mira's picture, she recognized her—and ran.

Soon they arrived at Prince's apartment. Davis stopped the car.

"You going into the office?" Prince asked, opening the door.

"No. It's Friday. 'Day is shot, but I thought I'd take a little drive."

"Have fun." The Gray Prince got out and went into his apartment.

* * *

It had been a long week and Lt. Doreen Foster was ready to go home. In fact, she wanted to leave a few hours ago, but her supervisors, the men who ran the department, summoned her upstairs to a big meeting earlier that Friday afternoon. All *men*, she thought. But she didn't feel sorry for herself, being the only woman in that room. In fact, those guys had given her plenty of responsibility, but not enough to leave her alone and let her do her job without interference. No, they didn't act superior—they were simply a pain in the ass. They wanted to know about Mira Ogilvy, and what the hell was going on with the investigation. She rubbed her eyes. What the hell did they think? That she had a hundred men to turn the city upside down? Just to find one more killer?

Then Samuels, the top political liaison to the Police Department from City Hall, suggested that if she thought about it long enough, she might figure out who killed that girl.

She answered him: "What exactly, Mr. Samuels, would you have me think about?" Samuels didn't like it, but he didn't say anything. Still, she knew he could make trouble.

The Lieutenant stood and approached the window that gave a view to the civic plaza outside, surrounded by tall government buildings. If Samuels only knew, she thought, what it meant to face death and violence up close. Guys like him never saw the horror, the pain, the fear. The supervisors were all torn up about a white girl found dead in the old neighborhood, a victim who may have been stupid, foolish, or plain unlucky. But how many violent deaths had Sloetown witnessed over the years? She noticed the file cabinet in the corner stuffed with stale crimes, homicides unresolved, barely acknowledged, and now forgotten. Except *she* remembered them. She knew about them. In a way, Doreen Foster knew about them long before she ever joined the Police Department, when she was growing up in Sloetown. And now Mira Ogilvy. What the hell? A terrible crime, but how was that girl any different, in the end? Another body found, another life lost. But those men upstairs wanted her to hurry up.

The Lieutenant straightened a few papers on her desk, then reached into a drawer for her purse and car keys. It would be good to get home and put her feet up, even though she'd been sitting down all day. As she left her office, she wanted to smile at the policemen who remained there at work, but she wasn't in the mood. Wilson jumped up from his desk as she walked by.

"And if they come back positive, Lieutenant?"

"What?"

"Those pearls, the ones I found with McDermott, the ones I sent to the lab."

"What about them?"

"If they come back positive. You know, if it's Miss Ogilvy's blood on them?"

"Then you know what to do, Wilson."

"Bring him in."

"Smart guy."

TWENTY GRAND

* * *

Late Friday afternoon, Gloria Orion sat amid a sea of papers in her husband's office at the Orion Pallet factory. Karl stayed home that day. He didn't feel like coming in. That morning she brought a glass of juice to his bedside and asked him again about Mira Ogilvy, but he told her not to worry. *It will be all right* he whispered, then turned away. He said he wanted to rest. The medicine was making him sick, but Gloria Orion wondered how they were going to pay for it. The insurance was gone. She'd come across the cancellation notice in the papers on his desk. She knew the cost for chemotherapy could easily hit a million dollars. And no health insurance! She felt as if her future was disappearing before her eyes, eating away at her flesh, sipping her blood.

O God, she gasped, not actually thinking of anything sacred or supernatural. She picked up the phone and called her brother. McDermott answered quickly. "What?"

"Richard?"

"What?"

"Are you all right?"

"Sure," he grumbled.

"Well, what are you doing?"

"Thinking."

"Well, why don't you come down here and think with me? I'm at the office, at the factory. Karl stayed home today. I'm looking through his papers, some old records. There's got to be something here about Mira and the money. Come help me. I'll be here for a while. Besides, I'm not sure I really have any place else to go."

"All right. I'll be there in about a half hour."

Gloria Orion leaned back in her husband's leather chair and surveyed the office as the last rays of afternoon sun painted the dreary paneling a dull orange. And what if Karl didn't make it? The company would be all hers—and she'd be stuck in Sloetown forever, making pallets. Even now, she heard hammering out in the warehouse that felt like blows to the stomach. She thought of her mother in Kentucky in the little house with the crooked porch and the leaky roof. The front window showed the hills in the distance, scarred from strip mining. She remembered her mother's Social Security payment—three hundred and sixty-seven dollars a month. Gloria Orion knew the number like she knew her own name. And

167

she wondered for a second if that would be enough to support them both if she had to move back there. No, they'd starve.

Surely these papers, Karl's records, held some clue about Mira Ogilvy. There must be secret accounts, money hidden somewhere. She'd find it, if it took her all night, if she had to tear the place apart.

She jerked open a drawer in her husband's big desk and a moth flew out. Another stack of papers. But these were yellowing, older. *Karl owed the girl? Jesus, he owes me.* She sighed and lifted the dusty papers, sorting through them rapidly, but they were meaningless correspondence. Then her restless fingers stopped, holding a letter almost ten years old, from an insurance company. It agreed to pay Orion Pallet a claim of almost five million dollars. For the fire.

Ah . . . there it is. That's what happened.

She kept digging in the old papers. More letters about the claim turned up; then she found estimates for the repairs. Finally, she found a summary quote from a general contractor—a little over 2.5 million dollars to rebuild the pallet factory. Her eyes narrowed. She checked the figures again. No, they didn't add up. A five million dollar settlement paid, but only half that needed to rebuild the factory. Well, my husband's no fool, she thought with grim irony. That would leave quite a surplus if Karl needed it—if he owed somebody. Maybe Mira Ogilvy. Was she a mistress? No. Gloria Orion knew her husband well enough to know that wasn't the case. Besides, the girl was young, beautiful, had her own money. She would never need or want an arrangement like that. Maybe she had something on Karl, something he wanted to keep secret. *Yes, blackmail, that's what it was! And that's illegal. Mira extorted that money—that money isn't hers at all.*

"It's mine!" Gloria Orion cried out in the empty room. She flung her arm across the desk, scattering papers across the room, and cursed through her teeth. Karl had no right! She fell back into the deep leather chair and closed her eyes and sighed. She thought for a moment she would cry. That would feel good, a release, and she deserved it. She felt something like tears welling up, but when she raised a finger to wipe her eyes, they were dry.

She got up and gathered everything from the floor, a cloud of dust rising around her. Then she noticed a manila folder, a clean one, new, with no label on the tab. She opened it, leafed through several wrinkled pages, and her hands started trembling. Records from Mira Ogilvy! Finally, a connection to the dead girl. Her eyes rifled through the contents. This must be it!

She heard a knock on the door and jumped. The door opened.

"You scared me!"

McDermott came in, went to Karl Orion's desk and sat down without a word. He slumped in the chair.

"What?" she said.

"Is there anything to drink?"

"Behind you."

McDermott turned around. From a low cabinet, he withdrew a bottle of scotch and glasses, then poured himself a drink. He slanted an eye at his sister.

"Sure," she said. He poured one for her, then drank heavily from his glass. He leaned back in the chair and stared at the ceiling.

"What, Richard?" she asked, tasting her drink.

"The police," he said, wearily. "They came to my office."

"A red-haired cop?"

McDermott grimaced. "Yeah. That's him. He wanted to talk about Mira."

"That little creep. I only told him she came to your house for dinner. A party guest."

"It wasn't just that, Gloria." He drank the scotch again. "They saw me down there one night."

"They *saw you*? Where?"

"In Sloetown one night. I was driving. They saw my Lincoln near where they found that girl, on Vinson Street."

"Vinson Street?! What were you doing there?"

"Just driving. That's all. I have a friend in Sloetown."

She glared at her brother. He finished his drink, then poured another one. His eyes appeared to rest on a distant horizon. "Her name is Cheryl. What about it?"

Gloria went to him, placed her hand on his shoulder and squeezed. "Look, Richard. I don't care what you do, in Sloetown or anywhere else. But we've got to find out about Mira—what she did with that money. We can't have the police involved!"

He muttered something and she turned away. She found her purse, dug through it for cigarettes.

McDermott rubbed his forehead. "I'm going to lose the

building too, Gloria. I don't have anything to pay the bank, and they'll foreclose soon."

"Oh for God's sake to hell with that. Help me find the money and we'll take care of it." She found the cigarettes and lit one. "Now look—" she said, reaching for the manila folder. "I found this. It's Mira's."

McDermott's eyes dilated as he opened the folder, examining the contents. "Jeez, it's all kinds of stuff." He shuffled through the papers. "Wait." She came to his side. "What's this?" He held up a bank statement, squinting his eyes as Gloria peered over his shoulder. "It's Mira's checking account. Look at the dates, look at—"

"There!"

"Yes. There is it is, Glo! The deposits. Look. Twenty thousand, month after month."

"God," she said bitterly. "Those must be the deposits Karl made." She reached into the pile of papers on the desk and withdrew a letter. "And I found this too. It's the insurance settlement, from the fire. Almost five million dollars."

McDermott studied it. "Whew."

"But that's not all. Here." She handed him the quote from the contractor.

"Two and a half million to rebuild the factory."

"Right. Quite a difference, huh?"

"Yeah. So you think that's where Karl got the dough he gave Mira? From the insurance? This surplus?"

"Well, there sure as hell isn't that kind of money in pallets. Believe me."

"All right, that kinda makes sense." Then McDermott remembered the picture he'd seen in the old newspaper in the archives. "But listen, I learned something else, about that fire. It wasn't just the warehouse damaged. Men were hurt."

"The workers? No, Orion Pallet compensated them."

"Maybe. But if Karl gave all that insurance money to Mira—"

"Are you saying they weren't paid? Richard, look. It was a long time ago. I'm not sure I care."

"'Not sure I do either. I'm only saying, maybe there's something else. We've got to consider what Karl did, why he—"

"Richard, the factory burned and Karl took the settlement. However it happened, Mira ended up with the money. We've got to find it."

"All right." He took another drink and picked up the bank statement again. "Wait a minute. Look there. What in the hell?" She leaned across the desk.

"Withdrawals."

"Yes. Debits, going back years."

"Wow. Jesus." They looked at each other.

"Twenty thousand, every month, year after year."

"All that money. How on earth could Mira spend—?"

"I don't know, but it doesn't appear she wrote checks to pay for anything, or deposited it elsewhere. She just took the money out. Cash, probably."

"Cash? Weird." Gloria found an ashtray and stubbed out her cigarette. "So Karl gave the money to her, paid her for some reason. He mentioned some work she did for the company, but I think it's a lie."

"Maybe she had something on him."

"Maybe, but she doesn't have anything now. She's dead." Gloria Orion crossed the room and parted the blinds. The last light of day fell beneath the trees at the edge of the big parking lot outside. "All that cash, all those years. She couldn't spend it all. She couldn't stuff it under a mattress. She must have given it away. It had to be for something, for somebody."

"Somebody—" McDermott said thickly, remembering Cheryl Lewis and how it felt to hold her and kiss her that night in the parking lot of Orion Pallet, the night she whispered *Mira*. He could smell her perfume as he returned the bank statement to the folder, his face clouded, his mouth a grim line. Gloria looked at him and said,

"What?"

"Nothing." The lawyer stood up from the desk and finished off his drink.

"Richard?"

"Keep looking," he muttered, nodding at the stack of papers. "You might find something." He moved toward the door.

"What? Where are you going?"

He turned in the doorway and looked at her. "I don't know." Then he was gone.

* * *

Baker Davis drove out along Kenner Boulevard in the late afternoon. He watched the landscape devolve into car lots, nail parlors, wing houses, check cashing joints, and storefront churches. The primary texture was chain link, with subtones of plastic, steel, glass and brick. Soon he was in Sloetown. He didn't enter the old neighborhood—he was there or it was around him and he was in it. The smell of the river and food rushed in through the window. Davis slowed the car. It felt like coming home, he thought, like going back to a place, to a time that doesn't change.

He passed Jackson Park, remembering that Michael Lewis's Cadillac lay hidden in the brush there, rotting and falling away into the land as Mira Ogilvy's body once decayed under the hot sun in a vacant lot. Everything changes, he thought, even in Sloetown, but one must look closely to see it. The sounds of the highway grew faint as the investigator cruised the back streets. Twilight had come and shadows gathered beneath the old trees. It was peaceful here. Then it wasn't. It was jarring, a kick in the stomach. He was on Vinson Street. He tapped the brakes. The faded diner loomed ahead, surrounded by tall grass—that's where he found Mira. As he neared the vacant lot, it reverberated with tension, inexplicable dread. His gut churned. He was afraid. *Run. Turn the car around and hit the gas.*

But something told Baker Davis to be still. It would be okay. It wasn't courage, whatever told him this, nor was it surrender. But he felt anchored, alive, his senses afire, and he realized then why he did it, why he stuck with the PI business year after year and why he couldn't let go. No one else in the city could do this, he knew, not the cops, not Prince, not McDermott, not Gloria Orion. Maybe this was something, after all, that his father had given him, his inheritance, though maybe it wasn't a *gift*. It's what I have, he concluded. *What I do. I operate.*

At the end of Vinson, a shape moved. Davis peered into the darkness. A solitary figure poked along the sidewalk with the jerky motion of a man either talking to himself or slightly intoxicated or both. He drew closer, pushing a shopping cart. Davis recognized him.

"Rico! What the—?"

"Bawss," he mumbled, staring at the ground. He approached the car.

"What the hell you doing out here?"

"Pickin' up cans and bottles." Then he looked up, his eyes rheumy and livid. "Dat white lady—she gone, man."

Davis leaned from the car window. "I know. The police know."

"Hell naw, they doan know! They ain't gonna find her. You ain't gonna find her."

"I ain't looking for her, and the police already found—"

"The police doan know nuthin!"

"All right. They don't."

His voice dropped. "But I knows, Bawss. Yeah I know."

Davis looked him over as he stood under the streetlamp there on Vinson Street. No telling how long Rico had been there. Maybe he'd always been there . . . even when somebody threw Mira Ogilvy in that weed-choked lot.

"Know what, man?"

"Hmm. Hmm." He reached into the shopping cart and found a can that wasn't quite empty. He drank it.

"How you know, Rico?"

"Ah know. In Sloetown, in the de junkyard, man. Hmm."

"What about it?"

"I show you Bawss. You take me up dere. Hmm. Ah show you. I know."

"All right. We'll go to the junkyard. You show me about that girl."

"Hmm."

"Get in the back," Davis said from the car window. He didn't want the man up front. Rico opened the door with shaky hands.

"Hmm. De junkyard," he moaned, tumbling into the back seat and becoming still. They left Vinson Street, Rico falling in and out of consciousness or sleep or sanity, and murmuring about the junkyard or that white girl or the police or related demons. Night had come to Sloetown. A few cars passed them, their headlights flashing a strobe pattern of darkness and light into the Buick. The neighborhood was quiet, but lamps glowed softly in a few houses, and people moved about inside, cooking dinner. They passed Jackson Park where Lester Lewis and his friends told the story of the fire and the men who got paid and the ones who never came back.

Rico stirred in the rear. "Lemme out, Bawss," he mumbled, coming around. Davis looked back at him. He was alert, his eyes open, his face gleaming in the darkness. "Lemme out," he said louder.

Davis glared back over his shoulder. "Let you out? You gonna show me about that girl."

"It's in the junkyard, Bawss, by de river. You go on down dere. You'll see."

"No man, you gonna show me what you been talking about, about that white lady."

"Naw Bawss. I ain't goin up in dat junkyard. I doan wanna see. Hmmm," he groaned as if in pain. "Lemme out."

They turned a corner and the junkyard loomed, enclosed by a high brick wall where the mortar had crumbled and washed away. It seemed the whole place was leaning over, about to slide into the river. A pallid moon hung above it all. At the front gate, the street turned to gravel and Davis stopped the car.

"Dat girl ain't comin back Bawss! Someone done shot her and she gone now."

"Shot her? Who shot her? How you know all that, Rico?"

"Lemme outta here!" He squirmed in the backseat fidgeting for the door handle. "I ain't goin' inside no gotdamn junkyard."

"Shut up. I'll let you out when we get inside." Davis looked back. Rico's mouth was drawn in a grim line and his eyes danced with fear.

"Boool-shit," he sneered. He grabbed at the door handle. At last, he found the lock, kicked the door open, and bolted. He ran, lurching down the street.

"Rico!"

"Naw Bawss. She gone!" he cried, his voice trailing off as he stumbled away beneath the high brick wall of the junkyard. He became a dim silhouette in the darkness, his image growing smaller and smaller under the canopy of big trees. At last the homeless man was a tiny figure at the end of a deserted street. Then Rico was gone, and it was quiet. A dog barked in the distance.

Davis got out of the car and looked around, remembering where he was, that he was alone. He peered through a metal fence into the old junkyard that extended back to the river, where a big crane loaded car wrecks onto barges that floated across the water to a plant where everything was crushed and melted down. He could smell the river itself, dank and heavy, blowing up through the yard. Rico wanted him to find something here, something about

Mira Ogilvy.

    No padlock secured the gate, only a rusty bolt. Davis jerked it, sliding it back, and the gate creaked open. Davis looked around again, his gut telling him that whatever Rico feared he probably ought to be concerned about too. Inside the fence, he found a gravel path which snaked through enormous piles of cars, trucks, and industrial debris of every kind. He stopped to yank a steel pipe from the mangled remains of a sprinkler system that had been ripped from a building. He swung the pipe around like a baseball bat, taking a few cuts through the night air. It would work, he thought, if he needed it.

    What in the hell did Rico want to show me in here, Davis wondered as he crept among the mountains of rusting vehicles that each told a story: the crumpled Chevy wagon which had paraded a family around town; a twisted old Mustang which had fired a young man's heart and perhaps a young woman's too; then a bashed-in Datsun which carried a student through early years of struggle; and finally a big Cadillac, the companion of an older man. All were empty now, rusting away into nothing, and Davis felt smaller and more alone with each step he took in the darkness.

    He walked to the end of the gravel path where it turned into a concrete ramp that descended into the moving river. The water was black like the night. Lights from tiny villages trembled on the far shore. Then about a mile upstream, a row of smaller lights glittered, moving toward him in the night, signaling the approach of a vessel riding high and empty in the main current. A big barge was coming to pick up a load of scrap. Then the smell rose around him, thick and old as if the river didn't flow by Sloetown but rested there, not spawning life but drawing everything to itself as if it was larger and more vital than the shoreline and the nearby fields and forests and towns. Davis breathed deeply, taking it past his lungs into his stomach. No matter how many times he'd come to the river over the years, he felt welcome here, familiar, as if he was seen, known, waited for, expected. The big, empty barge approached the concrete landing where he stood, its lights piercing the black night. Davis blinked and rubbed his eyes. No, it was still a half mile away.

    The entire scene felt restful and timeless—the industrial backdrop, the patient river. The water smelled fetid and fresh at once, bearing a strange cargo from upstream, from the far banks. Davis realized then that whoever killed Mira Ogilvy, whatever tormented Gloria Orion, whatever Rico feared, wasn't going to last, wasn't going to remain hidden but must find the light of day or even the darkness to be resolved into clear and painful relief. And then he would know. Everyone would know. Then it would be over. Only the smallest residue of life would remain, struggling to get free and begin again. But what would it be? And who, if anyone, would be there to see it?

The metallic thud of a car door boomed in the night. Nearby. Davis backed away from the riverbank and slipped into in the shadows, gripping the steel pipe. He got behind a row of tangled car wrecks the size of a house, his breath heaving in his chest. Then the boom again, metallic and hard. He crouched low and followed the sound, finally reaching an open clearing where a man stood about fifty yards away, leaning into a car with a flashlight. The man was searching the interior of the car, a white BMW. Davis stepped out into the clearing.

The man stopped; then he backed out of the white car, stuffing something into his pocket. He was a big man. Davis moved toward him. It was Karl Orion. Davis lowered the pipe.

"Find what you were looking for?"

"What the—?" he cried, jerking a pistol from his pants, waving it in the darkness.

"Easy! It's me. Baker Davis. Easy."

"Jesus! What the hell? You lost?" The gun trembled in the old man's hand.

"I know where I am."

Orion squinted in the darkness. "Good way to get yourself shot, Davis. 'Sneaking up on people." He lowered the weapon.

Davis approached, leaning his steel pipe against the fender of the car. He took a chance: "It's hers, isn't it? It's Mira's car."

"Yes." Orion sat on the trunk and wiped at his brow in the humid night. He stuffed the pistol back into his trousers.

Davis circled the BMW. The hood was open, the vitals stripped. The body was scarred and banged up, the windows broken out. It sat on rims. "Doesn't look like much is left, Mr. Orion. But maybe there's something here for you?"

"None of your business."

"All right. If you say so. But the last time we talked, at Roxanne's, you wanted me to help."

"Help, yeah. Not get in my way."

"So you're still looking, huh? For the girl's money?"
"It wasn't hers, Davis."
"You gave it to her, those deposits."
Orion's face hung heavy and gaunt. "That's right," he said. Spots bloomed under the skin of his neck, and Davis wondered if the man was sick. "But then she made all the withdrawals. That's what I want, what I'm looking for."

Davis reached into his pocket and withdrew the news article he'd taken from the archives, the image of the big fire at Orion Pallet. He handed the clipping to Orion. The old man grunted, his face becoming gray as he examined the photograph in the moonlight.

"What's this supposed to be?"
"I don't know. You tell me."
"A picture of the fire. So what?"
"Well, that looks like quite a loss to me, sir."
"Insurance took care of it."

Davis picked up his steel pipe and tapped the fender of the car. "Insurance, huh? So Miss Ogilvy knew you had it? Settlement money?" Orion glared at him. "And you gave it—"

"All right. I gave her the insurance money." He crushed the news clipping in his fist, threw it onto the ground beside the BMW. "What about it?"

Davis approached the old man, then stopped and reached for the crumpled paper on the ground. He slowly opened it up. "This story in the paper . . . quite a few men hurt that day."

"Things happen."

"But the girl ended up with the money. And those guys in the fire, the injured—?"

Orion's teeth clenched. "Those men? For God's sake, I couldn't pay them everything. They'd just go and spend it, get drunk, or lose it playing dice in Sloetown. So yeah, I gave them a little money. Then I told them to go home and forget about it."

"A few bucks for the injured. And the others? The missing? The guys who never turned up that day?"

"Missing? That's just a story, Davis, an angle the newspapers dreamed up. Look, everything was very chaotic that day. The factory was burning. Smoke was everywhere. Fire trucks were coming and going, the police. It was outta control. We couldn't account for everyone. Nobody could. Maybe some guys didn't make it out that day, I don't know. But a lot of guys did, and everyone was thrilled about that. The newspapers wrote up the firemen as heroes. Maybe they were."

"All right. If that suits you."

"It suits me fine."

"Did it suit Mira?"

"How should I know?"

Davis pointed at the ambulance in the picture. "Mercy Hospital? You took them there."

"Yeah. So what?"

"You took them to her daddy, Dr. Ogilvy."

"I don't know who—"

"Really?" Davis withdrew the other clipping from his pocket, the picture of Mira and Dr. Ogilvy and Karl Orion at the charity event. He held it up. "Looks like you knew him quite well."

"All right smartass, Winston Ogilvy was my friend. It was a party. So what? Look, the doc was a respiratory expert, and he was at Mercy Hospital that day the factory burned, at the ER. He helped a lot of people. Did he save them all? I don't know. Nobody knows."

"Huh. If the missing—the ones who never turned up—died at the hospital, then Dr. Ogilvy knew. He must have known. And you were his friend."

"You think too much, Davis," he sneered.

"Probably. But if those men died, somebody knew. Winston Ogilvy would have known. And maybe his daughter. Even you."

"Speculative!"

"Men died in that fire, Mr. Orion. They never came back to their homes in Sloetown. Did your insurance cover that?"

"Shut up. I've heard enough."

"But everything stayed quiet, right? Nobody ever took a close look at that part. But Ogilvy knew, so maybe his daughter knew too. And that's why you paid Mira—to keep it all real quiet. So you did your part, and she did hers."

Orion's face was hard, but his eyes went soft and watery. "All right damn you, all right. Yes, I paid the girl." Then he took a deep breath and stared out across the junkyard. "I paid her with the insurance money. She got wind of it. She learned about the men in the factory who didn't make it. Somehow she knew. Maybe her Daddy told her. I don't know, but she knew. And she was going public with it, to the police, the newspapers. So yeah, I paid her. To shut her up. And she took the money, all those years."

"Then you got tired of paying her and she ended up with a couple of bullets in her back. Now you don't have to pay her."

His body trembled with rage. "You think it's like that?"

"I don't know. Maybe the police would like to evaluate it."

"They don't know anything." His shaky hand moved toward his gun.

"Not yet they don't."

"And they're not going to—" Orion yanked his pistol.

But the investigator was on him. The old man was slow. Davis shoved his arm, pushed him back against the white car. The gun clattered onto the ground. Orion fell back, breathing hard.

"Damn you Davis." His breath came heavy and short. He wiped sweat from his face which had turned gray under the moon. His eyes were moist, heated, almost vibrating, struggling from within.

Davis picked up the gun. He popped the magazine loose, shaking the bullets out onto the gravel path. He handed Orion the empty weapon, and said, "And now you want to get that money back."

"That money wasn't Mira's, never was. She did something with it." He stuffed the pistol in his trousers and stomped away to his car that waited nearby. He called back over his shoulder: "And I'll find it, Mr. Davis." Then Orion got in and drove up the gravel road toward the front gate, his headlights careening among the rusty piles of old wrecks. He disappeared and the deserted junkyard was quiet.

* * *

Mira's car remained. Davis peered inside—it looked violated, outraged. The seats were ripped apart, the glove box hung open. The ceiling liner was torn away and the dash pried back. He climbed in and got behind the wheel. Mira sat here once, he thought, maybe even spent her last moment alive right here. It was sad and chilling. Did she know what was going on? Did she fight? Did she know her executioner? Did she even know what hit her when the bullets entered her body? What were the girl's last words? Her last action? Was there some brief awareness before the end that might give any meaning to the whole senseless episode?

Davis put his hands on the steering wheel. It was a nice car once. He imagined a joyful drive on a breezy, sunny day with a cute girl like Mira Ogilvy. As he reached for the gas pedal, his foot dragged against the floorboard. Part of the carpet was torn. Strange, he thought, for a late model car like this. He reached down to straighten the fabric and it came loose in his hand, separating easily from the floor. The light was poor and he couldn't see, but something lay beneath it. He reached down in the darkness between his knees and felt under the carpet. Something in wrapping paper—a small package? He withdrew it. Yes, it was a thick brown envelope, sealed and unmarked. His breath stopped as he turned around, surveying the junkyard through the busted out windows of the car. It was late. Orion was gone. There was nobody around. Davis opened the envelope.

Inside was money. A lot of money. He withdrew a handful of greenbacks, feeling his heart race; then he stuffed the cash back in the envelope and threw it on the floorboard. He jumped from the car and looked around the yard again. No movement. Far away, the deep horn of a barge rolled up from the river. The vessel had arrived for its load of scrap. But the junkyard was deserted. Empty. Davis reached back into the car.

Inside the envelope were thick bundles of hundreds. He counted about twenty thousand dollars, then stuffed everything back in the envelope and threw it into the car. He heard the river in the distance, lapping the shore. Above, the moon hung solitary and still in the black August sky. His jittery hands reached for a cigarette. Somehow, he managed to light it.

Jesus, he whispered. His mind raced back to Sloetown last year, and the night he helped the cops break up that heroin traffic in the old neighborhood. And how the money everyone knew those dudes made dealing junk turned up missing. He was sure the police would take care of the money. They had their rules and procedures. It was evidence.

But the cash disappeared. They had to find someone to pin it on and the PI was available. Then it got ugly. The arrest, and the cop who cracked him across the face with his stick when Davis confessed that sure, he'd hidden that money up his ass and invited the officer to climb up there and take a look if he wanted it so bad. They locked the investigator up for a night, then turned him loose.

That's when Lt. Foster got involved and the bad situation got better, or at least more real, he remembered. She knew Baker Davis had helped put those Sloetown dealers away. The bust looked good for her and she appreciated it and wanted to help him, but that dope money was missing and the PI was the last man this side of the law to see it.

"You *are* on the right side of the law, aren't you Mr. Davis?" the Lieutenant asked back then. He didn't know how to answer at the time—and he wondered if he knew now. In the end, the police couldn't tie him to a nickel of the money, but they were in a tight spot with the cash missing. They had to do something. So the Department brass made the phone calls and got his license suspended. Lt. Foster couldn't help him, but she did tell him the truth: "It's not the end, Baker, but you need a break. Take some time off. Go on a vacation. A long one."

Davis eyed the brown envelope lying inside the BMW and wondered what the hell it meant. As before, the money was evidence in an active investigation, but this time, a homicide. He drew on the cigarette and looked around the empty junkyard again. All quiet and still. There was nobody around, no eyes upon him. And the envelope lying in the car. All that money. Evidence.

But it wasn't drug money. Mira Ogilvy wasn't dealing heroin. And if he left the cash inside the car, it was destined for the scrap heap. The big crane would load the car onto a barge that would take it across the river to be compacted, melted, recycled. This twenty K wasn't going to help anyone that way. And if Lt. Foster needed it later to close the deal on this case, he could always give it to her. Baker Davis reached back into the car.

He shoved the envelope inside his shirt, threw his cigarette onto the ground, and picked up the steel pipe again. He walked quickly away from Mira's car, returning to the gravel path, almost breaking into a run as he passed heaps of twisted metal and debris. Finally, he reached the front gate. He looked around for Rico, but the streets were empty.

Davis felt relieved as he got into the Buick. A night wind blew up in the old neighborhood, cooling things off, so he kept the windows down as he drove away from Sloetown, taking his time but soon going faster and faster, leaving the junkyard and the river and Karl Orion further and further behind. Maybe that's what Rico wanted to show me, Davis wondered, the woman's car. He knew it was there. Or was it Orion he wanted me to see? Or maybe even the money. Davis reached down and felt the cash inside his shirt. He withdrew it, tossing the envelope on the passenger seat. No, Rico couldn't have known this part. But maybe. Who could tell anymore?

Davis made it out to Kenner Boulevard and the bright lights. It was good to be moving again, out on the highway, away from Sloetown. 'Good to be going home. It was late. But he knew for some the night was a beginning, a signal to begin errands or launch missions unwelcome in the light of day. Or maybe life was clearer then, in the darkness, revealing the other, necessary side of truths that appeared different in sunlit, waking hours. Davis couldn't tell.

But one must know both, he thought. Even if they were all tangled up sometimes, like Orion and that girl, like his memories and the money on the seat beside him.

* * *

After Karl Orion left the junkyard late that night, he drove quietly for a while, relaxing in the cool darkness of Sloetown. That Davis fellow got on his nerves. *He ought to mind his own business. And what the hell was he doing out there at night anyway? Someone must have told him about the car, and he knows too much about Mira. Maybe he's working for the police. He's up to something, that's for sure.*

Orion drove through the backstreets of Sloetown. He rolled down his window to get fresh air, and as he did, he heard strange sounds. He couldn't tell what they were, a man shouting, a woman screaming, the sound of a car, gunfire maybe. He rolled the window back up. At an intersection, he stopped and withdrew the revolver from his pants, then slid it under the seat, within easy reach. But as he bent forward, the pain shot through his legs and he winced. He drove on, breathing heavily.

Finally, he came to Orion Pallet. He looked at the clock in his dash. A quarter past twelve, about right. He turned into the parking lot of the factory—*his* factory, he reflected, though now, in the middle of the night, it seemed to have its own power, its own existence, as if Orion Pallet didn't belong to him anymore. He stopped and killed his lights. Again pain shot through his arms and legs, and another place he couldn't recognize. His cancer and the chemo drugs warred within him. He felt nauseous and rolled down his window in case he vomited. He breathed deeply and tried to relax. In a few minutes it would pass.

And then . . . ? What if he didn't make it, if he couldn't beat this disease, if the medicine coursing through his body failed? Then what? Orion Pallet was on life support too, hardly breaking even each month. If he was gone, the company wasn't much to leave Gloria. Maybe she could sell the place, but who the hell would buy it? And his medical bills would eat up whatever gain might come from that. In all, a dismal prospect. Then Orion remembered the payments he had made to Mira Ogilvy all those years, the numbers spinning involuntarily through his mind. Hundreds of thousands of dollars! And that blood-sucking girl took every penny of it. Maybe the whole thing was never worth it. Maybe he should have called Mira's bluff years ago, come clean about the men killed in the fire, the men her Daddy couldn't save. Yes, Winston Ogilvy knew, and told Orion everything. Together, they kept it quiet. The doctor carried weight at the hospital, so he kept a lid on it there. Orion took care of the men from Sloetown.

Then Dr. Ogilvy died, or killed himself with booze, and somehow Mira found out. Maybe her father told her in a weak moment. After her father was buried, she planned to tell the whole world about the men missing in the fire, and all the money Karl Orion made from it. She told him one day in his office right here at Orion Pallet that the money wasn't his, and that she knew the dead men—knew exactly who they were.

Hell, he thought, maybe I should have told Mira to go public with everything . . . then denied it all. Perhaps nobody would have listened to the young woman. No, a story like that would've opened an investigation. There would have been lawsuits, even the police. The truth would have come out. It would have ruined him, and Orion Pallet, and his life with Gloria too.

So he paid Mira, all that money. Now it was gone. No one knew where. And Karl Orion needed it now.

He saw movement in his rear view mirror. He wiped his eyes. He looked in the mirror again. It was the kid. He tightened. The kid was coming. He would bring the marijuana. It would help him endure the chemo drugs a little longer. Then Lester Lewis was at the window.

"Hey," Orion said.

"What's up Pop?" he said. "How'd that stuff fix you up?"

"It was okay. It wasn't bad."

The kid smiled. "All right, all right. Well, you lookin' for some more?"

"What you got?"

The young man scanned the parking lot, reached into his trousers and withdrew a brown paper bag. He handed it through the window. "Got you a little mo' this time."

Orion opened the sack and inhaled deeply the fragrant weed. He eyed the youth standing there in the parking lot. "Hhmm. All right. How much?"

"A hundred."

"A hundred? That's a lot of money."

"It's a lot of smoke, Pop."

Orion eyed him and said, "What the hell." But when he opened his wallet, he could only find a few tens. He cursed.

"What's up man?" Lester said.

"Damn."

"Whattup?"

"No cash." He held open his wallet for the young man to see.

"Aw man."

"I forgot to go to the durn bank." Orion handed the sack back through the window. The kid snatched it.

"That ain't cool, Pop."

Orion thought about the weed. He thought about the chemo drugs. "Wait a second. Hold up. I got something else." The kid sneered. Orion dug into his pockets, pain stabbing at his arm, and withdrew the contents. He reached through the window and showed the young man a handful of pearls—the same as he'd found in the white BMW.

"Here. Take 'em," Orion said. He dropped them into the boy's hands.

"What?"

"Pearls. They're valuable."

Lester examined them. His eyes grew wide. "Pearls, huh?"

"Yeah. They're valuable. You take 'em to a pawn shop or a jewelry store, and they'll give you money. A hundred bucks, easy."

The young man looked them over. He shook his head.

"Look," Orion said. "I'm good for it. You take these and get some money for them. If you can't trade 'em, I'll bring cash next time I see you."

"I dunno. I ain't never seen—"

"I tell you they're worth a hundred, maybe more."

"At a pawn shop, huh? They'll buy 'em?"

"Sure. All the time."

Lester Lewis stared long and hard at the pearls. He held one up to the moonlight.

"I dunno, Pop."

Orion fidgeted. Another shot of pain jabbed at his leg. He needed the marijuana. He glared at the youth standing there in the dark parking lot, but the kid was unmoved. He started to hand the pearls back.

"All right. All right. Look." Orion sighed. Then he reached under the seat and slowly withdrew his revolver. He looked at it, gripped it by the barrel and handed it through the window.

"Try this."

Lester stepped back.

"Go on. Take it."

"Whoa."

"For the dope sack."

The young man paused, then reached his hand out for the gun. Orion gave it to him: "Easy now."

"Mother —" the youth whispered.

"Yeah."

"Damn."

"That's right."

Lester stared at the weapon. It glinted under the moonlight. He massaged the blue metal with long tender fingers.

"The pearls and the gun for the sack."

"All right Pop," he said softly. He handed the marijuana back through the window.

"Thanks. Careful now." Orion started up his car.

"Of the gun?"

"No, boy . . . them pearls," the old man said, then laughed, and drove away into the night.

AUSTIN McLELLAN

NINE

No, it didn't happen. It was a dream, a strange tale from years ago whispered in his ear last night by a stranger. He didn't see Karl Orion picking over the remains of Mira Ogilvy's car in the old junkyard down by the river. The memory was insubstantial, completely unreal, never happened. And all that money? It materialized from thin air. That's all it was—thin air.

It was Saturday morning now as Baker Davis closed his eyes again, trying to get back to the dream, but he failed. He was awake, like it or not, and it was almost ten. The dog and the cat pawed against his bedroom door. He got up, opened the door and they tumbled into the room. They were hungry and ready to go outside, so he fed them and put them out. In the kitchen, as he made coffee, he noticed the drawer where he'd stashed the brown envelope last night when he got home. He didn't want to see it again. In fact, he hoped it wasn't there. *'Never found it in the first place.* For a long minute, Davis stared at the drawer. No, leave the money alone and it will disappear as easily as it had come into his life. *Don't touch it. Don't look.*

But the coffee was ready, and the spoons were in the drawer.

He pulled the handle slowly. There, the thick brown envelope, just as he left it last night. It was no dream. He withdrew it, reached inside and felt the cash, twenty tight bundles of greenbacks. It hadn't changed at all, still added up to twenty thousand dollars, enough to take him far away, out West maybe, where he could buy that ranch with his brother. Or, he could sit tight and lie low like

Lt. Foster warned him to do, out of sight, nice and peaceful. He wouldn't have to take Gloria Orion's money. He wouldn't answer the phone. He could let go.

But it wasn't *his* money. It was Mira Ogilvy's, or at least belonged to her ghost which seemed determined to linger about the city until someone or something let her go too. Or maybe her spirit had let go and it was the living who still held on to something restless and grotesque, hanging on with greed, or regret, or guilt, or fear.

Davis held the cash while the coffee brewed. A confused blur rang in his ears. There was no peace. Though a girl was cold and dead, and the police had taken her away, there was no rest. Mira Ogilvy knew about the fire and the men who died. She blackmailed Karl Orion. He paid her all that money over the years to keep quiet, and now he wanted it back—so did Gloria Orion and McDermott. They were all ready to fight or even kill to find it. But maybe Mira wanted someone else to find it, maybe Baker Davis. She addressed her last letter to him, and mentioned that she had set aside money for compensation. How ironic, he thought.

Wait, let it come, Davis remembered his father used to say, sitting in the office wearing a linen suit with his feet on the desk in the summer heat. It would come. They would come because the private investigator was the last stop. Then he would know, even if he didn't want to, even if he didn't care about them, even if he didn't feel like waiting them out. But no, Davis *wanted* to know, and plunge ahead like Prince with his *action* until he learned what drove Mira Ogilvy to visit Sloetown with twenty thousand dollars in her car that August night which was her last. But action had its risks, and he remembered again his father's words. *Wait, son.* He returned the envelope to the drawer and slammed it shut.

The coffee was ready and Davis examined the refrigerator. He found bacon and eggs to get breakfast started. The potatoes in the back had withered, but might do for hash browns. The milk didn't smell fresh, so he put it back. He discovered a few oranges in the crisper and a tin of biscuits in the freezer.

Then, on the counter, he noticed a light blinking on his answering machine. He depressed the message button. Gloria Orion's shaky voice came through the speaker: Would he come and meet for a drink later that afternoon? At the hotel? Then, with more confidence, *I know you'll be there, Baker. For me.* He didn't call back.

Davis got into the shower, taking a long time there, letting the hot water massage his neck as an image of Gloria Orion came to his mind. He saw her in the past, her eyes, her smile in the bloom of youth, hopeful, kind, even loving. Then the years had come and gone. Fortune had smiled on Gloria Orion, then frowned with money problems, diminished expectations, narrowing circumstances. Now she was hurting. He heard it in her voice on the machine. Would she find a way out? Maybe. Maybe in the arms of an unlicensed PI? And if that embrace came with a price, would he pay it? Could he? Clearly a deal with risk, he concluded, with that woman. But what real joy did anyone find? Real happiness unalloyed and complete? Pure and perfect, without cost? He weighed his chances. Finally, the hot water ran out in the shower. Then he dressed and assembled breakfast: scrambling the eggs, crisping the bacon, browning the biscuits, and charring the potatoes around the edges.

But his coffee was bitter.

* * *

Wilson picked up the phone when it rang in his office. It was Fortenberry in the forensics lab: "I'm supposed to leave early Detective Wilson, and go home. It's Saturday. I've got my kid's birthday party today and—"

"I don't care about your—"

"All right then, I don't care about your damn pearls! They can wait till Monday."

There was silence on the phone as Wilson collected himself.

"Sorry, bud."

Fortenberry took a deep breath. "Look, you just turned them in yesterday. The tests take time."

"I know. I know, but it's a homicide, the Ogilvy thing. Lieutenant Foster wants me on top of it."

"All right. All right. Jeez. 'Gimme another couple hours. Call back around one."

Wilson hung up.

* * *

Richard McDermott woke up Saturday and blinked hard, then rubbed his eyes as if trying to erase a vision. Dreams had troubled him all night: he was running through a blighted industrial landscape, past strange buildings and warehouses along a dreary waterfront. The sky was gray and freezing. Sleet lashed his face. His hands were cold and numb. Men were chasing him. He didn't know who they were, what they wanted. He didn't know where he was going—simply running hard, his heart pounding. He only knew he was in a foreign country, lost in a port where giant ships embarked in silence to cities across the sea. Maybe he could jump onto one of the ships, he remembered dreaming, and get away. They wouldn't find him there, whoever, whatever pursued him.

McDermott blinked again, and his head cleared. He was in his bedroom. After a few minutes, he made it out to the kitchen where he found orange juice in the refrigerator. He poured a glass and tasted it; then reached into a cabinet for the vodka, added a shot to the juice and drank deeply. Fear, anxiety, and desperation were upon him and he knew it. The police had questioned him about the murder, and he was likely to hear from them again. The loss of McDermott Center was only a matter of time. The money Gloria's husband had given away could be a way out, a solution, but the prospect of finding it receded each day. His empty hand opened and closed reflexively as if he was grasping a bundle of cash.

But *Mira*. That's what Cheryl said. She must have known the dead girl, but now didn't want to talk about her, or couldn't. And if she knew Mira—what about the money? Then McDermott remembered Cheryl's warm embrace, remembered the way his hand massaged the small of her back, the taste of her lips.

He had to get out, get moving. The house was too quiet, felt like a prison. It was Saturday, the weekend, when most of the world relaxes, but it seemed like years since he'd been able to relax, or rest at home. His office was the only place that made any sense, had any meaning. He would go there and think.

As McDermott's Lincoln moved through the city, he considered various streets, avenues, highways. Each one offered an alternative, some different way of making his life work out—if he would only take it. But as he passed by a multitude of intersections, it occurred to the lawyer that maybe he'd never pass this way again. His chances to take a different road, try something different, make things work out a new way . . . were fast disappearing. No, he

TWENTY GRAND

wouldn't come through here again, ever. With each mile a door closed. Events drew him forward. He wasn't sure how he got here, on this square in time, this place. He hadn't planned his life this way. And though this Saturday was bright and sunny, the world felt gray, as if it would never be otherwise.

He saw McDermott Center, twenty stories high, before he reached downtown. The big tower always made him feel better, to see it there commanding the skyline. A bright neon *M* stood on the roof. *M* for McDermott, he mused. And *M* for mortgage, *M* for money, *M* for Mira, even *M* for murder. A smile came to his lips.

He turned into the parking lot and noticed cars he didn't recognize. He stopped and got out, scanning the lot for the street people that annoyed him so, but everything was quiet. He looked up at the tower. Something didn't feel right.

McDermott approached the entrance. He jogged up the steps and reached for the door. He pulled, but it was locked tight. He pulled again, harder, with no luck. He glanced at his watch, barely eleven. The building was always open till noon on Saturday. He pulled again—the glass and aluminum doors made a loud clatter. He reached for his keys and tried them in the lock, no luck. He jammed the key in and turned harder, again no response. Then in the glass he saw himself and stopped. In that instant, he felt two dimensional, not quite whole, not a full man, merely an image that appeared in the glass.

He moved to the side . . . then he wasn't there at all!

McDermott grabbed the handle and shook it hard, making a terrible racket. Then he reached back and kicked the door. He turned around, fearful that someone would see him, but the street was empty. Again he stared at his reflection in the glass. He felt pity for the man there, as if he wanted to help him but couldn't.

Then inside the building, a man appeared, walking down a long hallway, coming toward him. McDermott didn't recognize him, then saw the man wore a security uniform. The guard came to the door and stood there.

"I need to get in," McDermott said loudly through the glass. He waved his hands. The guard was fat, his face the color of chalk. He shook his head. "'Need to get in!" the lawyer yelled.

Again the man shook his head. "Closed, sir."

"No, no, not closed, not till noon. My office is upstairs. I'm McDermott. My office —"

"Sorry sir," the guard said loudly. "Bank orders."

"Bank order?!"

"Foreclosure sir, on this property. That's all I know. We've secured the building."

"But I have a key," McDermott exclaimed. He held it up.

"Those don't work now," the man replied with a smirk. "Locks changed."

"Listen dammit! My office is on Twenty. I'm Richard McDermott. I've got to get in. Do you know who I—?"

"Come back Monday, buddy." Then the fat security guard turned away. He walked slowly down the hall and disappeared.

McDermott stood there on the sidewalk before the big glass doors. Again he saw his reflection. The image in the glass was smaller now, distorted. Again he looked up and down the block. He didn't want to be seen and, in fact, not a soul was watching him at all.

* * *

Karl Orion had a long night. He sweated and shivered with fever. Cancer and the powerful chemo drugs they'd given him made war throughout his body. He didn't know if the medicine would work. No one knew. Gloria and the hired nurse Suzy tried to comfort him, but sometimes he wished they would go away. He began to think there was little to be done. About three a.m., he finally drifted off to sleep. And then he awoke with light in the room, but felt confused. Did the nurse pull him from bed earlier that night? He seemed to remember a car ride, then a rush of people and a lot of movement, then he was still again. But his body ached. Karl Orion opened his eyes and looked around. Tubes and wires tethered his body to machines that blinked and whirred. He was in a hospital room. Now he wanted Gloria.

But the nurses had told her to go home. *We'll look after Karl today*, they said. *We'll get the fever down, treat the pain, get him stabilized. You go home and get some rest. You need to keep yourself strong. Stay hopeful. Pray.*

Gloria Orion turned the words over in her mind as she left the hospital that afternoon. She'd love a good nap, but when she arrived home, she poured a glass of wine, sat down at her kitchen table, and smoked. She didn't pray. Maybe they would stabilize

TWENTY GRAND

Karl; maybe he would come home soon. But she knew cancer didn't follow a steady, predictable path. Terrifying surprises and unexpected, fateful turns awaited. One never knew how it would go. She'd seen it before, with her uncle. Her husband might *not* come home.

Then she would be alone, the sole occupant of this home. She noticed the kitchen, the den, the formal dining room and the windows which gave a view to her garden and pool. Everything suddenly appeared to be a grainy snapshot that might fade away into nothing. The house *looked* like hers: the paint, the carpets, the antiques, the art displayed on the walls, but it always *felt* like her husband's. Karl bought it long before they married. She had simply moved in. Now, if Karl died, who would pay for it? She knew Orion Pallet was close to broke, and the man had no insurance. The hospital asked for coverage when they admitted him that morning. He mumbled something about forgetting his card. "Don't worry. I'll make it right," he said.

She sipped the wine, finished her cigarette. Somebody will come and take this place from me, she thought, like they will take Richard's building downtown.

Then it stung her like an ice pick. Mira Ogilvy. *That girl will pull me down into the grave with her. I can't run that factory alone. I'll die in Sloetown, as she did. And that money wasn't hers. It came from the settlement Karl received from the fire. He gave it to her— the sonofabitch gave it to her. And now the money is . . .*

Her mind reeled. Everything swirled around. *Maybe I'll go somewhere. Just stand up right now this minute, pack a bag and drive away. Disappear. Run. Go to the coast, or New York, or Chicago, and start over. Or maybe a small town far away where nobody knows me and nobody wants to. A place like that must exist somewhere, maybe out West.*

She imagined the empty plains stretching out before her, rolling away endlessly before the hood of the car under a comforting blue sky. She could drive on and on until she felt like stopping, until she was far away. That's all it would take, one irrevocable step in that direction, any direction, a single gesture, an act of will. Of that, she had plenty: will, determination, courage. Gloria Orion knew that. She'd pushed herself before. She could do it again. Movement—that was the answer. What did she have to lose, really? She performed a rapid calculation in her mind about her situation. It didn't add up. Nothing added up anymore. Maybe

Karl would never return from the hospital, and she would be left with the pallet factory. The smell of it came to her memory. The sound of it throbbed in her mind.

As she finished her drink, the phone rang. It was the hospital: *You better come back up here, Mrs. Orion. Now.*

* * *

Don Fortenberry sat as his desk in the forensics lab looking at the clock. *If Wilson doesn't call soon, I'm leaving. He can wait till Monday. I'm not getting paid overtime today. I don't care about his investigation, and truth be told, I don't really care who killed that woman. They found the girl's body in Sloetown? Well, what can you expect? What the hell was she doing up there anyway?*

Fortenberry looked at the small package sitting on his desk, the gay wrapping paper. It was a present for his daughter; today was her birthday. He imagined her smiling as she opened it at her party later that day. She was fourteen now. In a few years, she'd be driving. Fortenberry hoped she would never go driving in Sloetown.

The phone rang. He picked it up. It was Wilson.

"You got your positive on those pearls, Detective. It's the victim's blood on them."

"You sure?"

"No, I made it up, Officer. I don't have anything better to do on Saturday than examine blood-stained jewelry."

"All right all right. Relax. I'll take it from here."

Fortenberry hung up and went to a party.

* * *

McDermott walked away slowly from the locked doors of McDermott Center. It seemed to take forever to reach his car, as if maybe an hour, a year, or even a decade elapsed as he crossed the parking lot. He got into his Lincoln and sat there. Maybe for a minute, maybe an hour. He wasn't sure any longer. His eyes closed and it became Monday morning, and he saw the fat security guard again, letting him into his office on Twenty, where he entered and stood at the big window and enjoyed the splendid view of the towers nearby, the green trees of Sloetown beyond, and the

TWENTY GRAND

glittering river rolling by in the distance. He could reach out and touch it, make it his own. Then the security guard again, frowning, asking him to hurry up and get his things together—and move out.

His eyes opened. He wiped his face. Late afternoon surrounded him. He started his car and drove away, not sure when or how he would return. He felt exhausted as he drove through the city, hoping to get home and sleep all day and night. Surely everything would be different when he woke up Sunday. *Money will turn up. It always has. Gloria or that crooked investigator will find what Mira did with the cash. I can't help she's dead. The police are still hunting the killer, and she had pearls when they found her. So what? God, why did I let that stupid cop take those pearls from my desk? No telling where they came from, no telling where that creepy homeless man got them.* Then he heard the girl's name in his mind, interrupting his thoughts . . . *Mira.* There it was again . . . *Mira.* He wasn't sure where it came from, what it meant. But the voice that whispered the name belonged to Cheryl Lewis.

McDermott arrived in his neighborhood. But as his car turned onto the street where he lived, he saw police cars at the end of the block: one parked in his driveway, another in front of his house, their blue lights flashing.

They had come. To arrest him!

He slammed the brakes, stopping hard. They could see him. No, not yet! He instantly checked his mirror—no one behind him. He threw the car into reverse and backed down the street, rounded a corner, and moved away quickly, his heart beating in his chest.

He stepped on the gas as he cracked a window, listening intently for a siren, the sound of police cars rushing up behind him . . . but he only heard the wind. Then he realized he was doing sixty, and tapped the brakes. No need to draw attention, he thought, slowing. He found some back streets and got onto the highway, trying to be inconspicuous. He drove away from the city, not sure at all where he would go. He tried to focus on the road ahead, his hands turning white as he gripped the steering wheel, his eyes coal-black and empty.

* * *

Gloria Orion came slowly into her husband's room in the ICU, with a measured pace. Her face was unmoving behind dark glasses. She stood over the sick man in the bed, trying to feel sorry for him, sympathy, pity, something—anything. She failed.

"Gloria," he moaned. A machine at his beside blipped regularly, monitoring his heart.

"I'm here."

"Gloria."

"I'm here, Karl." She pushed her glasses back onto her head.

His eyes opened wider, but seemed focused on a faraway place. He raised a trembling hand and said, "That money, baby."

"I know. There's no insurance. Don't worry about it right now."

"That money—" His voice was weak, raspy.

"I know, Karl."

"It wasn't hers."

Her face twitched. "What did you say?"

"Mira."

"Karl?"

Orion leaned forward, his face sweating. "Paid her she Mira knew . . . the money all that insurance."

"Karl. What are you talking about?"

The sick man's feverish eyes burned. His words came rapidly: "Knew Mira her father knew the dead man paid them dead men money."

Gloria Orion grabbed her husband by the shoulders, jerking him up to her. "What money, Karl?! What happened —?"

"Mira was gonna tell dead men knew her father those men in the fire gone she knew and I paid that money—" Then he coughed violently, his eyes rolling deliriously.

"The money? You gave it to Mira. All right."

"She took it . . . the dead men . . . she knew," he panted, "every last penny."

"Dead men? What dead? Karl. What did Mira do?!"

But the sick man didn't hear. His head tossed, his eyes rolled. She let him go and he fell back into the pillows trailing wires and tubes behind him, saying, "The men Gloria dead keep it quiet money a deal Mira the men dead just from Sloetown."

"That was our money!"

"The police the whole thing, tell the cops the whole thing, the missing, the newspapers, the men in the fire . . . those payments—" She grabbed him again and his eyes bulged, seizing on her, as if he recognized his wife for the first time. "Oh God Gloria! I had to!"

Again she let him go and Orion fell back on the bed. His eyes twitched in his slack face. He stared at the ceiling, his breath short and labored. He was dying. He moaned, "Sloetown money dead men quiet Mira—"

"Karl. For God's sake, tell me! Karl!"

"Help . . . get . . . the nurse," he whispered, gasping for air. His eyes closed, his body convulsed as pink, bloody foam appeared at his mouth.

Gloria Orion slid the dark glasses back on her face. Then she smoothed her hair and left the room. As she closed the door behind her, she turned off the lights. She walked down the hallway where a nurse at the station asked her, "Your husband, ma'am? Is he doing all right?"

"Yes, Mr. Orion's fine. He's resting."

The nurse returned to her paperwork as Gloria Orion walked briskly through the clean, bright hospital.

AUSTIN McLELLAN

TEN

Cheryl Lewis was anxious sitting in church that morning. She had arrived late, and didn't like the eyes that fell on her as she worked her way through the crowded pews to find a seat. She was usually on time, but Lester hadn't come home until the last minute to take care of the baby. Where the hell was he all night? She was exhausted worrying about that boy. The sanctuary was hot, too. The air conditioner had broken down last year and the church didn't have enough money for repairs. Big fans, positioned in the rear of the sanctuary, blew warm air over the congregation with a steady hum. She tried to relax.

The voices of the choir rolled across the room like waves caressing her heart. She could feel the music, even though the singers these days were silver haired so the hymns didn't boom as they had in years past when the younger people sang. Lester should hear this, she thought. Attending service would help him. He used to enjoy church when he was little, but as he grew older—and after Michael disappeared—he stopped coming. Maybe teenagers were simply rebellious, she reflected, and hoped that God looked after young men too, even if they didn't come to His house. Maybe prayer would help. She bowed her head.

The music ended and the Pastor rose for the sermon. He was new to the church, a younger fellow the bishop sent down to breathe a little life into the aging Sloetown congregation. He was a good man and tried hard, Cheryl thought, as he spoke about "doin' right and gettin' right in your heart." She liked him okay, but would have preferred a more educated fellow.

She wondered where Richard McDermott attended college. He had never told her. Law school must take years of study she thought as the Pastor continued. Her fingertips touched her lips where McDermott kissed her a few nights ago, holding her under the stars in the parking lot of the Orion Pallet Factory. She felt his arms around her, and suddenly her skin felt different, as if it wasn't a part of her any longer. Where was he that morning? She didn't think Richard attended church anywhere. He never talked about anything like that. Maybe he was working on legal business.

"'Cause He knows when you ain't right in yo' heart," the Pastor shouted, his face gleaming with perspiration.

Cheryl Lewis looked out across the pews at the congregation. She knew most everyone there. She'd known them as long as she could remember. They were like parents to her, grandparents even, graceful old aunts and uncles. She didn't know how she was going to tell them. She didn't know how they'd take it. She wondered if they had come to rely on it too much over the years. They had memories too. And now it was over. Mira Ogilvy was dead.

The Pastor closed with the 23 Psalm. She liked that one better than the Lord's Prayer, which everyone knew so well they didn't put much feeling into it, just said it. And as he murmured "—He maketh me lie down in green pastures," and the people around her repeated the words, Cheryl Lewis heard it, felt it deep within, and remembered the green shade where her brother's Cadillac rested in Jackson Park. And when he concluded with "—dwell in the house of the Lord forever," she wondered for the millionth time if her elder brother would ever come home, or if he was gone forever.

The Pastor came to the end and everyone stood for the benediction. Then it was over, and Cheryl Lewis exhaled as if she'd been holding her breath. Voices rose as people made their greetings, sharing handshakes and laughter. The Pastor stepped down from the dais, moving among the congregation with smiles and embraces. Cheryl didn't want to speak to anyone but exchanged a few quick hugs with the ladies sitting beside her. Then she moved past them quickly and through the crowd to the classroom in the rear of the church where Sunday School began in thirty minutes. That would be enough time.

Each month Cheryl Lewis had come there. She couldn't

remember why they always met in church, except it felt like the right place. That morning, they slowly came into the little classroom. Danita Solomon entered, wearing a dress the color of ripe peaches. She was a proud woman who'd raised six children, but her son Derek never came home. Willie Houston crept in slowly, using her cane—she'd had a hip replaced last month. Her husband Cleo never came home either that day. Milton Ware came in too. He was always sunny and bright, flirting with the ladies even though he was past seventy. He joked around with everyone as if nothing bad ever happened to him, but his grandson was gone too. Then the others . . . they all came in that morning, as they had for years. No one ever said much about it. They knew the business. Cheryl Lewis knew too, and never explained when she laid the envelopes before them on those Sunday mornings after service. Sometimes they thanked her; sometimes they didn't, but it didn't matter. She knew what they felt because she too felt it every time she thought of the fire at Orion Pallet and her brother Michael. She only considered the question—*why her?* Why was Cheryl Lewis consigned to share the money with these people, strangers really, though she loved them as her own kin? Maybe because she was younger than most of them, and would be there as they aged and passed on. Maybe Mira Ogilvy trusted her because Cheryl also loved someone who never came home from the Orion Pallet factory that day.

But now the young woman didn't know what to say. Everyone sat around the little table but she didn't know how to tell them. She tried to recall the Pastor's words, seeking guidance there. She guessed she was *right in her heart* as he said, but that didn't help any. She could only whisper, "It's over."

Everyone looked at her in silence, their eyes wide and soft. She half expected them to burst out in anguish, anger, or grief. She felt everyone might blame her, now that the money was gone. Most of them, she knew, didn't have an old Cadillac to help with the memory, as she did. It seemed, sometimes, as if Cheryl Lewis was all they had.

"It's over and gone," she explained, summoning courage from somewhere. No one spoke. There was nothing to say, nothing to acknowledge. Everyone was quiet and peaceful in the Sunday school room as light poured in through the windows. The big fans hummed in the sanctuary.

"It's over and gone, and there won't be any more envelopes. For nobody. That girl . . . and the money . . . are gone." A tear came to her eye as she said it, knowing that together they had all come to the end of a long, strange road that started years ago when their loved ones disappeared and everyone forgot about them except Mira Ogilvy.

"We know honey," someone said quietly. "We know."

* * *

McDermott drove around the city all Saturday night. At one point, he felt he was driving in circles, but couldn't be sure. Finally, early Sunday morning, he turned his black Lincoln into Sloetown. The day was heating up already, even under the big shade trees in the old neighborhood. He slowed down and thought about Cheryl. She would be in church now, he thought, remembering the services she had told him about. He explored several nameless streets until he found the old chapel she had described, its wood painted a brilliant white. He heard singing from within. Cars lined the streets nearby. *They are still in there, attending services, or sitting in Sunday school, or having potluck dinner, or whatever they do. Maybe that's a good thing, but when the hell are they going to finish? When is Cheryl coming out?*

For a moment, McDermott considered parking the car, going into the sanctuary and finding a seat—but no. Earlier, at a convenience store, he'd grabbed a six-pack and started drinking the beers fast while they were still cold. The alcohol went to his head, and he guessed he smelled that way too, so, no, better not enter the church. Cheryl will come out soon, he thought, as he drove by.

He idled along the old streets, moving in and out of the sunlight and dappled shade from the trees overhead. He wondered why people lived here, in these old frame houses, their front yards run to dirt in many places. How did Sloetown get this way? There were plenty of other places to live. Why didn't the people leave? Money, he guessed. They didn't have any.

Then he realized he didn't have any money either. Richard McDermott, lawyer and landlord—bankrupt. He knew the newspaper always published Chapter 13 filings, and he visualized his name printed there in black and white. But he was more than bankrupt, he was broke. McDermott Center was gone. The bankers had seized it, and he didn't know when he'd get back inside, if ever.

They mentioned something about . . . maybe he could lease a little space from them. Maybe he could rent a small office, even a cubicle. Maybe he could work in a damn closet! It was a bitter image. He drained the beer from the can and threw it out the window where it made a tinkling sound on the pavement. He drove on.

A little boy chased a red ball across the street in front of him. He tapped the brakes.

"Damn kids," he muttered. The boy caught up with the ball, saw McDermott in the car, and flashed a big toothy smile. More kids ran into the street laughing, then as quickly disappeared. They don't care about anything, he reflected, driving by. McDermott turned a corner and saw them again in a grassy lot with the red ball, laughing in the sunshine. He sipped a beer and sneered at the vision, but it wouldn't go away: children playing in the warm sun, under the blue sky, laughing. He knew this was all they had—the red ball, a vacant lot—and it made him think of McDermott Center, his practice, his money, his reputation. They were all disappearing. In truth, maybe he had nothing more than these kids in Sloetown. 'Except they were laughing, enjoying life that Sunday morning.

But no, surely there was a way out. He'd find a way out. He'd do something, anything. Guts? Yeah, he had plenty. The lawyer opened another beer and took a long drink.

He turned another corner and recognized Vinson Street, with the empty diner and the weedy lot nearby. 'Too bad Mira Ogilvy ended up there, he thought. What a way to go. But now they wanted to arrest him! Why in the hell would he want that girl dead? He had no motive. The cops didn't know anything about her money, or did they? They didn't know he was in desperate financial straits, or did they? How much evidence did they actually need anyway, to arrest him? Criminal law wasn't his specialty, and he had no money to pay for a defense.

To hell with the police, he thought, driving away from Vinson Street. He turned another corner, then another, trying to find his way back to the church, but soon realized he was lost. He felt sweat dripping under his shirt, drank more beer to cool off. He passed by men on the sidewalk. They weren't children, and they stared at the black Lincoln with eyes that were old and hard. At the corner, McDermott searched for a street sign. No luck. He moved on, reaching for a cigarette as the confused streets grew narrower and narrower, as if they were going nowhere certain and would finally become nothing at all, only a dusty lot, an empty field, a dead end—like his life, he thought. Why was he even here? Why had things turned out like this? He felt as if he was a thousand miles from his office on the twentieth floor of McDermott Center. Would he ever get back there, he wondered, to the beautiful view from Twenty? He saw that view now. He shuddered with a hideous laugh.

Then, in an instant, he felt surrounded by . . . he stopped the car and looked around. Nothing, only the sunshine and a slight breeze that barely moved the leaves in the big oaks. He listened carefully . . . nothing, like a cemetery. Then he stepped on the gas and his vehicle hesitated. A spark of terror jolted him. Maybe this is what happened to Mira Ogilvy, what the end looked like—her car stalling and they were on her. Did she hear gunfire as the bullets entered her body? Does anyone? Did she look into the face of the killer and scream? Why the hell did she die? Why did the girl come to the old neighborhood anyway? Cheryl knew her. She mentioned her name. And why was *he* here now? Why, indeed, had God put Richard McDermott here on Earth at all, simply to end up on a deserted street in Sloetown?

He locked his doors. Where were the damn police now? He jammed the accelerator and the Lincoln surged forward. He felt better moving, the faster the better. The hot wind rushed in through the window, cooling the perspiration on his face.

He took a few turns, unsure of his location, unsure of everything, until he found the church again. A few people trickled out the front door; the services were concluding. *Cheryl will come out soon, she must.* He found a place to park along the curb and slumped into his seat, watching the congregation emerge from the church in their Sunday best. Everyone looked real nice, he thought, the men in suits and the ladies in dresses, as if today was a special occasion, a day that meant something to them. The faces of the men were serious but calm. A few ladies' hats bobbed in the crowd as children broke free from parents, glad to be outdoors.

An elderly gentleman approached from the church. He saw McDermott sitting in the glossy Lincoln. The lawyer sank lower into this seat, trying to disappear.

"Afternoon suh," the man said, leaning forward, peering into the car. He wore a black suit, a pressed white shirt, a green tie, even an old fashioned vest. It was hot that day, but the man looked entirely comfortable. His hair was white as snow as he repeated "Sir?"

"Yeah, afternoon," McDermott said.

The man looked him over, noticing the beer can between his legs. "You lookin' for something?"

"Uh, no. I mean, yes I am."

"In there?" the gentleman asked, glancing at the church. McDermott looked that way and nodded. "Somethin' I can help you with then?"

"No . . . no sir. I'll be all right. I'm lookin' for somebody. I just want to wait here."

The man scratched his snowy head. "Okay, all right . . . wait all you like. It's free parking. Wait all you want." He leaned away from the car, turning to go. McDermott swung his head back to the church, searching. *Where is Cheryl? Maybe she skipped church that morning.* The gentleman strolled down the sidewalk, humming a tune.

"Sir. Wait. Hey!" McDermott called out, leaning from the window. The man turned around. "Cheryl . . . Cheryl Lewis. You know her?"

The man turned, and the whites of his eyes expanded until they seemed as large as the bright sunshine that washed over them that afternoon.

"Miz Lewis?"

McDermott nodded, biting his lip. "Yes."

"Of course I know her, sir. 'Known her all my life. We all know Cheryl Lewis, and her brothers too."

"Brothers?" McDermott squinted into the sunlight where the man stood. It almost blinded him. "No, the Miss Lewis I know has one brother. His name is Lester, I think."

"No sir, two brothers. There's another. Michael Lewis." The man spoke in the present tense.

McDermott paused. "Michael, huh? Cheryl's brother? I thought he was—"

"Is that what you heard, sir? That Michael's lost? 'Not coming back? Or dead, even? Is that what you think?"

"No, no, I just meant—"

"People got memories around here, mistah. Real memories. I know. I been around Sloetown fo' a long time. 'Seems like just yesterday Michael Lewis . . . that boy had a red convertible . . . was driving up and down these streets with Cheryl. Him and those kids, they'd put the top down to catch the breeze." The man looked out across the neighborhood, as if he was staring across the ocean. "I know that's what a lot of people think, but no. Michael's gonna come back some day, sir. He'll come home. I know." Then he turned away and walked into the cool shade.

McDermott sensed a vague panic as the man disappeared, and he felt alone. He was on his own now. Most of the congregation had left the church. He looked around wildly for Cheryl, but the street was empty. He finished the beer. Then, as he reached for a cigarette, he saw her, standing on the sidewalk before the sanctuary. He sat up quickly, wiped his face, and got out of the car. He waved to her, and a smile came to the woman's face.

She walked quickly to him, looking up and down the block, wondering if anyone saw them, but most all the congregation had gone home. When she reached him, they embraced. Her rich perfume filled his head. She felt his perspiration through his shirt.

"How are you I wanted to see you . . . you've been in there all day," McDermott stammered.

"That's church," she whispered, averting her eyes, as if overcome with shyness.

He kissed her cheek. "Get in. It's hot." They drove away in the Lincoln with the windows rolled down and the air conditioner blasting away. McDermott didn't know where they were going. He didn't know what he was doing. He just drove, but he noticed the breeze coming into the car tousling her dress. Her skin looked like gold.

"I don't have much time," he said grimly. Cheryl noticed the smell of beer. Her eyes grew worried. She said,

"I don't either. I've got to get back home. My baby—"

"No, 'not much time . . . at all. I've got to do something." He spoke through his teeth. "McDermott Center . . . it's gone. It's over. Finished." The Lincoln made its way through Sloetown.

"Your office? Was it those bankers?" Her fingers twisted the handles of the purse in her lap. "No, Richard, they can't do it! It's yours. They have no right!"

McDermott drove on, his jaw tight, his eyes fixed somewhere

on the street before him; and in that moment he was not a sophisticated lawyer in the prominent building downtown, but merely another fearful, desperate man wandering around in a bad neighborhood, looking for something. The woman's mind raced, grasping for images of his fine office, the important meetings he attended, the way people looked at him, addressed him as *Sir*. But the images flitted by, faded, then disappeared. She couldn't find them. Still, the man was with her now. He had held her, kissed her, and waited for her outside the church all day. She reached across the car and touched his shoulder.

"You can do something! Don't they know who you are? Something will turn up. You'll find a way. There must be something—"

"Money," he said. The word appeared in the car with them, as if he had no control of what came from his mouth. "I've got to—"

"Money?"

"—find it, Cheryl. Orion gave it away, to that girl. It belongs to Gloria . . . and to me."

"You?"

He braked the car, stopping at an intersection, then turned on her, his eyes unanchored. Sweat glistened on his face. "I've got to find it—that money. Orion gave it to that dead girl."

Her mouth opened: "Mira?"

"That's right, dammit," he erupted. "Mira Ogilvy!" He stepped on the gas, the car lurched forward. He seemed made of stone.

"Orion? Ogilvy?"

But Richard McDermott was gone. He disappeared right in front of Cheryl Lewis when she heard the dead woman's name, as if someone killed a light switch and the man vanished into darkness. All he had been, all he had meant, all that he seemed to be and promise and hold out to her like something shiny and hopeful and proud died in that instant. His words lurched in her head: *money Mira gave it away belonged to Gloria.*

He turned again, his eyes wild and fierce, the blood rising to his face. "Mira Ogilvy. She had the money. Where is it now?!" Spit flew from his lips. "You know dammit. You said her name. You knew her! That money wasn't hers. What did she do—?"

Cheryl looked away, out the window of the car at the old neighborhood. It was late afternoon and shadows fell among the worn houses. She heard McDermott yelling but the sound made no sense. His words were like the barking of a stray dog far away.

"Yes," she finally said.

"What?"

"Yes, I knew Mira. She's gone now."

McDermott's face narrowed. "Somebody killed her, that's what the police think. 'Right here in Sloetown. But I don't care about that."

"Don't care!?"

"You heard me. I'm not worried about Mira. She's gone. I'm real sorry. But that money she had . . . it wasn't hers, see? She had no right to it," he said bitterly.

His words felt like acid. Cheryl Lewis remembered the money, yes. She knew it perfectly, thousands of dollars every month, and she remembered Mira waiting in her white car last Saturday night before her house, a night when it was too late to be out in Sloetown. Then the faces of her neighbors appeared before her, kind, wise faces she met in church every month.

McDermott glared at her, his mouth a black gash in his face. "You knew that woman, Cheryl. What happened? Why did Mira come here? To Sloetown? With that money? It wasn't hers. She had no right to it. It was fraudulent. I've got to get it back."

Cheryl Lewis covered her face, trying to hold off tears. His words *it wasn't hers . . . no right . . . fraudulent . . .* pounded against her heart like a metal rod against steel plate.

"What?" he demanded. "Why are you crying? Stop it."

"The money."

He looked at her, his face darkening.

"I knew her, sure I did. Mira. Yes, she came here to Sloetown with it, brought it here, came here with that money."

McDermott jerked the car to the curb and got out like an animal desperate to escape its cage. They were near Jackson Park. He stormed to the front of the vehicle, moving in spasms as if something electric was inside him. He slammed his hands against the hood of the Lincoln, making a terrific sound.

"What?" he shouted. "What happened to that money?" He came to the passenger door and yanked it open. He grabbed her wrist and dragged her from the car. "Tell me dammit!" His white fingers sank into her arm, holding her tight. His face was almost against hers.

Then right there on the sidewalk, a vision came to Cheryl Lewis, an image of Mira Ogilvy and her last moment in Sloetown, her last moment alive, as if they shared that moment, as if she knew right then who put the bullets in the young woman and watched her die. She saw it in McDermott's eyes.

"*You* killed her!" she screamed, tearing free of his grasp. "You—"

"No!"

"You and everybody like you that want the money!"

"Shut up." He swung at her, slapping her head with a glancing blow. She stumbled back, crying out.

"But you're never gonna find it!" she yelled, righting herself. "It's gone!" Then she turned and dashed across the street into Jackson Park.

McDermott stumbled after her, dizzy from the heat and the beer and the cigarettes.

"Cheryl!"

She ran into the green park, tears streaming down her face. She crossed the empty basketball court, then a grassy spot where the neighborhood children had left broken toys. The man followed, shouting.

"Stop! Wait!"

She came to a bench and collapsed there, exhausted. She turned to see McDermott as he came toward her, lurching across the basketball court, his face curdled in rage and despair.

"Cheryl, stop! Tell me where the . . . what did Mira . . . ?" He tripped over a toy in the grass and fell, cursing.

She picked herself up and lunged deeper into the park. She heard the man climb to his feet, yelling "That money!"

She ran past the old swing set flecked in bright paint and rust. She plunged into the shadows under the big trees. Twigs and leaves slapped at her face as she crashed through the underbrush. She heard McDermott shouting.

Then she stopped, panting quick and hard. Something large stood in front of her, blocking her way. Her brother's Cadillac.

There it rested, the red convertible parked beneath the vines and brush. She collapsed against the fender, breathing hard, her chest heaving against her dress. A few flowers had grown up around the old rotten tires. She heard the man coming. A broken beer bottle lay at her feet, among the flowers. She picked it up.

McDermott burst through the trees. His hair hung dark across his brow, his shirt fell loose from his trousers. Sweat covered his face, his body. He stopped, resting his hands on his knees, gasping for air.

"Cheryl," he sputtered.

She backed up, edging along the bumper of the old car, as if it protected her.

"Tell me," he said, breathing heavily. "That money . . . Mira had it . . . you know . . . I've got to —"

She didn't speak, but tears welled in her eyes as she remembered the man who kissed her, who held her tenderly under the moon that night in the parking lot of Orion Pallet, the man who touched her, who wanted to share the beautiful view from his office on the twentieth floor. That man stood before her now—but he wasn't truly there at all, not anymore. Her tears stopped. She gripped the broken bottle tighter.

"Mira . . . " he snarled, coming forward. "That money . . . it wasn't hers. I didn't kill that girl, but maybe she had it coming."

"She was my friend," Cheryl Lewis cried.

"Then tell me what she did with that money." McDermott saw the jagged bottle in her hand, then he stopped, his foot bumping something in the tall weeds. He reached down in the grass and picked up an old board, a splintered two by four. An iron smile appeared on his face.

"That's right, Mira had it coming. People who take money that don't belong to them—that's stealing." He crept toward Cheryl, brandishing the jagged board. The woman edged along the side of the car, keeping the man in her sights. She said,

"I don't know how Mira got the money."

"Uh-huh." He came closer. "But you know what she did with it. Maybe you were even in on it."

"No."

"Yes, by God." He slapped the wood against his open hand. It made a sick thud.

"You're never going to find out."

"Yes I am. Mira took that money from Karl Orion at the pallet factory. She came down here to Sloetown with it. You know what happened."

"No I don't."

"Yes you do." His eyes danced, the heavy board moving in his hand. He whacked it again in his palm. Cheryl felt her body slide to the end of the car, as if it wouldn't protect her any longer. Her feet groped for solid ground in the soft soil. Her knees trembled. The man moved forward, his eyes afire.

"And you *will* tell me, Cheryl."

"No."

"You'll tell me by God!" he spat, raising the jagged board, "because you love—"

She moved quickly, her arm shooting out like a bullet. The broken bottle crashed into McDermott's face.

Cheryl Lewis fell back, then ran, disappearing into the forest. She raced into thick woods, her arms flailing, pushing aside branches and limbs. It was dark, the green canopy overhead blocking the late afternoon sun. She ran and ran and ran—it felt like an hour. Then she slowed, hearing her lungs gasp for air, straining to hear the man following her. She collapsed on a dead log, the brush thick around her. Again she scanned the forest, searching for McDermott, her heart pounding . . . but there was only silence.

She rested on the log, catching her breath. She wondered if she'd injured Richard with that broken bottle. He was going to attack her and she was frightened, so she threw it and heard the man cry as he fell. She didn't plan it that way, but he was brandishing that jagged two by four, his eyes ablaze.

Her mind started to clear. What happened? Richard had been so kind. She remembered his fine hands, the beautiful suits he wore, the way he held her. What went wrong? It must be terrible, to own a place like McDermott Center, then lose it. She imagined a host of bankers, hunting him down with bloody knives. It made her sad. But something changed. She didn't understand it. Richard had been attentive, considerate, then became angry and desperate. Was it the money? Is that what money did to people? If so, she didn't want any, not like that.

The young woman stood up from the dead log. The park was silent all around as twilight settled over Sloetown. Darkness was coming. She walked through the forest toward the setting sun and after a while came to the last of the trees, the end of Jackson Park. She emerged from the woods onto a hill that overlooked the riverfront. She could see a great distance now. The sky was beyond measure, almost like the heaven the Pastor described. She watched the sun falling into the horizon far away, coloring the entire scene orange, red, and blue. She sighed. It was beautiful.

Then she brushed herself off and walked down the hillside toward the river.

* * *

Another hot day broiled the city, so Baker Davis drove toward Sloetown to look for a nice breeze. Surely the old neighborhood harbored a bit of cool shade, a place to relax. But he felt an urgency dwelled there also, a secret that brought no relief, put him on edge. Mira had brought that money to Sloetown. The twenty grand he found in her car was an outlier, made no sense.

Yet that afternoon, Baker Davis found no breeze as he drove past the tired streets, the fading houses. The day remained humid and still, yielding nothing but the memory of a dead girl on Vinson Street, and her corpse, pale as marble except where the blood had dried black. He left Sloetown, moving toward the riverfront where he knew it would be cooler. Perhaps a fresh scene might clear his head as he wondered, *Where does it end? How will it end? Maybe this twenty K leads to the rest of the money*—*Karl and Gloria Orion's desire, and McDermott's. The cops want it too after I laid that tip on Lt. Foster about Mira having the cash in Sloetown. They all want something bad. Maybe that's why they are no closer to finding it, finding what they want.*

He came to the river, where a parking lot on a hill gave a nice view. He stopped the car and got out. All around, the land and the river itself rolled away for miles in every direction. The riverfront was often crowded, but only a few people were visiting today. The sun sank toward the far horizon, its withdrawing light coloring the immense view in orange and red. And he felt a breeze!

He locked his car and walked down a long slope to the river below. It seemed like a mile away. At the shoreline a few boats were tied to cottonwood trees, their roots drinking in the moist soil. A worn path meandered along the water's edge where a few joggers and a few winos moved by. The wide river before him was huge, overwhelming, as if it was an artery for the entire continent. He saw a giant barge, the length of a city block, laboring upstream in the channel, its diesel engines roaring astern as it pushed foam before its bow, moving south. As he watched the vessel churn forward, it appeared to stand still in the water, making no progress. And it occurred then to Baker Davis that he was doing the same:

fighting upstream, banging his head against something immovable, against a secret, against a hidden story that was powerful, deep, below the surface, and might pull a man under like a dangerous undertow. Pushing, pushing, pushing—like Gloria and McDermott and the old man. Like the police.

The orange sky was melting into red and violet. Behind him, in the darkening east, the first stars appeared. As he stood beside the water, another great barge heaved into view from the north, rounding an island in the river a few miles up. This one moved downstream with the current, coming fast, making good time, its progress apparent. Davis waited, enjoying the breezes crossing the water. In a minute, the barge arrived at a point in the channel across from the riverbank where he stood. It was still hundreds of feet away, but the spray it kicked up reached his face. It was cool and refreshing. Strangely, the big vessel made little sound, as if its engines refused to strain. The investigator watched it pass by. It moved gracefully through the water; and he wondered if that was the way for him, if that was the right thing to do with Gloria, McDermott, the old man, even the cops. The dead girl and her money too. Find the current and stay there. Shift the engines into neutral and let something bigger be that way. And go with it, be a part of it—not separate, not apart. He watched the barge move away downstream silently, and felt a silence caressing his mind. Then it disappeared around a sandbar covered by willows, making its way toward the ocean hundreds of miles away.

 Davis walked along the dirt path, enjoying the view of the land as it sloped down to the water's edge. In the distance, green hills overlooked the riverfront. The violet dusk was turning blue as lights on the far shore winked on. More stars dotted the sky now. He realized it was almost dark and time to go when he saw movement in the trees that grew along the hilltops—a shape in yellow or white, he couldn't tell. He peered into the twilight. The shape was moving, emerging from the trees and the hills. He looked again. A figure, a person. He eased forward, curious about anyone who would be here, like him, at this hour. Maybe a tourist without a map. Then he saw . . . a woman in a yellow dress, picking her way carefully down the slopes toward the riverbank. Her steps were timid, as if she wore bad shoes, was barefoot, or lost.

 Davis went forward. He wasn't sure exactly why. Then the woman saw him, stopped, and in a moment resumed her hesitant steps. She was coming down to the water. The riverfront was empty, but they moved toward each other, compelled to approach, two people alone in the waning light. She reached the little path where Davis walked along the water's edge. They came closer. Then, in an instant, Davis recognized her—the waitress from Best Diner. Her eyes were anxious.

"You!" she exclaimed. Her voice was small against the sound of the river flowing beside them. "I saw you before . . . in the restaurant."

Davis managed a smile. "Uh . . . yes. Nice to see you again." He noticed the woman's shoes were dirty, her dress wrinkled. He said, "I'm Baker . . . Baker Davis."

"Yes, I remember you, and your friend, and—"

"—the pictures we looked at?"

"Yes." Her voice lowered. "Yes, I remember."

They stood there a moment as the water flowed past. Davis saw the woman's face glowing with perspiration, her hair loose. Tiny leaves and bits of grass clung to her yellow dress. Her breath was heavy, labored.

"Are you all right?" he asked.

"Oh yes, I just—well, I wasn't expecting to come down here." She smiled, catching her breath and smoothing a strand of hair that had fallen across her face. "Uh . . . my car stopped . . . back there." They looked up toward the hillside overlooking the riverfront.

"Ah. Well, if you need a hand—"

"No!"

The urgency in her voice surprised him. "Okay. No problem."

"No, sorry. I mean it won't start. I know that car won't start. There's no helping it."

"Oh. That's tough," Davis said, and stopped. The woman didn't seem to be going anywhere. "You got somebody coming to get you? 'A way to get home?"

Cheryl Lewis looked up and down the riverfront. Night had arrived. "I don't know. I'm not even sure how I got here."

He sensed her confusion. "Well, my car's right back up there . . . if you need a lift or anything."

She examined Davis carefully, watching his eyes that were still and quiet; then she remembered McDermott, his eyes burning with rage. She heard him scream again as the bottle smashed into his face, saw him go down in the grass, the heavy two by four lying beside him. But this Baker fellow, whoever he was, seemed calm, even relaxed. And no, nobody was coming to get her. She didn't know how she would get back home. She said,

"I don't know."

"All right." Davis shifted his feet and turned away. It was getting dark.

"Well, maybe . . . if you don't mind. I don't live far away."

"I don't mind. I was leaving anyway."

They turned and walked on the little path along the riverbank in the night. Downriver, another barge rounded the sand bar and came into view. They didn't talk much. She was nervous, didn't know what to think of this man, who he was, what he was doing here on the river, why he offered a ride. But he didn't look dangerous. He wasn't in a hurry. Maybe he was simply nice. She was glad he didn't talk much. The breeze felt good coming across the water. She told him her name.

They got back to the hill and Davis's Buick. They turned and surveyed the entire riverfront. Stars filled the sky now, shining on the gray river that flowed in the dark land. Beyond, lights from villages on the far shore twinkled on the horizon.

"I'm just over in Sloetown. Do you know where—?" she said as they got into his old Buick.

"Sure."

They made a little small talk as Davis left the riverfront, guiding his car toward the old neighborhood. But he noticed an edge to her voice, as if something held her back, troubling her. Between her words, her breath was labored, and he remembered the big barge moving slowly upstream, struggling, pushing. He stayed quiet and drove on. She grew silent, but still fidgeted, revealing agitation beneath the surface. Finally, she said,

"The other day . . . in the restaurant."

"Yeah, I was there. You left."

"Yes. 'Sorry about that."

"Maybe I said something?"

"No. I had to go." She was quite for a moment. "You remember those photographs, the ones you showed me?"

Davis nodded. "They're in the glove box if you want to see them."

It startled her and she froze. Her face grew hard. Then, in a minute, her hand moved slowly toward the glove box. She opened it and withdrew the old pictures, unfolding them on her lap. She stared at the images for a long time. Davis kept still, remembering what she said in the diner, about the fire at Orion Pallet and her brother who never came home that day. He listened for grief, for the inevitable tears. But her face was like stone as her eyes drank in the image of the burning factory. Then she touched the picture of the grand party, where Mira stood embraced by her father and Karl Orion, everyone smiling in elegant formal wear. Davis kept quiet, remembering the barge he saw moving downstream in the river, with the current, without effort.

"That girl—" Cheryl whispered.

Again Davis wanted to speak, wanted to draw her out. He recalled the words Prince said that day as they left the restaurant . . . *she knew her.* He gripped the steering wheel as they turned from the highway into the dark streets of the old neighborhood.

"Mira." she said. Then Davis heard a sob. A single tear fell from her eye. It dropped onto the photograph.

"You knew her," he said.

"My house is a few blocks over. Turn right." She folded up the news clipping, turning away to look out the window. "Yes. Mira's the one who got killed. She used to come in her white car and wait, every month. I don't know how she got it, but it always helped us. With our memories, you know? I never even knew her last name."

"Mira came . . . for you?"

Cheryl Lewis looked at him, her eyes moist, steady. "Yes. For me. For us. But she won't be coming anymore. Here's my street. Turn left."

Davis turned onto the block as she pointed at the bungalow. He stopped before her house as she opened the door and forced a smile.

"You know, Mr. Baker . . . twenty thousand dollars is a lot of money in Sloetown." She got out of the car, then walked briskly up to the porch and called back: "Thanks for the ride."

Davis watched her yellow dress disappear into the house. He drove away, his mind burning. *I found it! The money isn't missing. It never was. Mira brought it here. She brought that money to Cheryl Lewis. Those women knew about it all the time.* An image appeared in his mind like a dream, of Mira Ogilvy driving to Sloetown from her nice home in the Palatine, with all that cash in her car. Then it hit him: the insanity of Gloria Orion's desperate wish. She would never get the money back because it was gone. McDermott wouldn't find it either, nor the old man. It was changed now. It had woven its way like a bitter stream through the city, finally trickling out and disappearing in a vacant, grassy lot in the ghetto. But along the way, the payments had watered something, kept it alive, kept it going. Baker Davis wasn't sure what exactly, but that money found its way to Cheryl Lewis, found a way back to Sloetown.

Except for the last installment which sat in his kitchen drawer.

* * *

It was salty . . . salty and warm. McDermott licked his lips. Wetness covered his mouth and face. He wiped at it. Blood.

He felt the hard ground beneath him. It was night and his head ached. He sat up, his head pounding even more. He wanted to lie back down in the grass, and rest, but his eyes began to clear. He noticed a thick board lying in the grass beside him, and nearby, an old car, wreathed in vines. Broken glass covered his clothing. Then he remembered—Cheryl. That bottle knocked him out. He wiped his sleeve across his face, smearing it with sweat and blood and grass.

Slowly, McDermott got to his knees, then stood up. In the darkness, he scanned the trees in the empty park, but could only make out shadows among the mingled shades of black and gray. Someone might be there. He thought of the woman again. Where did she go? He wasn't going to hurt her. He just wanted to know about that money. *She knows about it. She doesn't need it. It's not hers.*

But she was gone. He wanted to call her name—Cheryl! But if he cried out, he might give himself away to . . . to whoever might be in Jackson Park in the middle of the night.

"To hell with her," he muttered, as he stumbled away from the old car. And in the same instant, he missed her, wished she was there to hold him for moment. His head ached, but he could feel the woman's arms around him.

McDermott came to the end of the green park and saw his Lincoln across the street under a streetlamp. He stopped and looked around. As he peered up and down the block, a vague, uneasy feeling gripped him that he wasn't alone. The lamp illuminated only a small area, and beyond the light . . . all was blackness. Yet a breeze had come up with the evening, rustling the trees and bushes, stirring the darkness. McDermott looked into the night again. He felt very alone, as if he was the only man in Sloetown, even in the entire city.

The lawyer made his feet move toward the car across the street. It seemed miles away. He tried to move quicker, but felt buried in sand. Then voices. Men were speaking. He wasn't sure what. He crossed the pavement until he reached a small pool of light under the streetlamp. And there Richard McDermott stood, alone, as if he lay on an examination table. Again he stared into the darkness, trying to make sense of the dim figures moving in the night. He heard voices murmuring in his ears. He tasted salty blood trickling from his nose. If he could only make it to his car—and get inside!

He reached the Lincoln, his sweaty hands pawing at the door, trying to get the damn thing open. He jammed a fist into his pocket, yanked out his keys, unlocked the door. He flung it open and threw himself inside, slamming the door behind him while his heart pounded and his breath steamed the windshield. He lay back in the seat for a moment, resting. He rolled down the window for a little air and closed his eyes. He listened for voices outside, but a different sound came to him now. Music. The notes of a piano floated through the old, tired streets like magic, like a song he had never heard before yet couldn't resist. It was a sad tune, deep in the minor chords, a blues, a rag, a dirge for . . . for whom for what he couldn't tell, but it seemed to knell an ending, as if nothing would be the same again. Then it disappeared. He heard a dog bark in the distance, but that was all. He stared into the darkness outside the car. Nothing. McDermott wondered if his time was up, if he had come to the end of the road.

He closed his eyes, and the music returned. But this time a horn joined in—a clarinet a saxophone a French horn—he couldn't be sure. The notes reached deeper inside him, touching a secret place he had wanted to see for the longest time, for years: a feeling a memory of something good and shiny and noble that he had known once long ago, then misplaced and couldn't recapture. He remembered his wife and family, his success, the beautiful view from his office. A faint smile came to his face. He wanted to linger there, and rest, but the harder he tried to remember, to imagine it .

.. the more it receded.

McDermott opened his eyes, sat upright, and stared outside. Quiet again. The voices, the music were silent, but a greater darkness surrounded him now, settling down in the old neighborhood. He reached into the glove box and felt inside—his gun. He withdrew it, taking it in his hand and feeling its heft. He jiggled the clip loose. It was full. It had been months since he'd fired it but he remembered. *Maybe this gun is a way out. Maybe this is the answer. Maybe this will pry the secret loose from Sloetown.*

His skin crawled . . . something touched him. Eyes were on him, watching him move, watching him think. No, he was alone. There was nothing. His hand gripped the weapon tightly. Then he looked outside. The darkness took shape. The shadows coalesced. Three men appeared in the emptiness and stood before the car.

McDermott's feet were outside on the pavement before he could think. His fear turned to fury. The dark shapes backed away as he showed the gun.

"Wait! Hold up!" the men cried.

"Shut up," the lawyer demanded.

"Hold on man. We don't want nothin'!"

"You! You're that Lewis kid. Cheryl's brother." McDermott brandished the weapon.

Lester Lewis backed up and raised his hands. "No! I don't know her."

"Liar! I saw you. You're her brother, damn you." McDermott stepped toward the youth. "And you know too."

"We don't know nothing!" the other youths cried. They saw the gun. Their eyes grew wide.

McDermott threw them a wild, hateful look. His eyes fixed on Lester Lewis. "You know, boy. You know about that white lady coming up here."

"No white lady. I don't know nothing 'bout that."

"You know, and you're gonna tell me." Spit flew from his mouth. He approached the young man, raising the pistol. "That white lady was coming up here. She brought that money. Cheryl knows about it. You know about it." Chaos raged in McDermott's face, his mouth was a snarl, his eyes black. The men stood in the dark humid night, breathing heavily. They were frozen, couldn't run. McDermott held the revolver heavy and grim beneath the putrid light of the streetlamp overhead.

"Now what the hell did she do with that money?" he leveled the gun at the young man's face. But Lester Lewis's eyes were quiet with something that was fear and not fear either, as if he was fully prepared to meet death. He stood perfectly still.

The lawyer trembled. He screamed, "Tell me boy!"

* * *

Baker Davis left the Lewis house. He drove through Sloetown thinking about Mira Ogilvy, noticing the bungalows that needed paint, the empty lots, the abandoned cars, the litter along the curbs. But the old neighborhood wasn't entirely like this, he knew. The next block over included older homes tended with care and love, tidy and gray like neat mice. But still Cheryl was right: twenty thousand dollars was a lot of money around here.

He passed a church painted brilliant white, its lawn thick and green and edged sharply along the sidewalk. Flowerbeds, cleanly weeded, led up to the front door. A sign out front displayed the hours for services. A spotlight shined on it all night long.

He made another turn, coming onto a street darker and more forlorn. He was near Jackson Park. He smelled the river. Then, ahead of him at the end of the block, he saw figures in the road, standing under a streetlamp near a big black car. He slowed, peering into the darkness. *Four men, maybe. This isn't my neighborhood. I don't need this. It's late. Maybe I can back up and turn around.*

Then he noticed one man among them, a white man. He was shouting, waving his arms at the others. It didn't look right. Davis edged forward. The little group came into focus. He could see now. It was his landlord! He pulled to the curb, stopped and got out. Slowly he approached the light where the men stood. He shouted,

"McDermott!" The men near the black Lincoln looked around, turning toward the investigator as he appeared in the light under the streetlamp. No one moved.

"You!" McDermott barked. "Davis!"

"Put the gun away."

"Mind your own business."

"This is my business."

"No it's not. These kids know what happened to Mira, what happened to the money." He waved the gun at Lester Lewis. "*That* boy. His sister knows about it. And *he* knows about it."

"No he doesn't. Now put the heat away."

"Shut up. Or you'll get some." He brandished the gun at Davis, his voice desperate. Then he swung around, approaching Lester Lewis, raising the weapon.

"Now you gonna tell me boy . . . what you know about that money . . . what that white lady did with it here. In Sloetown."

"I don't know nuthin!"

"Dammit, why'd she come here?!"

"Nuthin!"

McDermott whipped his arm, cracking the pistol against the youth's head. He fell to the pavement, clutching the side of his face, blood seeping through his fingers. The lawyer stood over him. He raised the gun.

"Now you got about two seconds to say what you know about that money—" His eyes were sunken and gray, his mouth a black scar across his face as he held the gun over Lester Lewis.

"Talk!" he shrieked.

Headlights exploded on them—two cars coming fast down the block. The police.

The young men scattered, their tennis shoes pounding the asphalt. Lester Lewis climbed to his feet and ran. McDermott jumped into his car and sped away into the night, gravel spinning out beneath the tires. The cops hit the sirens as their headlights blasted the street. One car roared to a halt where Davis stood, now alone. A wiry, red-haired cop jumped out, unholstering his weapon. Wilson. Davis remembered him. The other squad car flew by in hot pursuit of the black Lincoln.

"What the hell?!" Wilson cried, looking around wildly. He stared into the night, toward Jackson Park, but everyone was gone. He turned to Davis, his eyes on fire. Then a woman in civilian clothes exited the car—Lt. Foster, her eyes grim but still.

"You just missed the party," Davis said.

The Lieutenant came forward heavily. "I thought I told you we didn't need any help, Mr. Davis."

"I wasn't invited to this."

"But here you are," Wilson sneered, "right in the middle of everything."

Lt. Foster kneeled down and examined Lester Lewis's blood on the pavement. She glanced around at the empty street, frowning. Wilson scanned the park, searching. "Was that

McDermott who ran out of here? With the gun?"

"That's your man Lieutenant. Sorry I couldn't get him to stick around."

"He won't get far," Wilson said. They stood under the watery light from the balky streetlamp. The police sirens whined through the old neighborhood as Davis remembered the words from Mira Ogilvy's letter: the police, *heavy-handed and insensitive.*

Pop pop.

Gunfire. They froze, listening to the darkness. Then again . . . *pop pop.*

"That's not ours," the Lieutenant said, "It's McDermott." She turned for the car, giving Davis a ferocious look. He knew what it meant; he didn't move. Wilson jumped in behind the wheel. They tore away down the street in the direction of the shooting.

Davis watched them go. It was almost midnight as he stood in the street, alone. Everyone had left. McDermott had run away. Lester Lewis and his friends had escaped into the park, to their houses. Karl Orion had bolted from the junkyard. Rico ran into the darkness. Even the police had come, then gone. Mira Ogilvy too. The investigator remained.

At that moment a breeze broke through the moist night air, coming up from the river, stirring the heavy branches of the trees overhead. It bore the fragrance of ten thousand miles of streams and backwaters down into the street where Baker Davis stood that night. He sensed plains and mountains and swamps in the gentle, warm wind—and something else he didn't recognize, strange notes foreign and confused. He breathed deeply, trying to make sense of it all. Then, before his eyes, figures appeared in the shadowy park. He rubbed his eyes, his face damp. Black and shapeless, the images formed—then disappeared. They flitted by in the darkness among the trees, ghosts or living men, he couldn't tell. But he knew it was their time. Sloetown was their place. They had nothing but owned it all. They knew nothing but understood it all. The past was theirs and even the present, yet they had no future. They knew about Mira Ogilvy, her last words, her last thoughts, and they knew about the money. Baker Davis squinted in the darkness. Maybe they knew. Maybe they could speak! But the harder he tried to see them against the dark canvas of the old park and the worn out streets . . . the more they eluded him.

Davis got in his car and drove toward the gunfire. He

TWENTY GRAND

followed the sirens, not sure why, nor what he would find there. The sound made him sick to his stomach. His damp shirt stuck to his chest but his hands were cold against the steering wheel. Yes, fear. He recognized it and it carried him forward, even though he wanted to stop, turn around, go home, or run away. *Maybe I should leave it to the cops. They can handle it. If they want McDermott, they can have him. The Lieutenant—she doesn't need my help. That's what she said.*

He drove on. Dull pops echoed in the night. *McDermott. What the hell is going on in his head? What is he thinking? How does he know about Cheryl Lewis and the money? What does he know about Mira? Maybe he did kill her. Maybe he's come to the end of his rope, or the end of something, a final place created by his own ambition and desire and desperation. I'll go there too, if I have to.*

* * *

McDermott crouched low in the tall grass behind the brick wall of the old, white-washed diner. Sweat soaked his shirt, his breath came short and fast. He had jumped from his Lincoln and run up behind the diner when the police blocked Vinson Street, cornering him. He raced into the weed-choked lot, turning to fire upon them. They took cover behind their cars and screamed, "Put the weapon down! Put the weapon down now!"

McDermott looked around in panic. Everywhere was darkness. Across the street, the police crouched behind their vehicle. He squeezed off a round. *Pop.* Another squad car roared up, screeching to a halt, blue lights flashing. He saw a white cop jump out, then a black woman in civilian clothes. He turned, scanning the vacant lot. Behind him a rusty chain link fence guarded the rear of the property, but grass stood waist high all around. He gripped the revolver tighter. Overhead, the great old trees blocked out the stars and shrouded everything in gloom. He looked at the rusty fence again, noticing an empty space, a gap torn apart and never repaired. He squinted in the night. Yes, it was a gap, an opening . . . if he could make it through there, he could disappear into the thick brush and trees behind it. He could get away. Escape. Freedom.

"Put the weapon down McDermott!" a cop yelled.

He leaned out from the edge of the brick wall, peering through the grass at the police. They knew his location, his hiding place. He saw a cop run to the side. They were trying to outflank him! He gripped the pistol tighter, but the gun felt heavy in his hand, as if it were no longer protecting him, but had become a burden, a great weight around his mind and heart. But he had a couple of rounds left.

It will stop them. Let 'em get a taste of this. No, no—that's no good. But I can't give up, can't be arrested. They saw me with those kids back there. 'Saw me whack that boy. No, they can't take me in. I can't go to jail. They can't put me in there.

"Throw the gun down. There's no way out!" the cops screamed, but the lawyer didn't hear them. Their voices were distant and obscure, as if they were farther and farther away, receding into the night. He couldn't see them now. A memory seized his mind: Gloria telling him Mira Ogilvy was dead. She had all Karl's money, and they would get it back. Somehow.

McDermott stroked the steel gun. It was still warm from the shots he fired, but it was no comfort now. He looked at the chain link fence behind him, at the dark empty space there. Could he make it? He'd have to cross about forty yards to reach it. Running. Would they even see him in the tall grass? In the darkness? Maybe. Maybe not. Yes, he could make it!

He huddled low behind the old diner, leaning close against the brick wall. The white bricks were cool and felt good pressing against his damp shirt. Sweat dripped from his forehead into his eyes. He crouched lower, hoping maybe the cops wouldn't find him, wouldn't see him, might give up and go away and he could go home. That's all he wanted now, all he could think of—home. McDermott Center was gone. He'd never see his office again, never look out from the twentieth floor at the beautiful horizon stretched out below him for miles and miles, all the way to the river. He would never . . .

A twitch in the corner of his eye—movement in the rear, to the side, in the dark. That cop had flanked him, was now approaching, coming through the trees nearby! McDermott leaned out from the wall, peering around the corner at the men in the street. Another car had come up, an old Buick. Nowhere to go.

"McDermott!" he heard again. The voice came from . . . he couldn't tell. Then another sound, a man running in the grass, toward him.

The lawyer burst from behind the old diner. He exploded into the tall weeds, running away from the police, lurching across the grassy field in the darkness, heading to the rear of the vacant lot.

"McDermott! Stop!"

He crashed headlong through the weeds, stumbling, catching himself. He saw the fence in the distance, the empty gap coming closer. Yes, an opening! He was almost there. He could see it now. Escape. Freedom. If he could reach it!

"Stop! Now!"

They were gaining on him. His breath pounded in his chest. He'd never make it, never get to the fence. Right behind him!

McDermott turned and lifted the gun toward the street, toward the cops. He felt the trigger.

Pop. Pop.

The grass seemed very tall . . . grass all around him, dry and green. It made a rustling sound. He reached and grabbed a handful, just to hold on. Then music came to his ear, a melody beautiful and strange. But he liked it. It was soothing, like Cheryl's voice. And he heard the voice saying his name softly, "Richard," and he felt the woman's arms around him, and the fragrance she wore. And he saw the splendid view once again from Twenty, the glittering skyscrapers nearby, then in the distance Sloetown verdant and still, and finally the sunlit river on the horizon. 'Always there, since he was a boy. Yes, it was a great view from Twenty, from his office. *Big man on top,* that's what Dad used to say.

* * *

"It's about the same place, Lieutenant," Wilson said. He holstered his weapon.

"I know it," she replied.

"About the same place as we found that girl," he said.

"With her pearls," the other cop said, as if he were making a joke.

The Lieutenant frowned hard at the cop and he looked away. They stood in the vacant lot in the darkness. The lawyer lay in his black clothes before them in the tall grass. His eyes were fixed on some point he'd never see. His arm reached out along the ground, as if it were trying to reach something he'd never attain. Near his hand, in the weeds, the gun caught the moonlight.

Baker Davis came up, making his way to them across the

empty lot. He saw McDermott. He'd seen it all.

"It's no good," the Lieutenant said, looking at the body.

"No, Lieutenant," Davis said. "He turned on you."

"Who asked you?" Wilson remarked.

The Lieutenant shook her head. "It's no good, Mr. Davis. The man was here. In Sloetown. He knew that girl. He understood what was going on."

"And he was a murder suspect," Wilson added. "I'll take his gun to ballistics."

The Lieutenant kneeled beside the body in the grass. It took her a few moments. "That Orion woman is his sister, right. His next of kin?"

"I'll take care of it, Lieutenant," Wilson answered.

She stared at McDermott's cloudy eyes. "This one came a long way . . . to get here." She looked around the vacant lot. She saw the fence in the distance, noticed the gap in the chain link, about ten yards away. "And he almost made it."

"Why did he run?" one of the cops said. "Damn fool."

She stood up. "It's no good. Now we've got two dead; two dead and no answers." She looked at McDermott's body, then to Davis. "Those kids back there. What did he want with them?"

"I don't know."

"You're lying," Wilson said.

"Did McDermott know them?"

"I doubt it, Lieutenant," Davis said. "They were only neighborhood kids."

Wilson smirked. "This detective never knows anything, but he's always around."

"Well, Mr. Davis?" the Lieutenant asked. "What about it? You were standing there with those kids, with this guy." She nodded at the corpse.

"Is there a law against standing in the street?" And as soon as Davis said it, he wished he hadn't.

The Lieutenant approached him. "I told you before this is none of your business, Mr. Davis. I told you to stay clear."

"I'm doing my best, Lieutenant."

"Then tell me what McDermott was doing back there," she demanded.

"I don't know."

"What did he want? Why he was talking to those kids?"

Davis wanted to tell her, wanted to tell her about the money Mira Ogilvy brought to Sloetown, the money the dead man in the grass had sought, but Mira's words echoed in his brain: *the police, heavy-handed and insensitive.* And he remembered the dead girl's last installment, all that money, in his kitchen drawer. He kept silent.

The Lieutenant nodded at McDermott's body. "What was this man doing in Sloetown?"

"What the hell are *you* doing here?" Wilson added.

The Lieutenant's face was hard, angry, her eyes burning. "Are you hard of hearing, Mr. Davis?"

"He's hard of thinking." Wilson said.

"I just can't help you Lieutenant."

"Take him in," she blurted. "He can think it over in detention."

"Come with me asshole." Wilson grabbed the investigator by the arm. He didn't resist. The policeman jerked his other arm back, then slung cuffs on him. In a moment, Davis was in the back of a squad car moving through Sloetown again.

* * *

It was very late, but Lester Lewis felt good to be home now. He stood in his bathroom examining his face in the mirror, dabbing the cut on his head with a towel. The blood had dried. It would heal, might even leave a scar. That would be cool. But right now, it still hurt. Damn that crazy white dude, he thought as he looked in the mirror at the cut the pistol made when it slammed against his head. That's when the cops showed up, the man ran away, and the police chased him. His friends had scattered into Jackson Park, and he followed them. Soon he heard gunfire in the darkness, but that wasn't uncommon late at night in Sloetown.

Lester didn't want Cheryl to see his wound. He didn't want to tell her what happened, so he got into bed, turned off the lights, and pulled the quilt over his head. He wondered if the police ever caught that man with the gun.

AUSTIN McLELLAN

ELEVEN

The next morning, Cheryl Lewis stood in the doorway of her brother's room. She said, "Lester."

"Dude's crazy," he mumbled, tossing in his bed.

"What? Get up."

"That white dude's crazy."

She frowned. "Don't talk like that. C'mon now. I've got to go to work. It's Monday morning."

"What time is it?" He moved again under the quilt.

"Time to get up."

"I'm tired."

"Well, you wouldn't be tired if you'd get home at a decent hour." She turned and went into the kitchen.

"That man is crazy, Cheryl. He had a gun."

She came back into the bedroom. "What *gun*? What are you talking about?"

"I'm tellin' you. That friend of yours, that white dude, he had a gun last night."

"Richard?" A line plunged across Cheryl's brow while a sick feeling grew in her stomach. Lester sat up on the side of the bed, the quilt covering his face like a hood.

"Your friend with the black car. He had a gun." The youth stood and walked past her into the kitchen, the quilt over his head.

"Where?" she said, following him.

"In the neighborhood. Over by the park." He reached into the refrigerator for the milk.

"In the park? What happened?"

"Nothing."

"Lester, talk to me boy. What happened in the park?"

"Nothing. Dude had this gun."

He sat down heavily in the chair and poured the milk into a bowl of cereal. She approached him, then reached down and pulled the quilt away from his face. "Ah!"

"Uh . . ."

"Your head! What?"

"Nuthin."

"Lester, you hurt boy! Lemme see." She reached for him, but he waved her away. "Let me see!" she cried, and grabbed him. He held still. She examined the wound.

"What in the—?"

"Nuthin."

"What happened?"

"I got hit."

"Who?" Cheryl remembered the heavy board and McDermott waving it at her, his eyes ablaze. She saw him again falling into the grass, his face bloody.

"Your friend. He was crazy I'm tellin' you."

"Richard?" She trembled with anger and fear.

"Yeah."

"He did this? With a gun?"

"Uh-huh."

"Oh Lord." She touched at the wound.

"I'll be all right." Lester pulled away from her and dug into the cereal.

"You might need a stitch. He hit you—then what?"

"The cops came. I ran off."

"The police? Lord, Lord."

"We all ran off."

Cheryl backed away, unsure what to do, what to say, what to remember. She felt sick and guilty at the same time, as if she'd brought this on herself, on her brother. When she flung that bottle at Richard, she thought the fight was finished, over. How did she get into such a tangled situation? And now the police were involved. She was sure a bad end was coming. Something moved in her stomach.

Cheryl Lewis went to her bedroom to get ready for the day,

calling over her shoulder to her brother: "I've got to go to work. Get your head cleaned up. There's some rubbing alcohol in the bathroom and the baby will be up soon. She'll want breakfast."

* * *

As Officer Jeremy Wilson drove to the Orion place that morning, he realized how much he disliked this part of his job, notifying the next of kin. He hoped Gloria Orion wouldn't take the news too hard. He wasn't in the mood to offer sympathy. *Hell, if McDermott hadn't fired on us, he might still be alive. You can't shoot at the police.* And this was still a murder investigation, Lt. Foster reminded him. That lawyer had Mira Ogilvy's pearls in his office; he had been in Sloetown several times. Gloria Orion might know something about her brother and the dead girl, about the case. He still had work to do. But he was glad that Davis fellow was out of the way for a while. Now maybe he could get something done.

Wilson came to the Orion residence. He stopped, got out of his car, walked up a sidewalk onto the porch and knocked on the door. Then he remembered questioning the woman earlier that week, her dress, the lipstick she wore, the way she talked . . . as if she didn't care who he was. Wilson looked the house over. It was a very nice house.

* * *

Lester Lewis grew restless as the morning passed. He was tired of sitting in the house watching the baby. He flicked the channels on the television. He went to the front door and looked at the street; then he went to the refrigerator and looked in there. He wasn't hungry. In his bedroom, he withdrew a bag from underneath the bed and emptied the contents into his hand: six pearls, soiled but faintly glowing. He rolled them between his fingers. The old man said they were worth a lot of money. Lester knew where he could take them, a man who would know the value. Then from a drawer, underneath his socks, he withdrew the pistol the old man traded him. It was heavy and black, almost blue. It could be worth money too, but maybe he should keep it. A gun might come in handy some day. He stuffed the bag of pearls and the weapon into a small backpack, then checked again on the baby.

She was napping. In the living room again, he peered out the front window, waiting for Cheryl. Finally, he phoned his cousin Sheila. "You wanna make a few dollars?" he asked her. "Come and stay with the baby."

Sheila appeared in about twenty minutes. As she entered the house, Lester said,

"I'll give you some money when I get back."

"No, wait!" Sheila cried, annoyed.

But the young man was out on the porch already, then onto the sidewalk, carrying the backpack. His cousin stood in the doorway, yelling at him. He walked quickly through the old neighborhood. The summer heat made him sweat, but loosened him up too, so he walked faster, bouncing along the sidewalk. Then he slowed down; he didn't want to draw attention. He avoided Jackson Park, where the white dude whacked him on the head. His reached up and touched his wound delicately with his fingers. It had dried up fine. It would be all right.

Lester wondered about that crazy man who kept yelling about the money. His words gave him a bad feeling, as if the money was something he should know about, a secret that would follow him, haunt him. He took a backstreet around the park. His friends might be there shooting basketball—they'd be curious about the backpack. He didn't want anyone to know. He walked, almost running, down the long, narrow, shady streets.

Soon he came to a stretch of Kenner Boulevard where little stores huddled in a faded strip mall. He knew one of the places, a shop where the man inside once gave him five bucks for an old car stereo he'd found in the junkyard down by the river. Lester crossed the busy avenue and approached the store. The windows were tinted almost black, but he saw fluorescent lights within. As he pushed the front door open, he felt the gun heavy in his backpack.

Inside, merchandise was stacked in crooked rows: TV sets, golf clubs, stereos, tools, guitars, lawn mowers, bikes, and a motorcycle. Glass cases displayed watches, cameras, and gold chains. The air-conditioning was blowing hard and felt good. A man behind the counter looked up from a magazine as Lester came in.

"Got sumthin' for me today?" the man sighed.

Lester came forward, unshouldered his backpack and pulled out the little bag. He shook the pearls out into his palm. He laid them on the counter.

The man squinted. "Huh. We don't see much like these here. Pearls, huh?"

"Yeah."

The man picked one up and rolled it in his fingertips. He found a tissue and cleaned it. He held it up to the fluorescent light, then tried the same with another pearl. He rubbed two together.

"Hah." The man shook his head, and said "What you want for them?"

"Plenty," Lester said. "They're valuable."

"Is that so?" He gathered up the pearls, handing them over. "Here, take 'em. I can't use 'em."

"What?"

"I can't use 'em. They're fake." A smile crawled into the man's face.

"Aw man, bullshit. They're pearls. They're valuable."

The man shrugged. "No. It's costume jewelry." Lester wasn't sure what costume jewelry was exactly, but it didn't sound good.

"For real?"

"Yeah, they're plastic." He laid the pearls on the counter.

"Bullshit man."

"Take 'em to a jewelry store downtown if you don't believe me." He picked up his magazine.

"That's messed up."

"Fake."

"Aw shut up."

The man laughed. Lester reached into his backpack and jerked out the revolver. He pointed it at the man.

"Whoa now . . . take it easy."

"Shut up!" The gun was heavy and black. The man behind the counter raised his hands.

"Easy, boy."

Lester snatched the pearls off the counter and backed up, moving toward the door.

"You full of crap, man!" he cried. He kept the gun on the man as he moved away, his hand trembling.

"Sorry, bub."

"Bullshit," Lester spat, feeling his back against the front door. Then he stuffed the pearls in his pocket and pushed on the door. He stumbled out onto the sidewalk, in the bright sun. Suddenly, he realized the pistol was in his hand. He shoved it into the backpack and quickly walked away. When he reached the end of the strip mall, he ran. He didn't know where to go next. He ran back into Sloetown.

The man in the pawnshop lowered his hands. He wiped his face and exhaled, resting on the counter. *Damn kid* he muttered as he reached for the phone. He dialed the police. A woman answered.

"Police," she said.

"Hey, this is Jerry Noe down here at Jerry's Pawn on Kenner, near Sloetown."

"Yessir. How can I—?"

"We just had a man in here with a gun."

"Sir?"

"A gun, ma'am. In here. At Jerry's Pawn."

"A robbery. Got it. What's happening now? Where are you?"

"No, he's gone."

"Stay calm sir."

"I am calm. He's gone. The man with the gun is gone."

"Are you okay sir? We're on the way. A robbery—"

"No, he didn't take anything. It wasn't a hold-up. He had some pearls he tried to sell."

"Sir?"

"Then he pulled out a gun. Then he left."

The woman on the phone paused. "He left?"

"Yeah, that's it. 'Some black kid."

"But the robbery . . . the pearls?"

"No. The boy just had a gun. He got mad, took his pearls and ran off."

"Sir, what is the purpose of your call?"

"Well, hell, never mind."

"All right," the woman sighed. "We'll send a car over. But we're real busy right now, you know."

The man hung up and returned to his magazine.

* * *

When Baker Davis opened his eyes Monday, he stared at the cinder block wall. There was no need to turn over in his bunk—he knew what a nine-by-twelve jail cell looked like. He saw it last night when Wilson brought him here, shoved him inside, and slammed the door. And if he turned over on the narrow bed, he might fall onto the concrete floor. So he lay perfectly still and thought about Lt. Foster. Yes, she was mad at him, but at least his luck wasn't as bad as McDermott's. Soon, they would tell Gloria Orion about her brother. It would be nice to be there for her, but that wasn't in his contract.

Davis could tell it was morning, probably late. Sunlight streamed into his cell from somewhere. He smelled coffee, acrid or burnt even, but coffee nonetheless. He rolled over and sat on the edge of his bunk. Outside, beyond the steel bars, men lounged at card tables in a large common area. A few men wore dull orange jumpsuits, prisoners; others wore street clothes. No one had belts or shoes, and when Baker Davis looked at his feet he realized he didn't either. The men in the common area stared at a TV set that hung on the wall. They drank from paper cups. The coffee.

Then Davis recognized the place: the temp holding area at Police Headquarters. The cops had turned an entire floor into a detention area for minor offenders arrested over the weekend: drunk drivers, wife beaters, dope smokers, shoplifters, gamblers, pimps. A colorful lot, Davis reflected as he watched them, though right now they looked tired and gray. No one stayed here long; but if a man couldn't raise bail money, he could sweat out months in here. The investigator rose from his cot and approached the steel bars.

"Say guys, y'all got any coffee?" he remarked to the men in the common area. They were all watching television. No one answered.

"Hey man," he said, louder. "Coffee?" A man with a dirty moustache and bloodshot eyes turned and scowled, unhappy with the interruption.

"Coffee." Davis repeated.

Finally, an older black guy who looked like Santa Claus said, "They bring you some in a little while." He turned back to the television. Davis recalled then how detention worked: they locked you up most of the day, but let everyone out into the common room a few hours in morning and a couple hours after supper to watch TV, play cards, smoke. A janitor set out a plastic tray that held paper cups of coffee. His turn would come. It wasn't a country club, but wasn't exactly prison either. Davis rested on the cot and stared through the bars at the men in the common area. There was nothing else to see.

* * *

Lester Lewis exhaled when he got back to Sloetown, relieved to be away from the dirty strip mall and the noise of traffic. The trees in the old neighborhood made pools of shade on the sidewalks. This was his territory, his home, but the young man remained in the shadows, avoiding everyone. He wondered if he should have pulled that gun in the pawnshop. *No. Yes. Why not?* That man behind the counter pissed him off.

The streets led him to Jackson Park, a good place to rest for a while. Cousin Sheila can watch the baby for a little longer, he thought. The youth made his way past the rusty swing sets and the basketball court. No one had shown up to play yet. He came to a denser grove of trees which blocked out the sun. The shade here cooled the sweat beneath his shirt and eased his pulse. Then beyond, in the thick brush Lester saw the faded red paint of his brother's Cadillac. He walked through the grass, stepping over a broken bottle and an old board. Flowers grew nearby—magnolia or jasmine he couldn't tell but they smelled nice. He stopped, dropped the backpack and breathed deeply, then found a seat on the hood of the old convertible. Rich green vines snaked along beside him and he remembered the summers long ago when Michael came home from the pallet factory and gave them rides in the afternoons. Cheryl would go too, and they'd cruise around Sloetown with the wind in their faces. Most of all he remembered everyone laughing.

Now the silence reverberated. He listened for birds, children playing in the park—nothing. He shifted around on the rusty hood. It creaked, the only sound in the park. He picked up his backpack, withdrew the little bag, and emptied the pearls into his palm. *Fake*, the pawnshop dude said. So the old man at the pallet factory had tricked him, traded him plastic jewelry for the weed. Damn . . . he was out about fifty bucks. But he still had the gun, which must be worth something. It would bring some cash. Or maybe he ought to keep it. A gun might come in handy sometime. He rolled the little white spheres between his fingers. *Fake. Damn. Worthless.* He tossed the pearls into the back seat of the Cadillac.

TWENTY GRAND

Then Lester Lewis got up and left. He saw a few boys gathered at the basketball court, but he avoided them. Soon he was back out on the streets, going home, hoping to reach the house before Cheryl arrived. He wanted to get inside and hide the gun before she got home. Then he turned onto Vinson Street and felt a strange silence. He walked faster, the backpack swinging from his hand.

He heard a rumble behind him. He stopped and looked over his shoulder. It was a car. It came closer. A police car. Lester froze. The black and white vehicle eased up beside him. He felt as if he couldn't walk, as if his feet were in wet cement.

The car stopped. Two cops eyed him from inside. One of them had red hair. He leaned out the window, and smiled, and said "What you got in the bag, boy? Dope?"

* * *

Best Diner was slow on Monday. Cheryl Lewis was fine with that. She had one table, an elderly woman sipping tea, and hoped for no more customers. It had been a long weekend and she was drowsy. She stayed in the waitress station and looked at her textbook for class, but didn't feel like reading much. She polished the flatware and as she did, noticed her hands. This was the hand that threw the bottle that hurt Richard, smashed him in the face. She wondered how she could do it, how that hand could act so. But he picked up that board in the park, his eyes crazy, his speech slurred. He became a different person, vicious like an animal, and she was afraid. 'No telling what he might have done. Then she remembered him falling in the grass, his arms flailing as she ran into the woods. Those same arms held her once. He kept talking about the money. What right did he have to it? How did he even know about it? Maybe he knew Mira. She knew the man was troubled. Maybe the enemies he told her about finally got to him. Those bankers. Still, she wished she hadn't hurt him. It frightened Cheryl Lewis to get that angry with anyone, so out of control she would throw a bottle. She even hated it when Lester made her mad and she yelled at him. But McDermott had struck her own brother, drawn blood from his face, as if it was her blood. The very thought stabbed her in the heart. She wasn't sure she could forgive that. But still she remembered the lawyer; and the more she remembered, the more she thought about him: his voice, his nice clothes, and the way he touched her. He was tender once, more gentle than any man she'd ever known. He had an office downtown in the tall building with his name on it. He said he would take her up there, to his office on the twentieth floor where big windows gave a splendid view. You could look out over the city and see all the way to Sloetown, even the river beyond. It was beautiful, and Richard was going to show her.

Across the room, the old lady with the tea waved. She wanted more hot water. Cheryl went that way and wished she didn't have class tonight. She wanted Richard McDermott to come instead. Maybe he wasn't hurt too bad. Maybe he would get up from the ground where he fell and clean himself up and come into the restaurant as if nothing happened and be sweet again like she remembered him. She poured hot water into the lady's cup. It was going to be a long day.

* * *

Davis rose from his cot and stood before a steel basin welded to the wall. He punched a small lever that shot a jet of water into his hand. He rubbed his face, dried his hands on his trousers. There was another cot in the cell and he sat down on that for a change of scene when he noticed movement outside the door. A guard stood there, in police blues. Then another one, a huge man. They were bringing someone.

"Back up," they ordered. Davis complied. The cop unlocked the door while the big one led a young man into the cell. Davis recognized him. He was cuffed.

"Stand still," the cop said. He removed the handcuffs from the youth. Then he backed out and they slammed the door shut.

Davis yelled at them. "Hey, y'all know Lieutenant Foster?" They walked away. One of them laughed. The young man plopped down on his cot and massaged his wrists. It was Lester Lewis. Davis sat on his bed and leaned against the wall. He looked the kid over, noticing his face filled with anger and fear.

"Welcome to Holiday Inn," Davis remarked.

The youth looked at him, remembering him from Sloetown. Then his eyes turned to the men in the common room. He groaned and lay back on the bed. It was quiet for a minute, except for the

TV outside their cell.

"How's your head?" Davis said. The boy's hand touched the wound on his forehead where McDermott whacked him.

"Crazy white dude."

True, Davis thought. They were silent again. Lester Lewis closed his eyes as the television droned on. Davis stared at the men in the common room. There was nothing else to look at. Time passed. It could have been a few minutes; it could have been an hour. He said, "So what happened? 'Between you and the cops?"

"Nothing."

"They don't bring people in here for nothing."

"Then what the hell *you* in here fo'?"

Davis smiled and said, "Nothing."

Lester Lewis lay on his bunk, staring at the ceiling. He said, "I had a gun. They caught me. But it wasn't loaded."

Davis looked the young man over, his slim frame stretched out on the cot an arm's length away. He couldn't imagine a gun in his hand. He said,

"Policemen don't like guns."

The youth brightened. "Naw they don't."

"How long you gonna be in here?"

"I dunno."

"Have you been charged yet?"

"No. But they're talking like I held up this guy in a store. With the gun."

Davis felt his face twitch. He believed the kid. He remembered his sister Cheryl and guessed she didn't raise the young man like that, to commit armed robbery. But if the cops stuck him with a felony, it would not be good.

"But it ain't even my gun."

"Well, where'd you get it?"

Lester glared at him, then turned away and faced the wall. Davis thought *No telling how he got it. Maybe he found it in Sloetown. But if the cops tie that gun to the bullets they found in Mira Ogilvy, the boy is gone.*

"All right. Look, how you gonna get out of here? You got any bail money?"

The young man turned back to him, his eyes blank. Davis knew it was a stupid question, and said, "Look, you're gonna need money to get out of here. And a lawyer."

"I ain't worried."

"Well, good, but don't be stupid. You got somebody you can call?"

"They gonna let me make a phone call?"

"Yeah, they will. Later today probably."

"I guess I'll call my sister." Lester Lewis rolled over on the cot and faced the wall. "But she ain't got no money either."

"Davis . . . Baker Davis!" a big voice called. The sound came toward him, with heavy footsteps. It was two guards, including the huge one. They stood before the cell door. "Get up."

The investigator rose. They swung the steel door open and moved aside. Lieutenant Foster came forward, with Officer Wilson behind her.

"All right," she declared, jerking her head at Davis. "Let's go."

"Come on," the huge cop said.

Davis complied. He hitched up his loose trousers and shuffled out of the cell. He looked back at the boy once more.

"You better forget about him," Wilson said.

"Whatever you say, Officer."

"Asshole."

"Come on," the Lieutenant demanded. They marched through the common room and down a hallway with cells on either side. No one bothered to look at them. They approached a counter where a cop stood behind a bullet-proof window. He handed the Lieutenant a clear plastic bag through a slot in the glass; it contained the prisoner's shoes, his belt, his wallet, keys.

"Now go home, Mr. Davis," the Lieutenant ordered. "I don't want to see you again."

"Ever." Wilson added.

Davis took the plastic bag and said, "That kid back there, in the cell . . . robbery, huh?"

"Maybe."

"Or maybe not? Maybe just a weapons possession . . . right?"

"No. Maybe homicide, Mr. Davis. The Ogilvy case. Now get dressed and go home."

The huge cop nodded at a restroom the size of a closet. "Change in there," he said. Davis moved toward it and said,

"So it wasn't McDermott."

The Lieutenant frowned.

Davis added, "The lawyer's gun you picked up . . . it didn't check out, did it? He didn't shoot Mira Ogilvy."

"Shut up," Wilson said.

"Not McDermott's weapon, huh? Well, well. So then maybe it was *your* gun that shot an innocent man last night, eh Wilson?"

"Get dressed and get out," the Lieutenant growled.

* * *

When Davis got home that afternoon, he felt as if he'd been gone a month. He showered and changed, trying to clean away everything he'd seen in the city jail and in Sloetown the night before, even though he knew it all stayed with him, really. McDermott was dead, and probably innocent, but he did fire at the police. He knew the cops didn't appreciate that kind of thing. And the Lewis kid was in trouble.

In the kitchen, he made coffee. As he poured a cup, he noticed the drawer again, and after a few moments that felt like an hour, he pulled it open. Twenty thousand dollars, still there. He picked it up, felt its heft, but it didn't feel right hidden in his kitchen. It belonged to Mira Ogilvy and she was dead. No one knew about it, but if anyone broke in . . . this cash wouldn't be hard to find. Better take it downtown he thought, and lock it in the safe. He found his old briefcase, stuffed the money inside and left the house, feeling lighter somehow even though it was almost a hundred degrees.

When he reached McDermott Center, Davis wondered if they would change the name of the tower, with the owner dead now. He stopped the Buick, got out and crossed the parking lot with the briefcase, feeling self-conscious as if people knew the contents. Inside, the Gray Prince was firing on all cylinders, a phone in each ear:

"When they hear about this on the coast, they're not going to like it," he barked. "Find a way to get it done. Today. Better yet, before noon, before anyone finds out."

Davis walked past him. In his office, he approached his faded license hanging on the wall. He nudged the picture frame aside to reveal the safe. He dialed the combination, and it creaked open. Then he placed the briefcase inside the safe, wondering if Mira Ogilvy knew what had become of her money. Maybe she did. It was quaint to think maybe she knew all along; and as she wrote that last letter to Baker Davis she knew exactly how and where it would end. Maybe.

He closed the steel door and spun the lock as if he had some control over the situation, even though he knew he didn't. As he scooted the frame back into place, he remembered his license was no good. He remained a man on the edge, an illegal, an untouchable, and he reflected that it all provided him a kind of twisted freedom. Or was it a prison?

In any event, twenty K in the safe might keep him cool for a while. He could lie low, as he promised Lieutenant Foster.

* * *

Cheryl Lewis stood in the waitress station at Best Diner and turned the pages of her textbook. The dining room was still slow, and she didn't feel like studying. Math problems, meaningless numbers, covered the pages of her book. She remembered that Richard was good at math. Maybe I'll call him, she thought, see if he is all right, or still crazy. Maybe he's settled down by now, or come to his senses. But she didn't have his number. She wasn't even sure where he lived. McDermott Center was the only thing he ever mentioned, with his office up there on the top floor. He must be there by now, surely. Again she flipped the pages in her textbook.

She heard her name called from the kitchen. Danny, the manager, summoned her. "Cheryl!" She walked to the back. Danny stood at his desk, holding a phone. "For you." He handed her the receiver and left.

"Cheryl," a voice said in a harsh whisper.

"What?" she answered.

"Listen, you got any money?"

"Lester? That you?"

"I gotta have some money," he said.

"Money? Where are you boy?"

"I got picked up."

"What?"

"Picked up, dammit. The police—"

She paused to collect herself. The cooks in the kitchen seemed to be watching her. She turned away from them as she rubbed her forehead. Her voice trembled.

"Lester, are you in jail?"

"Yeah."

Again she stopped. A lump rose in her throat. Her knees felt weak.

"Listen, Cheryl, it wasn't no big deal. I just had this gun—"

"Gun?!" Again it seemed as if the whole kitchen staff could hear.

"Naw, naw . . . it wasn't loaded . . . I didn't do nuthin."

"Shut up. How much do money do they want? To get you out?"

"About twenty thousand dollars. I think."

"You *think?*"

"Yeah, that's it . . . twenty thousand dollars."

She closed her eyes. There were no tears.

"You got some money?" he implored. Suddenly, her brother's voice sounded very small and far away.

"Don't worry boy," she said. "I'll do something."

"Cheryl?"

"I'll do something. Sit tight."

She hung up the phone, then walked quickly from the kitchen, out into the big dining room, feeling as if someone had punched her in the gut. Twenty thousand dollars! A thousand maybe she could scrape together, borrow from relatives or friends. But twenty! She closed her eyes. *What the hell did the boy do? Oh God. Why did they arrest him? Twenty thousand dollars!*

Bail money. She knew about men who made loans for that, if you had a good down payment, maybe twenty or thirty percent. It still added up to thousands of dollars, an amount that seemed as far away as ever. She didn't want Lester involved with people like that anyway, so he might have to sit in jail. She heard his voice saying her name, *Cheryl,* and sounding so distant. Finally, she let a tear come to her eye. She wondered what McDermott would do. It would be a good time to have a lawyer, but Richard was crazy. She felt very alone.

In the dining room, she noticed only an elderly couple in a booth and a man alone reading the paper. The couple waved for more coffee and she took the pot there. The solitary man wanted ketchup and she brought it, along with his bill. She smiled at everyone but felt like a robot. She only smiled because Danny the manager ordered every waitress at Best Diner to smile, even if it hurt. It did hurt.

The solitary man stood up, approached the front counter to pay. Then he was gone and Cheryl Lewis went to his table for the tip. A dollar sat near his plate, along with the daily newspaper. 'Something to read, she thought, something to distract her as she thought about Lester. She took the newspaper and the dollar. It was a long way from twenty grand.

In the station she hid the textbook and opened the newspaper. It hit her in the face, there on page two . . . *Police Exchange Fire with Murder Suspect in Sloetown*. Her eyes froze on the story; the noise in the diner evaporated. She felt instantly alone. The customers seemed very far away, as if they were in another city. But there it was: the police shot it out with a murder suspect last night. The story didn't say what happened, how it ended, but the last sentence gripped her throat— the suspect was a local attorney. A cry rose in her mouth but she stopped it. She remembered Lester's words that morning . . . *crazy white dude had a gun*. Her eyes flitted across the article like lightning, but no name appeared. Her body shook.

She threw the newspaper aside and walked quickly to the break room, to her locker there. She grabbed her clothes, went to the restroom and changed. Her uniform lay on the floor as she ran from Best Diner, her hand over her mouth, her eyes streaming.

* * *

The low, muffled sound of traffic intruded from the city outside as Baker Davis considered the remnants of the afternoon and the sun streaming in through the dusty metal blinds in his office. It was late August now, long past the solstice, as the afternoons grew shorter if only by minutes. The waning sunlight was almost imperceptible, but there it was: an odd sense of something changing, withdrawn, or simply not there anymore. Summer was fading, and would soon be done. 'Like McDermott, Davis thought.

Wilson shot him. Maybe he had to. But now Lt. Foster's chief suspect was dead, and Davis knew this time the cops might not find the man, or woman, who put a bullet in Mira Ogilvy. Her death felt random now, arbitrary, meaningless. Baker Davis could live with that. He could live without a tidy ending, an explanation, a closed file. Others, like the police or Gloria, couldn't. They would keep searching, keep digging.

Rays of sunlight slanted in through the blinds, illuminating the dust in his office. No, the place really belonged to McDermott, Davis reflected. It was the landlord's property. He had taken the rent upstairs to him every month. Now what? There was still a lease to honor, after all. *Maybe I can get away without paying for a few days, a few weeks, but it's only a matter of time.* Then he remembered . . . McDermott's secretary was probably still there, up on Twenty. She can accept the payment. He shuffled around in the papers on his desk and found his checkbook. He opened it, looked at the register, and frowned. No money. Then his eyes went to the PI license hanging on the wall.

Davis rose from his desk and approached the framed document. He pushed it aside, unlocked the safe, withdrew the old briefcase and looked inside. All that cash—it could be rent money, but that much dough could also take him far away. He thought about Europe and spending quiet afternoons in museums contemplating the painting and sculpture of antiquity. He imagined wandering the clean, musical islands of the Caribbean; or the mountains, where he could stroll in alpine meadows carpeted in wildflowers under turquoise skies. Or maybe his brother's ranch out West.

He withdrew a pack of bills and caressed it. Maybe. Who would find out? Nobody saw him find that brown envelope in Mira's car. But he told the Lieutenant the victim had money, so this cash was material. And the last time evidence came up missing—when he helped the cops nail the heroin dealers up in Sloetown—it cost him big. He didn't want to live that over. Back then they took his license. This time they'd have his scalp. Davis fanned through the currency, thinking it would be a thin scalp indeed if he didn't find a payday soon. His mind began to whir: the rent was a grand, he was broke, but Mira's letter mentioned she'd set aside money for compensation. Maybe it was time to collect a little.

He took a thousand dollars and stuffed it in an envelope, then put the briefcase back. That's when he noticed the revolver, sitting quietly in the safe. He hadn't taken it out, or even held it in some time. He reached in and rested his hand on the weapon. It was cool, solid. He withdrew it and popped the chamber . . . empty, as always. It hadn't been fired in years. *If I'm going to keep it, I should take care of it. I'll take it home and clean it.*

The investigator stuffed the gun in his trousers, closed the safe and returned his license to the wall. He took the envelope of money, then left his office and went upstairs to find McDermott's secretary and pay his rent.

* * *

Cheryl Lewis jammed the accelerator, pushing her car over the speed limit. She didn't care. What did it matter? So what if the police stopped her. The police! They traded shots with a local attorney. No, it couldn't be Richard!

She wiped her tears with the back of her hand as she tore across the city toward downtown. Angry drivers blew their horns as she roared past. People yelled at her. She would find Richard, see him, touch him, make sure he wasn't the one in the newspaper. Crazy white dude, Lester said. He had a gun. He laid a gash on her brother's head and would have laid her out with that board in Jackson Park Sunday. No, Richard would never hurt her, not really, not if he was in his right mind. People were chasing him. He was all right. She would find him and make him calm down. She always could. It wasn't him! They couldn't have shot Richard McDermott.

Buildings and signs whizzed by as she raced downtown. Where the hell is McDermott Center, she muttered through her teeth. Approaching the business district, a tower with an *M* on the roof loomed before her. That's it, she thought, her hands tight on the steering wheel. *He's in there, surely, working in his office on the top floor. I'll find him, see him, touch him. It wasn't Richard in the newspaper. He can't be gone!*

The big tower grew closer. Then she was there, and wheeled her car into the parking lot. A security guard at the front gate noticed the woman driving in, her face twisted in anxiety. But she was moving fast. He didn't stop her.

She parked, found a tissue, wiped her face. She looked bad, she knew, but she couldn't wait. She got out and marched toward the front entrance of the big building in the hot sun, not knowing what to do next, not knowing what she would find inside. She only knew she wanted to see the man she remembered.

She pushed open the big glass doors. She was afraid to cry, didn't want anyone to stop her or ask questions, so she pressed her lips together hard, feeling the cool blast of the air conditioning as she stepped inside. The lobby was beautiful, she thought, three stories high and clad in creamy marble. Green palm trees stood along the walls in shiny black planters. A guard sat behind a counter of rich wood. He looked over his glasses at her, then looked away. There was a bank next to the lobby. She saw the tellers inside, but there was only one customer. She thought McDermott Center would be a busy place, but it felt quiet now. She wasn't sure why.

She walked to the elevators, trying not to look around much. She didn't want to appear nervous or attract attention. Then the terrible news in the paper came to her again. It made her sad and calmed her nerves at the same time. Maybe it *was* Richard. Maybe he was gone. Maybe it was over.

Cheryl Lewis remained perfectly still as the car approached. The doors whisked open and she stepped in, pressed the button marked 20 and felt her stomach move as the elevator ascended. It was like floating. This was the elevator Richard took every day, she thought, way up into the sky, almost to the clouds, away from the city, away from Sloetown. It was a very high place. She remembered a book from her childhood where the kids in a small village built a ladder to the moon with popsicle sticks. Or was it to heaven? She couldn't remember.

The elevator halted. She didn't want to get out. She didn't know what lay outside the car, nor what the lawyer's office would look like, nor even what she wanted to say. The polished steel doors opened and she stepped forward automatically, as if something pushed her. Then she stopped. She was on 18.

A silver-haired man stood there, waiting to get aboard. She winced and backed into the car. The man entered and they resumed, then stopped on Twenty. She looked at him.

"No, I'm going back down," he said, as the doors opened. It almost disappointed Cheryl Lewis, as if she wanted someone to go with her, to help. She stepped from the car, alone. The elevator disappeared silently.

Several offices stood before her, their tall oak doors arrayed along the hallway. They didn't invite a knock. They didn't invite anything. She couldn't tell which one belonged to the lawyer. She looked up and down the corridor, noticing a doctor's office, an accountant, and a shrink. Then at the end she saw another door with gold lettering. It seemed bigger somehow. She approached.

The gold lettering came into view. It was McDermott's.

She stopped at the door and listened. No sound came from within, no sound from anywhere. People should be around, but maybe they were hiding behind the big doors. She listened again . . . still quiet. She felt queer, as if someone was watching her there in the empty hallway. She couldn't stand it, better to be inside. She reached for the door handle and pushed. As she stepped in, a big, sleek counter loomed before her. No one sat there.

"Hello," she said. No answer. The entire suite was cool and silent as a vault, but her skin felt alive. And, strangely, there were no lights, only the afternoon sun coming through a window in the rear. She walked to the counter which displayed a phone, a stapler, a few pens, and that was about it. A steel filing cabinet held a potted fern which needed water. She placed her hand on the counter, as if she expected someone to greet her. But the office was empty. She withdrew her hand. It felt funny. It was covered with dust.

"Hello!" she repeated, and got the same answer—silence. Then she noticed another tall door behind the counter, marked *Private*. Maybe that was it. Maybe Richard was in there. Maybe. She looked around again. She was alone in the suite and wanted to give up, turn back, go downstairs and leave. It was crazy, she thought, coming here to this empty office. But that story: a local attorney, an exchange of gunfire with the police. And Lester said that crazy white dude had a gun. But no, it couldn't be Richard. He couldn't be the one! She walked past the counter, up to the tall door, and gave a soft knock.

Silence again, and she pressed an ear to the door as tears welled in her eyes. Her fingers caressed the glossy wood. She wiped at her eyes. It's no use, she thought, Richard's gone. They killed him. The poor, sad man—her lover! Her moist hand knocked again, harder. Then she turned away. She could hardly move. There was only silence as she remembered the way he kissed her.

"Come in," sounded a voice.

Cheryl Lewis jumped. She fell back from the door, almost tumbling onto the carpet.

"Come in!" the voice demanded, a man's voice.

She caught herself, leaning against the counter. Her breath stopped . . . then started again. Her tears were suddenly dry, her eyes clear. She came forward and reached for the handle.

Behind the door a man and a woman stood in a big office. The man was fat. His shirt fit tightly against his thick arms and his tie was dirty. He stood behind a large desk Cheryl knew must be Richard's. The woman was smaller, leaner, tougher. She held an armload of manila folders.

"What?" the man demanded.

"Uh . . . I didn't know there was anyone here."

"What do you want?" the woman said.

"Richard McDermott, the lawyer," Cheryl stammered. "I was looking for him. I didn't mean to . . . this *is* his office, right?"

The fat man and the woman stopped and looked at each other. He said,

"Yes, miss, you got the right place. But there's been a foreclosure on this property. We're Mr. McDermott's bankers."

"Oh, I see."

"*We* own the place now," the woman snapped. "It's not his."

"We're reviewing the financials," the man added.

"What do you want?" the woman asked.

"I just wanted to see him, Mr. McDermott that is."

"Did you have an appointment or something?"

"No." She looked at the bankers. They had the air of doing something they didn't want anyone to notice. The man appeared uneasy behind the desk, as if he didn't want to be there. The woman's eyes darted around behind thick glasses. Behind her stood a wall of windows that went to the ceiling. They'd drawn the curtains open, and Cheryl could see blue sky and sunshine outside. She knew it was Richard's office, his place.

"Mr. McDermott wasn't expecting me," she said. "I was hoping to see—"

"I'm not sure when he'll return, ma'am," the man said.

"Oh." She didn't want to hear that. Her knees grew weak and her stomach felt sick. She wanted to see Richard, wanted to make sure. Suddenly, she felt hot and flushed. An armchair waited nearby. She sank into it heavily, closing her eyes.

"And you can't stay here," the woman added.

A door opened from somewhere, from outside. Someone had entered the suite from the corridor. The bankers stared into the front room. Another visitor.

"Hello, can we help you?!" the fat man cried. A man came into the office. Cheryl remembered him from the riverfront—the man who took her home, the Davis fellow. The bankers repeated: "Can we help you?"

"Maybe," Davis replied, coming into the office, glancing at Cheryl in the chair. "Maybe not. Who are you?"

The thin woman's eyes narrowed. "None of your business."

The fat man raised his hand. "We're with the bank, downstairs. You're Davis, right? A tenant here?"

"Yep."

The man's cheeks quivered. "There's been a foreclosure, Mr. Davis, on the entire building."

"That's nice. So what are you doing here?"

"Looking over some . . . documentation."

Davis looked at Cheryl Lewis, noticing her eyes wet and sad. "'Afternoon."

She stood from the chair. "Hello. I came to see Rich . . . I mean, Mr. McDermott."

Davis heard the fragile hitch in her voice, the emotion, the man's first name she wanted to say. And he knew she wasn't going to see the lawyer that day.

"Sir!" the fat man blurted.

Davis glared at the bankers. "Look, I have a lease here. I came up to pay the rent."

"We'll take it," the tough woman said.

"I just wanted to see him," Cheryl said, to no one in particular. It was only a voice in the room. They all looked at her. "Mr. McDermott invited me up here, to Twenty. He wanted me to see the beautiful view. He wanted me . . . ." They watched her walk slowly toward the big windows.

"Ma'am," the woman said.

"Can this wait?" Davis asked, looking at the bankers and the papers strewn across McDermott's desk.

"We've got to get everything in order," the fat man said. The woman added,

"This office is under bank control now. We have our procedures."

Davis glanced at Cheryl Lewis standing before the windows, overlooking the city, and said again, "Can't it wait?"

"I'm afraid not sir."

Davis walked slowly toward the desk and stopped before the fat man and the woman. He looked them straight in the eye and said, "Are you real sure about that?" Then slowly he drew his jacket back, showing the big gun stuffed in his belt.

The bankers stopped breathing. The man's face turned white, the woman's face turned red. Davis moved his hand toward the pistol.

"Now now, there's no need for extreme—," the man stammered, wiping his brow. "Maybe we could . . . take a little break."

"Of course of course absolutely," the woman added, dropping the folders on the desk.

"A few minutes. I know Mr. McDermott would appreciate it," Davis said. The bankers grabbed a few papers and scurried from the room. Then they were gone.

The office became quiet and still. Cheryl Lewis stood at the windows that reached to the ceiling. She pushed the curtains back as blue sky and sunlight filled the room. The towers of Downtown, shimmering in glass and steel, stood nearby as if she could almost reach and touch them. She noticed tiny people on the rooftops nearby, while little cars inched along in the street below. But mostly it was blue sky, and she wondered how it might feel to touch one of the white clouds that drifted lazily above the city, right outside the window. Beyond, past the neighboring towers, she saw the suburbs with gabled rooftops aligned in an orderly grid, then a forest: the old treetops of Sloetown, like a deep green carpet, thick and comfortable. She tried to see her house and Jackson Park where Michael's Cadillac rested. Finally, away on the horizon, the river flowed past. The water appeared still in the distance, but sometimes the current caught a ray of sun and sparkled. Davis came to where she stood, and said,

"You came here to see—"

"—to see Richard, yes." She looked at the floor, then again at the beautiful view before them. "But now—"

"I know," Davis said, touching her shoulder gently. Her body trembled.

"He is . . . not here."

"No, he's not."

"I wanted to see him once more." A tear left her eye and trickled down her cheek. "I wanted to believe he might still be—"

"I know."

The young woman wept quietly, then stopped. She dried her

eyes. Again she took in the blue sky and sunlight pouring into the office, the white clouds floating by, and the world stretched out beneath her. Maybe heaven looked like this. The Pastor at church often spoke of it and she believed him. She wasn't sure why. It was hard not to think of a nice place when her parents were dead, and her brother Michael was missing so many years now. She had to think of something. They couldn't just be gone. Somehow in the blue sky, beyond the sunlight, among the clouds . . . .

"Richard wanted me to come here. To see this. He said it was a lovely view, from Twenty. You could see everything."

"It is beautiful," Davis said.

"And he used to stand here? Watching it all?"

"I expect he did."

"I often imagined it." She approached the window and touched it. "It's like the whole city is at your feet, and you're above it all, the entire world." Her eyes rested on a distant place. "I've never seen anything—"

They fell silent again. The investigator stood with her, taking in the view, a view fleeting and temporary, as if the scene might dissolve in an instant when they looked away. The splendid view, this world, a way of looking, an understanding—it didn't belong to them. It was Richard McDermott's. He had it, saw it, lost it, but he wanted to share it with this young woman. Maybe, in the end, Davis thought, he did. Maybe the man even had to die to do it. In a vacant lot in Sloetown.

"You can see forever," Cheryl whispered. "I could stay here . . . forever."

Maybe it *was* hers. Maybe it was his too, and Davis saw then how it would never belong to Gloria Orion, nor Karl Orion, nor the police. They couldn't see it. This wasn't their office. They had no appointment. Then he remembered the fat man, the tough woman. The place belonged to them now, a bank, an institution, a faceless pool of capital, as if it really belonged to no one. Maybe it was better that way, Davis thought. No one owns it, now.

"Maybe we should go," he said.

Cheryl Lewis turned away from the window and the horizon. She looked at Davis, her eyes still moist, but without tears.

"And now my brother Lester," she said, looking at the floor.

Davis remembered the young man who shared his cell not so long ago, but he didn't know what to say. She added, "He's in trouble. The police."

"Ah."

"He got picked up. It doesn't make any sense."

"Sometime it doesn't, with the cops."

"Damn fool boy had a gun, I think."

"Sorry to hear it." Davis remembered Lt. Foster and Wilson were looking to nail the kid for a homicide. He remembered the prisoners in the common area staring at the television with blank, empty faces. He said,

"You heard from him then?"

"Yes. He called me. He needs money. A lot. To get out." She sighed and looked away from the window, as if turning back to a reality she didn't want to face.

"Come on," Davis said. "We can't stay here." He yanked on the curtains, drawing them across the beautiful view, thinking *those bankers won't need this*. They left McDermott's office, closing the door gently behind them. They walked down the empty corridor to the elevator and waited for a car. One came, they got in, and felt it drop silently away from Twenty.

"So what are you going to do? For Lester?"

She looked at him. Her eyes were soft, but unafraid. "I don't know."

"Is there bail? Can you get him out?"

"Yes, and . . . well I don't know."

"Don't know what?"

"If I can get him out." She knotted her hands, but her voice was steady. "The money. It's twenty thousand dollars, Mr. Davis."

Twenty thousand, Davis thought. He stared at the floor as the elevator moved in silence, then stopped. "This way," he said, stepping from the car into the hall that led to his suite.

"Where are we—?"

"Just come."

They went to his office. Inside, Prince was barking into the phone: "Yes. Yes! We're swapping the debt for the balance for the credit . . . based on future earnings of course. Sure it'll vest. You bet your ass!"

Cheryl Lewis froze for a second. "This way," Davis said, smiling.

When they reached the back, she said, "Is this your office?"

"Depends on who you ask. Sometimes it feels like the

landlord's, when the rent is due. Sometimes it feels like my clients', when I have any. Other times, Prince up front there—he thinks he owns the place. Or maybe it belongs to my late father."

She looked at the investigator. She didn't know what to think, or say.

"But it's okay," Davis said after a moment. "I know whose office it is." Then he went to a framed document hanging on the wall. He considered it briefly, then nudged it aside to reveal a safe. He spun the lock on the steel door. It was open in a second. Cheryl Lewis watched him cautiously as he pulled an old briefcase from the safe and set it on his desk. Then he reached inside it. He withdrew something . . . her breath stopped. The man held a bundle of cash in his hand.

"What?!" she exclaimed, her eyes dilating.

Davis didn't say anything, but slowly withdrew more money from the briefcase until nineteen stacks of cash sat on his desk. Davis picked up a bundle and said, "Take it. You need it."

Cheryl Lewis blinked. She laughed. She had a beautiful smile, Davis thought. She shook her head and said, "Go on."

"Take it. Lester needs it."

Her smile went away. "You're not serious."

"Look, your brother's in jail. He can't stay there. How you gonna get him out?"

"I don't know." She approached the money as if was dangerous, a hazardous material.

"It's yours. Take it. For Lester."

"I couldn't." She withdrew, backing up toward the door. "I could never pay it back. You've been real nice Mr. Davis, but I could never—"

"Don't worry about that." He began stuffing the bundles of cash in the briefcase. "We'll say it's a little gift. Between friends, you know." He offered her the briefcase.

Her hand rose slowly to take it . . . then she jerked back, clouds in her face.

"No, Mr. Davis! That money ain't mine. It's yours. I can't take it, or even borrow it."

Davis looked sadly at the briefcase. He looked at the young woman. Then he looked around the office and sighed.

"No, Cheryl . . . it's not mine."

Her brow wrinkled. What a strange man, she thought, but not

like Richard, not crazy.

"It's not mine at all," he repeated. He offered her the briefcase once more.

Again she hesitated, her hand frozen in place.

"It's Mira's," Davis whispered.

The woman's lips parted, but made no sound. She felt as if she was in a faraway place, enchanted by a strange, wonderful mirage that would disappear if she looked away. Her knees felt weak.

"I'm sure Mira would like you to have it," Davis said.

"Mira?"

Davis pushed the briefcase at her once more. Her hands involuntarily rose for it.

"Go on. Go get your brother out of jail."

"I . . . I . . ."

"What about the rest? You need twenty, right? Do you have another thousand?"

"I . . . uh . . . maybe a few hundred in my savings, I don't know."

Davis thought about it for a moment, then reached into his pocket and withdrew the envelope with the rent money. He shoved it into the briefcase and said,

"Take it, Cheryl. Go down to the jail and get Lester out. Ask for Lieutenant Doreen Foster if you have any trouble. But don't mention my name."

She was silent. Davis quietly led her from the room, past Prince who was talking into two phones, and through the lobby of McDermott Center outside to the parking lot. Cheryl held the briefcase tightly. They didn't speak. There was nothing else to say. Finally she got into her car.

Then Baker Davis returned to his office. He withdrew the revolver from his belt and regarded it—still cool and dusty. He considered his work for the day. Not too shabby, he concluded, for an unlicensed investigator with an empty gun. He locked the weapon in the safe.

* * *

Rico was tired of pushing around his shopping cart that was heavy with cans he'd collected in Sloetown. They would bring a few dollars over at the junkyard tomorrow morning. Then he could buy himself a drink. But now it was late, almost midnight, and he needed a place to sleep. At least it was warm outside. He found himself in Jackson Park. Remnants of a breeze stirred the trees around him. It was a good place to spend the night.

He pushed the cart along a grassy path. He knew where he was going, sort of. Finally, he reached a place where the woods and brush grew thick. He hid the cart in a big clump of wild roses. Then, behind the brush he found what he'd been looking for, the old convertible. Often that teenager with the dope liked to hang out here, though sometimes he got angry and chased him away. But now the place was deserted, dark and quiet. The Caddy still had a little padding in the back seat that made for good sleeping. Rico looked around the park once more, then up at the moon. He scratched himself and climbed over the rusty door of the car into the back seat. He brushed away some leaves, then lay down for a night's sleep.

Yet as soon as he settled into the old cushions, he felt something sticking in his back, like small rocks. They hurt. He turned over and there they were—a handful of pearls, reflecting a soft glow of moonlight. *Huh*, he muttered, then stuffed them in his pocket. The homeless man rolled back over and went to sleep.

TWELVE

Doreen Foster answered her phone. It was Fortenberry, from ballistics.

"Lieutenant?"

"Speaking," she said.

"I guess it's strike two, ma'am. That piece your boys brought in yesterday . . . off somebody names Lester Lewis?"

"Yes, the Ogilvy case."

"It's not the one."

"What?"

"That gun, the one y'all brought in yesterday, it's not the murder weapon. No match on ballistics."

"You're certain?"

"That's my business, Lieutenant."

"Sure it is. Thanks." She hung up the phone and folded her hands on her desk, then pushed her chair back and stood up slowly as if it required great effort. So it wasn't the Lewis kid, nor was it McDermott—two guns and no murder weapon. She felt no closer to finding Mira Ogilvy's killer now than when her body turned up in that vacant lot. She stared out the window.

Officer Wilson appeared in the doorway. "Lieutenant?"

She turned. He said, "I tried to call Fortenberry. His line was busy. I'll go down there."

"Never mind."

"What?"

"Never mind, Officer. I talked to him." She frowned and

sighed. "It's not him. The Lewis kid's gun . . . it's not the murder weapon."

Wilson's face went blank.

"He's not the one, Wilson. Let him go."

"But the kid was on Vinson Street. That's where we picked him up."

"I know. It's not enough. McDermott was on Vinson too, and he looks innocent now. Charge Mr. Lewis with possession for the gun. That'll get him a court date. He's not going anywhere. If we get anything else for a homicide, we'll find him. But right now, that boy doesn't look like a killer."

Wilson frowned bitterly. "All right."

* * *

Cheryl Lewis sat at her kitchen table that morning, sipping tea. She had awakened early and put on a good dress because she was going downtown to Police Headquarters and wanted to look nice. She thought it might help get Lester out of trouble, even though part of her felt so bad about the whole thing that she wanted to wear old jeans and a t-shirt. She wanted to see her brother last night, but it was late when she arrived home; plus she was mad and concluded that a night in jail might not be the worst thing for the boy. She also planned to stop at the bank that morning and buy a cashier's check for Lester's bail. It would look better if she wore a nice outfit when she strolled into the bank lobby carrying twenty thousand dollars.

As she finished her tea, the young woman stared at the old briefcase on her kitchen table. Twenty thousand dollars! She hid it under her bed last night, slept on it, dreamed about it, and thought about what Baker Davis said in his office yesterday: Mira.

Yes, he said *Mira*, she was sure of it. But it hit her like a blow at the time; she was too stunned to speak or ask for an explanation. It must be the girl's money, the last installment. It would have been nice to share it with her neighbors as she had for years. That's what Mira wanted. The men who worked at Orion Pallet were dead, killed in the fire years ago. Then the police, the fire department, and men from City Hall came to Sloetown and talked about the fire for a while. A politician appeared and made a speech. Then they all went away. Long ago.

But Mira knew about it, knew the men who died or disappeared. Cheryl Lewis never knew why or how Mira knew, but she did, and because of her, the families got paid. She remembered McDermott, the lawyer, describing once how an injured client was made whole in a trial he won. She pondered the expression *made whole*, as if something important was missing or broken and somebody had to make up for it. Perhaps that was Mira. It seemed the right word all of a sudden. Richard did have a way of explaining things. There was no way to bring those men back, no way to bring Michael back, but that money helped. *Made whole.* Maybe it was the best anyone could expect, in Sloetown.

But right now, Cheryl Lewis had to get the last of the money to Police Headquarters. *Twenty thousand dollars! What the hell did Lester do?!* No, she didn't want to think about it.

She eyed the clock. Time to get moving. She drank her tea, reached for the old briefcase and heard steps on the porch outside. She started. Then a hand grabbed the door handle, shaking it. The hand pounded. She stood up, her heart skipping. Who would come here this early? Who would be this loud? She walked quickly across the room.

Her brother tumbled in as she opened the door.

"Aagghh!" she cried. "Lester!"

He stumbled across the living room and collapsed on the sofa, looking tired and dirty.

"Lester! What are you—?! I thought you were—"

He sank into the sofa and groaned. She approached him. She wanted to strike him and hug him at once. He waved her back and said,

"I'm all right."

"How did you—? You called me last night from the police! The jail!"

"I said I'm all right."

She stood back, folder her arms and glared at him. "Stop it. Sit up. Tell me what's going on."

He closed his eyes.

"Lester!" she demanded. She approached again, standing over him. Slowly, the boy sat up.

"It was like I said. I got picked up. Then they let me go."

"The police?" He nodded. "Well? What for? What did you do?"

"Nothin'."

"Don't give me that."

He rubbed his eyes. "I had a gun. They found it."

Cheryl Lewis let out a sigh. "Oh Lord."

"But it wasn't mine."

"Well, where was it?"

"In my backpack, but it wasn't mine I tell ya."

"Oh Lord." Again she wanted to strike him, and hug him too, but she was glad he was there, with her, on the sofa. "So you get beat up with a gun in Sloetown on Sunday night, and on Monday you got a gun yourself." Lester Lewis hung his head like a pitiful old man. "Let me see that bump on your head." She examined his wound with tender fingers. "I can see it didn't knock any sense into you. Now what about that bail? That twenty—?"

"I got a court date next month."

"Next month?! So nothing today? No money, no bail?"

"I guess not. They kept the gun though."

"Good." She blinked, then sighed. "How'd you get home?"

"The police gave me a bus ticket."

"All right. Go get cleaned up."

Lester Lewis pulled himself up from the sofa and went to his bedroom. Cheryl Lewis sighed again as if it were her very last breath. She reflected her entire life was filled with sighs now.

She rose and went back to the kitchen. There sat the briefcase, with all that money, and Lester didn't need it now. That moment, she recalled an afternoon in the graveyard behind her church. Her parents were buried there, and she visited sometimes. An old man worked in that cemetery. The church gave him a little money to take care of the plots. He was strange: no one ever saw him with a lawnmower or a rake. In fact he used to nap under the shade trees there, but somehow he kept the place looking nice. And when Cheryl visited that day, he stopped her and said, "What you doin' here in the graveyard?"

"I only came to—"

"This ain't no place fo' a pretty young girl."

"I'm just visiting my—"

"Ain't no need to visit the dead, honey. You live long enough, they gonna visit you. Now go on."

Cheryl Lewis thought about that old man in the cemetery and what he said as she considered the briefcase, filled with cash, in her kitchen. That's what Baker Davis said, *Mira*.

She finished the tea, and was surprised to find a smile on her face.

* * *

Baker Davis worked late that afternoon filing papers. He took out a new folder and was about to label the tab, name it, but he stopped. What should he write there? *Orion Case?* Well, Mrs. Orion hired me first, he recalled. She's the original client, but that felt long ago. Even before that, Mira Ogilvy had written him, asking for help. What did her letter say? She wanted to *bring everything to a peaceful, orderly conclusion*. Maybe that was done now, though her murder didn't exactly fit. McDermott was dead too. It wasn't peaceful. It wasn't orderly. But Cheryl Lewis had the money now, in Sloetown. The twenty K was Karl Orion's last payment. He had found it, as Gloria hired him to do, though he didn't *give her* the money—a fine distinction, Davis reflected. But maybe Mira Ogilvy wanted it that way. And he also wondered about that compensation the dead girl mentioned. He was broke now, or broke again.

His phone rang. It was Gloria Orion, her voice tremulous. Would he meet, talk with her, did he hear about Richard?

"Sure," he said.

"The Plaza Hotel, in an hour?"

"Sure."

* * *

The Plaza Hotel was an independent property that did a good business hosting small-time conventions and middle-aged tourists, but Gloria Orion considered it seedy. In the lobby the carpet was bright red in some places, worn dull pink in others. The air in the hallways was stale. Family photographs covered the dark paneling in the bar. They weren't an attractive family, she thought. She was glad that nobody she knew was likely to visit the Plaza and see her there.

She found a table in the bar and sat there alone, fending off the importunate eyes of two men lounging nearby. She noticed the heavy drapes over the windows, an odd maroon fabric—velour, she think they called it. It made her skin crawl, made her think *Is this what life will be like without money?* She felt relieved when Baker Davis entered from the bright lobby.

"Thanks for coming," she said, as he sat with her.

"No, I'm glad you called. It's good to get out. I'm not much for office work." He noticed her dress was white. A gold belt circled her waist. Her hair was brushed back and she wore sunglasses. Though her face drooped, her skin was firm and fresh. It had been watered with tears. But she looked nice. She always did.

A waitress appeared. She was young, and sported a cotton blouse that resembled a tuxedo jacket with a black bow tie except there was no tie. The design was merely printed on the blouse. Davis asked her for wine. She left to get it.

Gloria Orion removed the dark glasses. Her eyes were tired and red. She whispered,

"You heard."

Davis nodded.

"They came to see me, the police—" Something caught in her throat.

"I'm sorry, Gloria."

"My brother!"

"I'm sorry."

A sob gripped her. She held it in. A minute passed. "I never thought it would happen, that Richard would do something like—" She didn't finish, bringing a hand to her lips, choking it back.

"Gloria."

"He was so far in . . . with the bankers, with that girl in Sloetown. I don't understand."

"I'm not sure anyone does."

She sniffed. Another minute passed. "They said you were there Sunday night, in Sloetown. You saw what happened."

"Yes."

Her eyes grew clearer. "They said Richard had a gun."

"I'm afraid so."

"Did he—?"

"Gloria, listen. It was late, and yes, Richard had a gun. Could the cops avoid it? I don't know. It was dark. There was shooting back and forth. Maybe. I really don't know."

"Oh what does it matter? He's gone."

Gloria Orion sighed and looked away from him, toward the window. The sunlight streaming in past the red curtains turned her white dress crimson. She looked entirely relaxed, but different now as if sorrow and bitterness added something to her beauty, gave it a patina. The waitress came and placed two glasses of wine before them with a studied air that aimed to say the Plaza was a cut above the other hotels in town, the franchise places. Gloria reached for hers quickly. Davis offered her a cigarette. She took it and said, "And now my husband."

"Karl?"

"He's in the hospital, Baker." She paused, drawing on the cigarette. "He might not make it."

"Ah. I knew he was sick."

"Sick, yes," she said, her face hardening. "But he knows, Baker. Karl knows about the money. He tried to tell me, but he couldn't. His mind—"

"What did he say?"

"I don't know. He was confused . . . his medication, you know. But something about Mira's father, the money, and dead men in Sloetown. He was delirious. Mira knew about it too, whatever it was, and she ended up with the money."

"Gloria, look. I'm sorry about Karl, but that money . . . does it matter now?"

"It does matter dammit." Her moist face turned hard. "Don't you see? My brother is dead and my husband is dying. When Karl's gone, the only thing left will be that God-forsaken pallet factory out in Sloetown. I'll die there Baker!" She trailed off and for the first time, Davis noticed a tear in the corner of her eye. She brushed it away, finished her cigarette, focused again. "Karl gave that money away. He and I were married. It was my property . . . and I hired you to find it."

"You want to find it."

She didn't answer, just clenched her glass.

"You want to know, Gloria?"

She stared at the investigator, her mouth firm, her eyes smoldering.

"Then come with me." He stood up.

"Where?"

Davis threw a few bills onto the table. "Let's go."

She rose slowly, and he escorted her outside to the parking lot. He opened the passenger door of his Buick. She hesitated. He said,

"'Just a little drive. It's good for the soul.'"
"I don't think my soul can handle another visit to Sloetown."
"No bodies this time, I promise."
She looked at him and got in.

*   *   *

Lester Lewis spent most of the day in bed. The night before, in jail, he actually got a little sleep. There was nothing else to do, after all, in his cell, and no one to talk with either after the cops released that strange man named Davis.

But he felt worn out when he got home earlier, and slept most of the day. It was dark when he finally woke up. Cheryl was in class that night. Cousin had taken the baby over to her house. He was alone.

He went to the bathroom, washed his face, and examined the cut on his head, which had scabbed over now. It would be okay, might even leave a little scar. That would be cool, a scar from a gunfight. Or, it could heal up fine, and nobody would ask about it, or even notice.

He went to the kitchen and found cold meat loaf in the icebox. At the kitchen table, he sat and ate and thought about the gun. It was gone. He was hoping to sell it but now the police had it. He'd get no money from that. Then he remembered the pearls, but that guy in the pawnshop said they were fake, costume jewelry, whatever that was. That guy was a liar, Lester thought. You can't trust guys like that. He said take the pearls to a jewelry store, if he wanted to be sure. *All right. I'll find a good jewelry store downtown where they know about such things.*

The youth finished his supper, cleaned up, changed clothes and left the house, heading toward Jackson Park in the darkness. He walked quickly, anxious to retrieve the pearls from the backseat of Michael's Cadillac, where he left them. *Surely the man in the pawnshop is wrong; surely the pearls are worth something.*

Lester Lewis came to the old car at the far end of the park. He pushed the brush away and peered into the backseat in the darkness. He reached down and rustled the leaves on the moldy seat. The pearls were gone.

Damn homeless people, he thought.

TWENTY GRAND

* * *

Baker Davis approached Sloetown with Gloria Orion. It was night. The street lamps had flickered awake, but their light filtered down through the big trees with an anemic quality.

He turned off the main avenue, lowering his window to admit the cool air that lingered in the quiet streets, hearing a sigh of relief from Gloria. He drove on, the houses becoming smaller and grayer as if they had been settling into the land forever, like tombstones fading with time and rain. No one had built anything new in Sloetown in a century, and somehow, this was comforting. Davis slowed the car, his heart and mind slowing too. But it wasn't home. He was a stranger. Was there anything here for him? Maybe. If he could bear it, if the woman beside him could bear it.

He drove along the worn streets until he reached Jackson Park, the last green space in the city before the land sank away to the river. On the sidewalk, a few youths lingered. Davis knew he wanted to see them, wanted to be here with these kids because they wouldn't run a game on him, or if it was a game, they didn't know it. If there was something to know about a random killing in a vacant lot, or even about Mira Ogilvy's money, then it might be on this street corner. Davis guessed he'd find it here . . . because it started here. What was it Mira said? *Trees, fruit, flowers . . . all begin as seeds*? Maybe.

The Buick rolled up to four people on the sidewalk, two older teenagers and two children who all turned as one when the car stopped before them. Gloria Orion tightened and whispered harshly, "Baker what are you doing?"

One of the teens approached, a tall, thin kid. It was Lester Lewis. Davis leaned from the window and shouted,

"Good to be out, huh?"

"Yeah it is," Lester said, recognizing his recent cell mate. The other youth, a short, chubby young man Davis had seen before, held back. The two children, a boy and girl, remained on the sidewalk. Lester stepped up to the window of the car, looking in at Gloria Orion. "Who dat? You brought your girlfrien' tonight?" They both looked at her, the fear in her face.

Davis got out of the car. The other teen came forward and said,

"What you lookin' fo' mister?" He wore shorts that fell below his knees, almost reaching the top of his sneakers. The hair on the side of his head was shaved into a pattern of lightning bolts. "You know you done messed up . . . comin' around here."

"You're right. I prob'ly did." Davis answered. The remark stopped him. The youth wasn't prepared for anyone to agree with him. The passenger door opened and Gloria Orion stepped onto the sidewalk. Davis wished she hadn't, at this point, but there she was, the heels of her expensive shoes clicking on the pavement as she came around the car. It was an outrageous sound Davis considered had not been heard on the streets of Sloetown in quite some time, if ever. Lester Lewis checked out the strange woman, his eyes troubled. He knew she was different but he wasn't sure how exactly. Nor why. She was like a picture in a book he had never seen before. One of the children on the sidewalk noticed her and squealed.

"Yeah . . . you done messed up all right," the stocky kid said as Gloria Orion came to Davis's side.

"I'm used to it," Davis said.

"Then what you coming around here fo? To Sloetown?"

"I like it here."

"You don't belong here."

"That's right, but I'm looking for something."

"Well go on and look somewhere else."

"Shut up Daryl," Lester Lewis snapped. The children began laughing and saying: *Ssut-up. Ssut-up.* Daryl glared back at them.

"What you lookin' for?" Lester asked. "You want a little dope or something?"

"Not something. Somebody."

The young men eyed each other.

"Somebody you know."

"We doan know nobody, man," Daryl exclaimed. "This ain't nothing." His voice reverberated down the street and into the night. The children twittered nearby.

"What you talkin' about, man?" Lester demanded.

Davis came closer to them. "I'm looking . . . for Michael Lewis."

The youth's face glistened in the humidity, trying to remain hard as he shifted his feet. Something moved in his throat, but didn't come out. Davis said, "You know, right?"

"Maybe."

TWENTY GRAND

They were all quiet in the street in the darkness. Davis exchanged glances with Gloria. Then he moved away from the little group, walking toward the park, staring into the distance and saying, "*Maybe* huh? Maybe you know a story."

No one answered, but the children whispered. Davis turned and came back to Lester Lewis until he stood inches from him. He spoke easy and slow:

"Why don't you tell it?"

"Bullshit man," Daryl exclaimed.

Lester Lewis looked away and quickly walked toward the park. Davis followed him, grabbing Gloria by the hand. The others waited . . . then followed as the tall youth crossed the street. He marched past a grassy ball diamond, past a basketball goal with a bent rim, past a creaky swing set. They came to a grove of huge trees at the end of the park. Then Lester stopped. Davis felt Gloria's hand sweating, gave it a squeeze and let it go. The young man reached forward into the brush, beckoning to Davis as he pushed branches away. They peered into the darkness. Suddenly, an old wreck of a car appeared. Vines encircled the rusting red fenders, the hood and trunk. It was a Cadillac convertible.

Lester stood quietly. Davis and Gloria were silent as the others came up and stood behind them. The children made fretful noises. Far away, the rush of traffic along Kenner Boulevard filled the night.

Daryl said, "What you showin' them this old car fo?" Lester threw a hard look, silencing him.

"It's your brother's," Davis said. "Isn't it?"

"Yeah, it's his. Yeah."

"It don't even have no top," Daryl exclaimed. The children giggled.

"Never did," Lester said, his voice lowering. "Michael used to park it up under these trees, so it wouldn't get wet in the rain, but we had to dry off the seats anyway. On a nice day, he used to drive us around the neighborhood in it." He was quiet again. "I was a little kid then, but we had a lotta fun going around in that Cadillac. Me and Michael and Cheryl."

"Ain't goin' nowhere now," Daryl said, amused with himself. Lester told him to shut up. *Ssut-up* the children echoed.

"That's been about ten, twelve years now," Lester continued. "It ain't been driven since."

Gloria Orion spoke: "How come?"

The young man eyed Davis, waiting for him to explain, but the investigator stood silent. He said,

"My brother never came back."

"You ain't got no brother," Daryl interjected. Lester didn't respond. He didn't even acknowledge it, like a man who had been through such misfortune that insults couldn't touch him. He stood, like a rock. The children were quiet.

"My brother never came back from that big fire down at the pallet factory," Lester continued. "That's where he worked." A warm breeze rustled the trees in the night.

"At Orion Pallet?" Gloria Orion exclaimed.

Lester looked at her. "Yeah." He stared at the old Cadillac withering away in the underbrush. "I was little then, about seven or eight. My sister Cheryl could tell you more. But I know the day the big fire happened at the factory was the last day we ever saw Michael."

Gloria Orion's hand covered her mouth. "He never came back?" Her eyes darted back and forth, as if trying to discover something in her own mind. "And you never learned—?"

Lester Lewis shrugged his shoulders. Everyone looked at the strange blonde woman. She exclaimed, "No, those men got help! There was insurance. My husband paid—!"

"Paid who?" Daryl asked.

"The men, the fire, the ones who got hurt."

"Some of them," Lester said. "That was a long time ago."

Suddenly the color washed away from Gloria Orion's face, her skin white and pale against the night, against the dark green brush that covered Michael Lewis's car. She said to no one:

"Mira came here. That's what Richard said."

"Who dat?"

"She came here. Her father knew about the fire, the dead, and she knew too. Karl paid her. She took cash from her account."

"Nobody know nothin'."

"Mira brought that money here!" Gloria Orion cried. "For . . . for—"

Michael! one of the children shouted.

"Oh God!"

She screamed and ran away, lurching back through Jackson Park toward the car. They watched her go.

TWENTY GRAND

"This is messed up," Daryl sneered.

"Shet up," Lester told him.

Michael! the other child cried in the darkness.

Everyone left the old Cadillac, walking back to the bright area under the streetlight where the Buick waited. Gloria Orion sat in the car staring at nothing, her arms folded. She looked like a wounded animal. Davis got into the vehicle as Lester Lewis came to the window.

"What you know man?" he demanded, part tough, part teenager. "'Bout some money?"

Baker Davis looked at him, into his large, liquid eyes. He wanted to tell the young man, wanted to tell him about the men who got paid from that accident long ago, the ones who got Karl Orion's insurance money, and the ones who didn't. He wanted to tell him that's just the way things are: that if you worked in a pallet factory, and there was a fire, and some guys never came home, even your brother, sometimes after a while people just stopped asking. 'Like if you lived in Sloetown, maybe it was too much damn trouble.

"I don't know anything about it, Lester," Davis said. "Maybe ask your sister."

"Let's get out of here," Gloria Orion said.

The young man stood back from the car. Davis started the Buick and moved away, leaving them under the streetlight in the dark street. Gloria Orion stared straight ahead. The children on the sidewalk began to cry.

They drove through the old neighborhood in silence. The night was cooler now as the heat of day subsided. Davis exited Sloetown between an abandoned day care center and a used car lot surrounded by a chain link fence. A dog inside the fence barked at them. When they reached Kenner, it was good to drive faster, watching the city go by. Davis looked over at his passenger. She asked for a cigarette and he gave her one, then let it be quiet again. A few miles passed and they reached the Plaza Hotel. He entered the parking lot, easing in behind Gloria's car. She reached for the door handle.

"Good night," Davis said as she got out. Gloria Orion walked briskly to her SUV, throwing a brittle smile over her shoulder. Then she sped away into the darkness, the red tail lights of her vehicle disappearing into the night.

AUSTIN McLELLAN

THIRTEEN

One of these days Baker Davis planned to clean up his office. He was determined. He would put everything into the nice cherry wood filing cabinets and his desk would be clear. An impression of cool, clean professionalism would greet clients and visitors, impressing them favorably. He could raise his fees. One of these days.

Prince's voice rolled back from the front. By now, it had an ambient effect. Davis couldn't make out his words exactly, but the tone revealed when he was doing business, losing business, or when someone had entered their suite. That was the sound now: a visitor had come. Then hard shoes clicked in the hallway, but they didn't sound like a man's.

In a moment Lieutenant Doreen Foster stood in the doorway. She wore a gray skirt and jacket, all business. On her hip, beneath her the jacket, Davis glimpsed a black police revolver. From her belt hung the gold detective's badge. She couldn't smile, but tried anyway.

"Mr. Davis," she said. He stood up. "I hope this isn't a bad time . . . if you have a minute."

"My pleasure, Lieutenant. Have a seat."

She took the armchair as Davis settled behind his desk. They eyed each other for a minute that felt like a half hour. The room was very warm.

"Well, here we are again, Mr. Davis."

"Yes, ma'am."

"I guess it's better than last time, in jail."

"Yes, as a matter of fact, it is."

"You didn't really give me much choice. You know the rules about interfering in a police investigation."

"I know. It's all right, Lieutenant. I had it coming, but it's over now. I'm done with all that."

"Well, unfortunately, I'm not done."

Davis shifted in his chair. The Lieutenant's eyes didn't move. "The Ogilvy girl—she's still dead. Somebody killed her, Mr. Davis." She shook her head. "No, it doesn't look like McDermott. And no, it's doesn't seem like that kid had any connection to it either."

"The kid?"

"Yes, your bunk mate, in the cell. The Lewis kid. You know him, right?"

Davis paused, returning the Lieutenant's hard stare. "No."

"You sure about that?"

"I'm afraid I never saw him before that night in the street, with McDermott."

She shrugged. She had big shoulders for a woman. "And no idea why that lawyer whacked him?"

It was Davis's turn to shrug. "My guess is McDermott was drinking that night."

"That's probably safe to assume, but it doesn't help much." Lt. Foster stood up. She walked to the window and parted the blinds, looked outside and said, "And now the boy. We had to let him go. It wasn't his gun either that killed the girl."

Davis kept quiet, remembering the money he gave Cheryl Lewis for Lester. The Lieutenant turned and said, "Last week, Mr. Davis, you said that girl, the victim, had been in Sloetown before. There was money involved. I appreciated that, but the connections don't look good."

"Connections?"

"Yes. You were in Sloetown, with that Orion woman last Sunday. You ID'd the body, or she did. Then you showed up at the Ogilvy house in the Palatine. And then in Sloetown again, with McDermott and those kids, including the Lewis kid."

"Sloetown. Yeah I know it's strange, but I like to visit there sometimes, just to drive around."

She approached him. "Is that so? Is that what you like to do?

Do you think Sloetown is some kind of tourist attraction, Mr. Davis?"

"No, I uh—"

"Some place where you can just drop in when you feel like it, and enjoy the view?"

"No."

"Two people are dead Mr. Davis. We found that girl's body there, and McDermott died right on Vinson Street. That's two, and that's too bad, but you got any idea how many other pointless killings have occurred in Sloetown over the years? I'm not talking about the prominent citizens, Mr. Davis."

"I'm afraid I don't know, Lieutenant."

"I'm not surprised. But guess what: I don't know either. It's too damn many, and most of them are forgotten now. They're only files in somebody's desk at Headquarters. You think that makes any sense, detective? You think you're going to get a handle on that cruising around in your beat up Buick?"

"Sorry, Lieutenant. I'm just trying to make a living."

"And McDermott? He made his little excursions to Sloetown too. We saw his black Lincoln on Vinson Street last week. A man like that in the ghetto. Are you kidding me? He owned this office tower. What the hell?"

"I didn't know him."

"And Mira Ogilvy. She's in Sloetown too. What was she? Some kind of socialite? An heiress? A girl with money—in that neighborhood? It's absurd. Good Lord! And she ends up a bloody corpse in a vacant lot and who's going to make sense of that, Mr. Davis?"

"I know."

"No you don't."

"I simply meant—"

"Right. Everybody means well till it doesn't work for them anymore in Sloetown. Then they get in their cars and drive back home. But it's still there, the old neighborhood, the run-down ghetto. That Lewis kid is still there too. And the unsolved murders. And the endings that won't end."

She sat down and wiped perspiration from her brow. She stared at the floor as sunlight poured into the office from the window.

Davis kept quiet. He had nothing to say. The Lieutenant was

okay, even if she did lock him up Sunday night. Now he wanted to help her but couldn't. It wouldn't come out. Mira's little project was finished. She was gone and so was the money. The deal was done and he couldn't explain it. Yes, somebody killed that young woman and somebody knew about it, probably someone in Sloetown. Maybe her death was simply that way and meant to stay that way. It *was* too bad, like the Lieutenant said. Maybe the police and Mira Ogilvy, their worlds, would remain apart. Isn't that what the dead girl wanted, he remembered. What did Mira's letter say? She preferred the cops . . . *not be involved. I'm sure their efforts would be heavy-handed and insensitive. I want to avoid that.* Maybe she got her wish, Davis reflected.

The Lieutenant rose from the armchair. "Well, I've got a job to do, Mr. Davis."

The investigator stood. "Good luck Lieutenant. I hope you find what you're looking for."

"Oh I will. It may take a while, but we'll find out. It's a funny thing . . . over time, people can't keep quiet about this kind of thing. Not in this town, not really, not forever. There's always a story that wants to be heard. Someone's story." She turned to go. "So if you hear anything—"

"I'll call, Lieutenant."

Then she was gone.

* * *

Officer Jeremy Wilson threw his cigarette out the window of the squad car. Then he lit another and pulled his visor lower because the sun was very bright. *Find something,* Lt. Foster demanded earlier that day. "Go back to Sloetown again. See if you can find anything. Turn up something, Wilson! That girl's still dead."

So the policeman sat in his car on Vinson Street that sweaty afternoon and waited. Sure, McDermott drove by here one night, but he wasn't the killer. At least his gun wasn't the same that fired the bullets which put that girl down. But Christ, that lawyer shot at him Sunday night. He had to return fire, so now they were investigating *him.* Lt. Foster said not to worry, but it didn't look good. Wilson knew promotions went to guys with spotless records, cops that never rocked the boat, frigging boy scouts. But if he could break this case . . .

Maybe it will work again. Maybe the killer will come back here to Vinson. It was all he had, though he was sure that Davis fellow and Gloria Orion weren't telling everything. It pissed him off when somebody knew more than he did. He'd fix them. That PI was shady, was known for getting in the way; and the Orion woman— one couldn't trust her. If he connected them to the murder, it would boost his career. Plus, he'd been on the job long enough. It was time for a promotion, a raise. He imagined new carpeting for his house, maybe a patio.

Wilson stared down Vinson Street. It looked different now. He remembered Sunday night when McDermott ran into the vacant lot here. The grass was tall and thick. But since then, city maintenance had come through and whacked everything to the ground. There was no grass, no weeds. Everything was chopped low, broken and parched. The empty white brick diner stood alone.

Then he saw movement. A dirty man appeared from behind the diner, pushing a shopping cart. He noticed the squad car and stopped. Then he crept forward.

Damn homeless, Wilson thought. *They're nothing but trouble. They're always out here: one of them probably knows about Mira Ogilvy, who killed her.* And now this one approached, his walk unsteady, his cart empty. He was likely drunk and wanted money. The policeman threw his cigarette out the window as the man approached the squad car.

"Looky here!" Rico said. He reached for the cigarette butt on the ground. "Iss still good!"

"Beat it," Wilson said.

"Ain't doin' nothing," Rico answered, puffing on the butt. He leaned against the shopping cart. He could barely stand. He smelled like wine.

"Get lost."

"I'm lost now, man. I stay lost."

Wilson grimaced. The last thing he wanted that hot, sticky afternoon was a conversation. "I said go on."

"Go on where? This is *my* lot." His face twisted with anger. "I stay here. These bottles and cans 'round here are mine!" He sucked on the remains of the cigarette. "What the hell you lookin' fo' in Sloetown anyway?" Wilson got out of his car and said,

"You ever seen a white lady around here?"

Rico leaned against his shopping cart, mumbling "White lady white car."

Wilson squinted in the light, his eyes narrowing. "What did you say? Speak up."

"White lady white car and dem boys."

"What the hell are you talking about?"

"Yeah, I saw 'em, bawss—that white lady and her car and dem boys. And I saw a pistol."

"You're drunk."

"Naw bawss! I said I saw 'em." The homeless man swayed in the afternoon sun as if he was a tree in a breeze, except there was no breeze.

"You lying to me, damn you."

"Naw I ain't. 'Dat white lady she got shot in her car right around the corner. Then dose boys throw'd her body up here in dis vacant lot."

"How the hell you know?"

"I said I saw 'em you dam fool. Some kids and a pistol."

Wilson kicked the shopping cart. It turned over, crashing onto the pavement. "A pistol huh? Maybe it was yours. Maybe you had a pistol."

Rico backed up. "You crazy, man. I ain't got no gun, but them boys did and they kilt that white lady. But you ain't gonna find 'em cause you don't know how."

"You think you know more than me?" Wilson said, advancing.

"I know. And everybody in Sloetown knows too. It's just the way it is. But you ain't gonna know. Ever."

Wilson went after him. "You saw that girl die!" He jerked a sap from his belt.

"I saw and I know, but you ain't ever gonna know so go t' hell." Rico stumbled away, spitting curses. He leaned down to pick up a jagged bottle from the street, but Wilson was on him. He kicked the bottle away. The homeless man bawled as Wilson grabbed him, pushed him hard against the hood of the car. In a second Rico was cuffed.

"Maybe you got a gun, or a knife," Wilson snarled. He reached to frisk the man, gritting his teeth as he touched him.

"No gun! No knife!" Rico hollered.

"Shut up," he barked, his hand going into the man's pockets.

"I ain't done nothin!"

Wilson's face froze as he withdrew a handful of pearls.

"What? Jesus!"

"Naw bawss."

"Quiet!" Wilson fingered the dirty gems.

Rico wiggled around, facing him. "They ain't mine. Ah found 'em."

"By God, you saw that girl die and you stole these pearls from her."

"Ain't mine! I found 'em in an old car in the park!" He struggled in the cuffs.

"Shut up." Wilson grabbed his arm, dragged him to the car and shoved him in the backseat. Then they were going downtown, Rico cursing loudly, the policeman's face hard and grim and certain.

* * *

Late that afternoon Gloria Orion sat behind her husband's desk at the Orion Pallet Factory. The night before, Mercy Hospital had phoned. They said come quick. They asked about DNR. She told them she would come. She didn't. Then Karl Orion was gone.

Now she felt the man's absence. A heavy silence filled the office even as voices came from the warehouse in back. Occasionally the smell of sawdust and paint filtered through the air conditioning system, making her dizzy. She got up from behind the desk and walked around the room to clear her head. She took deep breaths and stared out the window. And every time Gloria Orion looked outside at the big parking lot and the trees in the distance she hoped the scene would change. But it didn't.

She had come in that afternoon to examine the current accounts—and discovered a dismal picture. The company had enough cash to make payroll Friday, but that was about it. When she projected costs and income to the end of the month, the picture was even gloomier. Then the month after that and the month after that . . . all the way to the end of the year. The grim picture didn't change, like the parking lot outside and the old trees beyond. She had enough to keep the place going. Orion Pallet wasn't bankrupt. She could keep the men employed building pallets for the handful of customers that remained. But for the owner, there was, and would be, almost no money left at all.

For a moment fresh ideas cascaded through her mind about cutting costs, making sales calls, drumming up new business. Maybe she could develop new products: tables or chairs or desks or coffee tables or something like that. No, the men didn't really know how to make anything except pallets. But maybe . . . with a little training, some new equipment. How hard could it be?

She sighed and slumped in her chair. Even if it worked, she would be stuck there running the depressing factory for years to come. As she studied the accounts, she felt as if she were reading her own prison sentence. Finally, she reached into Karl's desk, found his last bottle of good scotch. She got up, closed the door, poured a drink and wondered if she would have to learn to drink something cheaper.

Money, she thought. *Yes, Karl paid Mira all that money over the years. Then she gave it away. She took it to Sloetown, for some dead men, for that kid's brother and God knows who else. Maybe the girl thought she could help someone, but it wasn't her money. It wasn't even Karl's money. He was my husband—we were married. That money belonged to me too, and now it's gone forever.*

Again Gloria Orion heard the shouts of men from the warehouse. Their shouting sounded like laughter. They weren't dead at all. They were alive, and she was here with them. It was a connection she didn't want or understand. *But this is how my life has ended up.*

She sipped at the drink, lit a cigarette, and stared out the window at the timeless scene. It was ugly, felt like eternity. Then, in the distance, at the far end of the lot, a car eased through the front gate. It moved slowly, cautiously, as if the driver was lost, uncertain. Then it came into view.

* * *

Davis left the office late that afternoon. The city had been sunny, dry and parched for weeks, but now the air was heavy with moisture. Deep, thick clouds filled the sky, making it unnaturally dark as he got into his car. He drove out through town. The familiar imagery, the streets and the buildings, were like smooth, deep furrows in his mind, paths so worn they were hard to recognize. He began to see how none of it mattered without someone to live here, dwell here, suffer, love, and die here, giving everything but surrendering nothing and sometimes losing it all. The men and women he knew, their spirits, their acts, and everything they built or dreamed would all be gone someday, washed down the river to the ocean with time and by time. Even outside of time. Only a few remained strong or desperate enough to make a mark, stand against the tide, or stand up at all. It was all so clear, finally, though Davis wasn't sure what remained for him now, nor of his destination that afternoon, but he knew he was leaving something behind. He adjusted the rear view mirror in his Buick to get a better view and drove on.

Soon the shiny malls, the chain restaurants, the glowing gas stations devolved into nail salons, used car lots, laundromats, and finally became old churches, vacant lots, and liquor stores. The investigator had come to Sloetown again, and again he wasn't sure how he got there but it was okay. Warm, gray clouds blanketed the old neighborhood in suffocating humidity, holding the heat in, holding things still. He took his foot off the gas. There was no hurry. Everything rested at the end of the day under the big trees. He rolled down the window of the car and welcomed a fragrance of smoking ribs and fried chicken.

He passed Vinson Street, where Mira's rotting corpse summoned him barely ten days ago. Her letter said she wanted to bring everything to a close in a peaceful way. She had peace now, Davis reflected. But her project? Her desire? Her wish? Cheryl Lewis had that briefcase and her brother was free, but the girl was dead. So was McDermott, while the Lieutenant hunted the guilty. It all seemed like a mysterious equation scribbled in chalk on a dusty blackboard, with strange figures, odd symbols. But the equation wasn't balanced: the PI detected no $=$ sign. It wasn't clear, didn't make perfect sense. *Maybe it's not supposed to.*

He drove by Jackson Park. A few boys played basketball while children stood nearby. *Let them be. The Lieutenant is right. I'm no tourist. These people live here and I don't, even if I can touch them sometimes, feel this place, know it well.* He pictured the old Cadillac rusting away in the forest, and who it belonged to, and why they remembered it, and why Mira Ogilvy brought that money to Sloetown for all those years. That's what he knew. He couldn't change it. He didn't want to.

Finally, at the very end of the old neighborhood, the trees

parted and the Orion Pallet Factory appeared behind a big fence. Davis noticed the clouds overhead now, brown and gray and showing rain. In the distance far beyond the river, lightning twitched in the sky. It was late afternoon and the parking lot had emptied. Most of the men had gone home.

And there it was—her SUV, parked alone, as if waiting. Davis eased into the parking lot. He wasn't sure why, but at the end of Sloetown, there was nowhere else to go. He saw Karl Orion's office window under a metal awning, with a light on. Gloria Orion was inside. Her money was gone and maybe, by now, her husband too. He wondered if Karl Orion had made peace with Mira Ogilvy, with all the payments he gave her over the years. Or whether the old guy remained outraged till the end, secretly trying to find the money he gave away to return to his wife. And did Gloria ever know it? Did she learn that Karl wanted her to have something more than an old pallet factory in a run-down neighborhood? Maybe she'd never know. But the place was hers now.

Davis let his car stop next to her SUV and looked up at the office window. She was in there, alone, with probably no reason to go home. Then he recognized he had no reason either. He had his practice, what was left of it. The Lieutenant might let him back into the PI game some day, but what did it matter? There were no appointments, no business. It occurred to him that maybe he was done, it was over, a chapter ended. And he was broke too. Yesterday he had twenty grand nice and tight in his safe—but no, it was never his. It was police evidence, and now he didn't have a cent. All he ever got from the deal were painful memories of a dead woman in a vacant lot and, a week later, Richard McDermott dead in the same place. Maybe Lester Lewis remained, nearby in Jackson Park, standing watch over his brother's Cadillac.

Davis exited the Buick and saw gray clouds overhead. He felt the warm, moist air. He looked up at the office, the soft light inside. Gloria was in there. She had promised him so much, and yes, he knew it was a lie, a fake smile, an empty kiss. But now, she had nothing to promise him, nothing to give. Everything she had was gone. *Maybe it's a good place to start. The games are over. Maybe she can use a man around the pallet factory to make the place go, earn a little profit, keep her company. Her cold embrace . . . might become warm. What do I know about pallets? Not much. But how hard could it be?*

The sky darkened as the investigator stood in the parking lot.

It would be nice to bring her something. He reached into his pockets, but his pockets were empty. Maybe a flower, but there were no flowers in Sloetown. Then he remembered Karl Orion kept a bottle of good scotch in his desk. Yes, that could be a start. And Gloria *was* beautiful. He was sure of that, now more than ever.

Baker Davis ran up the stairs to the office and the woman inside as heavy drops of rain splashed onto the metal awning above him.

THE END

Acknowledgements . . .

A few good people who provided encouragement along the way . .

Richard Bausch, Emily Besh, Lou Chanin, Lillie Simmons-Dear, Donna Ellis, Lyman McLallen, Mark Nowell, Julie Ray, Aodhán Richardson, Ann Saccomano, Caroline Sposto, J. Lee Thomason, Stacey Wiedower, Lee Williams, and many others.

About the Author . . .

Austin McLellan has published fiction at Akashicbooks.com, and in the *Bangalore Review*, *Stepaway Magazine*, the *Monarch Review*, and *In Recovery Magazine*. His drama *King Henry, Mayor* was a finalist in the 2014 Tennessee Williams Play Contest. As an expert on healthcare technology and privacy, he has contributed articles to Memphis and Nashville newspapers, as well as national healthcare periodicals.

In a previous life, Austin taught English and writing at universities in Asia, Europe, and the United States. He has also operated an art gallery, developed software, and acted in a Shakespeare play. Today, Austin lives in Memphis, Tennessee, where he develops real estate in the inner city, and writes. He has a BA, Philosophy from Rhodes College; an MA in Literature from the University of Memphis.

More at www.austinmclellan.com

Wild Caught Press

AUSTIN McLELLAN

Cover image: Mulberry Street, Memphis, Tennessee
Photo by the Author